JANICE KAISER

EASY VIRTUE

MIRA

ISBN 1-55166-302-3

EASY VIRTUE

Copyright © 1997 by Belles-Lettres, Inc.

Printed in U.S.A.

"Can we be thinking the same thing?"

Dane thought about Mary Margaret's question before he answered, wondering if she'd be offended by what she heard. "I was thinking I'd like to pull over, take you in my arms and kiss you."

His words were received with a deafening silence. After several moments he asked, "What were you thinking?"

"That if you pulled over, you'd make us late. So then I thought, maybe if I give you a friendly kiss on the cheek, we'd both be content." Then, loosening her seat belt, she leaned over and pressed her lips to his cheek, her breast touching his arm. He could smell the soft scent of her hair and had to struggle to keep his eyes on the road. Why wasn't there a rest stop when he needed one? But Mary Margaret just settled back in her seat.

She must have sensed his desire for more, because she laughed and said, "Surely you aren't one of those guys who needs it all to be satisfied."

"Who, me? Of course not."

"Liar. There's not a man alive who won't keep going until he's stopped." She laughed again. "You know, I like you. The problem is the circumstances."

"So, what's the bottom line?" he asked.

"That you'd better wipe the lipstick off your cheek before climbing into the pulpit."

For Reverend John L. Young

Thursday

August 8th

The High Chaparral Hotel and Casino
Reno, Nevada

Mary Margaret couldn't help feeling sorry for them, even
the good ones. Of the twelve leggy girls prancing to one of
the chorus tunes from *Cats,* only two or three were passable.
The rest would have to be satisfied with that high-school pro-
duction of *Oklahoma!* as the high point of their showbiz ca-
reers. Poor things.

It was hard not to agonize right along with them. She'd
been there herself. Each was sure her whole life—at least her
whole musical life—was turning on this day, this moment,
this dance, the next kick, turn and kick. She could sense their
nervousness, even from the shadows at the back of the theater.

Artie Heartman was down there onstage with them, pretending he was Gene Kelly, circling the bouncing beauties,
as he called them, like a tomcat on the prowl.

"You, sweetheart, in the red," he shouted over the music.
"That'll do. Go on home and give it a rest."

The girl staggered from the line, her knees buckling, her
jaw slack. Artie waved for her to move out of the way.

"Thanks for coming," he said perfunctorily. "Thanks for
your time."

As the poor thing wandered off into the wings, Mary Margaret's heart went out to her. The girl would cry. The first
one given the hook always did. But she had to admit there
was method to his madness. Artie's girls had guts, the sort of
guts that would make John Wayne proud. They could dance

through God knew what—kids at home with hundred-and-two-degree fevers, cramps, bankruptcy, just about anything. Mary Margaret didn't have kids, and she didn't get debilitating cramps, but she knew all about financial pressure. Boy, did she ever. It was money worries that had brought her here before the noon hour, a time when normally she'd be just climbing out of bed.

She checked her watch. It was time to head up to the executive offices. She had an appointment with Muriel Eddy at eleven-thirty and didn't want to be late and offend her on top of everything else.

As she left the theater, Mary Margaret heard Artie giving the second girl of the morning the heave-ho. She cringed for her, but told herself maybe the girl, whoever she was, would be lucky enough to end up marrying that boy who'd gone into the navy last year and have his babies. Maybe that was a better way to live.

Mary Margaret walked through the casino, her purse slung over her shoulder, her long bare legs grabbing the attention of every male in sight. The clatter and jingle of the slots were like traffic sounds, the bell going off, like a siren, when somebody hit a jackpot.

A player at one of the blackjack tables, a stud with a mustache and cowboy hat, did a double take, drew his eyes up from her ankles to the cuffs of her white cotton shorts and then on to her curly mass of long red hair. He made a clicking sound and winked. *Yeah,* she thought, *and I love you, too, Jack.*

Mary Margaret tugged on the bottom of her little black cotton shirt and sighed. Well, she did know there were two problem areas she'd never likely escape. One was money. The other men. God definitely wasn't a woman.

"Hi, there, Mary Margaret," Lou Smitz said. He was a security guard, a friendly sort in his late fifties. "You're here kind of early, aren't you?" Lou was posted near the door that accessed the executive offices from the casino floor.

"Needed to hear the jingle of silver dollars," she said with a smile.

"Inspires you to pay your bills on time, don't it?"

"I should be so lucky."

Mary Margaret went through the door and up the staircase. Once she reached the office level, all evidence of gambling evaporated. She could have been in a high-rise on Montgomery Street in San Francisco. She'd left the world of Sam Sucker and entered the world of Archibald Accountant. This was where the real action was.

Bernie Solomon's office was at the end of the hall behind a set of double doors—"the pearly gates," as the kids in the crew called them. Nobody in their right mind ever went in there voluntarily, and virtually no one on the greasepaint side of the operation was ever invited. Bernie was God. He didn't exist unless you needed to pray.

Muriel Eddy, the woman generally regarded as his right-hand man, was the one who dealt with the mere mortals. Her office, appropriately situated to the right of Bernie's throne room, was where everything having to do with the human component of the operation began and ended. As the kids liked to say, the buck stopped, *really stopped*, in Muriel Eddy's office.

Mary Margaret stood for a second or two in front of Muriel's door and said a few Hail Marys, the way she used to in Catholic school when she was sent to the principal's office. Sister Beatrice and Muriel Eddy had a great deal in common, actually—they were both godless devotees of God.

Taking a fortifying breath, Mary Margaret rapped firmly on the door.

"Come in!" came a sputtering, coughing voice from inside.

Mary Margaret pushed the door open and stepped in. The air was so smoky it was opaque. It was like entering hell, or at least the lower reaches of purgatory.

"Hello, Mary Margaret," Muriel said, the cigarette between her lips wagging in time with her words. She was hunched over her desk, looking like a retirement-age troll. Gray hair sprouted from her head. She was sixty, give or take a year but, based on her weathered skin, she could have been seventy.

"Hi, Muriel," Mary Margaret said, closing the door.

The woman pointed to the leather armchair facing her desk. "Sit down."

The smoky chamber was littered with files, ledgers, computer printouts and a melange of memorabilia and personal artifacts, all languishing in the smog like an L.A. subdivision. Mary Margaret made her way to the chair, where she sat, crossing her legs. She put her purse on the floor beside her.

Muriel took a drag, the smoker's lines around her puckered mouth deepening, then blew smoke toward the ceiling. "You wanted to talk," she said, her voice dry and wheezy.

Mary Margaret studied her, summoning her courage. "I'll get right to the point," she said, her voice trembling. "I need an advance, Muriel. Two thousand. But I could probably squeeze by with fifteen hundred."

The woman took another drag, seemingly in no hurry to exhale. Finally she did. "I thought you were aware we don't give advances, Mary Margaret."

"I know it's against company policy, and I wouldn't have bothered asking if it wasn't an emergency, an extreme emergency, Muriel."

Again the woman contemplated her, her implacable expression showing nothing—not anger or pity or boredom or even curiosity. For several heartbeats she sat motionless. Then, "What kind of extreme emergency?"

Mary Margaret cleared her throat. "Because of the money I spent on my dad, the lawyer and private investigator, I'm behind on my bills. I borrowed from Anthony, who borrowed from somebody else, and the note's being called all the way down the line. I've got to pay him today. Or else."

Muriel Eddy carefully placed her cigarette in the corner of the ashtray, her splotchy, nicotine-stained fingers shaking slightly as she folded them on the old-fashioned green blotter. She took Mary Margaret in, appraising her. Had Muriel been a man, the evaluation could have had a sexual dimension, but it didn't. She was simply trying to decide if Mary Margaret was worth a patient explanation.

"That's not a very pretty story," she said.

"No, you're right. It isn't. But it's the truth."

Muriel drew a long breath and gave a little cough to clear her lungs. "Bernie would say no. Bernie would be upset to be asked. So that's the answer I got to give you. No."

"There must be a way," Mary Margaret said anxiously.

"Maybe if I talked to Mr. Solomon myself." It was false bravado. Muriel had to know she didn't mean it, not literally.

"You've been here what, four, five years now?" she said with the patience of a careworn prioress.

"Almost five."

"That's a long time for a showgirl. Five years. Two shows, eh?"

"*Fantasies* was in its third month when I joined the cast," Mary Margaret told her.

"A long time," Muriel said again, nodding her gray head.

Mary Margaret knew something unpleasant was heading her way. She was suddenly sorry she'd come. She'd taken a risk in asking, but the alternative had seemed worse, much worse. Now she wasn't so sure. What if they canned her?

"Well, I've been at the High Chaparral for twenty-two years," Muriel said. "Kids who were prancin' around in pasties when I started here are grandmothers. So I know how this place works, the way Bernie Solomon thinks."

"I know, Muriel. That's why I came to you first."

"I'm glad you were smart enough to do that," Muriel said, her expression critical. "But that don't change the problem, does it? The facts are the facts. And I've gotta do what I gotta do."

"But there must be some way I could—"

The woman held up her hand, stopping Mary Margaret. "Let me tell you a story, honey," Muriel said, "so you know where I'm comin' from."

Mary Margaret bit her lip, knowing she had to listen. But she couldn't stop the tears from flooding her eyes or the sick feeling in the pit of her stomach. All she could do was squeeze the arms of the chair, digging her long nails into the worn leather as she waited for Muriel to take a drag.

"Three, four shows back," Muriel went on, "maybe seven, eight years ago, we had a kid in the chorus line. Nice girl. Karen Something-or-other. Anyway, Karen has this little boy who gets hit by a car while she's here doin' a Sunday matinee. The kid has his pelvis crushed. Bad situation. Real sad. Of course, her old man's out of the picture. No insurance. Zip. Karen's down here dancin' her heart out, tryin' to hold things together, all the while her little boy's lyin' in the hospital, a cripple. Get the picture?''

Mary Margaret nodded, the image of Tiny Tim popping into her mind. She could see what was coming. Her heart began to ache.

"So anyway," Muriel continued, "the doctors tell Karen there's this experimental surgery they're doin' in L.A. Maybe the kid won't be a cripple if he has this operation. But it costs a hell of a lot. Karen's got no insurance, no money, no husband, no family. But she's got us. She's got Bernie, right?''

Mary Margaret nodded.

"Well, the kids in the crew pass the hat and come up with, I don't know, fifteen, eighteen hundred bucks. A drop in the bucket. The long and the short of it is, Bernie writes her a check for twenty G's, twenty thousand dollars! It don't cover everything, but it's enough for the doctors to go ahead. Twenty thousand's a lot of money, right?''

Mary Margaret nodded again, the faint hope she'd had rapidly fading.

"So Karen takes her kid to L.A., promisin' to pay back every cent. They have the operation. It's not a complete success, but the kid's better. Karen has to stay near the doctors for follow-up treatment, so she can't come back here and dance her way out of debt. She pays her rent by hustlin' cocktails at some whiskey joint in L.A. Bernie gets a couple of checks for two, three hundred dollars, then we stop hearin' from Karen. Bernie makes inquiries. Maybe Karen's in Phoenix or maybe San Diego. Maybe she's married to some insurance salesman, maybe she's not. Karen and her kid have disappeared. So what does that make Bernie besides a chump? He's Mr. Medicare, that's who he is.''

"But I *will* pay Bernie back," Mary Margaret insisted. "I'm not going to L.A. I'll be here, every night. Sprained ankle, broken wrist, I'll dance, no matter what. You know what kind of employee I am. I don't even have to have fifteen hundred. A grand will do. Enough to get Anthony off my back for a few weeks.''

"Then what? Another advance?''

"I swear, a thousand is all I need.''

Muriel shook her head. "You didn't hear a word I said.''

"Yes, I heard, but my situation's different. Bernie can take the payments right out of my paycheck. All I'm asking for is an advance."

"Mary Margaret, I don't mean to hurt your feelin's, but if Bernie pays for the operation of a crippled little boy and gets burnt, what makes you think he's going to give a girl a grand to make a payment to her ex because she had to borrow from him to hire a detective to prove that her old man didn't off the girl he's in San Quentin for murdering?"

Mary Margaret Duggan began trembling. She wasn't mad so much as she was hurt. "This is not about my father," she said as evenly as she could. "It's about Anthony. I've got to come up with a thousand dollars today, just to catch up, or he'll kill me. Maybe not literally, but…"

Muriel lifted her hand, signaling her to be quiet. "You've got a good job," she said, her tone firm. "You're a good performer and you've been a good employee until now. These kinds of problems are not what Bernie wants to hear. It says somethin' about you. I don't care how good the cause, how much it's not your fault. We don't expect our girls to be den mothers or sing in the choir Sunday mornin's. But we don't want them hittin' us up for money because their life's fucked up, either."

She picked up her cigarette, carefully tapped off the ash, took a drag and blew the smoke ceilingward. "Bottom line is, we don't run a welfare agency. The government's in debt for a reason. Everybody's got a crippled kid, a father in prison, a drug habit, cancer or some damned thing. If Bernie pays for all that crap, there won't be a show, no show means no jobs, no jobs means you and the other girls are waitin' tables or you're on the street hooking, or whatever. Which do you think is better, Mary Margaret, a job or no job?"

"A job, of course."

"Then we understand each other."

Mary Margaret could see there was no point in going on. She drew a long breath. "Yes, Muriel, we do."

Muriel took another drag. "Sorry to be so blunt, honey, but to my way of thinkin' straight talk is always best."

Mary Margaret picked up her purse. "I appreciate your taking the time to talk to me."

"Don't go just yet," Muriel said, stopping her. "I've got a few questions."

Mary Margaret settled back, for the first time wary. Everything seemed to close in on her. She had tolerated the tobacco smoke, but it suddenly became stifling, making her think of her poor asthmatic father whose first cell mate had been a chain-smoker. "Hell on earth," Jimmy Duggan told her during one of her visits to the prison.

Muriel studied her, squinting through the smoke snaking past her eyes. "Let me ask you this. You got money for groceries?"

"Yes, I'm okay."

"You sure?" Muriel opened her desk drawer and removed a small bundle of twenties, held together by a rubber band. She removed first two bills, then a third. "Bernie don't want any of his girls passin' out on the stage because they haven't eaten in two days."

"I'm fine. Janine keeps the refrigerator stocked. I've been sponging off her since Anthony put the squeeze on me, but she understands. She's cool."

Muriel reached across the desk and laid the bills in front of Mary Margaret. "Take this anyway and buy a few chops for the fridge."

Mary Margaret eyed the money. Sixty bucks wouldn't solve her problem with Anthony, but it would help Janine. Unfortunately, there was more at stake than grocery money. By coming to Muriel, Mary Margaret had laid herself open, planted seeds of doubt. She had put a big question mark by her name. "Mary Margaret Duggan's got financial problems," she could hear Bernie Solomon saying to the director. "Keep an eye on her, Artie. Make sure it doesn't affect the show, that her work doesn't slip."

Mary Margaret forced a smile. "It's sweet of you, Muriel. I know you don't have to do it, but I didn't come here asking for a handout. I just wanted an advance. I'll wait until payday."

"No strings attached, honey. It's not comin' out of my pocket. Bernie gives me funny-money to solve little problems. Take it."

Mary Margaret shook her head. "This town is full of gamblers who can't say no. I don't want to get hooked on charity, but thanks for caring.''

She got up and left Muriel Eddy's office, silently closing the door, hoping that she'd salvaged some shred of dignity. Sometimes that was all a person had.

The air in the corridor was fresh and clear. She took a deep breath, purging her lungs. It must have been the way her father felt when he'd finally been moved to a new cell. In prison, but free. Sort of.

Already feeling as if she'd been worked over by her ex-husband, Mary Margaret moved back down the corridor, her shoulders slumped, her spirits spent. She fought the desperation welling within as she searched for some reason to hope. She'd pretty well exhausted her options and that was almost scarier than the prospect of Anthony's anger. Hopelessness was worse than pain.

Reaching the end of the hall, she very nearly ran into Sean, the boy who worked in the mail room, as he came barreling around the corner.

''Whoops,'' he said, backing off, his eyes going right to her breasts. Sean, as every girl in the cast knew, was a voyeur. He liked to hang around after work to see the start of the early show each night, just so he could watch the girls going from the dressing room to the stage and back again.

Sean's rubbery mouth sagged open. ''Whoa,'' he said, unable not to stare at her breasts. ''Just the lady I want to see.''

''Yeah, I bet.''

She went on, but the kid grabbed her arm, stopping her. ''No, really,'' he said. ''You got another love letter.''

''From *him?*''

''Yep. No flowers this time.'' He pushed a lank of stringy brown hair to the side of his face. ''Just a letter.''

Mary Margaret would have told him to throw it away, but knowing Sean, he'd probably open it. Then there'd be gossip. Already most of the girls were aware that she had an admirer—a funny little man who came to the show every Friday, sitting at the same table and staring at her like some lovestruck teenager. Obsessions like that weren't without precedent, of course, but no girl, no matter how self-possessed, liked having a guy drool over her that way. It was creepy. Sick even.

"All right," she said, "get it for me, will you?"

Sean went off and Mary Margaret waited. A clerk from the ticket office, a young Chinese woman named Lin, went by. They exchanged greetings. Sean returned, holding out the envelope without really handing it to her. She gave him a look of annoyance and snatched it from his hand.

"Aren't we grabby, though."

She ignored him, studying the envelope instead.

The script was familiar—careful, ornate, almost calligraphic. She stuffed the envelope in her shoulder bag. "Thanks," she said without looking at him. She left for the stairway that led down to the employees entrance.

As she went downstairs, Mary Margaret began anticipating the hundred-plus-degree temperature outside. She thought of poor Janine, waiting at the trailer, as nervous about the money and Anthony as she was. Roommates had a way of getting sucked into each other's problems, and Janine had already loaned her twenty-five hundred for the retainer she'd paid Robinson Palmer, the detective. That had pretty well tapped out Janine's savings.

Mary Margaret had been living from paycheck to paycheck since her father's trial eight years ago. Lloyd Haskell, the attorney who'd represented Jimmy Duggan, had agreed to accept his $25,000 fee over time, taking a note at eight percent interest. Knowing she would need time to get on her feet, he'd agreed to give her three years' grace, interest free. After that she'd to pay him $506.97 per month for five years. She'd paid faithfully, month in and month out, telling herself that she was paying for another thirty days of her father's life. Somehow that made it easier.

As expected, the outdoor air greeted her like a blast furnace. Slipping on her sunglasses, she started across the parking lot, pulling her long red curls off her face and tossing them back over her shoulder. She was not looking forward to getting in her car, certain it would be like an oven. She'd bought the seven-year-old Ford Escort used. The air-conditioning had gone out in May and she hadn't been able to have it repaired. In fact, when she'd admitted the oil hadn't been changed in two years, the guy at the station told her she was lucky the car was running at all.

When she got to it, the first thing she did was roll down all the windows. She decided to wait a couple of minutes for it to cool down. While she waited, she watched the big High Chaparral sign atop the hotel tower slowly turn, catching the slanting rays of the sun. To the west she could see the downtown hotels, clustered at the parched feet of the Sierras. How in the hell had that little girl in Catholic school come to this inglorious end? she asked herself.

She thought about Anthony, knowing she had to face him that afternoon. It was going to be damned ugly, and that had her stomach in a knot. He was in a tight spot and he'd stop at nothing to get his money. Anthony Casagrande was fully capable of slapping her around. He had before. There wasn't anything he wouldn't do if it meant saving his own butt.

"Look, Mary Margaret," he'd said a couple of months earlier when she'd started having trouble making her payments, "why don't you put your bod to work? One night of tricks in a first-class operation, and you'd net more than you make in a month shaking your tits out at the High Chaparral."

"Don't start in on that again!" she warned.

"I'm not tellin' you to be a streetwalker, for chrissakes," he'd said irritably. "With your looks you could be a top-of-the-line call girl. Shit, you could retire after just a few months. Give me the word and I'll put you in contact with some people. Nothing but first-class clientele. Let's face it, what else are you good for?"

She'd blown up when he'd said that. "I'm not a whore!" she'd screamed. "The closest I ever came to prostitution was being married to you!"

He'd whacked her for that, knocked her right on her butt. It put a welt on her cheek that took Joni in makeup fifteen minutes to cover up. "You're a whore now," he'd sneered as she staggered to the door. "The only difference is you stay on the stage and make your johns jerk off under the table."

Marriage to Anthony Casagrande had been right up there among the biggest mistakes of her life. She'd been just plain stupid. Lonely and desperate. The worst possible combination. So of all the men in the world, who did she turn to when

Robinson Palmer had to be paid? Anthony. He'd been flush at the time. Had twelve grand in cash right in his apartment. "Hell, doll face," he'd said, "pay me back five hundred a month, no sweat. I'm cool."

He'd grabbed her ass playfully and said he'd be glad to take payment in kind if she ran short, but Mary Margaret had told him she preferred giving him a note. Truth was, she wouldn't have gone to bed with Anthony again for a hundred times five hundred bucks.

Deciding the car wasn't going to get any cooler, she opened the door and climbed in. "Jesus and Mary," she said when the hot vinyl seat burned her leg.

The sting only lasted a minute, but it was enough to send her over the edge. It was the last straw in what had been a real shitty day. Banging the steering wheel with her fist, she burst into tears, angry and frustrated at everyone—her father, Bernie, Anthony, and all the other rotten bastards who wanted a piece of her.

After a couple of minutes she stopped crying and opened her purse to get a tissue. She saw the letter Sean had given her. With all her anxiety she'd forgotten about it. She took it out of her purse and stared at it. In a way she dreaded opening it. Things like this made her skin crawl.

The first time she'd heard from the guy was three months ago when he'd sent flowers and a note to the dressing room. It was more a fan letter than anything. As with all those that were to follow, it started, "Dear Mary." It went on to say that he came to the show regularly and especially enjoyed her dancing. "You are a very pretty woman," was about the most personal thing he'd said. The card had been signed "Ramon."

A few weeks passed before she'd heard from him again. The second time she'd gotten a dozen long-stem roses. The note told more about him. Ramon was Basque, a sheep farmer. He was sixty-four, a widower. His wife had died five years ago. He came to the show every Friday because watching her dance made him very happy.

In the following weeks there were more roses and more notes, each more personal and revealing than the last. Finally, he told her he always sat at the same table in the front row, stage right. She danced one of the topless numbers on that wing, almost in its entirety. He wanted her to see him. He would be there the next Friday night with a rosebud pinned to his lapel.

Sure enough, that Friday Mary Margaret spotted her admirer. He looked harmless enough, his smile more angelic than sinister. But for some reason he unnerved her. She'd stumbled during the topless routine, almost falling on her face. Ramon must have loved that show of frailty because his note that night was particularly high in praise of her artistry.

The letter in her hand was unusual because it was mailed. There was no return address, but the script was unmistakable. She opened the envelope. It contained a letter and a crisp one-hundred-dollar bill, which fell on to her lap. She read the note.

Dear Mary,

I must tell you once and forever that I love you. This will come as a surprise because we have never spoken. And still, I know with all my heart that it is true.

I know also that nothing can come of this. I am old and I have nothing but a modest fortune to offer. Worse, I have a slow cancer and should die in not many years. I tell you this not for pity, but because I have a wish I want to realize before I become truly sick and die.

Every night I dream of touching your naked body. Do not be alarmed. It is not for immoral purposes. It is only so that my fingertips can know what my heart cherishes, to know the feel of the woman I love. And so, with the most respect possible for your dignity, I make this offer—

I send the one hundred dollars to ask you to come to my room (number 812) in the hotel after the performance Friday night. I will give you nine hundred dollars more if you will remove your clothing so I can see your beautiful body in the privacy of my room. If you will allow me to touch your breasts and buttocks in a respectful way (as a sculptor touches the marble) I will give you one thousand dollars more. I ask for no sexual favor, only what I have stated.

Mary, I beg you to understand my good intentions and
deep love for you, the woman I will carry in my heart
until my dying day.

Ramon

Her hands trembling, she folded the letter and put it back
in the envelope. Her chest felt tight. It was hard to breathe.
Good Lord. Nothing like this had happened to her before. Oh,
she'd been propositioned outright and had been offered large
sums of money for sex, but no one had propositioned her in
one breath and professed his love in the next.

Mary Margaret studied the one-hundred-dollar bill, then put
it in her wallet. Tears glistening in her eyes, she started the
engine and drove across the employee parking lot, heading
for the gate, a burning knot in her stomach. Love, cancer, a
dying man's wish or a cheap cynical trick? She didn't know
which it was and, in the final analysis, she didn't care. It
galled her to think that men, all men, seemed to want her for
one purpose and one purpose only—to satisfy their own selfish needs. Sometimes it seemed that even God saw her as a
whore. She didn't like that. She didn't like that at all.

Laurel, California

"I swear, I cannot picture you ministering to a bunch of
pig farmers," his mother said to him from Santa Barbara.

"Mommy, dearest," Dane said, pulling the phone cord taut
so he could swing his racket under it backhand before switch-
ing to the forehand side, "there aren't any pig farmers around
here to my knowledge. And if there were, I seriously doubt
they'd be Unitarian Universalists."

"Who *are* they then, for God's sake?"

"We're talking about my flock, are we?"

"Yes."

"Some of them grow raisins, I think. No, that's not right,"
he said, stepping over one of the boxes of books scattered
about the room. "One doesn't grow raisins. Dry them is probably more accurate."

"Raisin farmers."

"Plus the usual assortment of merchants, lawyers, teachers and widows," he said. "Lots of widows. I've hardly met anyone, though. A few people have dropped by, but most of them are waiting for Sunday, I guess."

"Oh, Dane, honey…"

He heard anguish in her voice, maternal anguish. "Yes, Mother?"

"Are you doing what you really want?"

He put down his tennis racket and, extending the phone cord as far as he could, managed to reach the glass of water on the table, nearly tripping over a box as he did. "This is the life I've chosen, Mother."

"I'm all too aware of that. But I still can't picture you conducting funerals and baptizing babies. It just doesn't seem like you."

"We don't baptize, remember?"

"Oh, that's right, I forgot. You don't believe in sin—so you can't very well believe in baptism, either."

He guzzled some water and wiped the perspiration from his brow with his forearm. It was the first time he'd spoken with his mother in a month. After his divorce her motherly instincts had risen from their slumbers and she'd telephoned regularly. But once she'd satisfied herself that he was neither suicidal nor given to bacchanalian excess, she'd backed off. Now Constance Barrett's concerns had gone back to his choice of career. She had never understood what prompted him to become a minister.

Dane put down the glass and picked up his racket again. For some reason, it had always been hard for him to talk to his mother without doing something else at the same time, like building a house of cards or solving a crossword puzzle. Though he loved the woman dearly, something about her drove him to distraction.

There was a silence on the line, then Constance Barrett said, "Dane, I worry that becoming a minister has made you too…too…"

"Too what?"

"I don't know. Accepting maybe."

He couldn't help chuckling. "That's the paint, Mother. A person who learns to accept his lot—whatever that may be—is truly happy. That's what Buddha taught, the denial of self, sublimation of ego to the greater reality."

"Yes, Dane, but are you happy?"

"I thought I just explained that I..." But then his voice trailed off.

"That you what?"

"I haven't reached nirvana, Mom, and I occasionally sink to lower levels of consciousness, but...well, I'm fine."

"The Presbyterians wouldn't have put up with that sort of gibberish."

"You got that right," he said.

She hesitated, then said, "You know, I still wonder sometimes if your father wasn't right."

He had a wary feeling, but he wasn't going to cut her off unless he was sure. "About what?"

"About you, your career, and that whole terrible money thing."

"Mother, do we really want to get into that?"

Constance sighed. "No, you're right, we shouldn't. We've managed to avoid it and our relationship is the better for it."

"Look," he said, "try not to worry. I'm a big boy now and I'm very much in control of my life. Things are going just fine."

"I can see you're trying to keep your spirits up," she said, "and that's good, but you miss Toby, don't you?"

"Of course I do." Dane pulled at the neck of his T-shirt, trying to get some air around his sweaty body. He was in shorts and sandals, which was about all he could do to ventilate his body until the repairman came to fix the air conditioner in his new house. "Being at peace with the cosmos does not necessarily mean you think everything is hunky-dory," he said.

"Hmm," his mother replied.

Dane hadn't realized it before, but a conversation with one's mother was a hell of a way to test one's personal belief system. Still, he could only endure so much at one sitting. He began wondering how he could gracefully end the conversation.

"So how was Kathy?" Constance asked before he came

up with something. "Did she show any…remorse when she picked up Toby?"

"You mean because she was taking him away for a year?"

"That, too."

"What besides that?"

"Oh, don't be dense," Constance said. "Was she sorry to be going off to Japan and leaving you?"

"She'd sort of left me already. That's the point of divorce."

"Dane, you're being deliberately obtuse. You know what I mean."

He tugged at his T-shirt again. "No, I'm afraid I don't."

"I mean, was she doing what she wanted or is this trip just to spite you?"

He groaned, wondering if his mother would ever be able to let go of her animosity. "Frankly, I think Kathy was rather blissful about going. But if what you're really asking is does she have any regrets, the answer is no."

The ensuing silence was the longest yet. Constance Barrett had not been a fan of his wife, but the two women had developed an understanding. And Constance, as it turned out, was greatly upset by the divorce—blindsided by it.

For Dane, Toby had been the only factor in the equation he'd anguished over. But then, it hadn't been his decision alone. Kathy, if anything, had pushed harder for a divorce than he. In a way, she'd done him a favor. "Since you damned Unitarians are so guilt-free, I should've let you carry the burden," she'd said, understanding the situation perfectly. But then his wife had never liked being passive about anything. Even if the boat were headed into the rocks, she liked having her hand on the tiller.

"At least Kathy will be getting away from that Latin boyfriend of hers for a while," his mother said.

"No such luck, Mom. She took Osvaldo to Kyoto with her."

"She did *what?* How could she do that?"

"She bought him a ticket."

"Oh, Dane, don't be flippant. How can she have a man who isn't her husband living under the same roof with your child? Aren't you incensed?"

He was starting to get annoyed. His mother's misplaced piety, which was usually scantily disguised pique, could wear thin. Dane decided to end the conversation before it really began to disintegrate. "Perhaps, but that's a topic for another day, Mom."

He picked up the nearly empty glass and pressed it to his forehead. As he did, he saw a car pull up in front of his house.

"So are you keeping up with your tennis?" she asked.

"Haven't found a partner yet."

"There must be some raisin farmers who play, or are they all into polo?"

"Don't be too snide, Mums, some of the raisin farmers around here are richer than you."

"How terribly impolite of you to say so."

To Dane's surprise the man getting out of the car was in clerical garb, though in deference to the weather the sleeves of his black shirt were short. Judging by the collar, his demeanor and the Plymouth, Dane figured Roman Catholic. What was worse, he was headed up the walk. Dane realized he was about to get his first professional courtesy call.

"Listen, Mom, I've got to get off the phone," he said. "One of the pope's minions is here for a look-see and I'm not exactly dressed for communion. Be thinking about when you want to come up and we'll talk Sunday evening. Bye."

Dane no sooner hung up than the doorbell rang. He wondered whether he'd easily be able to put his hands on the box with his liquor stash. Probably not. And the chances weren't good his guest was the only padre west of Nevada who was a teetotaler.

Stepping over boxes, Dane made his way to the small entry hall and opened the door. The roundish, florid man on the porch was wearing an expectant smile. He only secondarily took note of the way Dane was dressed.

"Is this the residence of Reverend Barrett and might he be in?" the man asked.

"It is and I am," Dane said, pressing his hand to his sweaty T-shirt.

"My, Unitarianism seems to be getting more and more unpresuming, doesn't it?" the priest said, laughing with genuine good humor. "I'm Father Muncey, from Saint Aubin's parish church up the street," he said, extending his hand. "Tom Muncey. I came by to say hello."

"How nice, Father Muncey," Dane said, taking the man's hand. "Please forgive my informal attire, but I don't normally put on clerical garb to unpack."

"Forgive an impertinent question," Muncey said with a twinkle in his eye, "but do you own any clerical attire, Reverend Barrett?"

Dane chuckled. "I'll be honest with you. I've only had a collar on once in my life, and that was while I was at seminary. I went trick-or-treating with one of the *women* on the faculty."

Muncey roared with laughter. "That's priceless! Truly."

"Come in, Father, please," Dane said gesturing for the priest to enter.

"It's Tom," Muncey said, wiping his eyes.

"And I'm Dane."

The priest stepped into the hallway. Glancing into the front room, he saw the boxes. "My, I have caught you in the middle of unpacking, haven't I?"

"My housekeeping leaves something to be desired, so the excuse is a blessing, believe me. Let's go in the kitchen. I think there may be two chairs in there that aren't covered, and the beer in the fridge might even be cool. God in his wisdom has not yet blessed me with a functioning air-conditioning system." Dane led the way through the mess.

"You Unitarian chaps claim the only heaven you'll ever know is here on earth, so it's only fair, I suppose, that this is the only hell you'll know, as well."

Dane laughed over his shoulder. "Decent of you to spare me the threat of eternal damnation, Tom."

"Never insult a man before you drink his beer," the priest replied. "That's what they taught us in seminary."

Dane removed a tray of utensils from one of the kitchen chairs, moved the boxes to the far end of the table and motioned for Tom Muncey to sit. The priest took the seat and Dane got a couple of Heinekens from the refrigerator.

"My, my, imported beer," Muncey said, perusing the bottle Dane held for him to examine. "You're no ascetic, I see."

"It's one of my few concessions to the good life," Dane

said with a grin as he pried the caps off the bottles. Then he handed Muncey one and tapped his against it. "To intergalactic peace, Father," he said.

"Seems a safe enough point of departure."

They both smiled and sipped their beers.

"Well, down to business," the priest said. "I have another reason for dropping by besides welcoming you to the neighborhood. A parishioner of mine has brought a matter to my attention that probably falls more into your purview than mine."

"Oh? What's that?"

"A woman in my congregation, Elena Perez, is a nurse in a convalescent hospital in Lodi. She came to me with a story about one of her patients, an elderly woman who'd had a stroke."

Dane drew on his beer as Father Muncey went on.

"It seems the patient, Ledi Hopkins, despite her speech being impaired, somehow managed to convey to Elena that she wanted to make a confession. Elena contacted me and I went to the hospital. This was last week. In conferring with the staff, I discovered Miss Hopkins was not Catholic, but rather a Unitarian Universalist. Anyway, I phoned your church office and was told that your predecessor, Reverend Shallcross, had gone back to New England."

"Jane Shallcross. The previous interim minister."

"Yes, lovely woman. I only spoke with her once or twice, but I was impressed." Muncey glanced toward the door, then leaned toward Dane and, in a conspiratorial tone, said, "Off the record, Rome is missing a bet not allowing women into the priesthood. Some of the best priests I've ever known have been nuns."

"The people at the top are usually the last to realize that sort of thing," Dane said.

"It's generational for the most part." Muncey took a long drink. "Same with celibacy. The old boys sacrificed, and they don't want to see things changed when it's too late for them."

Dane admired Tom Muncey's candor as much as his wit. "Most things in life are relative," he said.

"Unless they're absolute," Muncey replied with a sly smile. "But then, we digress."

"Yes, you were about to tell me that one of my flock was in need of confession."

"When I learned that you would be here in a matter of days, I decided Miss Hopkins's spiritual needs could await your arrival."

"I'll be happy to take care of it," Dane said.

"Sadly, it's too late. Miss Hopkins, I'm told, passed away yesterday."

"That is unfortunate," Dane said. "I hope she didn't feel abandoned in a time of need. The last thing I'd want is for her to feel we'd let her down."

Muncey nodded and sipped his beer. "I'm sure. But alas, there's more to the story."

"Oh?"

"Upon questioning Elena Perez further, I discovered that prior to her last stroke Miss Hopkins had talked a great deal about a murder that had taken place here eight years ago. A high-school student named Donna Lee Marshall was stabbed to death. Elena said that Ledi Hopkins was obsessed with the crime. At one point she insisted to Elena that the convicted man was innocent.

"I personally knew nothing about the case—it was before my time. But being the son of a policeman, I have a natural curiosity about these things and talked to the police chief, Carl Slater, about it. This was on Friday. To make a long story short," Muncey went on, "Ledi Hopkins was a witness in the case against the convicted killer, a man named Jimmy Duggan."

"But on her deathbed she recanted her testimony."

"That's right."

"Did you tell the police chief?"

"I told him, yes, but he wasn't familiar with the case, having come to town only a year and a half ago himself. He did me the courtesy of perusing the file, but basically he pooh-poohed the whole thing. Old people involved in a life-and-death matter will often become obsessed with it in their last days. He said that even if there were something to Ledi Hopkins's story, as a practical matter there was nothing that could be done about it. Her condition would make anything she said suspect."

"But you don't buy it," Dane said.

Muncey shrugged. "I'm the son of a cop. I guess I have a naturally suspicious mind." He stroked his chin, reflecting for a moment before pulling on his beer.

"Is Duggan facing execution?" Dane asked.

"No. The chief told me he was sentenced to life in prison. But that's no picnic, either, particularly if the man is innocent."

"I guess not," Dane said.

The priest took another drink of beer.

"So," Dane said, "your father was a cop."

"San Francisco P.D."

"Mine was a lawyer."

"Criminal law?"

"No, Dad was into making money. He was a securities lawyer. And he was very good at it."

"Oh?" Muncey raised an eye brow.

Dane laughed. "We were rich, had a wonderful home in the best part of Santa Barbara. I was so sheltered growing up, I thought all kids spent their summers in the country-club swimming pool."

Muncey reached over and patted Dane's knee, chuckling. "And then you blew it all by going into the Church."

"I haven't exactly taken a vow of poverty, Tom, but I've…well, let's say I've taken another road. A road my parents wouldn't have chosen for me."

"Much to their chagrin, I imagine."

"That, my friend, is an understatement."

"Really, now?"

"My father's been dead for over five years, but Mother and I are still contending with the fallout. He had a slow, difficult death, which in itself was hard on everybody, especially my mother. But to make things worse, my father essentially disowned me."

"Disowned you?"

"He didn't much care for my decision to go into the ministry."

"Ah," Muncey said, sipping his beer, "I see. And how did you feel about that?"

Dane laughed, shaking his head. "You're the first priest

I've said more than two sentences to, and you've already gotten me in the confessional."

Muncey blushed. "Sorry," he said. "Habit. I suppose there's a part of me that likes delving into people's souls."

"That's fortunate, considering. But I can say, Tom, even without knowing you, that you're probably pretty good at your work. You invite confidence."

"Thank you, but it's no special talent, just a matter of practice. Hearing confession, like saying confession, becomes routine after a while. It's cheap therapy."

Dane laughed. They both swigged their beer.

"I haven't talked much to anyone about my father," Dane said, his tone more sober. "Mother and I mostly skirt around the topic, but I have to say it still weighs on me."

"I'm drinking your beer," Tom Muncey said. "The least I can do is listen to your story."

Dane grinned. "You've got finesse, Tom, real finesse."

"It's up to you."

"Why not?" Dane said with a shrug. "I always wondered what it would be like to be in a confessional booth."

"Not a lot different than talking to the guy on the next bar stool at times. All that's different is the trappings."

"Well, here goes," Dane said, putting down his bottle on the table. "Like most young fellows, in finding my own way, I had to reject my father's. Money was never important to me in spite of the environment in which I was raised. But there was a lot that was expected and a lot that was assumed. My father wanted me to follow him into the law, but I rejected that right away. Instead I went to business school and became a stockbroker."

"A rather mild sort of rebellion."

"I was choosing my own life, but I didn't really think of it as rebellion. Dad accepted it. Considering his father was a doctor and a man who wanted his son to go in to medicine, how could he complain?" Muncey asked.

"Were you successful?" Muncey asked.

"Yes, reasonably. To the extent it can be measured in dollars. But I wasn't happy. Something was missing. Matters of the mind and spirit had always interested me, though I hadn't been terribly religious in the conventional sense. I happened

on Unitarian Universalism by chance and found the openness
and intellectualism appealing. One thing led to another and
the next thing I knew I was leaving the brokerage business
for the seminary.''

''And got yourself disowned in the process.''

''My father's attitude was, fine, do what you want with
your life, but not on his money. Psychic pleasure would have
to be my reward. And when I took him up on that, I got
written out of his will. Mother was instructed to pass on to
Yale and charity whatever she didn't spend.''

''Quite a tragic story,'' Muncey said, finishing his beer.

''Not really, I made enough during the five years I was in
business to put myself through seminary and buy a modest
place in Berkeley. I still have a few bucks socked away, but
I expect to get by nicely on what I make as a minister. Enough
to keep a few Heinekens in the fridge. Speaking of which,
may I offer you another?''

''No thanks. Seeing as we've just met, I've got my reputation to consider,'' Muncey said drolly.

''I won't tell if you don't.''

The priest shook his head. ''Thank you, though.''

Dane reflected on their conversation. ''Well, I've spilled
my guts, but I haven't done much to help solve the problem
you've brought,'' he said.

''Frankly, it's Jimmy Duggan I'm concerned about,'' Muncey said. ''And there may be an additional reason for you to
be concerned, as well.''

''Oh?''

''At the time of the murder, Jimmy was an employee of
your church. The custodian, I believe.''

''Really?''

Muncey grinned. ''What I'm saying, Dane, is that the thing
has Unitarian Universalist fingerprints all over it. I suppose
the business about Ledi Hopkins has the weight of gossip,
but I couldn't allow it to go unnoted. What you do with it,
if anything, is your business.''

Dane scratched his head contemplatively. ''If I didn't know
better, I'd say you're trying to lay a guilt trip on me.''

''Guilt is a very personal thing, my son. Only you know

which way your conscience is tugging you. But unless I misunderstood, helping those in need is the life you've chosen.''

Dane grinned, shaking his head. ''You not only have finesse, Tom, you can be downright diabolical.''

Muncey's eyes twinkled. ''Please, Reverend, any word but that. The bishop would have apoplexy.''

''Let me put it another way, then. You've flat outsmarted me.''

Muncey rubbed his jaw to hide his smile. ''I'm not used to having people see through me so easily.''

''It's not easy to kid a kidder, Tom. I feel duty-bound to make you work a little harder for this.''

''Well, I've got another trick up my sleeve,'' Muncey said deviously. ''But first I've got to ask a question. If my information is correct, you're single.''

''Divorced.''

''That's good enough, I suppose.''

''What's your trick?''

''As luck would have it, there's a girl involved,'' the priest said. There was a lilt in his voice. ''She's a beautiful young woman, from what I hear.''

Dane folded his arms over his chest. ''Reverend Muncey, you are really scraping the bottom of the barrel. First you try to draw me into this thing by laying a guilt trip on me, now you're dangling a woman in front of my nose. I knew the Catholic church could be pretty Machiavellian, but honestly, isn't this going a little far?''

Muncey beamed, looking very pleased with himself. ''You're already a lost soul. Besides, it just might work. Who knows, one day you might even thank me for dragging you into this.''

''All right. I'll bite. Who's the girl?''

''Jimmy Duggan's daughter.''

''His *daughter*?''

''That's right. I don't know the lass myself, but I've certainly heard about her. She's a showgirl up in Nevada. A real stunner from what they say. Her name's Mary Margaret.''

Dane was surprised. For a second he thought Tom Muncey might be joking, but then he saw that he wasn't. ''Duggan's daughter is a showgirl.''

"That's right. She was just a teenager when he was convicted. She's absolutely convinced he's innocent and, according to the chief, has been doing everything in her power to
prove it. She recently hired a detective to see if he could
uncover anything. Carl Slater had one of his officers talk to
the guy, but not much came of the investigation, apparently.
The poor girl's really in a desperate state."

"You paint a very alluring picture, Tom."

Muncey smiled.

"All right, so what is it you want me to do?"

"Well, it makes sense to me that young Mary Margaret
would be very interested to know about Ledi Hopkins's
deathbed confession, if that's the term."

"And because there are, as you put it, Unitarian fingerprints all over the case, I should be the one to tell her about
it," Dane said

"There's that, and the fact that I'll be leaving shortly for
a retreat in Southern California for a few days, a sort of bus-
man's holiday to L.A., and won't be around to follow up on
the matter."

They exchanged long looks.

"I guess you're looking for a commitment from me to take
up the Jimmy Duggan case in your stead," Dane said after a
while.

"I'd sleep better knowing a man of conscience was on the
case."

"A man of conscience, or a bachelor who might be enticed
by the thought of a desperate showgirl?"

"Papists, like everybody else, do the best they can."

Dane laughed, slapping Muncey on the shoulder. "You're
my kind of priest, Tom."

"I think we've got a lot in common despite our theological
differences."

"You're talking about Christian charity, not women, I take
it."

Muncey ran his tongue around his cheek. "I won't bite on
that one," he said evasively. "I have to run along. Strange
as it may seem, God has a claim on a few hours of my time
each day."

"She can be a tough boss," Dane said with a wink.

Father Muncey shook his head, amused. "It must be nice to have all that scriptural freedom."

"It's true salvation, but that's a whole other conversation, isn't it, Tom?"

"And not one for a budding friendship, you're right." Muncey slapped his knee. "Well, I'll be off."

He got to his feet, as did Dane. They went to the front hall.

"Do you play tennis, by the way?" Dane asked.

"No, golf's my game. I'll play with anybody who'll pay my green fees."

"My father was a golfer, which is why I'm not, I suppose. Too bad."

The priest nodded. Then he extended his hand. "Well, good meeting you, Dane. And welcome to Laurel. I trust the next time we meet I won't be bearing congregant problems."

Dane shook his hand. "Thanks for coming, Tom."

"Let's get together again soon."

Father Muncey opened the door and went out onto the porch, then down the steps. Dane looked after him. The priest had gone only a few paces when he stopped and turned. "Can I assume you'll look after Mary Margaret, then?"

"Yes, Father, you can rely on me to take care of it."

Tom Muncey beamed. "I'm grateful, Dane. And I hope you'll forgive me for resorting to the lowest, most wretched means of enticing you to take on the job."

"Don't worry, Tom. I'm sure you'll burn in hell for it."

The priest waved him off. "I'd better go before I've been completely corrupted." He started down the walk. "I hope she's the girl of your dreams," he called over his shoulder.

"You haven't told me how to get hold of her," Dane called back.

"Talk to the police chief, Carl Slater." Muncey got in his car.

Dane stood at the door until the man was gone. Then he glanced at the huge elm that cast a shadow over the bungalow. A light breeze had come up, rustling the leaves. In a few more hours the cooling ocean air would arrive. For the moment, though, it was still blazing hot. The street was quiet, the only signs of life a white dog ambling along the sidewalk and a few birds twittering in the trees.

Dane watched the dog disappear behind a hedge, and thought of the puppy he'd had as a boy, which in turn made him think of his father. He could almost hear Wilson Barrett laughing in that deep Zeusian baritone of his. "Every decision a man makes has its consequences," his father had told him in their last conversation. "Had I gone to Cornell instead of Yale, I never would have met your mother and there'd be no you."

"Anybody can step off a curb at the wrong time, Dad," he'd replied.

"A man still has to mind his decisions," his father had shot back. "There will always be choices."

Fate had always seemed a curious thing. There were times when you could almost feel the weight of a moment, when you could sense it was pivotal to the course of events. There was something about Tom Muncey's visit that struck Dane that way. In saying he would go to Nevada, he'd set something in motion, something important, but at the same time something mysterious and obscure.

Desert Rest Mobile Home Park
Reno, Nevada

As she turned off South Virginia Street into the trailer court, "Social Security Haven," as Janine called it, Mary Margaret wondered if God in his wisdom might have given Anthony a big night at the craps tables. If the pressure were off him, it would be off her, but she knew that was too much to hope for. When you got to the point where your life depended on the roll of the dice, you were in trouble.

Turning her Escort off the court's main thoroughfare into Date Palm Lane, Mary Margaret saw what she was dreading—Anthony's bloodred Corvette parked in front of Janine's double-wide. Even though she knew it would be there, her heart lurched and she stopped the car. "Damn," she muttered, hitting the steering wheel with her fist.

She was tempted to turn around and run as fast and far as she could, but she could not leave Janine holding the bag—there was no telling what Anthony might do if she didn't show up. No, she had to face him, for Janine's sake if for no other reason.

Proceeding down the lane, she parked in front of their neighbors' place, the home of a retired nurse and a retired teacher, a lesbian couple named Candy and Colleen. What brought the four of them together initially was a shared contempt for Anthony Casagrande. Mary Margaret's ex had earned Candy and Colleen's eternal enmity by calling them "shriveled-up old dykes" when they had complained about him backing over their rosebushes.

There were a handful of residents under fifty at the Desert Rest, but Janine and Mary Margaret were the baby chicks of the coop. Most residents were the garden-variety grandmother types, the blue and white hairs who played bridge. There was also a good number of old dolls—aging beauties with brightly dyed hair, false nails, false eyelashes and false teeth. The faded belles tended to be the friendliest, though the two residents who made the most serious effort to socialize were Mary Margaret and Janine's lesbian neighbors.

Colleen, the former teacher, a large woman with thick glasses that were always sliding down her nose, was the only person Mary Margaret knew who liked to read even more than she did. They talked about books whenever they had the chance. On her day off, Mary Margaret sometimes had lunch—really breakfast for her—with Colleen and Candy. Afterward, the two "bookies," as Candy called them, would sit around drinking Dr Peppers and comparing impressions of famous female characters in literature.

Mary Margaret got out of her car and saw Candy watering the hanging plants on her porch.

"Trouble's waiting," Candy said ominously, inclining her head toward the Vette.

"Tell me about it."

Candy, who was even fatter than Colleen, though not as tall, had a penchant for wearing shorts and basketball shoes. "I'd be careful if I were you, honey," she said. "I had a glimpse of him. Looked to me like he came loaded for bear."

"How long's he been here?"

"Half an hour or so."

"Poor Janine."

Bracing herself, Mary Margaret carried the dry cleaning and milk she'd picked up on the way home. She opened the trailer door and went in. Anthony was sprawled in Janine's recliner, the fingers of one hand wrapped around the neck of a beer bottle. Janine sat on the arm of the sofa across the room, her shoulders slightly rounded. She wore cutoffs and a tank top. Her feet bare. At twenty-eight, Janine Russo was a couple of years older than Mary Margaret. She returned a worried smile, but said nothing.

Mary Margaret turned her attention back to Anthony, whose taciturn manner and intransigence told her he was determined to play the hard guy. He stared at her, his jean-clad legs splayed open, his yellow silk shirt unbuttoned halfway down, revealing a small wooden cross on a leather thong.

Mary Margaret put the dry cleaning and the milk down on the chair by the door and took off her sunglasses. The trailer was cool compared to the searing heat outside. She wiped the fine sheen of perspiration from her lip.

"I see you've dropped by," she said.

"Very observant," he replied.

Anthony watched her. He had great eyes and cheekbones. And great hair. It was jet black, thick and pulled into a short ponytail at his collar. He was not smiling. No surprise there.

Anthony drew on his beer, his eyes taking her in with a languorous, yet carefully unfriendly look. She was a lot more nervous than she let on, but she indulged him, letting him look at her ass as she turned to glance at the mail on the little table by the door. After several moments she lost patience and abruptly faced him, folding her arms under her breasts.

"So," she said, almost sounding defiant.

"Which is it?" he replied. "Do you have the money or don't you?"

Mary Margaret removed her purse from her shoulder, realizing the time for a decision had come. Ramon was her best shot. "Part of it. The rest you can have tomorrow night after the show," she said, opening her purse. Her fingers trembled. She hated that she'd let him intimidate her. Weakness was the last thing Anthony should see.

She took the hundred from her wallet, walked over and handed it to him. Anthony plucked the bill from her fingers and held it in front of him as if it were a dead mouse. He turned it to see the denomination. "What the fuck's this? A tip?"

"Earnest money to show my good intentions." She hoped he couldn't hear the tremor in her voice.

"Good intentions, my ass!" Crumpling the bill, he threw it at her. The wadded bill bounced off her chest and fell to the floor. Then he got to his feet very suddenly. She recoiled, thinking he was going to slug her. "I want my money, Mary Margaret," he roared. "All of it. I want it *now!*"

Janine, who'd heard every story about Anthony that Mary Margaret had to tell, interposed herself between them. "Let me get you another beer, Anthony," she said, taking the bottle. She ran her fingers through her light brown, pixy-cut hair, giving Mary Margaret a sympathetic smile.

"Get out of here, Janine," he grumbled, half pushing her aside with the back of his hand.

Janine gave Mary Margaret a look of dread, then, taking the carton of milk, limped off to the kitchen. Years ago she'd been a dancer, but in a freak accident she'd fallen off a runway and broken her hip. Harrah's had compensated her, providing her with enough cash to buy her mobile home. The other part of the settlement included a cashier's job in the casino for as long as she wanted it.

"Listen, Anthony," Mary Margaret said when her friend was gone, "you got a problem with me, fine, but get off Janine's case. This is her home and you and I are guests here. Try to act like the gentleman you've never been."

He turned red and stepped toward her, his fists clenched. But he stopped short of hitting her. "Fuck you, Mary Margaret," he snarled. "You promised me the money today and you're saying you don't have it. What gives? Wouldn't they give you the advance, or are you holding out on me?"

Mary Margaret took half a step back. "I've made other arrangements," she told him, "but I won't have the money until after the show tomorrow night."

"Yeah, why's that?" he said. "What happens between now and then?"

"Let's just say I've got something lined up."

Anthony frowned, weighing the remark. "You've got

something lined up? What kind of…" Then, thinking he got her drift, he broke into a smile. "I don't believe it. Mary Margaret Duggan's actually going to flop for a buck," he said, the corners of his mouth lifting. "Never thought I'd see the day." He sat back down in the recliner, looking almost mirthful.

"That isn't what I said," she replied, picking up the crumpled bill from the floor.

"But that's what you meant," he said triumphantly.

"Think what you want," she said. "How I get the money is none of your damned business."

He chuckled, sensing he'd gotten something on her. Mary Margaret flushed despite herself. She'd given him exactly the leverage she didn't want him to have. Tossing the bill onto his lap to cover up, she retreated to the sofa.

"Janine, I'll have another beer after all," Anthony called to her in the kitchen as he stuffed the bill into his pocket. "And bring Mary Margaret one. It looks like the girl I once married has finally become a woman."

"Oh, stuff it, Anthony," Mary Margaret said. "You don't know what you're talking about."

"Yeah? Then why are you so red?"

"Because I'm embarrassed to be talking to you about anything concerning my personal life."

"Nice try."

Janine came to the door. "You want a beer, Mary Margaret?"

"No thanks."

Her friend retreated into the kitchen.

"So, tell me," Anthony said in a casual tone that bordered on intimate, "you working freelance, or have you signed on as a regular somewhere?"

"Shut up, Anthony, just shut up!"

He hooted. "Christ, I never thought I'd see the day Mary Margaret Duggan would spread her legs for money."

"You haven't seen the day, smart-ass, and you never will."

"Oh really? What're you saying, then, doll face? That you're going to spend tomorrow afternoon typing?"

"If you think I'd become a whore just to keep some flat-nosed creep from kneecapping you, you're dumber than I thought." She shook her head. "Hell, I'd be smarter to let whoever bought your ass have it."

A scowl came over his face. "Wait a minute..."

"You don't see that, do you, Anthony?" she said, shaking her head.

He scratched his jaw, his brow furrowing with deep creases. "So why *are* you getting me the money?"

"Because I owe you. I borrowed it and, being an honorable person, I'm paying you back. I guess while we were married you never noticed I had integrity."

He wasn't sure he believed her, she could tell.

"I didn't marry you because you had integrity, for chrissakes," he protested.

Mary Margaret groaned. "Why am I not surprised?"

"What's that supposed to mean?"

"Nothing. It doesn't mean anything."

"You were making fun of me," he groused.

"Look, Anthony, just forget it. I'm going to pay you your money and that should be all that matters."

He scowled, then waved a threatening finger. "I damned well better get the grand tomorrow, 'cause if you stiff me, I'll beat the shit out of you, even if it means I never see my dough." He thought for a moment until an idea came to him. When he faced her, he had a big smile on his face. "No, come to think of it, I'm not going to beat the shit out of you. I've got a better idea."

Dread came over her. Whenever Anthony got an idea, it almost always meant trouble. "What idea?" she said.

He snickered, seeing he'd thrown her a little off balance. "I don't know why in the hell I didn't think of this sooner."

"Think of what?" She was reacting just how he wanted, but she couldn't help herself.

Anthony slapped his leg. "Jesus, it's beautiful. And so obvious."

"What, already?" she asked.

"You know what I'm going to do, doll face?" he said gleefully. "I'm going to sell your goddamn ass myself."

"You're going to *what?*"

"To the highest bidder. I'm going to repossess you, just like you was a car. Then I'm going to goddamn sell you."

"Anthony, you're out of your mind."

"No, babe, that's exactly what I'm going to do. You didn't give me no security, so I've got no choice but to take what you *do* have. Your fucking body."

Janine came back, a bottle of beer in her hand. Mary Margaret saw her, but Anthony wasn't paying attention. He was busy celebrating his brilliance.

"Anthony changed his mind about the beer," Mary Margaret said, getting to her feet. "He has to go." She walked over to her friend, took the bottle from her hand and put it on the table behind her. Then she turned to her former husband. "You might as well know, Anthony, I want to pay you every bit as badly as you want to get paid. If it was in my account, I'd write you a check right now for the entire debt, just so I'd never have to see your face again."

Anthony stood, uncoiling his lanky body, shifting the fit of his tight jeans. Then he walked over to her, taking her jaw and squeezing it hard. Mary Margaret's pulse pounded, her stomach knotting up again.

"I'm not shitting you about putting you on the market, babe," he said. "If I have to sell your ass to a carload of brothers to get my bucks, that's what I'm going to do. And I have ways of doing that. I think you know."

Mary Margaret nodded, though he still had her face in his grip. He let go of her and sauntered to the door. Stopping, he turned.

"Better hope you're a goddamn fast typer, doll face," he said with a sneer. Then he went out, softly closing the door behind him.

Several moments passed before Mary Margaret exhaled. Janine looked ashen. She went to the door and turned the dead bolt. Mary Margaret sat on the arm of the chair and pressed the bridge of her nose with her fingers. She closed her eyes, wondering how in God's green earth she got herself into these messes. Her intentions were always good. She'd never knowingly hurt anybody in her life.

"You all right?" Janine asked.

She picked up the untouched bottle of beer from the table and handed it to Mary Margaret, who took a long drink, then

closed her eyes, waiting for her heart to find its natural beat.
"Yeah, I'm okay."

"Maybe I'll have one, too," Janine said. She went off to
the kitchen, leaving Mary Margaret to contemplate what had
happened. When Janine returned, she put her hand on Mary
Margaret's shoulder. "I bet if you'd had a gun, you'd have
shot him."

"Yes and no. Anthony's being squeezed, so he doesn't
know what to do except squeeze me."

"I don't care, he's still a prick."

Mary Margaret took a swig of beer. Anthony Casagrande's
problem was that his only God-given talent was knowing how
to screw. He was as deep as a rain puddle. What charisma he
had was good for only three or four changes of sheets—which
was about how long their marriage had lasted.

She shook her head, feeling defeated. "If my mother saw
me now, she'd wonder what in the hell happened to that little
girl in the white lace communion dress," she said, wiping her
cheek where a tear had fallen.

"Don't beat yourself up, Mary Margaret. You're doing the
best you can."

Mary Margaret drew an uneven breath. "My best is pretty
damned shitty," she said, her voice shaking. "I'm living off
the charity of friends and the most I can hope for is to get
out of debt. If I'm lucky."

Janine took her hand. "You'll be fine, honey," she said.
"I promise."

Mary Margaret stood and they hugged each other. It wasn't
much, but it made her feel better. Kissing Janine on the cheek,
she went over to the sofa and plopped down.

"So, have you figured out a way to get Anthony his
money, or were you bullshitting him?" Janine asked.

"Oh, I know where I'm going to get it."

"Where?"

"Ramon. The Basque sheep farmer."

"The guy who's obsessed with you?" Janine said with
alarm.

"Yep."

"Doing what?"

"He sent me a letter with an offer. For a thousand dollars

all I have to do is go to his hotel room and take off my clothes.''

"Mary Margaret, are you *nuts?*"

"No, I'm desperate, to be perfectly frank."

"Not *that* desperate. I'll get a loan on the trailer before I let you go to some guy's hotel room and undress."

"Bull," Mary Margaret said. "I'm not taking another penny from you. I'll be fine. I'm bigger and stronger than he is."

"That doesn't mean a damned thing, and you know it."

Mary Margaret took a long pull of beer, letting it flow down her throat until it started to burn and her eyes flooded. She choked and wiped her mouth with the back of her hand. "Sometimes a girl has got to take a chance," she said.

"You could lose your job in the show."

"I know."

"You've completely lost your mind. You know that don't you?"

Mary Margaret stared off at the trees through the windows. Her eyes shimmered. The lump in her throat got bigger and bigger. "No," she finally said, shaking her head, "I'm just a sucker for any guy who says he loves me."

Friday

August 9th

Laurel, California

Just before the phone rang, Dane Barrett heard the sound of the bells of the Campanile drift across the campus to his North Side apartment, announcing the dawn of another day. That moment of transcendence—going from the world of his dreams to reality—could be deflating, he'd discovered. Even if the dream was not pleasant, there was a certain freedom in sleep that was lost in wakefulness. "Oh, yeah," he would think upon awakening. "This me, this life." And there he'd be again, facing the problems he'd left on his pillow the night before.

The first ring of the phone sent the guy in his dream running for cover. It took a couple more rings before he figured out those weren't the Campanile bells at all, but Saint Aubin's up the street. And this wasn't Berkeley, it was Laurel, a farming community in the San Joaquin Valley. "Oh, this me." He reached for the unfamiliar phone next to his familiar bed in the unfamiliar room of his new house.

"Hello."

"Dane, Toby wants to talk to you."

That took a moment to register. It was Kathy's voice. Yes, his son wanted to talk to him. Yes, they did that on the phone sometimes. And yes, Kathy usually dialed to make sure their four-year-old's conversation wasn't with someone in Finland. But although his ex-wife's voice was clear, it had a disjointed quality that threw him off balance. It was only then that he realized she was calling from Japan, not the house they'd once shared in Berkeley.

"Dane?"

"Yeah…"

"Will you please speak to Toby?

"Yes, sure."

"I'll put him on."

Dane was still internalizing the reality behind Kathy's mechanical, perfunctory manner. She was a cultural anthropologist, but considered herself a scientist and therefore unassailable in matters of the mind. She'd been an assistant professor at Berkeley the past two years and was spending a year doing research at the prestigious Suguri Institute in Kyoto. Out of habit, she spoke to him as she would a baby-sitter or the signatory of the child-support checks, both of which he was.

Dane heard the receiver being passed from one hand to another, way out there beyond the Pacific, in the Land of the Rising Sun.

"Daddydoo," came his son's exultant voice over the line.

"Hi, Toby, how's my boy?"

"Fine."

"So, is Japan neat?"

"Uh-uh. I don't like it."

"No? Why not?"

"Mommy said we can't go home, so I want to come to your house."

"Oh."

"Can I, Daddy?"

"I wish you could, Toby, but that would be kind of hard. Anyway, you have to try to give Japan a chance."

"Just tell Mommy you want me to come home," the boy said. "You're bigger than her."

Dane heard more fumbling of the receiver on the other end. Then Kathy's impatient voice.

"Dane, I'd like a little help on this, please." It was more a command than a request. "You can put an end to it right now, if you will."

"Kat," he said, using his familiar name for her reflexively, "I was just trying to get a reading on the problem, trying to understand."

"What's to understand? We agreed to present a united front, did we not? Just explain to Toby that this is what we both want for him."

Dane was annoyed. Kathy was trying to use him to hit his son over the head. But then, using him had been her MO—since the divorce more than ever. He was about to tell her that was unfair, but then he realized this was not something that could be handled from a distance of six thousand miles—not when she could slam down the receiver in the middle of the conversation, as she surely would. Toby would suffer most and nothing could be gained.

"Put him on," he said perfunctorily.

The phone was handed back.

"Did you tell her, Daddy?" Toby asked, coming on again.

"Listen, sport, we've got a problem."

"What kind?"

"Remember how long you were on the plane? It was a long time, right?"

"So?"

"Well, it's not like riding across town. You and your mom will have to work things out there, son."

"But I don't want to stay," the boy said, starting the cry.

"Toby, Daddy loves you. In a year you'll be home and you can stay at my house as long as you want. Japan can be a lot of fun, if you let it. I'm sure Mommy's got a lot of fun things she wants you to do."

There was sniffling, but Toby's resistance seemed to be breaking. Dane felt like Heinrich Himmler. It really pissed him off that Kathy put him in this position.

"Can Mead come here then?" the boy asked.

The cat! Dane had forgotten completely about the cat. He'd put Mead out while unpacking the previous afternoon and hadn't seen him since.

Mead, as in Margaret Mead, was Kathy and Toby's neutered cat that had been left in his care. Kathy had acquired the animal at the time of the divorce as a kind of father substitute. Dane had never understood the logic of naming a neutered male cat after a female anthropologist as a substitute for a missing father, but he was sure Kathy's Jungian analyst had worked it all out nicely.

"Mead's keeping Daddy company, short stuff," he said casually. "You wouldn't want Daddy to be all by himself, would you?"

"No," came Toby's thin little voice in reply.

"Well, you look at the pictures you have of Mead, and we'll look at our pictures of you, okay?"

"Okay," Toby replied tearfully.

Kathy came back on the line. "I can see this was a bad idea," she said. "I thought you'd be able set things right with a word or two."

"The boy's in a strange environment, Kat. He's seeking familiarity. And I'm no magician."

"It was a mistake. I won't be doing it again. This call is costing me a fortune. I've got to go. Goodbye, Dane."

The phone went dead in his ear. "Yeah, well, goodbye, Kathy." He put the receiver back in the cradle.

Dane had only a moment of reflection before he recalled that Mead was out there somewhere in the great outdoors, coping with the dangers of Laurel alone, abandoned by his protector. Jumping from the bed naked, he looked around for something to throw on. Already he had visions of poor Mead as a corpse, lying in the street with tread marks scoring his body, or slumped dead in a vacant lot, his limp carcass torn to shreds by the neighborhood dogs. A little house cat, newly arrived from Berkeley, wouldn't have a chance in the country. How could he have failed Toby so?

Grabbing a pair of jogging shorts and a T-shirt, Dane first started for the door, then decided he couldn't wait to go to the bathroom, so he made a detour. Moments later, on his way out of his room, he stopped, taking the time to put on some sneakers, not bothering with socks. Dane made his way to the back door. Looking into the yard, he saw no sign of Mead. "Kitty, kitty," he called. "Here, kitty."

Nothing.

He went to the front door. No cat was waiting on the stoop. A sick feeling went through him. How would he explain this to Toby? Fortunately he had a year, and the solution was obvious. He'd get a substitute cat. A new kitten. It would mean a year of lies, but that was a small enough price to pay.

Dane went to the curb and peered up and down the street.

No cat corpses in sight, though he did see a squirrel make a dash in front of an approaching pickup. "Shit," Dane said under his breath. Then aloud, "Mead! Here, kitty, kitty!"

He watched the truck pass, then he perused the neighboring yards. No cat to be seen. He remembered the white dog from the day before and a shiver went through him. Poor Mead. How could he have forgotten? Toby and that cat had been inseparable.

Dane began walking, deciding to scout the neighborhood. Kathy's call came to mind and he fought the temptation to blame her for everything, including Mead's disappearance. The whole Japan business had been sticking in his craw for months.

A year to the day after their divorce was final she'd told him she was going abroad and that she was taking their son with her. This posed a problem because Toby had been spending three days each week with him since the separation, and God knew he was not eager to give up his three-sevenths of his child's life.

"It's only for a year," Kathy had said. "It will be good for him to be exposed to another culture at the formative stage of his life. He'll come home speaking Japanese. He'll have a second language."

Easy enough for you to say, Dane had thought. *You'll have him. I won't.* Besides, who gave a damn about acculturating a four-year-old to Japan when he hasn't even grasped the fundamentals of baseball? But Kathy considered that two years of "Sesame Street" and Toby's ability to read at the first-grade level were all the cultural grounding he needed to venture out into the wider world of sushi and karaoke.

"Better we put him in a Zen monastery with Buddhist monks than some Nippon nursery school where he'll get his identity totally confused," he'd said when they'd first argued about it. "At least that way he'd come home with a higher level of consciousness."

Then Kathy, who could give as well as take in the sarcasm department, had replied, "A vacation from God is the best thing about this trip."

The real problem wasn't Japan or even Toby. It was history—their history. Dane's dear former wife had a blind spot when it came to religion. This was ironic, considering she was fully aware that the man she'd allowed to impregnate her was on his way to becoming a divinity student. Then she'd added insult to injury by proceeding to marry him only weeks before he actually entered seminary.

Dane, of course, had to shoulder his share of the blame. He had first knocked up, then married a woman who had no sympathy whatsoever for his life's goal—the most profound mistake a man could make. But then, there had been mitigating circumstances. When they met, Kathy had a teaching fellowship and he was in his last few weeks with his brokerage firm and had already been accepted at the Starr King Seminary, making for geographical compatibility. They were also compatible in bed. In retrospect it seemed incredible that religion was simply something upon which they agreed to disagree—a blueprint for divorce, if ever there was one.

Dane came to the corner and looked in both directions. "Mead, you little bastard, don't forsake me," he muttered under his breath. Then aloud, "Here, kitty, kitty!"

Nothing.

Naturally, Toby's innocent little face began searing Dane's soul. Getting off the plane a year from now, the first words out of his son's mouth would be, "Where's Mead?"

Damn.

He crossed the street and started back down the block, calling to the truant feline from time to time, his hope rapidly fading. He'd have prayed for Mead's return, but Dane did not pray as a rule, believing that the God of creation did not need the petitions of human beings to bestow grace. Dane's God surely did not employ the same mental processes as mere humans—heaven help the cosmos if he/she did—making prayer useful only as a form of therapy.

Dane concluded that Mead, if not dead or on a pilgrimage back to Berkeley, was definitely laying low. Somehow it seemed within the cat's character to run Dane around the neighborhood for spite. If Mead still lived, Dane could only hope hunger would bring him home. Reaching the other end of the block, he crossed the street again.

Headed homeward with a sad heart, he mechanically re-

peated his pathetic mantra—"Kitty, kitty. Here, kitty, kitty."
It was to no avail.

Finding himself in front of his house and still Mead-less,
Dane peered up and down the street one more time, grumbled
an oath and went inside. He glanced around the front room,
now nearly cleared of boxes, wondering if the cat might have
slipped inside unnoticed. There was no sign of him. Mead,
he feared, was history.

After Tom Muncey's visit the previous day, Dane had put
away most of his books. It was amazing that during those
hours of unpacking he hadn't once thought of Mead, or heard
him mewing or yowling. He'd been preoccupied with that
curious story the priest had told. There was no denying that
an innocent man being put in prison for a crime he didn't
commit made for a compelling tale. Equally compelling was
the business about the daughter, a showgirl frantically trying
to save her father.

In the kitchen he tried to remember where he'd stowed the
coffeepot, checking several cupboards before he found it. The
coffee was easy. He kept it in the refrigerator, mainly because
Kathy had. He once asked her why she did that and she'd
told him she'd developed the habit while living with
Brian—the teaching assistant she'd nearly married only
months before Dane and Kathy had met. Amazing the way
little things like coffee-making habits spread through a culture. He was surprised Kathy hadn't turned that nugget of
wisdom into an article.

Oddly enough, Dane had questioned Kathy's reasons for
marrying him more at the time of their divorce than when
they'd tied the knot. It had simply never occurred to him that
she had married on the rebound until she'd said as much the
day she told him she wanted to call it quits.

As recently as the day she'd left for Japan, Toby under one
arm, the galley proofs of her book on mating rituals in post-
industrial society under the other, he'd learned something in-
structive about his ex. "I was never meant to be married,"
she'd said. "This escape is necessary for me to find myself
again." Funny. She'd never bothered to tell him she was lost.
On the other hand, maybe that was the real message of their
divorce.

It had struck him as ironic that Kathy could be so acutely cognizant of the behavior patterns of society at large, yet so blithely ignorant of what was happening in her own life. Worse, what did it say about him that it had taken so long to discover it? Part of the problem may have been that Kathy had deceived him for her own selfish purposes, but only a part. What it really came down to was that she had been one person and he had seen another, entirely.

The telephone rang about the time the coffee began to boil. Dane went into the front room to answer the phone.

"I hope I'm not calling too early," the caller said. "It's Tom Muncey."

"Ah, Father Muncey, a good morning to you. And no, it's not too early. As a matter of fact, I've just come back from my morning walk."

"Calling a clergyman of a morning can be dangerous, I find. There's no telling what prayers or rituals they might be going through."

"If it would be of comfort to you, Tom, when you called I happened to be thinking of hell."

"Jesus and Mary, Dane. That's one subject I think as little about as possible."

"A Catholic priest?"

"Off the record, mind you."

Dane chuckled. "What I said about hell is off the record, too."

They both laughed.

"I'm calling to give you Mary Margaret Duggan's address," Muncey said.

"I thought you wanted me to get it from the police chief."

"This'll save you the trouble. I know the chaplain at San Quentin, a priest by the name of O'Grady. I asked him for the girl's address, and he phoned with the information a few minutes ago."

"If I didn't know better," Dane said, "I'd wonder if you aren't getting some sort of vicarious pleasure from sending me up to Nevada to see her."

"Holy Mother, am I that transparent, Dane?"

"I gotta tell you, at times you sound more like a *schatchen* than a priest."

"A what?"

"*Schatchen.* That's Yiddish for matchmaker."

"Good Lord, you do think I'm perverse, don't you?"

"Not perverse, no. But I've got this funny feeling about what you've got in mind."

"I admit, I have a funny feeling myself," Muncey said. "Deep in my soul I sense that this is something you're meant to do."

Dane remembered his own feelings along those lines. Funny that the priest should have them, too. "When did you decide that?"

"Last night, as soon as I saw you."

"You *are* a *schatchen,* Father. Like it or not."

"Well, maybe I am. So, let me give you her address." He read it off and Dane jotted it down.

"Tell me, Tom, do you have any telepathic powers with cats?"

"Cats?"

"Yes, I lost one last night. My son's cat."

"Oh, he'll be back. Sooner than you think. Cats have strange minds. If he's your son's cat, he'll know how important he is to you. Don't worry, my friend."

"I can see how your parishioners might think you walk on water, Father. You have a very convincing manner."

"Thank you. But I'm not as inflexible about God as you might think. In fact, someday I'm going to slip off my collar and come hear you preach."

"Are you sure you'd want to risk it?"

"The devil couldn't reside in the heart of a nice fellow like you, Reverend Barrett, I'm sure of it."

"I appreciate the vote of confidence. I'm touched, actually."

"We'll talk again, but now I've got to run," the priest said. "There are sick awaiting my blessing."

"Good luck, Tom."

"Don't forget our lass, Mary Margaret, now. With a name like that, she's got to be an angel."

"I thought I'd drop by the police station today and have a chat with the chief, anyway," Dane said. "You don't mind me doing a little independent research, do you?"

"Not at all. In fact, let me know if you turn up anything interesting."

"By all means."

"I'll be off, then," Muncey said. "And don't worry about the cat. I've got three of my own. I know the way they think. He's probably outside the door right now. Have faith."

"And you have a good trip to L.A."

Dane shook his head as he hung up. In his view there were two kinds of clergymen—the worst being those who took themselves seriously, the best being those who didn't. Tom Muncey definitely fell into the latter group.

Dane returned to the kitchen where the coffee was boiling vigorously. Too vigorously. He cursed himself for not having turned down the burner. Taking the pot off the stove, he wondered if the brew could be salvaged.

He went looking for a mug. As he was poking through the cupboards, he heard something at the back door. Rushing over, he opened it, only to find Mead sitting there, looking up at him indulgently.

"Thank God," Dane said aloud. "Or maybe I should say, thank Father Muncey."

Mead casually sauntered into the kitchen, and Dane bent down, lifting him into his arms, hugging him the way he had Toby when he was a baby. He was surprised how relieved and happy he was.

Mead soon tired of the affection and Dane put him down, then watched him amble about, sniffing the air. Father Muncey understood the minds of cats, all right. Dane couldn't help wondering if he knew the minds of women just as well.

He reached into his pocket and pulled out the slip of paper—the one on which he'd copied the information Tom Muncey had given him. Mary Margaret Duggan, Desert Rest Mobile Home Court, South Virginia Street, Reno, Nevada, it said. Why, he wondered, did he find the ring of that so damned compelling?

San Quentin State Prison, California

He watched the younger men running from one end of the basketball court to the other, their bare torsos gleaming with sweat, shouts of encouragement, playful taunts and oaths hurled back and forth as rapidly as the ball itself. At the other end of the yard, iron weights clanked and jangled, reminding him of halyards slapping the masts of sailboats down at the marina on a windy day.

He circled the yard slowly, his initial burst of energy having been spent in the first twenty minutes or so of walking. Always moving, always clockwise, against the grain of traffic of the other walkers and joggers. The oddball, the walker, the old man who didn't talk much.

Jimmy Duggan lived for these three hours. The three hours when he could feel the sun, the fog, the rain on his face. The three hours they let him out of his box to pretend he was alive again.

The maximum-security exercise yard at Quentin was no Garden of Eden, but in a universe in which everything got compared to something else, it sometimes felt like paradise. Jimmy mostly thought about the world beyond the prison walls in the dead of night when he lay clinging to his blanket, hating how long it would be before the exercise period came, when he could breathe again.

In the night, and only in the night, would he think about being at sea, the salty air blowing in his face, the coastline of Sumatra or Portugal or Alaska on the horizon. On some nights he thought of walking down Market Street in San Francisco or along the vast sandy stretches at Ocean Beach. Sometimes, at two or three in the morning when the close air of the cell block was slumbering through a muted chorus of snores, punctuated by an occasional cough or sob, he would even allow himself to think of the town of Laurel and the final, painful months of his other life—the one he'd lived before the death of prison.

In those same dark hours in the netherworld of unlife, Jimmy Duggan would think of Mary Margaret. For most of her life he'd been off at sea, or in and out of county jail, on probation or off, but never much of a father. She had not lost much in losing him, but she had rallied to his cause just the same. Maybe because she was her mother's daughter. Moira had stood by him through thick and thin, never turning him away, always willing to open her heart. And now that she was gone, Mary Margaret was doing the same. She'd suffered right along with him, and she didn't deserve that. It pained him.

Whenever he saw Mary Margaret, Jimmy did not speak of his innocence because the injustice made it worse for her. Death, even, was not so bad, he had come to realize. The real suffering was not in death itself, it was in denying death. And only the living could do that. That was his legacy to his daughter, her cross and his to bear.

On the other side of the yard, Rut Coleman got up from the bench he'd been sitting on, smoking a cigarette, and began moving clockwise around the yard, same as Jimmy. Duggan was always aware of Coleman—where he was, what he was doing, who he was looking at. Rut Coleman had been his cell mate briefly when Jimmy first arrived at the prison, and he got to know him well enough to hate him deeply.

There were some fearsome characters in the maximum-security block at San Quentin—sadistic killers, rapists, thugs, the worst sort of men—but there were few who took pleasure in making their evil personal, the way Rut Coleman did. He didn't so much rage against the world, as he orchestrated misery on an individual basis. He liked to see suffering up close, and for some unknown reason he'd singled out Jimmy Duggan. To Rut, another man's peace was his sorrow. "I'm not alone if I can hear you cry, Jimmy," he'd once told him. That had said so very much about the man.

As Duggan was passing alongside the basketball court, one of the players, a young black man of twenty the men called Ace, went down after a collision, clutching his ankle. The other players gathered close, watching him writhe in agony. Another, older black inmate named Lester who couldn't shoot worth a damn but who, by common agreement, was a "demon on the boards," looked up at Jimmy and broke into a wide smile.

"Wanna play a liddle ball, ol' man? They needs somebody to slow 'em down a liddle. Whoopin' our ass, they is. Oh, Mama!"

Duggan shook his head and kept walking. It wasn't a serious question. Lester was ribbing the opposition, using him to do it, the way he used the ball. Gamesmanship. Wordplay. Friendly competition. Everybody had some kind of jive, some mode of expression, even if was only silence.

With help, Ace limped off the court under the scrutiny of the guards in the gun tower—the "referees with guns," as the players called them. "Another foul like that and I'll have 'em shoot your black ass," or "Clint up in the tower's got twenty bucks that says you're goin' to miss the free throw, Slick. And Clint's got a rifle. Say your prayers."

Even when he was young, the rough-and-tumble of a playing field wasn't Jimmy Duggan's world. He'd been in his share of bar brawls in his youth, especially when he was in the merchant marine, but basketball and handball and lifting weights were not his thing. Walking round and round, like the hands of a clock, wearing an invisible path in the asphalt, wearing an invisible path through time—that was *his* sporting life.

As he approached the corner of the yard, Jimmy heard footsteps. He glanced back and saw Rut Coleman approaching.

"Nice day, Jimmy, isn't it?" Coleman said, putting his arm around Jimmy's shoulders.

"Yeah, great."

Coleman sucked on his cigarette and blew the smoke in Jimmy's face. Duggan didn't flinch. He just kept walking. Coleman stayed right with him.

"Heard the good news?" Rut Coleman said as they strolled past the bodybuilders.

Duggan shook his head.

"Got my release date, man!" he enthused, squeezing Jimmy's shoulders. "It wasn't supposed to be for eight more months, but they moved it up. Tomorrow I'm outta here!"

"That's great, Rut. Congratulations." Jimmy meant it. If there was anybody he'd like to see killed or released, it was Rut Coleman.

Rut, a bulky man of forty with rounded shoulders and gangly arms, sighed like a dreamy schoolgirl. "Yeah. Me and my brother already got the first week planned. Figured we'd go to Reno and have a look at Mary Margaret's tits. 'Course, I'll get some ass while I'm there. Maybe hers, if she's interested. Think she'd want to do it with a former roommate of her daddy's, for old time's sake, Jimmy?''

The words went through Duggan like a knife. He'd seen a man killed with a bedspring, the blood spilled all over the shower room. Had Rut Coleman thrust a bedspring in Jimmy's side just then, it couldn't have hurt him more.

For several years Coleman had taunted him about Mary Margaret. In the first few weeks they were cell mates—when Rut had put on the friendly act he used with new prisoners to ferret out their vulnerabilities—Jimmy had let down his guard and talked about life outside. They'd lain on their bunks in the dark, Coleman listening as Jimmy told him how his daughter had given up her chance to go to college to become a showgirl so she could pay his legal bills.

Jimmy should have wondered at Coleman's questions about Mary Margaret, his fascination with her. "You mean she dances nude on stage?'' Rut asked, that first night they'd talked.

"It's not a strip joint," Jimmy had told him. "It's a musical review, legitimate stuff.''

"But topless, right? Nothing on their tits?''

Rut's insistence on hearing details was the first warning sign, and Jimmy had tried to back off, but Coleman became obsessed. He'd begged to see Mary Margaret's high-school graduation photo. One afternoon he'd stared at it so long, rubbing his crotch as he did, that Jimmy lost his cool. He jerked the picture away and tore it to pieces right in front of him. That had been the beginning of the end.

Jimmy wasn't supposed to get a cell of his own, but he had a couple of asthma attacks, making them seem worse than they really were to get the attention of the prison staff. The ploy worked and they moved him to his own cell, away from Rut and his tobacco smoke.

It was only a reprieve, though. Rut Coleman chided him about Mary Margaret's dancing and her bare breasts every chance he got, especially in the shower, while he played with himself. In time, Jimmy realized it was as much Rut's sadistic impulses as his obsession with Mary Margaret that drove him, but that didn't lessen Jimmy's anguish. Mary Margaret was Jimmy Duggan's Achilles' heel and Rut Coleman knew it.

"So, are you happy for me?" Coleman said, slapping Jimmy affectionately on the chest with the flat of his hand, all the while keeping the other arm clamped around his shoulders. "Bet you wish it was you going to Nevada to see the girl dance, don't you?" He gave a false laugh. "Ever get a hard-on thinking about her boobies bouncing while she prances around? Maybe since you're her daddy you don't think about things like that." Rut laughed again. "But then again, maybe you do."

"You're sick, Rut."

Coleman took Jimmy's jaw in his large hand and squeezed it, making it seem affectionate on the surface, but secretly digging his nails into Jimmy's flesh. "All I need is a little loving from your long-legged baby girl, Jimmy."

"You won't be able to leave the state while you're on parole," Duggan told him.

Rut took a long drag on his cigarette and blew smoke in Jimmy's face again. "They don't follow you around, jerk-off. You ought to know that. Nobody'll know if I slip over the border with my brother for a little nooky with a showgirl. Unless you plan on telling, of course. You aren't a fink, are you, Jimmy? Lord, the boys would hate to think they're living with a fink."

Duggan fell silent. There was no way to outsmart Rut. His mind was too sick and twisted and focused on evil. Silence was the best antidote.

Passing the handball courts, gambler's corner, as the men called it—mostly because the game, a one-on-one contest, attracted the hustlers and bettors—Rut leaned close, his stale tobacco breath washing over Jimmy as he whispered in his ear. "You going to give me your blessing with Boobsie, old man?"

Duggan refused to answer.

"Are you? You gonna think of me up in Reno havin' a ball ballin' your baby girl, Jimmy?"

Duggan still didn't speak, he just kept walking.

"Well, I'll tell 'er her daddy sends his love anyway," Rut said. "I'm sure she'll be real eager to hear all about you, how friendly you and me were."

With that, Rut made an about-face and headed in the other

direction, probably to find one of his other favored pigeons to torment. That was Rut Coleman's life, preying on people. He'd spent fifteen-plus years in maximum security for robbing and pistol-whipping a woman in a Stockton parking lot. He had a prior for rape.

Jimmy tried to put Coleman's words from his mind. Coleman was just talking, he reasoned, finding a way to torture him. But what if he was serious and did try to contact Mary Margaret? She might respond to an appeal to meet with her father's former cell mate. Rut could be disarming, even charming if it suited him.

Should he warn her? Jimmy wondered. It might upset her for no reason. On the other hand, what if a word of caution spared her a horrible experience? Whatever suffering he endured because of it would be nothing in comparison.

But how could he warn her? A letter could tip off the staff and Rut could be questioned. That might cause problems with a lot more people than just Rut Coleman. Maybe he could talk to the prison chaplain and ask him to phone Mary Margaret. Father O'Grady was a decent enough man. That was the only way he could do this sort of work. But the priest also had loyalties to the system. After all, anything Jimmy said wouldn't exactly be like confession and therefore privileged. Still, Mary Margaret's safety was at stake.

The tower buzzer rang, indicating that the exercise period was up. Grumbling, the men stopped what they were doing, the shooters on the basketball court taking a final shot before a shout from a guard brought them to heel. Everyone began moving in the plodding cadence of a chain gang toward the entrance to the cell block, the vigor of only moments earlier bottled up until tomorrow.

Nearing the door, Jimmy glanced back over the prison walls at the mountaintops of Marin. The afternoon fog was in, spilling over the rounded peaks like an ethereal gravy. He would feel the fog in his bunk that night as it embraced the prison, and he would shiver under his coarse blanket and worry about his little girl. That was his lot in life. God's punishment for being the man he was.

Laurel, California

Dane Barrett had never known any policeman personally—the extent of his direct contact with one was getting a traffic citation. Nor were there any stories about cops around the dinner table when he was growing up. His father rarely saw the inside of a civil court, let alone a criminal one. And so he had little to compare with what he found at the Laurel Police Department when he dropped by that afternoon.

"Curious how the Duggan case has caught the imagination of the clergy," Chief Slater said. "Is it something in the air, Reverend?"

"The possibility of injustice, I believe."

"I haven't studied the case closely, but it looked like a solid one," the chief said. "Which is not to say mistakes weren't made. But then, there's not much—outside the Church maybe—that's perfect."

"Human frailty is rampant everywhere, Chief. Some say in the Church more than any place else."

Slater chuckled. "Now that I wouldn't know."

Carl Slater was in his mid-forties, a neat man with a neat gray mustache to go with his neat gray hair. There was a military precision about him, yet an affability that was more in the mode of a politician. He'd made it clear right up front that he didn't have a lot of time. "I'll have you speak to Sergeant Jones, though," he'd told Dane. "Granville's been around here longer than anyone else and is much more familiar with the case than I am."

They left the chief's tidy corner office and went down the hall to the office of Granville Jones, a wiry little man in his fifties with a persona that was more typically small-town than Slater's. Granville had large protruding ears, narrow shoulders and thin slicked-back hair that made him appear rodent-like. It was immediately apparent that Sergeant Jones took himself very seriously.

"Coffee, Pastor?" Granville said, thumping a pencil on the desktop in front of him.

"No, thank you."

"Mind if I have one?"

"Not at all."

Jones got up, hitching up his pants before striding from the office, leaving Dane to peer around in search of clues to the man's character. They were everywhere. Framed certificates, honors and photos covered the wall behind the sergeant's desk. Dane checked them out.

A citizen-of-the-month award from the Laurel Chamber of Commerce, June 1987. Honorable mention in the Little League coach-of-the-year contest. Certificate of completion in the basic course at the state police academy. Second prize in animal husbandry, poultry division, at the San Joaquin County Fair. His high-school diploma. Pictures of him in uniform with a group of grade-school crossing guards. Granville in uniform posing with a group of beauty queens—one would imagine the Miss Laurel contest. And prominently placed in the center of the wall was a plaque in recognition of Granville Jones as the 1982 Laurel City Government Employee of the Year, complete with photo of the recipient shaking hands with the mayor.

The man himself returned, a steaming mug of coffee in hand. "Sure I can't get you a cup, Pastor Barrett?"

"No, thank you."

Granville took his seat behind the desk, carefully setting down his mug down on a kitchen tile he used as a coaster. He folded his hands on the desk, leaned toward Dane and said in a solemn voice, "Let me save you a lot of grief, Pastor. Jimmy Duggan killed Donna Lee Marshall. He *was* guilty. He *is* guilty, and he'll *be* guilty till his dying day."

"You seem awfully certain, Sergeant."

"I was there when they brought him in and present at the interrogation. If I've ever seen a guilty man, Jimmy Duggan was the one."

"Was it his demeanor that makes you say that?"

"First, of course, it's the evidence. He still had the girl's blood on his clothes, for chrissakes. Oops, sorry," Granville said, clearly thinking his language might offend. "There was the evidence, but yes, the way he acted, too. A cop can look in a man's eyes and know. That don't mean a thing in court, of course. The law says we have to prove the crime and that's exactly what Ted Gotchall did. He was chief detective on the case. Teddy retired a few years back. He's no longer around."

"I see."

The sergeant took a careful sip of coffee, then placed the mug back on the tile. "The chief told me about the old lady mumbling something about Duggan being innocent, but I don't put any stock in it, Pastor. You shouldn't, either. She wasn't critical to the case, anyway. At the time of the trial she was just another nail in Duggan's coffin."

"I'm afraid I'm at a severe disadvantage, Sergeant Jones," Dane said. "I don't know a thing about the case except that a girl was stabbed. Could you fill me in?"

"Yep. It's in my brain like it happened yesterday" he said, pointing to his head. He folded his hands over his stomach, his rodent-like face growing pensive. "The Marshall girl's murder was one of the biggest cases ever to hit Laurel. I don't mean to say there aren't other murders. Every few years a Mexican gets knifed in a bar brawl, but that's common in the valley and hardly gets much attention. The Duggan case was hot for months. People wanted justice."

"Could it be they wanted it too badly?"

Jones shook his head. "We had him dead to rights, believe me. Here's the story." He cleared his throat and leaned back in his chair self-importantly. "I'll start with the background. Duggan's got a long list of priors, see. A string of misdemeanors that could've been felonies if the prosecutor had really gone after him. That's not proof of guilt, but it reveals the man, if you know what I mean."

"What sort of crimes were they?"

"Assault. Drunk and disorderly. There was a sexual battery when he was nineteen. A few years later he was going to be tried for burglary, but the charges were reduced to criminal trespass. He was arrested once for armed robbery, but his lawyer worked out a deal in exchange for his testimony against his accomplices and he did a year in county jail. He was arrested for rape over in the Philippines, but never went to trial. It was a hooker and he bought her off was the story I heard."

"The pattern of violence led finally to the murder of a high-school girl—is that the theory?"

"That was the prosecutor's angle, yeah. Mr. Wainwright did a hell of a job, by the way. It's no surprise he went on to be attorney general."

"Scott Wainwright was the prosecutor in the Duggan case?" Dane said, surprised.

"Yep. He was prosecuting attorney of San Joaquin County before going up to Sacramento. Lot of people say this was the case that launched him. Made political hay about the need to protect our young people from violence. I remember him going up to the legislature and testifying about the need for tougher legislation."

"You know," Dane said, "I'd forgotten that. But now that you mention it, it sounds familiar." He shook his head. "So all that political hoopla years ago was about the Duggan case."

"One and the same."

"I guess I repress anything having to do with politics and politicians. They give mothers, apple pie and the Fourth of July a bad name."

Granville Jones scratched his head. "I feel the same, I guess. Once Scott Wainwright got into big-time politics, he sort of lost my respect. But he did one hell of a job on the Duggan case."

"The jury must have thought so."

"It wasn't a stretch, believe me. Not considering the evidence." Jones nodded solemnly.

Dane scanned the achievement wall behind Granville as he tried to think what else he should ask. The business of crime was new to him, but the pursuit of truth wasn't. Investigators, while not exactly employing the Socratic method in questioning people, did have to understand the human mind, and perhaps the human soul, as well. Still, he wasn't sure what he was after. He and Tom Muncey were working on the hypothesis that Ledi Hopkins's deathbed revelation was somehow significant. If it was, he wanted to be able to relate that to Duggan's daughter.

"Tell me, Sergeant," he said, pressing on, "except for the rape in the Philippines, were the other crimes committed here in Laurel?"

"No, no. Duggan's from San Francisco. He was sent over

here on some church rehabilitation program. The do-good Unitarians.''

Dane smiled. "Yes, we do have that failing."

"Oops. Sorry, Pastor Barrett, I forgot you were Unitarian."

"No harm, Sergeant Jones. We've been called worse."

Granville Jones grinned sheepishly.

"That explains why Duggan was working for the First Unitarian Church, then," Dane said.

"Right. I think his kid was a big factor. You see, her mother died when she was in high school and there was no other family. The parents had been separated off and on for years and the girl hadn't spent much time with her old man. Since he was out of work when his wife died, he wouldn't have been able to support the girl. This program was supposed to give them the chance they needed."

"But it seems to have backfired."

"Roger that."

Dane contemplated the man. "So how did the murder occur, Sergeant?"

Jones took another drink of coffee, setting the mug down carefully, as he had before. "It was a crime of passion, Pastor Barrett. Ted did a hell of a job putting it all together. Seems the victim, Donna Lee Marshall, was sort of wild. Her father had run off and the mother didn't do a very good job of keeping her in line. The girl got mixed up with a fast group at school—nothing real bad, the usual high-school petty-drug scene, wild parties, skinny-dipping out at the lake, things like that. Anyway, the mother puts her in a youth group at the Unitarian church, hoping it'd be a good influence. The pastor and his wife kind of took Donna Lee under their wings, though Mrs. Ragsdale was already pretty much bedridden by then. She had that muscle disease where your face and throat and lungs get all spastic."

"Myasthenia gravis. My aunt had it."

"Yeah, that's it. Sad story. She finally died a few years after the trial. Left behind the pastor and their daughter."

Dane nodded solemnly. "Somehow, though, Donna Lee got involved with Duggan."

"Yep. We aren't sure how they got connected. She spent a lot of time around the church, and with Duggan there, living in the basement, I guess one thing led to another, and he seduced her."

"But he was living with his daughter, wasn't he?"

"Yeah, but like all teens, her friends were important to her. She spent a lot of time with her best friend, slept at her house, that sort of thing. Point is, Duggan was on his own a lot."

"And ended up having some sort of romantic or sexual relationship with Donna Lee Marshall," Dane said.

"That's the theory."

"Did Jimmy Duggan admit he had a relationship with the girl?"

"No, he denied it at first. Then, when we started throwing things at him, he backed down pretty damn quick," Jones said with a self-satisfied grin.

"Explain."

"Well, he was forced to admit that Donna Lee had been in his apartment after we found...well, some of her pubic hairs in his bed."

"Did he have an explanation?"

"He said a few days before she was killed he'd been working in the church and went down to his apartment and found Donna Lee in the bed, buck naked. Claimed nothing happened, that he ran her out. We knew she was a wild-ass kid, pardon the expression, but who's going to believe it was all her doing—that he was being sexually harassed by her? I sure don't buy it."

"Evidently the jury didn't, either."

"No siree. You gotta admit it strains the imagination."

"What about the day of the murder?" Dane asked. "What happened?"

"Donna Lee was killed in the kitchen of her house over on Hemlock Street. She staggered out the back door and actually died in the yard. Happened in broad daylight. She was stabbed twenty, thirty times with a kitchen knife. You'd have thought somebody would have heard something," Jones said, "but the mother was at work, as were most of the neighbors. The old lady next door, Theo Bledsoe, claimed she was taking a nap and didn't hear any screams.

"Donna Lee was in a bikini, probably sunning herself, when Duggan arrived. We figured they argued, had a lover's quarrel, she fled into the house. Duggan pursued her, breaking in the screen door to gain entry...in other words, committing a burglary. That's important, Pastor, because a murder committed during the commission of a felony makes it first-degree. They call it the Felony Murder Rule.''

"Otherwise it's second-degree?"

"Or even manslaughter. Mr. Wainwright worked real hard to get first-degree. He wanted a finding of special circumstances in order to get the death penalty, but the jury didn't buy it. He got the first-degree conviction, though, and Duggan got life without possibility of parole. Personally, I think it was the brutality of the crime that tipped the scales. Evidence was she put up a hell of a fight. There was blood all over the kitchen and in the yard.''

"Did they find the murder weapon?"

"Yeah, it was on the floor, a kitchen knife.''

"With Duggan's fingerprints on it?"

"Hardly any prints to speak of. Some of the girl's, as I recall. The knife was covered with blood. The coroner thinks Donna Lee pulled it out of her stomach herself before staggering out the door.''

"What did Duggan say?"

"At first he denied he was even there. Claimed the blood on his shirt was from a cut he got shaving. He had a fresh cut on his neck, all right, but we knew where he got it. When we told him a neighbor had seen him running from the crime scene, he changed his story again, admitting he was there but insisting that Donna Lee had already been stabbed and that he found her in the yard, dying. That's why he had blood on him—he came in contact with the body, trying to give her first aid, if you can believe that.''

Dane pondered that. "Did Duggan say what he was doing at the victim's house?"

"That's the best part. He said the minister sent him.''

"Ragsdale? From the First Unitarian?"

"Yep. Pastor Stephen Ragsdale. According to Duggan, the pastor asked him to take some books and papers and things having to do with the youth group over to the Marshall place.''

"Was that true?"

"We did find books and papers with Donna Lee's name on them in the yard, but Pastor Ragsdale denied asking Duggan to take them to Donna Lee's house. Said he left the stuff with Duggan to give to the girl when she came by the church."

"Is the distinction significant?"

Granville Jones clasped his hands behind his head, grinning. "That's where things get interesting. The defense claimed it was Ragsdale who was sexually involved with Donna Lee, not Duggan. They tried to make Duggan out to be an innocent bystander."

"They said Reverend Ragsdale killed the girl?"

"There was no evidence of that. But Duggan's kid, Mary, came to us the day of her dad's arrest and told us a story about seeing Donna Lee and Ragsdale together. Said she'd seen Ragsdale fondling the girl. And Mary also claimed Ragsdale had made a pass at her. I was the first to talk to her. She was passionate about it, I admit, in tears during most of the conversation, which is understandable, considering. But in my professional opinion, she was trying to save her old man's butt."

"So Mary Margaret tried to blame the murder on Ragsdale."

"She said he could have done it as easily as her father, that he was the one Donna Lee was involved with."

"Could she have been right?"

Granville Jones got out of his chair, stretched, then he ambled to the window and peered through the venetian blinds at the sunny, leafy streets of Laurel. "Ted Gotchall talked to Pastor Ragsdale, of course," the sergeant said. "He denied being involved with Donna Lee. He admitted the girl had some emotional problems and had been sexually aggressive toward him, but that nothing shady had happened."

"So you felt Duggan succumbed, but Reverend Ragsdale didn't."

Jones turned from the window. "Basically, yes."

"Where was Ragsdale at the time of the murder?" Dane asked.

The policeman broke into a broad grin. "You have this question thing down pretty good, don't you, Pastor Barrett?"

"Sorry," Dane said, embarrassed. "I hope I'm not being pushy."

"No, it's just that I'm used to asking questions, not answering them so much," he said with a shrug. Jones returned to his chair. "Ragsdale had an alibi. He was in his study at home, working on his Sunday sermon."

"I assume he was able to prove it to your satisfaction."

"His wife corroborated his story. She said he came into her room several times during the critical hour or so when the crime was committed. But Teddy didn't leave any stones unturned, as they say. He checked things out real carefully, talked to every girl he could find who'd been in Ragsdale's youth groups. Not a one said he ever came on to them. If he was playing around with the Marshall and Duggan girls, they were the only ones."

"I understand Reverend Ragsdale is deceased," Dane said.

"Yep. He was killed in a hunting accident a few years after the murder, shortly after his wife died."

"Unfortunate."

"Yep."

"Strange sport for a Unitarian Universalist minister, hunting," Dane said.

Granville Jones stroked his chin. "Yeah, why's that?"

"Ours is a liberal religion. UU's tend to be ecology-minded."

"What's that mean? Animal rights?"

"Some UU's are advocates of animal rights, but not all by any means. As a religious denomination, we're diverse."

"Seems to me I heard Unitarians are different," Granville Jones said. "The wife, who's into all that stuff, says they aren't Christian. Is that true?"

Dane smiled. "I'll spare you the details and give you my two-bit summary of the subject. Historically, Unitarian Universalism was considered a Protestant denomination, and many modern UU's are Christian, but it's not a requirement of membership."

"You don't have to believe in God, in other words."

"I would say most UU's believe in a spiritual dimension to human existence—that there's something bigger than us out there, that life has transcendent meaning, and that God or creation is behind it. But the individual member is free to define God as he or she sees fit, and to relate in a way that meets his or her own needs.''

"So what about heaven and hell?" Granville Jones asked, his curiosity clearly piqued.

Dane thought of the many conversations he'd had in Berkeley on the subject. Once he explained that he regarded God to be a good deal more complex than the classic Renaissance image of an old man with a white beard that had become a fixture in western culture, it always seemed to come down to heaven and hell.

"Let me put it this way, Sergeant," he said. "We believe what's important in life is the way you live it, that all religions have something to offer and that there is no one single truth.''

"Boy, wouldn't that give the wife fits? She's an old-time Methodist. Goes to church every Sunday. Always nagging me to go, but...well, let's say I don't buy all the devil-and-angel stuff. Being a cop and seeing the things I see, I figure all the hell there is, is right here on earth. Like the Donna Lee Marshall murder, for instance.''

"Yes," Dane said, "that *is* our subject, isn't it? Didn't mean to sermonize.''

"Don't sweat it, Pastor," Jones said with a grin. "Gave me a chance to *ask* some questions instead of just *answering* them, for a change.''

"I'll try not to abuse your indulgence, Sergeant.''

"No problem. We're here to serve the taxpayer. Fire away.''

"Well, what I was getting at is that Reverend Ragsdale being killed while hunting strikes me as a bit strange for a UU minister.''

"I don't know anything about the circumstances," Jones said. "The department wasn't involved. Happened up in Amador County.''

"I see.''

Granville Jones leaned back in his chair, his hands again folded over his stomach. "So, any more questions, Pastor Barrett? This is your chance.''

"We haven't talked about Ledi Hopkins," Dane said. "How did she figure into the case?''

"Oh, yeah, the deathbed statement. That's why you came here in the first place. Like I told you, Ledi wasn't critical to the case. She was visiting her sister, who lived next door to the Marshalls. Theo Bledsoe. Ledi was just arriving when she saw Duggan run down the driveway of the Marshalls' house and head up the street.''

"In other words, she was the eyewitness placing him at the scene of the crime.''

"Roger that.''

"So, why would she now say he's innocent?''

"Who knows? She was old and senile and dying. I'm no expert, but how trustworthy can she be under those circumstances?''

"In my experience, Sergeant, people tend to be more truthful as they approach death, not less.''

"If they've got all their marbles, yeah.''

Dane nodded, seeing that the officer was more than convinced of Jimmy Duggan's guilt. "You don't see any room for doubt, do you?''

"I gotta be honest. Donna Lee Marshall may not have been the most innocent girl in town, but we know one thing for sure—she was brutally murdered. She didn't deserve it.''

"No,'' Dane said. "We can agree on that.''

"As far as Duggan is concerned—'' Jones held up his hand and began ticking off the points one by one "—he had the motive, the means and the opportunity. All the essentials. We had enough evidence to hang him twice over, in my opinion. The man was lucky to get off with his life. Damned lucky.''

"You make a convincing argument.''

"If you were in the jury box, you'd have voted the same.''

"Perhaps,'' Dane said. "Probably, even. But I have to tell you, Ledi Hopkins recanting her testimony gives me pause.''

"Did you talk to her before she died?''

"No, unfortunately not.''

"Babbling something about a convicted man being innocent is not exactly recanting testimony,'' Jones said. "She either saw Duggan leave the Marshall place minutes after Donna Lee was killed, or she didn't. I don't think she changed her mind on that, did she?''

"It's a little vague, I admit, Sergeant, but I intend to find out."

"How?"

"For starters, I'm going to talk to the nurses who cared for Ledi before she died."

"I'll be interested to hear what they say. Be sure and let me know."

"I will, Sergeant." Dane checked his watch. "I'm sure you have more important things to do than indulge a would-be sleuth, so I'll get out of your hair."

"No problem," Granville Jones said, getting up. "Like I said, our mission here in the department is to serve." He came around his desk to shake Dane's hand. "It was a learning experience for me, too. Now I can say I've met a Unitarian minister and got the God's truth...or somebody's."

Dane laughed as he went to the door. "I should introduce you to my mother."

"Why's that?"

"She's one of those folks who directs her prayers to her stockbroker. I'm her prodigal son, you see. She's waiting for me to come to my senses."

"So, even ministers have those problems."

"That's a twenty-dollar lecture in itself, Sergeant Jones."

"Maybe some Sunday, then."

"Sure," Dane said with a wink, "services are at eleven. Drop by anytime."

Dane had walked to the police station and found the temperature even hotter as he retraced his steps to the First Unitarian Church, eight blocks away. He liked walking and felt it was the best way to get to know a place. Of course, there wasn't as much to get acquainted with in Laurel as in Berkeley or San Francisco, but he'd vowed to get to know both the town and the people. A minister, he'd learned in seminary, had to be devoted to his community, as well as to his congregation.

On the surface, Laurel was a sleepy town of fifty thousand people, not a real city, but not a village, either. There was more affluence in Laurel than first met the eye though. The tip-off was that it had as many banks as restaurants or churches.

On a hot summer afternoon with the temperature approaching a hundred and five, there wasn't much activity. Everyone was enjoying the air-conditioned comfort of their homes, offices or businesses. Thank God the repairman had fixed his unit that morning. Life without air-conditioning was a little too ascetic for his taste, to put it mildly.

At the corner of Broadway and Park, he turned west and went a block to Elm. From there it was only a few blocks to the church. He'd already spent a little time with Claudia Rosenfelter, the church secretary, and he had met the office volunteers. Sunday he'd be delivering his first sermon, but it was one he'd written the previous year and had delivered before.

As he strolled, Dane couldn't help wondering if the concern he and Tom Muncey had developed for Jimmy Duggan wasn't misplaced. Could the priest have been aware how strong the case against Duggan was?

Dane came to the city park, a square block of shade trees and grass with a playground in one corner and a bank of tennis courts in another. Two teenage girls were playing. He stopped under a big tree to watch them.

Eight years ago they might have been Mary Margaret Duggan and Donna Lee Marshall, two innocent girls playing tennis in a leafy park in small-town America, a place where people put their money in the bank and went to church. Now one was dead and the other was a showgirl. Was it their failure? he wondered. Or had America failed them?

Having had his respite from the sun, Dane continued his trek. Reaching the corner, he looked up at the sound of a horn. There was a car at the stop sign. Father Muncey was waving his arm out the window.

"Dane," he called. "Do you have a minute?"

Muncey proceeded across the intersection and pulled over. Dane crossed the street to speak with him.

"Glad I ran into you," Tom Muncey said, squinting into the sun. "There was no answer at your house and the woman in the church office said she didn't expect you for a while."

"I've been at the police station. What's up, Tom?"

"I had a disturbing call from Elena Perez. She told me a

man came by the convalescent hospital last night and threatened her.''

"Threatened her how?"

"Warned her to stop talking about Ledi Hopkins," Muncey said.

"You're kidding."

"No. Told her if she didn't there might be trouble for her relatives. Apparently, she has a cousin or a nephew or something who's an illegal and living in fear of being deported. Said if she kept her mouth shut, there wouldn't be any problem."

"Jesus."

"Well," Father Muncey said with a puckish grin, "yes, I suppose."

Dane smiled. "No offense, Father."

"None taken, my son."

"What do you make of it?" Dane asked.

"I haven't the slightest."

"It's safe to say somebody out there is not at all comfortable with Ledi's crisis of conscience."

"I'd say that's a fair assumption."

"And still more reason to wonder," Dane said.

"Yeah."

They both reflected.

"How did it go at the police station?" the priest asked.

"Frankly, I'd decided the business with Ledi Hopkins was a tempest in a teapot. If the police are to be believed, all the evidence against Duggan was overwhelming. I don't know if we'd be doing the Duggan girl any favors by raising her hopes, when nothing can come of it."

"What about this guy who threatened Elena?"

"It suggests there's something going on, doesn't it?"

"Go see Mary Margaret, Dane. She should know what's happened."

Dane sighed. "Maybe I can drive up to Reno tomorrow and talk to her."

"It's not the sort of thing to be handled on the phone," Tom said with a wink. "Far less personal."

Dane ignored the chiding. "What does Elena Perez plan to do about the threats?"

"Needless to say, she was unnerved by the visit," Muncey replied.

"She doesn't know who the guy was?"

Tom Muncey shook his head. "He wouldn't identify himself. Elena said he was totally unfamiliar."

"The poor thing."

"She knows I'm going to be out of town, but I told her there was a possibility you'd want to speak with her. I gave her your name and said she could trust you." Muncey handed over a slip of paper. "Here's her home address and phone number. I also jotted down my numbers in Southern California in case you need to reach me."

Dane took the paper, then stuffed it in his pocket. "I was mentally prepared to drop the whole thing. Now you've got me right back in it."

"No rest for the wicked," the priest said with another wink.

Resting his hands on the open window, Dane glanced into the back seat of the car where he saw a large suitcase. "You're on your way, I take it."

"Yes indeed. Hollywood, here I come."

"The next Bing Crosby."

Tom Muncey chuckled. Then, patting Dane's hand in a friendly way, he said, "Happy hunting, lad."

He stepped back and Tom took off up the street. Dane thought about the priest's last words. Happy hunting was about the size of it. There was his curiosity about Duggan's daughter, yes, but that wasn't the essential point. Donna Lee Marshall had been murdered eight years ago in this sleepy little town and it was becoming clear that somebody didn't want her grave disturbed. And though Dane couldn't explain it, he was developing an irresistible urge to find out why.

Reno, Nevada

Mary Margaret carefully applied polish to Janine's nails, glancing at the clock between fingers. They were at the kitchen table, the oscillating fan sitting on the counter slowly weeping over them. It was nearly five.

"Am I going to have time to do you?" Janine asked.

"No. Maybe tomorrow. I have a feeling I'll be in the mood for a complete makeover by then."

Janine gave her a very displeased look. Mary Margaret ignored her.

"I wish I could find a way to bring you to your senses," Janine said. "I'm a thousand percent opposed to this business with Ramon."

"So you've said."

"I have a proposal."

Mary Margaret glanced up as she dipped the brush into the polish. "A proposal?"

"Let me go with you to his room."

"Janine, he might panic or get pissed off. I can't take that chance. Anthony's been relatively gentle up to now. But I guarantee you, if he gets the hell beat out of him because he couldn't make his payment, he'll come after me."

"But it's so risky. And, forgive me, stupid, too."

"I'm in a corner and you know it," Mary Margaret replied.

Janine pulled her hand free. "Listen, you might have financial problems, but you've lost all sense of proportion. I'm telling you, Mary Margaret, I won't let you go to that hotel room alone. If you don't want me to go in with you, fine, but I'll be outside the door and the first sign of trouble I'm calling for help."

"That's silly. This is not your problem."

"You're my problem," Janine rejoined. "I've got big bucks invested in you. I want you dancing, earning the bread to pay me back. This isn't altruism you're hearing."

A smile touched the corners of Mary Margaret's mouth. "Lord, a few college courses under your belt and you're using big words on me."

"Don't try to change the subject."

Mary Margaret leaned back in her chair. She folded her arms under her breasts. "If I let you go to the door with me, will you get off my case?"

"Yes."

"All right, we have a deal. Now give me your other hand."

Janine seemed to feel better and so did Mary Margaret. A good friend was the most valuable resource a woman could have. Since her mother had died, Mary Margaret had pretty much been on her own, and she'd learned the hard way that the secret to *being* strong was to convince herself that she *was* strong. As a result, it was sometimes hard for her to let her guard down, to admit her fears and her pain, even to someone she trusted, like Janine.

Doing a private strip show for a stranger was not just your everyday walk in the park. Sure, other girls had succumbed to temptation—especially when the dollars were big. She hadn't known anyone who'd actually fallen into prostitution, but she had heard tales about girls who'd "dated" customers and subsequently lost their jobs.

Bernie Solomon ran a clean operation and the High Chaparral had a good reputation because of it. In fact, most of the cast was as moral as any other group in their twenties or thirties. Four women in the chorus line were married, and Dora Thomas had two kids. As Artie Heartman often said, "Keep your waist trim, your legs in shape and the fat off your butt, and you can do chorus 'til you're fifty."

The phone rang.

"Your nails are wet," Mary Margaret told Janine. "I'll get it." She went to the phone on the kitchen counter. "Hello."

"Could I speak with Mary Margaret Duggan, please?" It was a man's voice. Unfamiliar.

"This is she."

"Oh, Mary Margaret, hello. This is Father O'Grady, the chaplain at the state penitentiary at San Quentin."

Mary Margaret's heart went stone cold. She'd met the priest and his solemn face was instantly in her mind's eye. He wouldn't call unless there was trouble. "Something has happened to my father," she said, fighting back her panic.

"No, no. Jimmy's fine, my child. Nothing like that."

"What then, what is it?"

"Your father's asked me to pass along a message."

"What message?"

The priest sighed. "I really shouldn't be doing this. I'm taking a risk myself."

"Father, what message?"

"There was an inmate here at the prison who was released today, paroled, a man named Rut Coleman. A rather unpleasant human being, I must say. I didn't know him well, so I can't speak from personal experience, but your father certainly can. They were cell mates briefly some years back.'' The priest took a calming breath. ''The long and the short of it, Mary Margaret, is that Coleman amused himself by tormenting your father.''

Her heart began to ache. Her dad's having to endure a life in prison was one of the hardest things for her to deal with and she tried not to think about it if she could avoid it.

''Anyway,'' Father O'Grady went on, ''as a parting shot, Coleman told Jimmy he was going to go to Reno to look you up. Threatened to…well, let's say do some unpleasant things.''

''Like what?''

''Molest you. I don't know how specific he was, but the point is, it wasn't the sort of thing a father wants to hear. Jimmy and I both think it was idle talk, but he felt you had to be warned, just to be safe. The man is evil, but he can be charming when it suits him. Point is, if Coleman calls or tries to contact you, don't see him. That's essentially what your father wanted me to convey.''

Mary Margaret was stunned. Never once had she felt as if she was in danger because of her father's problems. ''I appreciate you letting me know, Father O'Grady,'' she said as calmly as she could. She glanced at Janine, trying hard to keep her anguish in check.

''Goodbye, Mary Margaret, and God bless.''

She dropped the phone into the cradle and turned to Janine, who'd been listening to every word.

''What happened?'' Janine asked.

Mary Margaret told her the gist of the conversation.

''Just what you need, somebody else to pester you.''

Mary Margaret sat at the table and took Janine's hand. She had one nail yet to do. ''God doesn't give you more than you can bear,'' she said stoically. ''That *is* what they say, isn't it?''

Janine reached over and touched her cheek. Mary Margaret looked up. Tears started welling. She tried to smile through them. It didn't work. They rolled down her cheek. ''Damn,'' she said, reaching for a tissue.

"You poor baby."

Mary Margaret blew her nose. "You know what? I've cried more today than I have all year. It's getting embarrassing."

"You're entitled."

"At Saint Catherine's the nuns used to say everything happens for a reason," she said, shaking her head. "What they didn't say was that sometimes the reason is pretty shitty."

Janine's eyes were glistening, too. "If this guy, Coleman, is stupid enough to come around, we'll be waiting for him. You know where I keep the gun, in the drawer in my bedside table. Speaking of which, I've been thinking that maybe you should take it with you tonight."

"You mean so that if I don't fall in love with Ramon, I can shoot him?"

"I mean in case Ramon wants to do more than look."

"God, what a crazy life, huh?"

"It beats a lot of things," Janine said.

Mary Margaret took Janine's last finger, pulling her hand closer. "I'm going to tell you something you won't believe, something I never told anybody but my mother, so you'd better not repeat it. Under penalty of death."

"What?"

"When I was a little girl, I wanted to be a nun."

Janine started laughing. "Mary Margaret Duggan...a nun. That's priceless."

"Laugh all you want, but you know what? I'm beginning to wish I'd done it. I wouldn't be worrying about Ramon, Anthony Casagrande and some deviant con right now if I had."

"You sure as hell wouldn't be doing the sisters' nails, either."

Mary Margaret groaned. "You're headed for hell, Janine. You might as well know."

"You really think you'd like the life of a nun?"

"Why not?"

Janine shrugged. "Well, maybe it's not all that different from the way you live now. You haven't been getting any, anyway."

Mary Margaret took a swipe at Janine's face with the polish brush. Giggling, her friend leaned back out of the way.

"Bitch," Mary Margaret said.

"I still have hope for you," Janine said. "You're due for a turn of good luck."

Mary Margaret beamed at her, having finished the last nail. "Yeah, maybe I'll marry Ramon."

Janine pointed at the clock. "You won't be marrying anybody unless you get your butt over to the High Chaparral, sugar."

Mary Margaret jumped up. "Fired before I can snare Ramon, now *that* would be a tragedy."

Laurel, California

Dane had spent half an hour setting up files and listening to Claudia Rosenfelter and the other women gossiping in the outer office. Church ladies had a certain quality the world over, he decided. Unitarian Universalist women were more independent and less deferential toward the clergy than most, but there was still a quality, maybe something in the genetic makeup of the female of the species.

When he heard the office volunteers leaving, Dane figured he would have some quiet time, so he got out his sermon with the intent of reading it over. The last time he'd delivered it, he'd practically had it memorized.

He was halfway through the text when Claudia Rosenfelter, a large woman of sixty with a rather officious manner, knocked on his door. She'd assumed the role of master sergeant, taking the new scrubbed-faced lieutenant under her wing.

"It's after five, Reverend Barrett," she said, "so I'll be going."

"Okay, Claudia. Good night. And thanks for the help."

She nodded. "I hope you have everything you need."

"I think so. You've been very helpful."

"Summer services aren't well attended, so you can ease into the swing of things. I want you to know how pleased the whole congregation is that we were able to get you as an interim at the last minute," she continued, seemingly more interested in talking than leaving.

"Yes," Dane said, "I'm glad it worked out."

"Reverend Shallcross was very popular," Claudia said, "and people were sad to see her go. Still, I think having a few interim ministers before calling a permanent one is good for a congregation."

"Especially considering the way Reverend Ragsdale's ministry ended. I imagine it was a bit traumatic for everyone," Dane said.

Claudia Rosenfelter looked embarrassed.

"I guess I've gotten into a sensitive area," he said.

"It was a very difficult time for the church, Dane," she said.

It was the first time she'd addressed him by his first name, making him wonder if he should have invited her to do so earlier. Judging by her demeanor, it was a signal she might want to engage in a more candid conversation.

"If you aren't in too much of a rush, why don't you sit and talk a while?" he said, offering her a chair.

She jumped at the invitation, taking the chair across from his desk and putting her purse on the floor. "It's best you're apprised of everything," she said. "You can hardly serve the congregation well if you don't know the history of the place."

"I've heard all about Jimmy Duggan from the police," he said.

Claudia shook her head. "One of our saddest chapters...not only for the church, but for the town."

"I can imagine."

There was a long silence. Claudia seemed unsure where to start. Dane wanted to get clarification on some of the murky areas of the tale, so he decided to take the initiative.

"Tell me," he said, "is the story about Stephen Ragsdale dying in a hunting accident true?"

Claudia pushed back the strands of kinky gray hair at her temples. "You homed in on the central issue," she replied.

"You have doubts about it, then?"

"Reverend Ragsdale was not a hunter, nor an outdoorsman. The gun was his, all right, but only because it was a family heirloom."

"Then what does everyone think?"

"Therein lies the problem," she replied. She drew a long

breath, hesitating. "I might as well say it straight out. Most people felt it was suicide. The investigators in Amador County probably thought they were doing everybody a favor by ruling it an accident, and perhaps they were. Nobody objected, of course. What was to be gained?"

"Why would he kill himself?"

"His wife, Margo, had just died after a long, heartbreaking illness. Myasthenia gravis. And so, among other things, he was coping with the loss."

"What other things?"

"Reverend Ragsdale's ministry was never the same after Donna Lee Marshall was murdered. I think he and Margo both felt somehow responsible for not preventing it. He seemed to age twenty years in the five before he died. Tragically, he left a daughter behind. Sally was married and expecting her first child at the time. That's why some doubted the suicide theory. Sally foremost among them."

"Who would have murdered him?"

"That's the problem. He wasn't robbed. It happened in the backwoods. There was no evidence of foul play, but some folks couldn't accept the suicide theory. And it doesn't make sense that a nonoutdoorsman would be in the woods with a gun he never used. He didn't even have a hunting license."

"What do *you* think?" Dane asked.

"Something was troubling Stephen," she replied. "I worked with him very closely for years. In the weeks before his death he was involved in something...shady."

"What do you mean?"

"That's just it. I don't know. He didn't confide in me, which in itself was strange. He'd always spoken freely with me."

"What, exactly, happened that made you think something was going on?"

"He was making and receiving mysterious calls. The only reason I noticed was because he'd be very agitated afterward, which was not at all like Stephen."

"I'm sure you mentioned this to the police."

"Of course. But without specifics what I had to say was basically meaningless."

Dane pondered the situation for several moments, thinking

that Granville Jones's certainty about the case might be a bit too facile. "You said Reverend Ragsdale and his wife took Donna Lee's death hard. I take it you don't buy the story that he was involved with the girl."

"Good heavens, no. I knew Stephen for the better part of twenty years. There's not a fiber of my being that can accept the notion he'd done anything improper toward Donna Lee or any other girl."

"What about Mary Margaret Duggan's assertion that—"

"A fabrication," she replied without hesitation. "An attempt to turn suspicion from her father."

"Then you accept as fact that Jimmy Duggan was guilty."

"Absolutely."

Dane wondered if he should share what Tom Muncey had told him about Elena Perez being threatened over Ledi Hopkins. He had to be able to trust someone. "If I share some confidential information with you, Claudia, can I count on you keeping it between us?"

"Certainly."

"It's come to my attention that Ledi Hopkins recanted her testimony against Jimmy Duggan before she died."

Claudia contemplated him. "What do you mean, 'recanted her testimony'?"

"Ledi told a nurse at the hospital that Duggan was innocent."

"How could she say that?"

"I don't know," Dane said. "I've gotten all this secondhand."

Claudia pondered the news. "Ledi was always strange, though not half so strange as her sister, Theo. Frankly, I never cared for either of them."

Dane glanced at the text of his sermon and felt a strange indifference toward it. This conversation about Jimmy Duggan seemed so much more relevant. Claudia pushed the hair back off her temples as she waited.

"Do you know anything about Mary Margaret Duggan?" he asked. "I assume she left Laurel as soon as her father was convicted of murder."

"Yes, she stayed with a family through the trial. I must say I did feel sorry for the poor thing. She was a beautiful child with the most lovely fiery red hair you've ever seen. Though she was underprivileged, she had a certain dignity. She didn't belong in a town like Laurel. There was nothing here for her.''

"I understand she's living in Nevada now," Dane said.

"A performer, I believe. I have no idea if she has talent, but she was as beautiful as anyone in the movies. Still, you have to wonder what sort of life she leads. She was considered intelligent and was a very good student. She was headed to college when tragedy struck.''

"Really?''

"She had a hard time when she first came to Laurel. Starting at a new school, living with a father who'd spent as much time in jail as out. She was the object of great envy by the girls and...well, lust, I suppose you'd say, on the part of the young men.''

"You paint a fascinating picture, Claudia.'' Dane was finding himself more and more intrigued with Mary Margaret Duggan. Each piece of information added to her mystery. "I'm curious,'' he said, "if she was alienated from her father so much of the time growing up, why did she sacrifice so much for him? Giving up an opportunity to go to college is no small thing.''

"Jimmy was her only family and, to tell you the truth, Dane, I think she was as protective of him as he was of her. She took what happened very personally. When the community turned against her father, she felt that it was turning against her. Mary Margaret is—or was—very proud. And she was absolutely convinced Jimmy was innocent. Unfortunately, I believe it was wishful thinking on her part.''

"I can see that passions run very deep.''

"You should have been here at the time,'' she replied.

"Actually, I'm glad I wasn't.''

"You may be wise.'' Claudia Rosenfelter took her purse. "Well, Reverend, I've got a puppy to feed, so unless you have other questions, I'll be running along.''

"No, you've been very informative.''

She nodded and headed for the door. "Good evening, Dane.''

"See you Sunday.''

Dane sat pondering the conversation and more especially the picture Claudia had painted of Mary Margaret Duggan. A girl too pretty for her classmates and her surroundings—a poor outcast who was highly intelligent and deeply loyal to her father. What could be more intriguing?

Mary Margaret Duggan was beginning to obsess him. Could Tom Muncey have been right? Was it a sign of the devil at work?

Dane laughed out loud. It was a damned good thing he didn't believe in hell. A damned good thing.

Reno, Nevada

As the curtain came down for the final time, the *Dream Girl* dancers made their way toward the exit, upstage right, which led to the dressing rooms. Mist still hung in the air from the waterworks in the finale, leaving a dewy sheen in everyone's hair. Months ago wardrobe had gone to vinyl costumes to spare replacement expense, which only meant more sweating and chafing.

"Artie should have to dance in one of these damned things just once," somebody would grumble. "With his period," somebody else would add under her breath. They'd titter and groan and one of the boy dancers would slap another one on the butt and make a crude joke, but mostly they were tired and wanted to get the hell out of there.

Mary Margaret hung back a little as everyone else bunched at the top of the stairs. Then she suddenly turned on her heel and went back onto the stage, making her way past the stagehands already at work with mops and squeegees. One of them glanced at her as she went to the curtain, downstage right.

Finding the spot where she could look out into the house, she peeked through the heavy fabric. Though most of the audience was heading for the exit into the casino, Ramon was still seated at his table, third from the end, a rosebud in his lapel. He was gazing wistfully at the curtain at about the spot where she had been dancing only minutes before.

This was her first good look at the man. She was relieved to confirm that there was nothing glaringly sinister about him.

To the contrary, his melancholy, dreamy expression evoked compassion. Infatuation, she realized, could be a very sad thing.

Mary Margaret studied his face, desperate to know if he was a monster, but realizing there would be no way to be sure until they were alone and she was naked.

"Watch your feet, sweetheart," one of the stagehands said as he came by, pushing a squeegee.

Mary Margaret stepped out of the way. The man, whose name was Ed, gave her a friendly grin, ignoring the fact that she was wearing nothing but high heels, earrings and a few square inches of pale blue vinyl.

"Sorry," she said.

Ed, an avuncular man in his fifties, pivoted in front of her and pushed the water back toward the middle of the stage. "Hollywood agent out there?" he asked, gesturing toward the house.

"No, an admirer."

"Oh?" he said, raising his brows.

"Are you a good judge of character?" she asked.

Ed shrugged.

"Take a look and tell me what you think. He's sitting at the table in front."

He stepped to the curtain and peered through the slit. After observing for ten or fifteen seconds, he turned to her. "Kind of old. Sort of reminds me of Charlie Chaplin. You know, sad and funny."

Mary Margaret considered that. "Chaplin was a ladies' man, wasn't he?"

Ed shrugged again. "I wouldn't go on any dates with this one, if I was you." He idly pushed his squeegee a couple of times, making a squishing sound. "Reminds me of a guy who lived in my neighborhood when I was growing up. Had a big vegetable garden. Real quiet old guy."

"And?"

"He was molesting all the little girls in the neighborhood."

Mary Margaret wasn't sure why he made the remark, unless he really feared for her. But what made him think going on a date with Ramon was what she had in mind? But then, maybe there wasn't any other reason she'd even notice him.

"I see your point. Don't worry, no danger of me ever seeing this guy." She nearly choked on the words.

"I'd forget it, if I was you," Ed said, obviously seeing right through her.

Mary Margaret hated it when she was transparent. It always made her feel dumb. She was beginning to feel chilled in the cooled air and was glad for an excuse to leave. Rubbing her arms, she said, "Gotta go." After a perfunctory smile, she headed off.

"Take care," Ed called after her.

She heard the squeegee behind her and hurried past another man with a mop. She was almost running by the time she reached the stairs leading down to the dressing rooms.

Back in her cubicle after her shower, Mary Margaret took her bra from her locker and put it on. Then she slipped into a simple little beige cotton T-shirt dress.

Other than being fairly short, it wasn't particularly provocative.

She'd debated between wearing something dowdy, to project modesty, and something sexy, which would be more in keeping with the spirit of the evening. The latter seemed less hypocritical, and hypocrisy was something she cared about. Face it, Ramon was hiring her to put on a show, and she either did it right, or not at all.

On her feet she wore sandals. No panty hose. She didn't want to fool around with extra clothing. Dress, bra, panties, sandals, gold hoop earrings, a thin gold chain around her neck. No cross, though she'd considered it. That, too, would have been hypocritical.

Mary Margaret checked herself in the mirror. Her hair was still damp—she'd half dried it with a diffuser—and so she fluffed it with her fingers. Because of the natural curl, it looked good wet or dry and she never had to do much with it. She looked into her eyes once more, seeking reassurance, though she knew perfectly well she was more likely to find uncertainty and self-doubt. Truth be known, this was like the very first time she'd danced topless—and she was nervous as hell.

"You're just a mannequin," Artie Heartman had said that night as she stood trembling in the wings. "The line between the dots in some guy's fantasy. You're not selling sex, you're filling a canvas. Fantasy art. Yours and all the other bodies are simply part of the illusion."

Mary Margaret had been surprised at how easy it had been once she'd gotten on the stage with the other dancers, wearing nothing below her neck but a G-string. She'd been with thirty other girls—and they'd each had enough feathers on their heads to embarrass an ostrich. Strangely, that had helped. Between the costume, the music and the pretense of being clothed, she'd discovered that dancing bare-breasted had nothing to do with sex. Shame was a state of mind. Like happiness. Or sadness. Or false modesty.

She left the dressing room and headed for the corridor leading to the stage door, but instead of going outside, she made a turn and went up the metal staircase to the floor where the administrative offices were located. The hallway was silent as a tomb, the big double doors of Bernie Solomon's office suite ominous and disapproving.

She went around the corner to the small elevator next to the mail room and took it up to the mezzanine level. From there she went round to the mezzanine lobby where the main hotel elevators were located. Janine was waiting in a celadon linen suit, her light brown hair slicked back.

Seeing Mary Margaret approach, she appeared more annoyed than relieved. "I was hoping you'd gone home," she grumbled irritably.

"What? And leave you to contend with Ramon alone?"

Janine gave her a heartsick look, but said nothing. Mary Margaret smiled to cheer her. It was better than focusing on her own fear.

"Well, let's get this over with," she said, walking over to the elevator and pushing the call button.

They waited in silence until the bell sounded, then they went to the doors of the arriving elevator. Two men were in the car, paunchy, middle-aged conventioneer types. They perked up at the sight of two young, attractive women. The men had obviously been drinking.

"Going our way?" one said.

Mary Margaret saw that the sixth-floor button was lit and pushed the eighth. "Not for long," she said.

The more outspoken of the two men inhaled their perfume in a vulgar, suggestive way. "Too bad, because you girls smell good enough to eat. Right, Bob?"

The other man chuckled. The elevator stopped on six and the men stumbled out.

"Ramon is starting to look good," Mary Margaret said to Janine as the door closed.

The car went up two floors. The doors opened again. Mary Margaret intended to march out of the elevator with determined strides, but she found herself unable to move. When Janine regarded her questioningly, Mary Margaret finally stepped out. Her heart was really pounding now. She tried not to let her sudden failure of courage show. But Janine knew.

"You all right?" she asked.

"Just a little nervous. I'll be fine."

She started toward the wing where room 812 was located. Janine took her arm, stopping her, and unzipped her shoulder bag. She opened it wide enough for Mary Margaret to see the automatic pistol inside.

"Jesus, Janine, you shouldn't have brought that. You could shoot somebody and then where would we be?"

"I can think of a few worse things happening than that."

"Oh, God," Mary Margaret said under her breath. She knew Janine was waiting to hear something from her like, "The hell with it. Let's get out of here," but she couldn't back out now. This was something she was going to do. Period. "Come on," she said, and headed down the hallway.

Strangely, she felt like a condemned prisoner going to her execution. She was running on guts, determined not to make a fool of herself. Pride almost seemed more important than anything else. When they were a few doors from Ramon's room, she stopped.

"Let me go to the door alone," she whispered. "You can move down closer after I step inside."

Janine, her expression dark, nodded.

Taking a deep breath, Mary Margaret went to the door. She lifted her hand to knock and willed her knuckles to rap. For a full thirty seconds nothing happened, then she heard the doorknob turn. Her stomach clenched.

There was instant joy on Ramon's face when he saw that it was she. "Mary, you came," he murmured, smiling. He was in a white long-sleeve shirt, a plain navy necktie neatly in place.

She searched his face for clues, clues to anything—danger, innocence, dishonesty, uncertainty, fear, friendliness. All she could see was unmitigated joy. It came as a relief in an odd way.

Ramon's eyes teared and his lip quivered as he stared at her. His reaction gave her courage. And a sudden feeling of control.

"Do you still want to do it," she said with businesslike impatience, "or have you changed your mind?"

"Oh, no, of course," he said apologetically. "Do come in, Mary. Please come in."

He stepped back to allow her to enter.

Mary Margaret realized that to walk into the room would be, as Colleen would say, like "crossing the Rubicon." That was a strange thing to have pop into her mind, but even if Ramon was as harmless as he seemed, it was a very big step she was taking. She knew she wasn't here to fill a canvas, to create a fantasy art. She was here to sell herself, albeit in as pristine a manner as she could get away with.

"Are you coming in?" Ramon asked when she hadn't moved.

She studied his dog-sad face. Even when he smiled, there was pathos in his eyes. The huge discolored bags sagging beneath his lower lids didn't help.

Ramon was not quite so small as the impression he gave from afar. She still had a couple of inches on him, which seemed even more given the fact she wore heels. But he did not strike her as frail. His color was bad—the veins in his face and hands purple under his sallow skin. She remembered him writing that he was dying, though, of course, she didn't know if it was true. She sensed in him a resilience, the sort of quiet strength of a man who'd spent much of his life outdoors.

"Move on into the room," she said, gesturing for him to back off.

Ramon seemed surprised by her command, but he complied. She crossed the threshold and, as he backed into the room, she opened the closet door and peered in. Apart from some clothes on hangers and a suitcase on the floor, it was empty.

Next she moved to the side of the entry opposite the closet and stuck her head in the bathroom. Satisfied that no one was there, she closed the outside door.

"What are you doing?" Ramon asked as she came to the main part of the bedroom. He stood waiting by the large king-size bed.

"I'm making sure you didn't invite any friends along," she said.

"Oh, no," he said. "I would never."

She realized he didn't understand her point, but she wasn't going to explain that women had a special fear of men in groups. They were braver in packs and more prone to violence. Like wolves. That's why hookers never did more than one john at a time. It was a sure recipe for rape.

She glanced around. In her five years as an employee of the High Chaparral, it was the first time she'd seen the inside of a guest room. She pointed to an armchair that sat to one side of the large window covering most of the outside wall.

"Sit down over there, Ramon."

He complied again, only this time with reluctance. His joy had changed to wariness. Perhaps she'd already destroyed the illusion.

"Why do you speak with me so harshly?" he asked, sounding hurt.

Mary Margaret decided to set her cards on the table. "Because I don't know you and I'm not sure I can trust you."

"But you had my letter. I told you my feelings."

"Talk is cheap, Ramon. I'm taking a chance coming here. You must realize that."

He looked the saddest yet. "What can I do to make you trust me?"

"Let's see your money. I want to know you're serious."

Ramon reached into his pocket and pulled out a thick

money clip, holding it up for her to see. "All hundred-dollar bills," he said.

Obsessed or not, he seemed almost too willing to part with large amounts of money—just for stripping. Most women in her shoes would have assumed he'd want a lot more for the kind of money he was offering. It made her wonder, too.

"For a thousand bucks you could get a classy call girl," she said. "Someone who'd give you the full treatment. I'm just going to strip. You understand that, don't you?"

"Oh, yes, Mary," he said, his voice trembling slightly. "You have my word."

"All right," she said, "tell me exactly what you expect me to do. Just undress, or do you want me to dance?"

"Would it be too much to ask you to dance a little? Softly. Slowly. Like you love me."

Mary Margaret swallowed hard. She wanted to scream at him that he was sick, that by dancing nude she was corrupting not only herself, but him, as well. It was like bringing candy to a diabetic, heroin to an addict.

"You can turn off the other lights if you want," he said, pointing. "This one behind me is enough. And the radio's there, if you want music."

"Do you want music, Ramon?"

"Yes."

She switched off the light in the entry hall and the one on the writing table. She turned on the radio alarm clock next to the bed, moving the dial until she found some soft jazz. Then she turned off the lamp on the bedside table. She did all that, keeping an eye on Ramon. He hadn't moved.

Mary Margaret went around the bed and stood before the strange little Basque gentleman. All the light in the room was coming from the floor lamp behind him. His face was in shadow. He sat motionless in the armchair, the money clip in his hand.

She wanted very badly to leave, to prove to herself that she wasn't corrupt. She craved being bigger than her need, bigger than her fear. But she wasn't a saint. She was just a girl who danced and had a chance at some easy money.

Mary Margaret began swaying her hips to the beat of the music. Ramon, the dark bags of skin under his eyes tragically sad, seemed so melancholy, so pitiful. And at that moment she realized she was more than a sex object. She was an antidote to his pain, the dessert of a dying man's last meal.

It helped for her to think of him that way. What she was doing was a gift. She was just a pretty girl willing to give an old man pleasure, willing to do for him in private, and for money, what she did for thousands of faceless men in public—display her body.

In truth, this wasn't personal, she told herself. It had nothing to do with Mary Margaret Duggan, because to Ramon, Mary Margaret Duggan didn't exist. Only her legs, her breasts, her navel, her lips, only the sway of her body and her unbreachable allure meant anything. And they weren't even her. Not really.

Mary Margaret pulled the hem of her skirt up to the top of her thighs as she gyrated. She'd never done an erotic dance for anyone but Anthony, so she went more on instinct than experience. But she was in tune with her body and so she allowed Ramon to be in tune with it, too.

The Basque sheep farmer seemed scarcely to be breathing. He was still—his only movement the occasional quiver of the money clip. Ramon was mesmerized, in a trance. Knowing that made it easier to pull her dress over her head and throw it on the bed. Now she was swaying and twisting in nothing but her bra and panties. It was only then that she realized she was in a sort of trance herself, acting at being somebody besides herself.

Next she removed her bra, tossing it aside. She thought she heard Ramon gasp, but wasn't sure. She did see his mouth sag slightly. He wheezed.

Mary Margaret knew he was becoming aroused and it frightened her. She wanted to stop, but she was afraid they'd fall out of their trance, their illusion, and what was left would be dirty.

"When can I stop?" she asked, her voice beseeching, not commanding like before.

"You must take everything off," he said softly. "Everything."

Mary Margaret sighed with resignation and peeled down her panties, knowing that if she didn't do it right then she wouldn't be able to do it at all. It took all her willpower to begin dancing again.

"Turn around as you dance," he softly commanded.

Mary Margaret did as he asked, though she was alert to the possibility of him getting up and jumping her from behind.

"Make it more sexy," he said, growing more sure of himself.

She checked over her shoulder to make sure he hadn't moved. Though her heart cried out for her to run, she made herself stay, made herself pretend she cared. Staring at the wall, she ran her fingers up through her hair and gyrated her hips, allowing him to stare at her ass in hopes he would get his rush and let her go.

After giving him a good long look at her backside, she turned slowly to face him. Ramon stared at her pubis, trembling, though it was hard to tell whether with emotion or lust. After a minute, she stopped dancing.

"Okay," she said. "That's it. Now give me the nine hundred."

Ramon began removing the one-hundred-dollar bills from the money clip, one at a time. She counted with him. He held the nine bills out for her to take. Something about the way he was holding them, waiting for her to draw near, alarmed her.

Screwing up her courage, she stepped forward and swiped them from his hand. She stepped back, checking to make sure they were all hundreds.

"Don't be afraid of me, Mary," he said. "There is nothing to fear."

"We had a deal and we each lived up to it," she said, going to the bed. She put down the money and picked up her clothes.

"Mary," he said, starting to get up.

She pointed her finger at him like it was a gun. "Don't move!"

Ramon extended his hand, offering her another handful of hundreds.

"Let me touch you," he said, his voice quavering. "As I wrote in the letter, it will be respectful. Your breast, your skin. Nothing more."

She stared at the bills.

"Here is another twelve hundred," he said. "That's more than I promised in my letter. You can have it, if you let me touch your body."

Mary Margaret heard her mother's voice mimicking the men she was warning her about—"Candy, little girl?" Poisonous words. Sinful words. Words that led to terrible things.

She shook her head. "No, Ramon."

"Fifteen hundred then," he said, peeling off three more hundreds. "Just to touch you, nothing more."

"Jesus, Ramon," she said, "you're making me feel like even more of a whore than I am."

"You're no whore!" he said sharply. His voice was almost angry.

Oddly, she found his anger heartening. But she wasn't going to give in. "Go down to the bar," she said. "You'll find five girls who'll let you feel them up for a hundred."

"I want you," he said insistently.

"No, Ramon."

"Two thousand," he said. "It's all I have."

She gritted her teeth, hating herself. That, plus what he'd already given her, was a third of what she owed Anthony. If she took it, she could even give some money to Janine. In the fall she could take a course at the college. And hate herself.

"Please, Mary," he said.

She saw the tears running down his cheeks.

"Jesus," she muttered under her breath, feeling the horrible, gut-wrenching allure of temptation.

"Please."

She folded her hands over her pubis. "All you'll do is touch me?"

"I swear on the Virgin."

"God," she said, "anything but that."

He held out the money, beseeching her to come take it. Mary Margaret slowly moved toward him, her eyes boring into him, fearful and threatening.

"One false move, Ramon, and I'll deck you."

"I swear I won't hurt you," he said, almost crying.

She pointed a threatening finger. "Stay seated. Don't get up."

"I promise."

She stood before him. Ramon slowly leaned forward and, with a trembling hand, touched her breast. Her body was so taut she was shaking, too. He sobbed as he lightly caressed her breast, making the nipple harden. Her own eyes began to flood.

"Dear God," she muttered.

Ramon ran his dry parched hand down over her stomach and hips, feeling her skin, little sobs welling from within. Mary Margaret slowly turned to allow him to stroke her backside. She looked at the ceiling as tears streaked down her face. They ran down her neck and chest, between her breasts.

His hand continued to caress her, his sobbing turning to weeping. She faced him. Ramon had one hand to his face. The other, the one with the money, he extended toward her. Mary Margaret took the bills and went back to the bed, tossing the money on the pile with the other bills. She quickly dressed.

Ramon, slumped in the chair, was crying into both hands. Once she had on her shoes, she picked up the stack of bills. Ramon was so lost in his misery he seemed oblivious to her presence.

Mary Margaret counted out nineteen hundred dollars, stuffed it into her bra and went back to him. She lightly tapped his foot with the toe of her sandal. "Ramon."

He looked up at her. She put her hand on his shoulder.

"Here's your change." She put the rest of the bills in his open palm.

"What do you mean, change?"

"Our deal was nine hundred to strip, a thousand to touch me. I didn't earn the rest." She folded his finger over the bills, patted him on the head and went to the door.

"Mary," he called. "Can I see you again?"

"No, Ramon."

"I'll pay you again. The same."

She shook her head. "I sold my self-respect. About all that's left is my soul, and it's not for sale. Not yet, anyway."

"I love you," he said with a quavering voice.

Mary Margaret's heart ached. She couldn't speak. Ramon knew how miserable this rotten life was. They'd just been through a little heaven and a lot of hell together. There was nothing she could say to make things better. The moment spoke for itself. So she turned and went out the door, not bothering with goodbye.

Saturday

August 10th

Desert Rest Mobile Home Park
Reno, Nevada

"I don't think that makes you a whore," Colleen said, pushing her glasses up off her nose. "I think it took courage to do what you did. After all, you didn't want to do it. You were desperate."

"Hookers are desperate by definition," Mary Margaret said with a groan.

"But you didn't sleep with him, did you?" Candy interjected. She was listening from across the room, leaning against the counter.

"No, but I might as well have." Mary Margaret put the college catalog down. They were in Candy and Colleen's kitchen. After Janine had left for work, Mary Margaret had come over to ask advice about literature courses she might take at the junior college, but she'd ended up telling them about Ramon instead. She'd spent a miserable night, and Janine's assurances that she wasn't a slut hadn't been enough to soothe her conscience. She'd needed another, more objective opinion.

"Men have exploited women since the beginning of time," Colleen said. "And sometimes you just don't have any choice."

Mary Margaret stared into Colleen's eyes, wondering if she really meant it. She thought of when she was a kid, the time she'd taken a *Playboy* to school to show her little girlfriends. The nuns had confiscated it, of course. They told her she had a dirty, sinful mind and sent her home with a note. When her mother had asked why she'd done it, Mary Margaret, her cheeks burning, had told the truth—she and her friends had wanted to see what their bodies would look like when they were grown. Moira Duggan had simply said, "I hope it was worth it, Mary Margaret."

It was her first lesson in the basic truth that everything has a price, and sometimes the price was self-respect. That was probably the highest price anyone could pay, and it was the reason she'd hardly slept after letting Ramon feel her up.

"You always have a choice," Mary Margaret said. "If not, nothing you ever did could be immoral. Everything would be God's fault."

"I think if you made a mistake," Colleen said, "it was not taking all the money. The guy obviously wanted you to have it."

"Amen," Candy added, shifting her weight. "I'd have taken it."

Mary Margaret shrugged. "Maybe I'm a whore with a conscience."

Colleen picked up the college catalog, giving her a disapproving look. "I advise against calling yourself a whore. You can't change the past, but you can control the way you think about it. Besides, some good came of what you did. You paid Anthony and got him off your back."

"Yes, I guess I should look at it practically."

"This is not nineteenth-century England and you're not living in a Thomas Hardy novel," Colleen said. "Be glad of that."

At Colleen's suggestion Mary Margaret had read *Tess of the D'Urbervilles* and had fallen in love with Hardy's brooding passion. "Oh, but at least things were clear in those days. You were either a lady or you weren't."

"I think I'll go water the roses," Candy said.

Mary Margaret and Colleen exchanged amused looks as Candy left the kitchen, her basketball shoes squeaking on the linoleum floor. When the conversation turned to literature, she usually excused herself. Candy had her roses and Democratic politics, Colleen her books. Those parts of their lives they kept separate.

"So," Colleen said to Mary Margaret, "it must have felt good to give Anthony his money."

"I can't tell you."

"You see, it was worth it."

Mary Margaret pictured Ramon's doleful eyes and the tears running down his pallid face. She shivered. "You know what was even worse than when Ramon touched me? When he told me he loved me."

Colleen regarded her with surprise. "Why?"

Mary Margaret rubbed her bare arms. "He said it, he may even have believed it, but it wasn't me he loved. He doesn't even know me. It was all inside him. It was his imagination running away with him. Do you know what I mean?"

"I think so."

"It's sort of like when I'm on stage. I'm not a person up there," Mary Margaret said. "I'm an object. It's my body people see, not me. But that's fine. At least nobody's telling me they love me, because nobody has the slightest idea who I am."

"You know," Colleen said, "you're very wise, very smart."

"Get out of here."

"No, I'm serious. I really think you should teach English lit. You're a natural. You've got poetic insight. Not many people do."

"That idea's just a dream. Something that keeps me getting up every day."

"Tomorrow is today's dream, Mary Margaret," Colleen said. "It's how you get from here to there."

Candy, her faced flushed from the heat outside, hurried into the kitchen just then, looking upset. "Problem," she intoned.

"What's the matter?" Colleen asked.

"There's a man down at your place, Mary Margaret," she replied breathlessly. "Well, he's sitting in a car out front, actually. He'd gone to the door and knocked. Now he's waiting. I saw California plates on the car and thought it might be the guy that priest warned you about."

Mary Margaret's heart turned to ice. She'd told Colleen and Candy about Rut Coleman under the theory it wouldn't hurt if others in the neighborhood were on the lookout for him, too. "Oh, jeez," she groaned. "If it's not one thing, it's another."

"I really think it is him," Candy said, going to the sink. She ran some water, splashing it on her florid face, which she then wiped with a tea towel.

"Why?" Colleen asked.

"Because I went down and asked him if he was looking for someone."

"And he said?"

"That he was looking for you, Mary Margaret. I told him you were shopping. Said I was a friend and that I might be getting a call from you. I asked him if there was a message."

"And?"

"He said he wanted to talk to you about your father."

"It's probably him, then," Colleen said ominously.

"He gave a name," Candy said, "but it was different than the one you said."

"Coleman?"

"No. He gave the name Barrett, I think."

"He wouldn't be stupid enough to give his real name," Mary Margaret said. "Damn." She started to chew her nails, but realized what she was doing and pulled them from her mouth.

"Should we call the police?" Colleen asked.

"I don't see how we can. He hasn't done anything. Yet." Mary Margaret got up from the table and went to the front room of the small mobile home. Colleen and Candy followed her. Peering out the window, she saw a car parked opposite Janine's, but it was a rear view and all she could see was the back of the man's head. "What did he look like?" she asked.

"I couldn't tell much because I didn't have on my glasses. Sat on them yesterday," Candy said, embarrassed.

"You must have gotten some impression," Colleen said irritably.

"I was afraid to look right in his face," Candy rejoined. "But he didn't seem real scary or anything. Actually, he was polite."

"Father O'Grady said he could be charming," Mary Margaret said. "But underneath he's a sadistic son of a bitch. He tormented my father."

"What are you going to do?"

Mary Margaret stared at the car, then began pacing. "I can't hide forever. He might lose patience and go away, but then he might not." She made a couple more passes across the living room. "Maybe I'll confront him," she said. "Give him a taste of his own medicine."

"Is that wise?" Colleen asked.

"You never accomplish anything in life if you don't take chances," Mary Margaret said. "Frankly, I think the way to deal with a stalker is to scare the piss out of him. They thrive on their victim's fear, so the thing to do is throw them off balance, make them play your game."

Colleen wrinkled her nose. "Where did you hear that?"

"It wasn't reading Jane Austen, I'll tell you that," Mary Margaret said. She went to the window again and observed the scene, thinking. After a moment, she said, "Listen, I'm going to sneak out back, go down to Janine's and get her gun."

"Gun?" Candy was horrified. "And do what?"

"Turn the tables on Mr. Coleman. After I'm inside, Candy, would you go back and tell Mr....what name did he give you?"

"Barrett, I think."

"Yeah, tell Mr. *Barrett* that you got a call from my roommate and heard I'm home, after all, probably sleeping. Tell him I work nights, but that I should be getting up anyway."

"Why do you want me to do that?"

"Because I want him to walk into a little trap. Then I'm going to scare the holy hell out of him."

"I think you'd be better off calling the police," Colleen said.

"The most they'd do is ask what he was doing here, then maybe tell him to leave. All that would accomplish is to make him jump me in the dark next time. No, some things are best accomplished by taking matters into your own hands."

"Like with Ramon."

"Yeah," Mary Margaret said. "Like with Ramon." She patted Colleen's arm. "I might be a fast woman, but I'm not going to be anybody's patsy." She turned to Candy. "You up to sending Mr. Fly into Spiderwoman's web?"

"I guess so," she said weakly.

"Give me three or four minutes before you go out."

Feeling a rush of adrenaline, she turned sharply on her heel and returned to the kitchen with Colleen and Candy trailing behind tow. Mary Margaret went to the back door. "Think of this as a blow for womankind," she said, searching for a formula that might appeal.

"Why not call a female cop?" Colleen said.

Mary Margaret shook her head. "Do all literary types lack a sense of adventure, or is it just you, Colleen?"

"I didn't get to retirement age by busting balls," she rejoined.

Candy tittered and turned red. Colleen actually looked pleased.

"Well, now's our chance to right the scales of justice, ladies," Mary Margaret said. "One for all and all for one!" She gave them each a high five and went out the door.

The giddiness of adventure soon gave up to the soberness of reality. As Mary Margaret made her way along the back hedge to Janine's, she wondered if the psych job would last. She'd never considered herself particularly courageous, but the challenges seemed to be coming at her fast and furious of late. "Hell, just living takes courage," her father once told her in a moment of rare insight.

She entered the back door of the mobile home and made her way to Janine's bedroom. Her friend was doing an extra shift as a vacation substitute to earn overtime, something she relished. "Overtime," Janine often said, "is the next best thing to sex."

The gun was in the drawer where she kept it. Mary Margaret made sure the safety lock was on.

Janine, who'd been raped the year she left Boise for the bright lights of Nevada, was security conscious. She'd made Mary Margaret go to the firing range with her as a condition of moving in. "Being raped is one thing," Janine said, "shooting yourself or an innocent person because you don't know how to use a gun is another. The house rule is we only shoot muggers and rapists."

Rut Coleman, Mary Margaret decided, might well qualify.

She was certainly going to give him every chance to earn a bullet, if it came to that.

She went to her room and got her terry robe from the closet. She was wearing a pair of shorts and a tank top, which meant there was no place to hide a gun. The pocket of the robe was perfect. Besides, Candy was going to tell Coleman she'd been asleep.

Mary Margaret went to the front room and peered through the curtains. She could see his face in profile. His head was bowed and, for a moment, she thought he was dozing. Then she realized he was reading. He was younger than she expected and, from what she could see, rather good-looking. Of course, every ex-con didn't necessarily have a flat nose and a jagged scar running down his cheek.

Just then Candy appeared, going to the driver's side of the car. Coleman looked up at her. Mary Margaret couldn't hear the conversation, but after a minute he opened the car door and Candy went scurrying back up the lane.

As he climbed out of the car, Mary Margaret got a good head-on look at Rut Coleman. She was surprised. He was really, truly handsome. She watched him close the car door and come around. He was in a polo shirt and jeans. Coleman was tall and slender, with nice broad shoulders and narrow hips. A hunk and a half. Funny, her father had never said anything to her about him being good-looking.

Coleman moved toward the front porch with a graceful, almost athletic stride. There was something else, too, an elegance or sophistication that was totally unexpected. Not that she was an expert on men of that ilk, but if she had to put a label on it, she'd say he had class. She pulled back from the window, nervously fingering the weapon in her pocket.

The screen door rattled open and there was a firm rap on the door. Then the screen door closed. Taking a fortifying breath, she went to the door, hesitated, then pulled it open, immediately sinking her hand in her pocket and gripping the handle of the gun.

"Miss Duggan?"

Even through the screen his blue eyes seemed startlingly pale. She knew that he couldn't see in as well as she could

see out, and she was glad, because Rut Coleman was a pleasure to behold—a prime-grade, double-A hunk.

Mary Margaret looked him over, despite knowing the image and the reality were two entirely different beasts. The
man had high cheekbones, a jawline that was just rugged
enough so that he wasn't too pretty, a sensuous lower lip and
those wide-set, magnificent eyes. What a color! His nose was
a bit too narrow to be perfect and it gave him an almost
haughty air. "Yes?" she said.

"My name's Dane Barrett," he said, running his fingers
back through his dark hair. "I have some news about your
father I think you ought to hear."

"Oh, yeah?"

"Yes. I don't want to raise false hope, but I've learned
something that raises questions about his guilt."

"Is that a fact?"

"Yes. I'd like to tell you about it, if you'll allow me."

"Want to chat with me about my dad, is that it, Mr. *Barrett?*"

Her tone seemed to perplex him. "Yes, I drove in from
California just to speak with you about your father's case."

"I see. And I guess you want to come inside and discuss
it, right?"

"If you don't mind."

"Sure," she said. "I'd love to hear the latest. Come on
in."

Mary Margaret stepped back and Coleman gingerly opened
the door. The first thing he did was look her over and, seeing
she was in a bathrobe, he hesitated.

"I hope I'm not imposing," he said, "but your neighbor
assured me that you were in and would have to be up by now.
I knocked earlier."

"No problem, Mr. Barrett," she said, backing away without taking her eyes off him. The hand in her pocket squeezed
the handle of the gun. "Come in."

Coleman entered tentatively. He seemed to sense something was amiss, and she wasn't going to keep him wondering
for long. What an actor! The man had innocence written all
over him. If he'd told her he was Jesus Christ, she'd have

half believed him. No wonder her father wanted to warn her about this guy.

"Sure it's not an inconvenient time?" he said.

The little smile on his lips contained a trace of mischief as he checked her out. It was subtle, certainly not the leer of a man who'd been locked up for years in the maximum-security wing of a penitentiary, but he was interested just the same. The bastard.

"So, you want to talk about my father," she said airily. "Are you bringing his regards, Mr. *Coleman?*" As she said it, she pulled Janine's gun from her pocket and leveled it at him. "You wanted to let me know Dad says hi, is that it?"

The man's mouth sagged open at the sight of the weapon. He was speechless. It was just as she wanted it, and it pleased her immensely, even as her anger toward him raged.

"On your hands and knees, you sonovabitch!" she shouted, seething with all the venom she could muster.

Coleman was frozen, unable to move.

"I said, on your knees, Coleman! Are you deaf? Get on the goddamn floor before I blow a hole in you the size of the Grand Canyon!"

"There's s-some mistake," he stammered as he lowered himself to the floor. "My name's not Coleman."

"Get down!"

Coleman got down on the floor, looking up at her like a terrified animal. The pretty boy suddenly seemed pathetic and she couldn't help reveling.

"You've got me confused with somebody else," he insisted.

Mary Margaret went around behind him and, leaning over, she grabbed a handful of his thick dark hair, jamming the muzzle of the weapon into the side of his neck as she did. "Listen, you deadbeat sonovabitch, if you think you can come waltzing up to Reno and get your jollies harassing me, you've got another think coming. For two cents I'd blow your head off right now—if only for the things you've done to my father, you lowlife scumbag."

She jerked hard on his hair, making him wince. He looked back up at her, the whites of his eyes showing. "Miss Duggan, please…"

She yanked hard on his hair and pushed the gun into his neck. "No, you listen! This is your one and only warning," she said. "If you so much as drive past this trailer park again, I'm going to let you have it with an elephant gun. You'll wish you never got out of prison. I'll make being some blood-thirsty psychopath's girlfriend again sound good to you. Understand?"

"If you'll just—"

"Shut up!" she screamed. "I don't want to hear a word from you. Just get on that pony of yours and ride on back to California. Understand?"

Coleman nodded as best he could with her yanking on his hair.

"Now I'm going to let go of you," she said. "When I say so, I want you to get slowly to your feet. Then you're going to turn around and meekly walk out the door without saying a word. Not a word. Because if I hear one teeny tiny sound pass your lips, just one, I'm going to blow you away. Of course, if you're still alive, you can talk then, but not before. Get the picture? A nod will do."

He attempted to nod again.

"Okay," she said.

Then she let go of his hair and moved back to where she was before. Coleman was on his hands and knees, looking like a whipped pup. He stared at the floor.

"Good boy, Rut. You're learning. Now it's time to stand."

Coleman slowly got to his feet. He looked terribly sad, which struck her as strange. She wanted terrified and she was getting sad. Or maybe bewildered. It didn't compute.

Mary Margaret made a circular motion with her finger, indicating that he should turn around and leave. The poor man gave her the most forlorn look she'd ever seen. She actually began to feel sorry for him, which only made her mad because the last thing she wanted to do was allow herself to be manipulated.

Then, to her surprise, he mouthed the word "please," not once, but twice. Then, holding a finger to indicate he wanted her to watch, he slowly reached for his hip pocket.

"Careful," she warned. "No sudden moves or you're dead."

Coleman produced a billfold, which he held out like a magician about to show that his top hat was devoid of rabbits. Then he carefully opened the wallet and extended it.

Mary Margaret realized he wanted her to look at his ID. She took it, the gun still pointed directly at his midsection. It was a California driver's license with Coleman's picture on it, but the name wasn't Rut Coleman. It said "Dane Barrett" and had a Berkeley address.

Mary Margaret blinked. What kind of trick was this?

"Miss Duggan," he whispered, "if you'll let me speak, I'll explain."

Now Mary Margaret was stunned. She stared at him dumbly.

"I'm Reverend Dane Barrett, minister of the First Unitarian Church of Laurel," he said calmly, but in a small voice. "I've come to discuss your father's case with you."

She looked incredulous. "You mean you aren't Rut Coleman? You didn't just get out of San Quentin?"

"Not unless my mother's been lying to me all these years."

"Then..." She looked down at the gun. "Oh, my God!"

"I tried to explain."

"Jesus Christ," she said, dropping her gun hand to her side.

"Buddha and Mohammed, too," he said. "And there's always Confucius and Moses."

"God," she repeated.

"Well, if you insist. We can stick to the basics."

"I can't believe this," she said, feeling weak. She handed back his wallet.

"I'm struggling a bit myself," he said.

Mary Margaret looked into Dane Barrett's wonderful pale blue eyes. He didn't just look innocent, he *was* innocent. "What have I done?" she murmured, realizing what had transpired was totally incomprehensible.

"To put it in...well, terms you can relate to, you scared the crap out of me, Miss Duggan."

She put her hand to her chest. "Good Lord, how am I going to apologize?"

"Somehow, I think we're beyond apology," he said.

"Maybe a prayer of thanks that I'm still alive would be sufficient. Of course, you may have other priorities."

Mary Margaret went to the sofa and sat down. She put the gun down next to her and buried her face in her hands, but she was too mortified to cry. The earth swallowing her up wouldn't have been enough. There was only one solution. She glanced up at him.

Dane Barrett was smoothing his hair, trying to pull himself together. He was as shaken as she was, though of course for entirely different reasons.

Mary Margaret took the gun, got up and walked back over to him. "Here," she said, handing it to him. "There's only one way to end this with dignity. You'll have to shoot me."

"What?" He was baffled.

"Really," she said. "Just point and pull the trigger. You might want to take off the safety first."

Finally understanding what she was saying, he laughed. Really laughed.

"Please," she said. "Put me out of my misery."

"Honestly," he said, "an apology will do."

Mary Margaret pulled her bathrobe over her head to hide from him. "Believe me, I've never been this embarrassed in my life. I'm not kidding, a bullet would be a relief."

"You give new meaning to the term *coup de grâce*," he said.

Mary Margaret peeked at him through the opening in the robe. Dane Barrett had the most adorable grin. She caught him checking out her legs. She slipped the robe off and tossed it on a chair. He managed to look into her eyes.

"No serious harm done," he said with renewed confidence. "A minister can't expect a warm welcome on every call. This will, however, go down in my annals as a most memorable one."

"How can you ever forgive me?"

"I think it was Pope who said, 'To err is human, to forgive divine.'"

"Pope?"

"As in Alexander Pope. Not the big guy in Rome."

Mary Margaret laughed. "Yeah, I know the one. He also said, 'At ev'ry trifle scorn to take offense.'"

Dane's brows rose with surprise. "Very good. You're a Pope fan."

"Not really. My mother used to quote that when I was a kid, and I *did* think she meant the big guy in Rome. It was only a few years ago that somebody explained otherwise."

Dane chuckled. "You're as adept at candor as you are with a gun." He handed the weapon back. "There must be a holster somewhere this goes in. Being an advocate of gun control, I don't even like looking at the things, much less holding one."

Mary Margaret decided he was criticizing her. "Apparently you've never been raped."

"No. I grant you I haven't."

Mary Margaret lightly slapped the pistol against her palm. "Well, my roommate has and this is hers. It makes her feel safe and I don't question that."

"I don't either. But I think a world without guns would be a better world."

"So would a world without sin," she replied. "But I'm not too hopeful."

"You're a pessimist."

"No, a realist."

"A realist's perspective, like everybody else's, is relative," he said. "This was once a country where slavery, illiteracy and back-room abortions were commonplace. Those things didn't pass because of a realist's perspective."

Mary Margaret smiled. "It's a good thing I didn't shoot you. Who would have saved my soul from the sin of realism?"

"It's an aside, Miss Duggan, but I don't happen to believe in sin, either. However, I didn't come here to preach."

"Or to get shot, I guess."

He grinned. "No, I think we can agree on that."

"Gee, Mr. Barrett, I hope I didn't hurt you. I was yanking your hair pretty hard."

"I won't need a scalp massage for a while," he said, rubbing his head. "Let's put it that way."

Mary Margaret felt a tug inside as they regarded one another. Embarrassment followed. She had to look away. "I'd feel like a fool trying to be hospitable after what I did," she said. "That's why I'm not offering you anything."

"I might demand a cold drink anyway. It's not often a guy has an attractive woman beholden to him, begging to make amends."

She gave him a wary look. "Maybe I should have insisted you shoot me."

"I'll have whatever you've got that's cold and wet," he said.

"All right. Sit down and make yourself at home," she said, pointing to the sofa. "If that's possible. I'll be right back."

Mary Margaret went off to the kitchen, feeling the heat of Dane Barrett's eyes on her. She checked the refrigerator. Four bottles of Bud Light. Three Dr Peppers. A bit of orange juice and an unopened can of V8.

"It looks like beer or Dr Pepper," she called to him.

"I'll have what you're having."

She glanced at the clock. In just over an hour she had to be at work. If anybody showed up there with booze on their breath, they were out. Artie was stricter than the Department of Motor Vehicles. "Dr Pepper," she called to the man in the front room.

"Fine."

She took the soft drinks from the refrigerator, but before opening them, she carried Janine's gun to the bedroom and put it away. On her way back to the kitchen she stopped in the bathroom to check herself in the mirror.

Her face was flushed and her hair mussed. Mary Margaret splashed water on her cheeks and ran her brush through her hair a couple of times. Before leaving, she smeared on some lip gloss and put some of Janine's Caleche on her wrists and neck. Then she asked herself what she was doing. Hadn't Dane Barrett said he was a minister? Or was that something she imagined in all the confusion?

No, she was sure she'd heard him say that. The minister at the First Unitarian Church in Laurel, where her father had worked—where all their trouble had begun. And Dane Barrett said he'd come to talk about her father. Concerning what? The question had been lost in the excitement of the moment. A soberness came over her. What about her father?

As she left the bathroom, headed for the kitchen, she heard a commotion in the front room. There were shouts and scuffling.

Mary Margaret hurried out to find Dane Barrett sprawled on his stomach on the floor, a police officer over him, pressing a knee into his back. A second officer was standing over them, his gun drawn.

"Get back, lady!" the cop with the gun shouted.

"What's happening?"

The officer that had Dane pinned was slapping cuffs on him. Mary Margaret couldn't believe what she was seeing. Then, out the open front door, she saw Colleen and Candy outside. Suddenly she understood.

"Oh, my God," she said. "Officer, that's not Rut Coleman."

Both cops looked at her.

"The ladies outside said this guy was an escaped convict and that he had a woman trapped inside," one of the cops said. "Are you saying that you aren't the woman, or that this guy isn't the convict?"

"I'm the woman but he's not the convict. He's a minister and the confusion is all my fault."

The cop with the knee in Dane's kidneys got to his feet. "Where's the con, then?"

"There isn't one."

"You mean this is a false alarm?"

"I'm afraid so. You see, I thought Reverend Barrett here was my father's former…uh, well, it's complicated, Officers. Believe me, there's no problem."

"The lady means well," Dane said, craning his neck to look up at the cops, "but she's having a bad day. You could probably do both her and me a favor by shooting her."

"You can say that again," she said.

"What gives?" the cop with the gun said, holstering his weapon.

"You explain, Miss Duggan," Dane said. "I'm indisposed at the moment."

"Oh, the hell with it," she said woefully. "Just take me to jail. His chances of getting out of Reno alive would be better."

"So this guy's okay?" the other officer said. "He's not harassing you?"

Mary Margaret bit her lip, shaking her head woefully.

"No," Dane said. "And I've got the bleeding wounds and broken limbs to prove it. The one saving grace is I might get a sermon out of this."

"Let him go, Officers," Mary Margaret said miserably. "It's all a terrible mistake and it's entirely my fault."

The cops looked at each other.

"Did this even happen?" one said to the other.

"I don't think so."

"Maybe we should go."

"Do take your handcuffs with you," Dane said. "Preferably without my wrists in them."

The officer who'd cuffed Dane took out his key and unlocked the bracelets. "Our apologies, Reverend," he said. "Perhaps you'll take up any complaints you have with the lady here."

Dane sat up on the floor, rubbing his wrists. "It'd be my pleasure, Officer."

The cops headed for the door. The last stopped before going out. "Want us to tell your neighbors it was a false alarm?"

"Please," Mary Margaret said.

"Have a good day, folks."

Mary Margaret clutched her hands to her chest in supplication. "Maybe this time I should offer to shoot myself and save you the trouble," she said.

"What? And leave me with that on my conscience for all eternity?"

"My feelings are beyond words," she said. "I guess my neighbors thought you were raping or murdering me or something."

"I wonder how they got that idea? Maybe it's my sinister looks."

"No, I'd told them I thought you were Rut Coleman, my father's former cell mate. I'm sorry."

Dane smiled stiffly. "Fortunately, I have Job's example to guide me." He got to his feet, brushing the front of his shirt.

"It's a foolish question, but is there anything I can do to make amends?" she asked.

"That Dr Pepper would be a start. There's something about being in handcuffs that whets the appetite."

She was completely at a loss. "Well, sit down and I'll get your drink."

Dane glanced at the sofa. "I tried that last time. I think I'd rather come with you—unless, of course, the kitchen is booby-trapped."

"Frankly," Mary Margaret said, "I'm afraid to promise you anything."

"Your karma leaves a little to be desired," he agreed. "Did you have a tendency to fall off of roofs as a child?"

"Thanks for keeping a sense of humor about it," she said.

"It's not humor. I'm whistling in the dark."

Mary Margaret's shoulders slumped. "And I used to be such a nice person."

Dane took her arm. "I'll come with you," he said. "It's somehow easier to accept when you see the punch coming."

Mary Margaret led the way. He climbed onto the stool at the kitchen counter, and she got some glasses from the cupboard. She filled them with ice. When she turned, she caught Dane looking at her backside.

"So, you're the minister at the church in Laurel."

"Interim. I arrived this week. Tomorrow I'll be giving my first sermon."

"Then you're just starting." She popped the tab of one of the soft-drink cans and poured the effervescent liquid into a glass.

"Yes. I'm in the process of getting acquainted. Folks in Laurel seem a bit dull, so I decided to come to Reno, thinking it'd be a little more exciting to have my first pastoral visit here." He gave her a wink as she handed him the glass.

She poured the second drink, thinking the guy was pretty sexy.

"You're an awfully good sport, Reverend Barrett."

"Well, when you spend your workdays wrestling with sin, you're always on the lookout for something to lighten the spirit."

"I thought you said you didn't believe in sin," she said.

"Only as a figure of speech. But really, who could have planned a more charming diversion than you and your gun?" He touched his glass to hers. "Cheers."

They sipped their soft drinks. Mary Margaret watched him, telling herself that this was a minister and that she shouldn't be having feelings of attraction for him. Just as disconcerting, he seemed to be having a parallel reaction to her.

"Not to put a damper on the mood," she said, "but I believe you mentioned something about wanting to talk about my father's case. That's really the reason you came to see me, I take it."

He took a drink. "Yes. I don't want you to get excited, because the Laurel police assure me that it's insignificant, but Father Muncey, the parish priest at Saint Aubin's, and I felt you should know about it." He put his glass down. "It seems that Ledi Hopkins, the woman who testified to seeing your father leave the murder scene—"

"Yes, I know who you mean. I sat through every minute of that trial, Reverend."

"Well, Miss Hopkins died recently. But in the days before she passed on, she started telling people that your father was innocent."

Mary Margaret was astounded. "Innocent?"

"She didn't exactly recant her testimony about seeing him at the murder scene," Dane went on, "but she was adamant that your father did not kill Donna Lee Marshall."

"He didn't."

"But the point is, Ledi said so."

Mary Margaret considered that, wondering at the significance. "So, why are the police discounting it?"

"The dying words of an old, ill woman whose testimony wasn't critical to begin with, or words to that effect. I think you get the picture."

"God forbid they admit they could have been wrong." Mary Margaret drank her Dr Pepper. "You must think it's important, or you wouldn't have come here to tell me about it."

"I'd like to say unequivocally, yes," Dane said, fingering his glass, "but the truth is, I don't know what to make of it. But there are two other things that bother me. First, the nurse who Ledi Hopkins confided in received an anonymous threat to stop talking about it. This was in the past few days. The other thing is, the circumstances of Reverend Ragsdale's death—perhaps his role in the case... I can't put my finger on it exactly, but something about it's a little strange.''

"He was a liar, if that's a help," she said bitterly. "A goddamn liar, forgive my French." She knew the anger she felt did not serve her well, but it had been a long time since she'd talked about Stephen Ragsdale. Hardly more than the mention of his name was necessary before she began to seethe.

"Tell me about it," Dane said.

"I hate the man," she replied, "but he's dead, so what's the use of going into it?"

"Allowing people to vent is part of a minister's job."

"All due respect, Reverend, but you're not my minister."

"Well, Father Muncey was really the one who—"

"I'm through with priests, too, thank you very much," she said, cutting him off. "I don't see why we're talking about me, anyway. I'm not the issue."

Dane was obviously surprised by the sharpness of her tone. She looked off, out the window. A jet making its approach to Reno Cannon International floated across the frame of the window. She turned back to him. "Look, I don't mean to be bitchy, especially after I all but shot you, but why talk about that bastard Ragsdale?"

"I suppose because I know so little about him. Most of my information came from the police and a conversation I had with the church secretary. I'd like a balanced view. That's all."

"All right, if you're that eager to talk about it, we will. What d'you want to know?"

"Did you see him...well, let's say, in a compromising position with Donna Lee Marshall?"

"He had his hand under her dress and in her panties. Is that compromising enough for you, Reverend?"

"This was at the church?"

"In his study one evening. I was walking by the window. I saw them. He opened her dress and kissed her breasts, too."

Dane stroked his chin, apparently pondering the information. "According to the police, you claim Ragsdale came on to you, as well."

"He didn't get that far with me, I can guarantee you that. It was before the incident with Donna Lee. Dad and I had only been in Laurel a few months and we had an argument. I was upset. Ragsdale saw me crying in the parking lot behind the church. He told me to come into his office. He counseled me, if that's the term. Then gave me this fatherly hug. But the next thing I know, he's running his finger under the collar of my blouse, then fiddling with the buttons in front. I was so surprised, I didn't know what was happening. When I tried to pull away, he grabbed me and kissed me on the mouth. I ran outside to get away."

"Then what happened?"

"Nothing, really. He came outside and apologized. Told me he meant to be loving in a respectful, pastoral way and that his mind wandered, and he got to thinking about his wife who was ill and who...well, who hadn't been able to have sex with him. He didn't put it in those words exactly, but that was what he was getting at."

"Did it end there?"

"I didn't do anything about it, and he didn't try it again, if that's what you mean. I figured if I told my father there'd be trouble for him instead of Ragsdale. And it's not like guys hadn't tried to feel me up before. Until then it had been fuzzy-cheeked boys, not old goats. That was the only difference."

Dane Barrett frowned.

"I was seventeen, what did I know?"

"So when you related the incident to the police later, they took it to be creative storytelling to save your father."

"Is that what they told you?"

"That was the gist of it, yes."

Mary Margaret shrugged. "I'm not surprised."

Dane Barrett contemplated her. She saw priestly compassion on his face and she wasn't sure she liked it. The plain fact was she didn't trust "men of the cloth," as they called themselves. Hypocrites was a more apt description as far as she was concerned.

Dane cleared his throat. "If no one has ever apologized to you for what you went through with Reverend Ragsdale, I do now," he said. "I know it's years after the fact, but you're owed an apology by the Church, the community, the whole male population, for that matter."

Mary Margaret was amused. "Decent of you to take on the sins of mankind, Reverend. I hope it doesn't mean you have a Christ complex."

Dane laughed. "Not considering my main prophet is Buddha."

"You're a Buddhist?"

"I'm a universalist. I take my spiritual wisdom wherever I find it, whether in the Bible, one of Shakespeare's sonnets, or a novel by Erica Jong. But I do believe in the importance of righting wrongs, whenever and wherever I can."

Mary Margaret gave him an appraising look, wondering about the man. Was he a phony or was he for real? Maybe he had lines he liked to use on women, the same as any other guy. "Have you read *Fear of Flying?*" she asked.

"When my wife and I were first married, we gave each other five books the other had to read. That was one of the books Kathy gave me."

The word *wife* brought her up short. "Oh, so you're married."

"My *ex*-wife I should have said. We've been divorced for over a year."

"I guess the only ones immune from that are Catholic priests," she said with a smile.

Dane nodded and drank more of his Dr Pepper.

She was glad he was single, not that it really mattered. But if she was going to be attracted to someone better that than a guy who was married. Even a fantasy was less fun if it involved cheating. "So, what books did you give her?" Mary Margaret asked. "If that's not too personal a question."

He stroked his chin, a bemused little grin forming on his lips. "The *Kama Sutra* wasn't one, if that's what you're alluding to."

"I'm not sure what the *Kama Sutra* is," she said. "Unless it's that Chinese sex book." Mary Margaret never apologized for her ignorance. Pretense always struck her as the worst sin.

"Close. It's a classical Hindu treatise on sexual love. It's become a new-agey thing in recent years."

Mary Margaret was becoming intrigued. "So, what did you give her?"

"Let's see. *The Education of Henry Adams*, Jung's *Memories, Dreams, Reflections*, *Shōgun* by James Clavell, *The Prophet* by Gibran, and *Siddhartha*.

"I haven't read any of them."

"Read *Siddhartha*, by all means. It's a story about the soul's search for meaning, spiritual exploration. A Buddha story."

"Sounds like something a minister would read."

"No, it's for anyone with a passionate soul, Miss Duggan. It's short and simple, elegantly simple. I think you'd like it."

There was something about his earnestness she liked. He was respectful and he didn't patronize her. And he seemed willing to talk to her about things that mattered to him. Guys normally didn't do that—at least not the ones she knew.

"Thanks," she said. "Maybe I will."

They fell into a contemplative silence. Mary Margaret felt a little self-conscious because she sensed Dane was thinking about her and she wasn't a hundred percent sure in what way. He was a man, so of course he'd leered a little. But to his credit he had tried to treat her like a person, not just a piece of meat. That was something to be thankful for.

"I appreciate you apologizing for what Reverend Ragsdale did," she said. "That was considerate."

"I want you to know I don't in any way condone his actions."

"He denied it, you know."

"Yes," he said. "I know."

"So you believe me, not him?"

A quirky smile touched his lips. "You're here and alive, he's not."

Mary Margaret wasn't sure if he was being glib or just plain honest. She chose to believe it was honesty, perhaps because she wanted to think well of him. "Well, I accept your apology," she said, "under the condition you'll accept mine for what happened earlier."

"Done," he said, offering his hand across the counter.

Mary Margaret took it. Dane gave her fingers a firm squeeze, then let go.

"In some small way the scales of justice have been at least partially righted," he said.

She returned his smile, watching as he took another sip of his soda. Dane Barrett was not your everyday minister, even a Unitarian minister, though she'd only had one example of those. He had a depth to him, she decided, an obvious intellect. That part was credible enough. His stealthy glances at her breasts were an indication he wasn't a eunuch, though. And since she'd told him about Ragsdale coming on to her, he'd been more careful with his eyes. Maybe that meant he was a gentleman.

"Getting back to Ledi Hopkins," he said, "you see my news isn't startling, but as I said, Tom Muncey and I thought you were entitled to know about it."

"Actually, it *is* interesting. Too bad she's dead. I'd like to ask her what the heck she meant. Especially considering she was partly responsible for the conviction."

"I've been thinking of talking to Elena Perez, the nurse at the convalescent hospital, to see if I can learn more."

"When?"

He shrugged. "Maybe tomorrow after church."

Looking into Dane's eyes, she felt a connection between them— different than before. Stronger.

"Do you have any interest in talking to her?" he asked.

"You mean, go with you to see her?"

"If you like."

Mary Margaret wondered if things weren't starting to head in the wrong direction. Her instinct for caution arose. "I don't know..."

"When's your day off?"

"Monday."

"Hmm."

"Normally I work the Sunday matinee, but this is my week off," she said.

"Then you're free the next two days."

He seemed a tad too pleased. "Yeah, but I've got other problems," she said. "My car's a bit under the weather. I doubt it would make it over the mountains."

"You can ride down with me," he said. "And I'll bring you back."

"Yes, but you're going back today, aren't you?"

"I was planning on it, yes."

"Well, I've got a show to do tonight."

"Hmm." He thought for a moment. "Well, we could leave first thing in the morning. Early enough that I'm comfortably back in Laurel by, say, ten."

"We'd have to leave by seven or so," she groaned.

"Is that a problem?"

"Seven is the middle of the night for me, Reverend."

"Only you know how important this is to you," he said.

She couldn't help being suspicious. Was this a Good Samaritan thing, or did he have something else in mind? She hated being suspicious of everybody, but her life had been one long, cruel lesson in human nature...or maybe in the nature of men.

"I'm not pushing," he said. "I just thought because of your passion over the issue, it might be something you'd want to do, Mary Margaret. You don't mind if I call you Mary Margaret, do you?"

She shook her head. "You wouldn't have to bring me back. I could grab a bus in Sacramento."

"Whatever works."

She realized that what had started out as an unlikely development was now practically a done deal. The trouble was, she didn't have a lot of time to negotiate. She looked at the clock and saw she was already running late. "I hate to be a party pooper, but I've got a show tonight. I don't know if you're aware, but I'm in the chorus at the High Chaparral."

"That's what I understand."

She didn't know whether to be relieved or concerned. "I hope that's not too off-putting for a minister."

He shrugged again. "I'm going to be doing my gig tomorrow morning from the pulpit. I hope that's not too off-putting for a showgirl."

Mary Margaret liked his sense of humor. What she hated most about priests was that they were usually ponderous and Dane Barrett didn't seem ponderous at all. She had just about decided she liked the man, which was a strange admission, considering the way she felt about guys in general and clergymen in particular. Not that she was incapable of rising above her prejudices, but she hated disappointment. It all came down to a simple fact—she'd been burned too often.

"You sure you don't mind staying over?" she asked as doubt crept in.

"Not at all."

Mary Margaret felt herself giving in. She rationalized that it wasn't really a bad thing because this was about her father, not about Dane Barrett and whatever was going on in his agile mind. It wouldn't be the first time she had to put up with a man's flirting to get what she wanted.

"Okay, what time do we leave?"

"Six-thirty?"

"Ugh," she said. "That's about twenty minutes after I usually fall asleep."

"Let's make it seven, then."

"Much better."

He smiled; she smiled.

"This is your leisure time then, I presume."

"Yes, but I have some things to do before going to work tonight." She glanced again at the clock.

"I'll get out of your hair."

Dane got up and Mary Margaret followed him into the front room. He stopped at the door and extended his hand. "The afternoon was...well, let's say different."

"I won't even comment further on what I did, Reverend Barrett," she said, shaking his hand.

"You don't have to, if you'll call me Dane."

"Okay. Deal."

He gave her a wink, looking just adorable. Mary Margaret felt a shameful rush. She watched him go down the steps and out onto the walk. When he got to the lane, he stopped and turned around.

"Since I'm staying over, maybe I should take in a show this evening. Any recommendations?"

"Any but mine."

"Is that a demand or a request?"

"Considering I can't very well put a gun to your head again, I guess it's a request."

"It *is* a free country," he said.

"I've had so many embarrassing things happen already today, what's another? I mean, every woman who meets a minister would be just thrilled at the thought of having him see her dance practically naked, don't you think?''

"If you don't want me to go, I won't.''

Mary Margaret thought for a moment. "I'll leave it to you, your conscience and God to decide.''

Dane chuckled. "I may have to pray over that one, Mary Margaret.'' He waved and went on to his car.

His reaction made her wonder if she'd hit on the right formula or the wrong one. It could be this particular minister had God in his pocket. Or thought he did. Now *that* was a real scary proposition.

The High Chaparral Hotel and Casino
Reno, Nevada

"More coffee, sir?''

Dane looked up into the long-suffering face of the middle-aged waitress. "Please.''

With her free hand resting on her ample hip, she filled his cup. "Having any luck?''

He gave her a quizzical look. "Pardon?''

"At the tables.''

"Oh. No, I haven't been gambling. Came to see the show.''

"Just as well. At least you get something for your money.'' She glanced around, a bored expression on her face. "But don't tell 'em I said so.'' Then she left.

Dane chuckled. Then he noticed a little old couple in their late seventies coming through the buffet line, tottering by at half speed, seemingly as familiar with each other as a person's right hand is with the left. They settled into a table nearby.

An Hispanic busboy silently cleared away Dane's dirty dishes. Two tables away, the elderly woman tucked the man's napkin in the collar of his shirt and began cutting his meat. Dane sipped his coffee, observing them. He couldn't help wondering if fifty years earlier she'd been doted on by the feeble man who was now practically her child.

He thought of Mary Margaret Duggan and an odd image came to mind. He pictured himself as a tottering old man being cared for by an elderly version of her. It seemed crazy to be thinking of her that way—especially since he didn't even know the woman—but for some reason he couldn't get her out of his mind.

His obsession, if that's what it was, had actually started before they met, thanks to Tom Muncey. The notion of a beautiful woman dancing her heart out to save her father really got him in the gut.

And yet, it wasn't simply a charitable impulse on his part. The truth was, he'd come to Reno to see Mary Margaret, not help her father. And now he was prepared to take her back to Laurel, not for her sake, but rather for his own. It was easier, he found, to face up to the fact than to dance around it. He'd come to see the show for the same selfish reason.

It wasn't the first time he'd been infatuated. He'd been strongly attracted to Kathy when they met. But it had been different than this. There had been an intellectual dimension right from the start. Being able to talk about trends in French deconstructionism or evolutionary psychology over coffee was the cachet of a Berkeley relationship. It lent substance to sexual attraction. Without it there was only lust which, in the final analysis, was boring and very male.

He'd learned from Kathy that the feminine was the higher virtue, the feminine in everything—orgasms, spirituality, art, consciousness, politics and intellectualism itself. But even the Berkeley falling-in-love experience had to face up to the realities of life. Things like burnt toast, hurt feelings, dirty diapers and overdue bills. Dane never could figure out if his marriage had crashed on those rocky shoals, or if he'd simply deluded himself about his wife from the beginning.

What he felt for Mary Margaret Duggan was of a different order entirely. And the distinction was not just one of body and mind. He liked Jimmy Duggan's daughter. He liked her a lot—even if she had practically blown his brains out. He liked her fierceness and her sharp tongue because there was a softness underneath that belied the tough act. He'd seen her vulnerability. Sure she was beautiful, the most beautiful woman he'd ever laid eyes on, but that was only a part of it.

Unless he was kidding himself, of course.

Maybe that was the part that had him somewhat confused.

The feeling of lust was easily understood. But what did these other feelings mean? And why did they make him so uncomfortable? He needed to find out. So here he was.

He checked his watch. The doors to the theater wouldn't be opening for twenty minutes, but he'd grown tired of sitting in the buffet, rationalizing the fact he had a ticket to *Dream Girls* burning a hole in his pocket. He decided to walk around the casino to stretch his legs.

He left the restaurant, which opened directly onto the casino floor. There was a discernible energy in the hall, a sort of muted tension underlying the hum of activity, a curious mixture of boredom and expectation. He studied the faces of the people standing around the craps tables. There was a certain grimness about them that made him wonder how much fun they were having. There were cries of joy when the dice came up right, but gambling struck Dane as work as much as pleasure, especially for the people seated in front of the slot machines, looking for all the world like factory workers on an assembly line.

A cocktail waitress with her breasts bulging out the top of a skimpy little outfit brushed past him, her eyes passing over him without really engaging his. Dane glanced over his shoulder, taking a peek at her legs. Ah, the temptations of Gomorrah.

Which brought him back to Mary Margaret Duggan again.

Was it really so bad he'd come to titillate himself? If he felt any shame at all, it was because he didn't have sufficient willpower to stay away. The temptation of seeing her with her clothes off was simply too great.

Did that mean he was no better than Stephen Ragsdale? he wondered. Was he succumbing to temptation, preying on the weak, pursuing his own desires at the expense of hers? If so, it was a sad commentary on the man he was. Dane didn't want to believe that was true. It was safer to cling to his confusion and uncertainty. For the first time he actually felt a twinge of compassion for Jimmy Swaggart and Jimmy Baker.

Carried by the momentum of his own misgivings, Dane wandered over to the theatre. It was still a little early, but several dozen people were already in line. He was glad to see that, for the most part, they looked to be average middle-American types, as many women as men—people who drove motor homes and had grandchildren, people who got their cars serviced at Jiffy Lube and flew American flags on Memorial Day and...well, maybe went to church, at least a few times a year.

He was relieved he wouldn't be seeing Mary Margaret in the company of a bunch of men with red faces and bulging eyes, or with tattoos on their forearms, grease under their fingernails, smelling of beer and sweat. It wasn't going to be like attending a Rodin exhibit, he knew, but at least it wasn't going to be like sitting in a sleazy strip joint, listening to the grunts and groans of other men.

He tried to recall exactly what Mary Margaret looked like. A general impression of her beautiful face remained in his mind, but her precise features were somewhat blurred. The red hair and porcelain skin he recalled vividly. He remembered the furor in her green eyes as she swore at him. She seemed more a termagant than an angel, a real hellion. Based on her acid tongue alone, his mother would have said she was common. And she probably was in some respects. Yet, he sensed much of what she presented was a mask. After they'd talked a while, he'd begun to feel that the person beneath the facade was more genteel than the persona she'd assumed.

His recollection of her pulling her robe over her head to hide from him after she'd discovered her mistake was his most delightful remembrance. Even if he never saw her again, he'd savor that memory, the woman-child, the innocent, the victim.

Funny how he'd been able to both forgive and idealize her. Mary Margaret Duggan was without flaw because even her human frailties were a form of perfection.

The line behind him was getting longer, an air of expectation rising. Dane felt it. Everybody, it seemed, loved a show.

Within a few minutes the doors to the theater opened and the line began moving. Dane had purposely asked for a seat in back, so as to be as unobtrusive as possible. He was merely there to satisfy his curiosity, after all. As the theater filled, the wait persons began hustling drinks. Feeling impulsive,

Dane ordered a martini, though he'd probably not had more than three or four his whole life. The last time was in Santa Barbara on a date with a young CPA his mother had fixed him up with the summer before he'd met Kathy. "This girl is levelheaded," his mother had told him. "Just what you need to balance your excesses."

"Excesses" was his mother's code word for his propensity to do things his own way. Charlene—he was fairly sure that had been her name—was slender and moderately attractive, but more important, had a penchant for martinis. They'd had quite a few that evening and ended up having sex on her sofa when he took her home. It was one of the few times in his life he'd made love with a woman for whom he had no real affection. Maybe he'd done it to spite his mother, which, after it was over, made him feel twice as guilty as he otherwise might. Interestingly, he'd never heard another word from Charlene or about her from his mother. Perhaps Constance Barrett had intuited that her son had somehow blown it and found the situation more easily ignored than explored.

Finally the lights in the house went down and the curtain went up. Dane, his hand wrapped tightly around the stem of his martini glass, scooted to the edge of his seat as the music began and the costumed beauties in full plume spilled onto the stage. His eyes jumped from one long-legged siren to the next. They all were so much alike, all pleasing to look at, all wearing less than the average person wore on the beach, yet which one was she?

At last he spotted one girl in the chorus with a smidgen more grace, a dash more elegance and with a touch more presence. He wanted to believe it was Mary Margaret Duggan, but with her hair covered by the feathered headpiece and her face painted he couldn't be sure. He followed her with his eyes, wanting to believe her to be the woman who'd jammed the handgun in his throat that morning. Could she be the painted lady who'd joked with him about Pope and the pope, whose intelligent eyes were both shy and fearless, who could just as easily have been the Virgin Mary or Gypsy Rose Lee? Yes, it had to be.

The first number, the opening extravaganza, ended and the curtain came down on the performers, leaving Dane feeling cut off, dependent on his memories. His heart was beating nicely and he found himself feeling strangely anxious. It was only then that he realized he had not seen Mary Margaret as a sexual being, despite her nudity, but rather as a symbol of the feminine ideal—or perhaps more accurately, as a symbol of *his* feminine ideal.

Next, the master of ceremonies, who doubled as a comedian, came out and did a stand-up comedy routine, which Dane scarcely heard. He couldn't get Mary Margaret Duggan out of his mind. How could a human being be so perfect? Clearly she couldn't. She was an illusion, his own needy creation more than reality.

When the curtain went up for the next number, Dane was again at the edge of his seat. This time he spotted her more quickly. The girl he had watched before was indeed Mary Margaret. The costume she wore in this number did not include a headpiece and so he could see her fiery hair, and her face was more clearly that of the girl in the trailer that morning.

And so it went through the entire show, number after number interspersed with circus acts or comedy routines. But he was there for only one thing—to see her. Whenever Mary Margaret Duggan was on the stage, he watched, transfixed, helpless. She might as well have been up there alone because he saw nothing else. Just her. Just the graceful woman with the lovely body and the curious air of dignity. The goddess. *His* dream girl.

The finale of the show was a waterworks extravaganza, a virtual medley of fountains and geysers, one huge aquatic ejaculation. That, clearly, was the intended subliminal message. The symbolism was probably more powerful than most people realized. Though the majority, he imagined, went back to their motor homes, having no idea what had hit them. It was an unconscious thing, probably intentionally so. Elitist thinking? Most likely, but in all probability, accurate.

Dane left the theatre with the others in the audience, feeling more spent than elated. An uncomfortable anxiety gnawed at his heart. He'd come for titillation and was leaving wanting. It was an evening of empty calories—lots of promise and no payoff. Which made him wonder if he'd really come to see her perform, after all. Maybe what he truly wanted was to talk to her. But that would have to wait until tomorrow.

The light wind outside the High Chaparral was surprisingly warm and dry. The stars shone brightly in the high desert sky. It was a different world from Berkeley. As disparate as, say, the casino floor and the chapel at Starr King Seminary. By the time he found his car and got inside, Dane was mildly depressed. It wasn't the intense sort of depression that had occasionally plagued him during his separation and divorce. It was more like the pang of sadness he'd felt when he'd watched Kathy drive away with Toby on their way to the airport and Japan.

Starting the engine, he drove off, headed for the freeway. That afternoon he'd taken a room not far from the Desert Rest Mobile Home Park. He would go there now, get in bed and wait to see Mary Margaret Duggan by the light of day.

Sunday

August 11th

Reno, Nevada

When her alarm went off at 6:15 a.m., Mary Margaret decided she hated Dane Barrett. But then she told herself that was unfair—the trip was for her father's benefit, after all. The real problem was that her car was on life support and she couldn't drive to Laurel at her leisure, which meant if she wanted to go, she'd have to go with the good reverend.

Getting out of bed, she staggered into the bathroom. In the twenty-some hours since she'd met Dane, her guilt over nearly shooting him had worn off. He was now simply a man whose motives were unclear, as unclear as her feelings about him. But he had to be dealt with, she told herself, like any other Tom, Dick or Harry.

Having given it some thought in the shower, Mary Margaret still wasn't sure what to wear. It could be blistering hot over in the valley in August, which meant shorts and a tank top. But this situation called for modesty. She settled on white cotton pants and a simple cotton blouse. No makeup. Just straight vanilla. She wanted to get their relationship off on the right foot and that seemed the best approach.

When Janine had come home from work the previous evening, Mary Margaret had told her what had happened, laying more emphasis on the developments in her father's case than on her impression of Dane. "Maybe the time and money you've expended is finally paying off," Janine had said. Mary Margaret was reluctant to get her hopes up, because the disappointment would have been painful, so she'd played it down. But the truth was, she'd thought a lot about it, even wondering if a new trial could result.

With about ten minutes before Dane Barrett was to arrive, Mary Margaret headed to the kitchen for a cup of coffee and maybe a bite to eat. These daylight hours, she'd discovered, could be very confusing to the digestive tract. She was poking around in the refrigerator, trying to decide between breakfast food and a late-night snack, when Janine limped in, still half-asleep, but looking concerned.

"So, you're off," she said.

"The reverend should be arriving any minute."

Janine yawned. "I heard you in the shower and thought I'd see if I could make you some breakfast or something."

"Thanks, honey. That's really sweet, but I'm just going to have a piece of toast and a cup of instant coffee. Go on back to bed."

"I'm awake, I might as well help," Janine said. "How about if I toast you a bagel while you put the water on to boil?"

"Okay. Have a cup with me?"

"Sure."

The two of them went about their respective tasks in silence until Janine said, "So, what's this guy like?"

"He's a guy. What can I say?"

"He's a guy," Janine said, rolling the phrase through her mind. "That's it?"

"All right, he's nice-looking. Pleasant personality. Friendly. What do you want, his chest measurement?"

"My, but aren't we testy this morning. Is it the earliness of the hour or the dimple in the reverend's chin?"

Mary Margaret turned red. She quickly bent over the tea-kettle to cover her embarrassment.

"Ooo," Janine said, "we're talking Elmer Gantry, are we?"

"No," Mary Margaret insisted. "Nothing like that."

Her friend hooted. "I can't remember the last time I saw you blush this way."

"Will you shut up!"

Of course, that made Janine laugh even more. Mary Margaret peered into the kettle again, keeping her back to Janine. The water was far from boiling.

"He's single, I take it," Janine said.

"Divorced," Mary Margaret replied, trying to affect a nonchalant demeanor.

"That's good, considering you are, too."

"Half the world's divorced."

"So, did he come on to you?"

Mary Margaret glanced back at her. "You're really getting off on this, aren't you?"

"Oh, so he *did*," she said with a laugh. "He must not have been too obnoxious. How many men are there who could get *you* out of bed at six-thirty in the morning?"

Mary Margaret spun around. "Look at me," she said. "Do I seem like somebody out for a good time? I didn't even put on any makeup."

"You don't need to."

Mary Margaret put a spoonful of instant coffee in each of the mugs she'd taken out of the cupboard. "I'm not going to argue with you. Think what you want."

"A little fling with a minister *would* be different," Janine observed. "There hasn't been much going on in your love life of late."

"Not since Ramon, anyway."

Janine reached in the oven with a fork and moved the bagels a little. "I think a roll in the hay would be good for your disposition. Seriously. And what could be safer than a minister?"

Mary Margaret put her hands on her hips. "Janine Russo, what's with you this morning? Did you wake up horny or something? God, it's usually men who are trying to get me in bed!"

"The reason," Janine said, "is because I've been worried about you."

"Worried?"

"It's been months since you've showed any real interest in a guy. The only person I ever hear you talk about is Colleen."

"Janine!"

"I'm not suggesting anything like *that*. It's just that after that business with Ramon, you need something wholesome."

"And you think jumping in the sack with a minister is wholesome?"

"If the guy's a hunk, why not?"

"Because I'm not interested," Mary Margaret said.

Janine groaned, then checked the oven. Mary Margaret decided the water was hot enough and took the kettle off the stove. Janine grabbed the bagel, burning herself. She stuck her fingers under the tap, then dried them on a tea towel, examining them.

"I can see I'm going to have to check this guy out myself," Janine said. "I obviously can't believe anything you say. I bet he's adorable."

Mary Margaret handed her a mug. "Well, I hope you fall for him, because he's all yours."

Janine gave her an appraising look. "The lady doth protest too much."

"Dammit, Janine, I couldn't care less if I ever saw this guy again! Why can't you accept that?"

Janine scoffed. "My God, you're in love!"

Mary Margaret flushed. She took a breath, prepared to lash back, but was suddenly struck by the absurdity of the situation. She began to laugh, and soon Janine was, too. "You can be a little bitch at times, Janine Russo," she said, wiping her eyes.

Janine pushed the plate with the bagel toward her. "Eat your breakfast, Juliet."

Hap Coleman began drumming his fingers on the steering wheel of his van and glanced over at his brother, Rut, who was staring down the lane in the direction of the broad's trailer. He wondered how long he should let this go on.

"What are we going to do, sit here all day so you can get a glimpse of her going to the outhouse?" he said. "She's in bed, for chrissakes! What are we doing sitting here?"

Rut Coleman didn't reply. He continued to brood, rubbing the stubble on his chin as he gazed blankly out the window.

"Please, Rut, just tell me what you plan to do, will you? This shit's getting to me."

"I'm thinkin', all right?"

"Tell me what you're thinking. I don't like sitting here, not knowing."

Rut remained silent.

"Rut?"

"Jesus Christ, Hap," Coleman shot back, "I told you last night. I'm going to fuck the bitch. You know how long it's been since I've had a piece of ass. And this is the broad I want. I decided that even before I got out of the slammer. You knew that before we fucking came up here."

"Yeah, right, but I don't understand why it's got to be her."

"Because I said. *That* broad. The one sitting in *that* god-damn trailer. Mary Margaret Duggan. Got it?"

"All right. So how? When?"

"I'm thinkin'. I'm thinkin'."

Hap sighed. He wondered if his brother had gone a little nutso. Jesus, Rut hadn't been outside the walls of Quentin five minutes before saying, "Let's go to Reno." The last time he'd seen Rut before his release, he'd said to him, "What do you want to do your first night on the outside? Want a party? Want me to buy a case of beer and have some broads over at my place?" Rut had shaken his head and said, "I don't give a shit. Buy some beer. Get the broads. Whatever. But you might as well know, what I really want is up in Reno."

Rut hadn't said why until they'd gone to the High Chaparral. Hap couldn't believe it. "You think some showgirl will go to bed with you? You don't have enough bread, Rut. Those broads don't do it for peanuts, if they do it at all. This ain't no whorehouse."

"One way or another, it's going to happen." That was all Rut had said.

But then they'd gone to see *Dream Girls* and after that Rut was like a zombie. Going to their car afterward, he'd kept muttering over and over, "I gotta have her, Hap. I gotta have her."

Then, when they were sitting by the employee parking lot waiting for her to leave the casino, Hap had said, "Just tell me one thing—why her? There were fifty broads bare-ass naked up there. A guy could fuck any of them.''

"It's gotta be her. Gotta be." That's all the poor bastard could say.

Hap drummed his fingers some more, telling himself that if he didn't give Rut some slack he'd probably explode. And Hap sure as hell didn't want to be standing there when it happened. But he wasn't so sure he wanted to be around when Rut did whatever he was going to do to the girl, either. Jesus, this could get hairy. Maybe even dangerous.

"Well," Hap finally said, "you sit here and stare at her house, if that's what you want, but I'm going to crawl in back and catch a few winks."

Rut grunted his consent, but Hap wasn't sure he'd even heard. He moved out of the driver's seat and climbed in back of the van. Fortunately he kept a mattress on the floor. He'd just gotten down on his knees when his brother called to him.

"Hey, Hap, look at this."

He crawled forward and peered over the front seat. "What?"

"That Camry just pulled in and stopped in front of the trailer. Look, there's a guy getting out. Who the fuck could that be?"

"Maybe it's her boyfriend."

"What's he doin' comin' over at seven o'clock in the morning?"

"Maybe he likes boffing her in the morning. How the hell should I know?"

"That ain't her boyfriend."

"How do you know?"

"The car's got California plates."

"Maybe it's her out-of-town boyfriend."

"Zip it, Hap. You don't know shit."

"Well, what do you want me to say?"

"Nothing," Rut said, snatching his pack of cigarettes from the dash. "Just let me think. I gotta see what happens. I'm tellin' you this, though. No boyfriend's going to stop me. Nothing is. Nothing."

* * *

Mary Margaret had just taken a huge bite of bagel when there was a rap on the front door. She gulped, reaching for a paper napkin to wipe her mouth.

"Why don't I get it?" Janine said, pulling closed the flaps of her robe. "You appear to be indisposed."

Mary Margaret nodded and took a slug of coffee, trying to wash down the bagel as Janine headed for the front room. She heard her talking to Dane, but couldn't understand what they were saying. So she took another bite of bagel, knowing she shouldn't hold Dane up.

She was in the middle of chewing when they entered the kitchen. "I offered the reverend a cup of coffee," Janine announced.

Mary Margaret tried swallowing quickly and nearly choked, her eyes watering as they fell on Dane. Through the blur, she saw he had on a white Polo T-shirt with an American flag across the chest, jeans and loafers. No socks. He was smiling as though he was happy as hell to see her.

"Morning!" he said cheerily.

She gulped again but couldn't speak, settling instead for a little wave.

Noting the reason for her plight, he grinned. "We have a habit of catching each other at awkward moments, don't we?"

"Hmm," Mary Margaret mumbled.

"I hope instant's okay, Reverend," Janine said, sounding inordinately chipper.

"Fine," he said.

"Take anything in it?"

"Black's fine."

He turned his attention back to Mary Margaret, taking her in with a cautious sweep of his eye. She suddenly regretted not putting on a little makeup and maybe dressing more carefully than she had. But it was too late now. She managed to swallow the last bit in her mouth.

"Sorry, I was having a quick bite," she said. "I don't recommend the bagels if you want to talk."

Dane chuckled. "Reminds me of a dog I had when I was a kid. Barney loved peanut butter but it always stuck in his mouth. Sometimes he couldn't bark for an hour after taking a bite."

"I know the feeling," she said, taking another quick sip of coffee.

He laughed, recalling. "I used to give him a big old spoonful just to watch him smack his lips."

Mary Margaret observed him, already intrigued in spite of the fact that she had worked so hard at diminishing him. But Dane Barrett kept surprising her. He was so different from the men she was used to.

Janine handed him a mug of steaming coffee.

"Thanks," he said, but his eyes returned to Mary Margaret.

She felt self-conscious. Janine, who'd retreated to the sink, behind Dane, silently mouthed the word "Wow!" Mary Margaret took a hasty sip of coffee, splashing the liquid over the rim. Coffee trickled down her chin. Embarrassed, she reached for a napkin.

Dane seemed bemused. "This is the middle of the night for you, isn't it?"

"Yeah. For all I know, I'm sleepwalking."

"You are a dream girl, after all." He had the decency to wince at his own bad pun.

In the background, Janine clasped her hands together and gave a silent romantic sigh, batting her lids. Mary Margaret could have slugged her.

"Well, I guess we should be going," she said. "Don't want you late for your first mass."

"My first mass is probably one I'll never see," he said.

For a second she didn't understand, then realized she'd used Catholic terminology. "Sorry, I meant service."

Dane took a healthy gulp from his mug. "I've allowed a margin for traffic problems, but I don't suppose we should push it." He consulted his watch.

Janine still had a silly, blissful look on her face. Mary Margaret decided to ignore her. "Well, I'm ready," she said to Dane.

He turned to Janine, who erased her sappy lovesick expression just in time.

"Would you two like to take a bagel or some fruit or something with you to eat in the car?" she asked, sounding perfectly dignified.

They both declined. Mary Margaret led the way back into

the living room. Dane and Janine followed. Oddly, she'd been dreading the thought of being cooped up in a car for several hours with a man she didn't know, but now she couldn't get out of the house fast enough.

"Don't you have a bag, an overnight case or something?" Dane asked as she reached for the doorknob.

Mary Margaret gave him a quizzical look. "What would I need that for?"

"I thought if we didn't get everything done this afternoon, you might want to stay over a night in Laurel."

"Stay over where?"

He shrugged. "I don't know. Wherever you'd like. A motel?"

Mary Margaret saw that she had misread his meaning. "I don't think it will be necessary," she said.

"Wouldn't hurt, though," Janine chimed in. "Better safe than sorry."

Her tone was innocent on the surface, but Mary Margaret knew Janine could just as easily be suggesting she take her diaphragm.

"You never know," Janine added wryly, "when something big might come up."

Mary Margaret flushed. To hide from Dane's eyes, she spun on her heel. "Maybe it wouldn't hurt to throw a few things in a bag," she said, walking away. "Excuse me."

She headed for her room, wishing she could strangle Janine. Instead, she dug out her worn overnight case from the closet and tossed in a change of underwear, a pair of shorts and a tank top. Since she had room, she added her favorite turquoise silk blouse and her beige linen skirt, some heels and a pair of panty hose. Then she went to the bathroom and scraped her toiletries into her makeup bag, pausing long enough to dig the lip gloss back out and spread a little on her lips. How was it she always allowed herself to get manipulated when it came to men? she wondered. Were they to blame? Or was she?

In less than two minutes she was back in the front room. The way Janine had her hip cocked as she looked up at Dane told Mary Margaret that her roomie had discovered his charms. A wave of annoyance went through her, giving her pause. It couldn't be jealousy, she thought. It absolutely couldn't, because she honestly, sincerely, positively had no serious interest in Dane Barrett. It was impossible.

"Well, here I am," she said, trying to sound cheery.

The other two looked at her, Janine less sanguinely than Dane. Mary Margaret realized this was ridiculous. As far as she was concerned, Janine could have him. At least she was Protestant—sort of. Dane might even have decided he liked her already. And why not? Janine was pretty. The limp had to appeal to his Good Samaritan soul. Besides, she was so devoted and conscientious she'd probably learn to play hymns for him on the piano.

Dane offered Janine his hand. "Really nice to have met you."

"If you're ever in Reno again, drop by and say hello," she said, her voice positively saccharine. "We can always throw an extra hamburger on the grill."

Mary Margaret winced, embarrassed for her. Janine hadn't been as resolutely celibate as she, but her roommate had never come across as cloying or desperate before. What had happened to her dignity?

Dane took Mary Margaret's overnight case from her. "I'll toss this in the car."

His departure gave Mary Margaret and Janine a chance to exchange a few words. Janine wasted no time.

"God, what a hunk!" she said, slapping her chest with her hand, her eyes round as walnuts. "And *you* get to ride with him to Laurel. *Bitch!*"

"Look, Janine, if I could, I'd send you in my place."

Janine was incredulous. "Don't you get wobbly in the knees just looking at him? Mary Margaret, he's so *nice!* God, I'd be on him like a leech."

"So I gathered. As it was, you didn't exactly play the shrinking violet, kiddo."

"Did I make a fool of myself?"

"No. He's probably used to church ladies hanging all over him."

They both looked out the door at Dane, who was putting her case in the trunk of his car. Janine actually sighed like a teenager.

"I'll tell him you're available," Mary Margaret said dryly.

Janine shook her head as though she knew she was over-doing it a bit. "I guess I did wake up horny. A cold shower should take care of that, though."

Mary Margaret, who'd been feeling a mixture of annoyance and jealousy, suddenly felt sorry for her. It's not as if Janine was pitiable. She wasn't a wallflower or anything. She went out more than Mary Margaret did, but she had long hungered for a meaningful relationship. Her loneliness made Mary Margaret sad. But they couldn't talk now, so Mary Margaret gave her a conciliatory hug and headed for the car.

Dane had opened the door on the passenger side and was waiting for her. He seemed perfectly oblivious to what had happened inside—which was so typically male. She glanced at him as she slid into the leather seat of the Camry.

"So," Dane said after climbing in on the driver's side.

So? She waited but nothing more was forthcoming. "So, what?" she said.

"So, you look awfully nice," he said, starting the engine.

Compliments were the last thing she wanted under the circumstances, but how could she be offended? "Thank you."

The way he hesitated told her he'd read something in her tone. He started the engine.

They went along Date Palm Lane. Past Colleen and Candy's place, past their rosebushes and along the row of palms. There was a dark blue van parked at the corner. The only reason Mary Margaret noticed it was because parking wasn't allowed along the median strip of the park's main thoroughfare. She'd found out the hard way when she'd parked a U-haul there overnight the day she'd moved in. This van probably belonged to a relative of one of the blue hairs. The management always looked the other way when it came to them.

Dane was silent as they proceeded to the entrance of the trailer park. Mary Margaret noticed he had an ardent expression on his face, as though he was struggling with something. Then he gazed directly at her. He looked tormented.

"What's wrong?" she said.

"Nothing's really wrong...."

She wondered what the hell that meant. God, he wasn't going weird on her, was he?

"You'll have to direct me to the freeway," he said.

Mary Margaret took that to mean he wasn't prepared to explain himself, at least not yet.

Come on," Rut said, giving him a whack on the shoulder, "get the fucker started. They're getting away."

"Okay, okay," Hap said, turning the key in the ignition.

The engine came to life and he jammed the transmission into gear. The vehicle lurched ahead and they sped to the entrance of the mobile-home park. The Camry was still in sight, only half a block or so away.

"Get a move on," Rut growled, drawing on his cigarette. "Follow them."

Hap stomped on the gas pedal and the tires squealed as they roared up the street in pursuit of the Camry.

"Not too close," Rut said, coughing smoke from his mouth as he spoke. "I don't want them to know we're following.

Hap's veins bulged at the temples. His brother was fucking nuts. But he'd already decided to go along with him. Maybe he'd come to his senses.

"What are we going to do?" Hap asked. "Follow her everywhere she goes?"

"I wanna know what she's doing."

"Probably going to his place to get laid. Or to fucking play golf. What difference does it make?"

"It makes a difference to me, all right?"

"Rut, you don't even know the bitch. How can she be so goddamn important?"

"She just is. I gotta do this. Then I'm done with her. Do it and I'm done. Okay?"

"Shit, whatever you want. Whatever you want."

"Thanks."

Hap was trying to be understanding, but the truth was he was annoyed. "You'd think I was a goddamn prison guard the way you talk to me."

"It's not personal, Hap, okay? Just do this. I got this thing in my gut, eatin' me. This is the only way I know to take care of it. Just give me a little slack. This is how I get Quentin out of my system. I know what I'm doin'. I fuck this broad and I'll be all right. Trust me."

She could see that he was wrestling with something, and it perplexed her. They'd gone a few blocks and he hadn't said a word. He was agonizing over how to say it. That's all she could figure.

"Well," he said at last, shooting her a nervous smile, "I guess the best way is just to say it. I've got a confession to make."

Mary Margaret was wary. "Okay..."

Dane cleared his throat. "Last night I saw your show."

"Oh."

"I thought I ought to get that out right up front."

Mary Margaret was disappointed, but she told herself she shouldn't be surprised.

"I see," she said mildly. "And now that you've bared your soul, you want me to forgive you your sins. Is that it?"

"I wouldn't quite put it that way," he said, grinning. "Like I told you, I don't believe in sin. But I do feel guilty."

"Well, you're forgiven."

"You really don't mind?"

"I try to take things like this with a grain of salt. You went, you saw, like thousands, *many* thousands, of men before you."

He considered that for a moment. "Thousands, huh?"

"There's no point in sugarcoating it," she replied. "I'm a showgirl. I make fantasies for a living. You may not like it, but that's the way it is. Turn here," she said, interrupting herself, "if you want to get over to the freeway."

He hung a sharp right. Mary Margaret directed him to the on-ramp. Within moments they were sailing along a virtually empty freeway.

She glanced out at the unfamiliar sight of Reno in the early morning, but inside she felt empty. The bit of euphoria that had rubbed off on her from Janine was already gone. She and Dane Barrett had gotten down to basics in record time. It was established now who she was. Not that he hadn't seen for himself last night.

Dane remained in a contemplative silence for several heartbeats, then said, "If you're so blasé about it, why didn't you want me to go to the show?"

He obviously couldn't let go. Or was he trying to provoke her? Whatever his motive, she decided the best response was dead honesty.

"Because I knew I'd be spending several hours with you today, *in my clothes,* and I'd rather you think of me as the person I am *in my clothes.* Okay?"

"I'm fully capable of making the distinction," he said.

"Oh? That's a surprise. You look pretty normal to me. A clergyman, maybe, but still a man."

"And all men are oversexed jerks?"

"Well, you said it."

"I see."

"At least you have the decency not to deny it," she said, meaning it.

"Hey, I'll be the first to admit I find you very attractive. You're a beautiful woman. You have a lovely body, wonderful grace and presence. I was thoroughly entranced, watching you. But that doesn't make me a monster, does it?"

"You can look at it your way," she said. "I'll look at it mine."

They soon came to the Interstate 80 interchange and headed west toward California. Soon they were passing the heart of the city. The Sierra, dead ahead to the west, was majestic in the morning sun. Dane stared up the undulating ribbon of asphalt that rolled toward the mountains.

"But what I said is not the point I was trying to make," he explained.

"Then what is your point?"

"That I'd like to get to know the woman in the clothes. But I couldn't say that without admitting that I'd seen the other one."

"The bad girl?"

"Not bad. Unabashed."

"Meaning?"

"Unashamed."

"Yep, that's me," she said. "There's no point in doing what I'm going to do if I'm going to be ashamed."

"And what about *this* you?"

"It's the same me. One with clothes, one without. The difference is what's in *your* head, not mine. That's what guys don't understand."

"Well, let's put it this way then, Mary Margaret, I'd like to get to know the whole you."

She regarded him. "Why?"

"I don't know. Curiosity's part of it."

She considered that. "The dazzle got to you."

"Not the dazzle, the mystery."

She wasn't used to this kind of conversation and it had her a little off balance. There'd been plenty of guys who'd opened with a line like, "Hey, babe, you turn me on like nobody I've ever seen before. What say we go someplace and boogie?" But that didn't seem to be what Dane Barrett was saying, unless an educated man of the cloth simply said these things in an infinitely more subtle way.

"So, what's the point?" she said, beginning to see this was a bit more complicated than she thought. "I mean the *real* one? You making a pass or what?"

"I think 'or what.'"

She groaned. "That helps."

"I'm obviously not getting through," he said.

"Look, Reverend Barrett," she said, seeing they might never get on track, "last night you got your fantasies stimulated. That show you went to is a business. It's a machine and I'm one of the cogs. This is not rocket science. In fact, there's nothing fancy about it but the costumes and special effects."

"I know all that, but it's what's in your *head* that interests me. Do you really think of yourself as just a cog in a machine? It seems to me there must be more to it than that."

She was beginning to understand. She'd been asked before if she felt like a slut when she was on the stage, but nobody had tried to get inside her head the way he was. In a way, it was flattering. Still, she wasn't sure she liked it.

"I like dancing," she began. "I guess I'm an exhibitionist, to be perfectly honest. A girl couldn't do what I do for long if she didn't get some satisfaction strutting her stuff. But it's not like I live for the minute I'm up there onstage with the whole world staring at my boobs. Nobody makes me do it. Not even economic necessity. It's a job, basically, hard as that may be to believe.''

"I see."

She noticed his pensive expression as he gripped the wheel. "I hope you're not disappointed. If you were expecting some big intellectual Freudian thing, I'm sorry. I'm just a working girl," she said.

"You're unduly modest, Mary Margaret. It's not so much *what* people do in life that matters, it's *how* they do it. Even the most menial tasks can be performed with joy. When there's something special inside a person, it comes through. They radiate. After watching you last night, I'd say that of you. You were absolutely sensational."

It was silly, but his words put a lump in her throat. God, the guy was either the slickest hustler she'd ever encountered or he was some kind of mystic or saint. She traced his profile with her eye, lingering on his lower lip, which protruded ever so slightly. And she noticed his long lashes, his well-shaped ears and head. Dane Barrett was something to look at. But lots of guys had the physical part. Lots had money and balls. Some were even funny and clever. But those were just superficial qualities. Every once in a while a guy came along who found a way to touch a girl, who seemed to know her. She'd never had it happen before, but this guy had her thinking.

"You're skeptical, aren't you?" he said.

"Maybe I am. But don't take it personally. In my world everybody's got an angle."

"Everybody does have a hungry heart, you're right," he said. "*Everybody.* We all have needs and desires and we're all trying to satisfy them. That's what makes us human."

"So, what are yours?"

"Not that different than anybody else's when you come right down to it."

"That's reassuring."

"But there are different ways of approaching a situation.

You can do it selfishly or with kindness, care and understanding.''

"And that's you?"

He chuckled. "My ego comes right through, doesn't it?"

Mary Margaret fingered the hand grip on the door. "Maybe what you're trying to say is you'd be willing to think of me as just a person and we could be friends," she said, almost afraid to hope.

"That's a good way to put it."

"It's what you want?"

"I'd like that, yes," he said.

"Really?"

"Really."

God, she thought, wouldn't that be nice? She put her head back and reclined the seat, realizing she felt good about herself, which was astonishing considering how low she'd been since Ramon.

Ramon. God, what a contrast that night was to this. Staring out at the parched, sagebrush-strewn mountainsides, she pictured the little Basque fellow sitting in that chair, gazing at her naked body and weeping. She remembered the feel of his cold bony fingers on her breasts, her stomach and her butt. "Do you want to know who I *really* am, Dane Barrett?" she wanted to say. But she couldn't. She wouldn't. She didn't want that to be her, even if it was.

Closing her eyes as a heavy fatigue came over her, Mary Margaret tried not to think of Ramon. She wasn't even sure she wanted to think about Dane Barrett. Things were much too complicated to understand. Maybe it was easier and better not to try.

San Quentin State Prison, California

Jimmy Duggan sensed that something was coming down. It was in the air. The past few days things hadn't been quite the same. Little things. Sideward glances. People looking the other way when he approached. What was going on?

The men in his cell block were on their way to breakfast. As they shuffled along, going from one barred gate to the next, the chatter was the same. The morning people were wide-awake and at it. The night people—of which there were only a few because of the enforced routine of prison— dragged themselves after the others. Jimmy counted himself among them. But this particular Sunday morning even the sleepyheads seemed to be shunning him. Why? What had he done?

By the time they reached the dining hall, Jimmy found himself at the rear of the line. Willy Green, a small, wiry black man in his early sixties who Jimmy counted among his few friends, was just ahead of him. Willy had cast a glance in his direction when they'd first exited their cells, but hadn't said good morning as he usually did.

"Willy," Jimmy said under his breath. "What's going on?"

"Damned if I know, man," Willy replied in a low tone. His voice was deep and gravelly from years of smoking. He'd spoken without turning around.

"You must know something."

"Word's come down to keep away. That's all I know."

"Why?"

"Beats me."

"Who put out the word?"

"Them, man. How the fuck do I know? Just them."

Them had to mean those who had influence and made decisions. Some were faceless, some were known, and who called which shots depended on the issue and the parties involved. Jimmy had a sinking feeling.

The men moved steadily forward, quickly taking a tray and sliding it along the cafeteria-style counter. Jimmy had lost his appetite, but took a tray anyway. Willy's unwillingness to turn and face him, and his ominous tone, told him it was serious, whatever *it* was. He wondered if maybe Rut Coleman had been arrested in Nevada. That would explain everything.

When Jimmy got to the server, a sloppy man with a heavy stubble of beard on his chin and jaw, he waited for a plate. The man, who most of the inmates called "Pig," looked at him with flat eyes but didn't move.

"Yeah?" he said after a long pause.

"Could I have some eggs?"

"No eggs left," Pig said.

Jimmy looked down at the serving pan which was still half-full of the runny pale yellow curds that passed for scrambled eggs in Quentin. The next pan had several dozen greasy bacon strips.

"Bacon?" Jimmy said.

"All gone," Pig said.

Jimmy knew it was a signal he was being shunned, he just didn't know why. "Is there anything to eat?" he asked.

Pig turned to a scrap pan on the counter behind him and grabbed a couple of pieces of charred toast that had been discarded. He plopped them on a plate and handed it to him. Jimmy took the plate without a word and proceeded along. Willy had already gotten his coffee and had gone off to a table. Jimmy filled a cup with some "governor's java," as the inmates called it, and ambled to the table where Willy Green and two other men were sitting. When he put his tray down, Willy and the other men got up and moved to another table. Willy did him the courtesy of looking woeful, which told Jimmy he had no choice. Jimmy sat down, his back to the center of the hall.

He hated burnt toast and tried scraping off the worst of the charcoal with a spoon. Having scraped one side, he knew there'd be nothing left if he scraped the other, so he took a bite. It wasn't worth the effort. He picked up the coffee cup and pushed the tray away.

Jimmy sat glumly sipping his coffee when a figure appeared at the table directly across from him.

"Mind if I join you, Duggan?"

It was Larry Hicks, a pale giant of a man with a shaved head who the men called "Mr. Clean," mostly behind his back. Hicks was one of the ringleaders of the Aryan Brotherhood, but Jimmy knew him mostly as a buddy of Rut Coleman. He sat down without waiting for a response.

"So, how you been, sport?" Hicks said with a faux-friendly lilt.

"I've been better."

"No kiddin'?"

Jimmy sipped his coffee and waited, knowing this little

social call wasn't accidental. Hicks grinned at him as though they were longtime pals.

"So tell me, Duggan," he said, his gold incisor gleaming, "you planning on going to mass this morning?"

Jimmy sometimes did go to mass. He went for no particular reason except that it was a relatively safe place to be and a change of scene. "I'm thinking about it," he replied.

"Figured you would, since you and Father O'Grady are so tight these days."

An icy chill went down Jimmy Duggan's spine. He blinked, making Hicks's smile broaden.

"You see, Duggan, we got no problem with you gettin' in the confessional and stickin' your hand under the padre's robe, or whatever the fuck it is you two do, but we do got a problem when you discuss prisoner business with the son of a bitch."

Jimmy stared into Larry Hicks's hard, cold eyes. "We're talking about Nevada."

"Damned fucking right we are!" He said it loud enough that the men at the nearby tables all turned to look. Hicks lowered his voice and continued. "I'll put it straight and simple, Duggan. You mention Rut to O'Grady or anybody else on the other side of the bars again and they'll be carrying you out of here in a box."

"Rut said he was going to attack my daughter and I warned her the only way I could without going to the prison officials."

"What do you think O'Grady did, jerk-off? Put it in his diary?"

"I was trying to protect my daughter."

"Well, you got shit for brains. If the worst thing that happens is Rut having a party with your baby girl, you can consider yourself damned lucky."

Jimmy glared, a silent rage filling him. He knew it served no purpose to argue with Hicks, but it was all he could do to keep from leaping over the table and strangling the bastard. Not that he'd get very far. "Mr. Clean" could crush him with his thumb.

"I got one last piece of advice, Duggan," Hicks went on. "Unless you want the rest of your days here to be living hell,

I recommend you kiss Father O'Grady's fat ass goodbye."
He hesitated, his eyes hard, then said, "Do we understand
each other?"

Jimmy did not respond.

Hicks reached across the table and picked up Jimmy's coffee cup. Then he spit in it and returned it to where it had
been. "Have a nice day, Duggan." With that, he got up and
left the table.

Jimmy sat frozen for several minutes, his rage building.
Finally, unable to keep it in any longer, he took the tray and
hurled it against the wall. The crash brought a sudden hush
over the room. Heads turned. Two guards came over to him.

"You got a problem?" one of them asked.

Jimmy didn't respond. The next thing he knew they had
lifted him to his feet. With one on either side, he was led
away.

The High Sierra

Dane glanced over at the sleeping beauty from time to time,
trying to decide what was wrong with the picture. She was
easy to look at. That wasn't the problem. Truth be known,
he relished the sight of her, amazed that the long-legged
beauty on the stage last night was here, beside him. Part of
it was that he didn't trust his own motives, which was why
he'd taken the super-honesty tack with her. But he knew in
his heart that she was as right about him as she was about
every other guy—the overwhelming emotion he felt for her
was lust. But with a twist. It was the twist part he was struggling with.

Which was not to take anything away from Mary Margaret.
His mother would have dismissed her as a pretty little thing
without class—by which she'd have meant a girl with looks
but no pedigree. He would have put it differently. She was
real. She'd lived, she'd suffered. She didn't get lost in pretense. And she had substance. The last wasn't patently obvious, but if you talked to her for a while, it came through.
In fact, she was clever. And underneath the tarnish there was
a refinement about her, a nobility.

So, was the problem his guilty conscience? Or was it that she knew that he knew that she knew the friendship thing was questionable at best. She distrusted him. Maybe with good cause. That was the problem. But what did he do about it? Perhaps the solution was to ignore his glandular impulses, but that would be asking a lot of any man, even a mature one with a son and an ex-wife and a cat and a church to keep him grounded.

When Mary Margaret awoke and, rubbing her eyes, sat up, he was relieved. Somehow he felt less dangerous when she was awake and able to fend for herself.

"Good morning," he said.

She squinted at him. "God, I really conked out, didn't I?" She looked around. "Where are we?"

"Just past Donner Lake."

"Oh." She stretched, thrusting out her breasts as her head rolled back.

He wanted to touch her.

Yawning, she said, "Do you think the chances are good that something might come of this nursing-home business? Something that might clear my father?"

She was asking a question he could not answer. Worse, having met her, he found he cared less about what had happened in the nursing-home. Ledi Hopkins's revelation had become the justification for being with her. But he couldn't tell her that.

"I don't know what might come of it," he said. "But I think it's worth looking into."

There was consternation on her face. "Don't take this wrong, but why do you care about my father, anyway?"

He felt a twinge of guilt. Maybe more than a twinge.

"The world is full of injustice," he began tentatively. "And I'm a person who fights it whenever and wherever I find it." No, he thought as soon as he said it, that sounds too noble, too self-important, too much like bullshit.

"Really? That's why?"

She knows, he told himself. She knows I'm as hollow and self-serving as the next guy. "It's part of the reason."

"What's the other part?"

God, she was like a D.A. pinning him to the wall. "I think you know."

Mary Margaret didn't reply. Dane stared up the road, but her silence was wearing on him. He sneaked a peek at her. She was stone-faced. Finally the pressure got to him.

"Look," he said, "I'm only human. Besides, a person can have more than one motive," he said. "Is it really so bad that I want to get to know you better?"

She began laughing.

"What?" he said, bewildered.

"Nothing."

"No, tell me why you're laughing."

"I can't decide if you're a complete bullshitter or a nice guy. Usually I know right away, but you're harder to read than most."

"Thank God."

"So, which are you?"

"My motives are good."

"Good for who?"

"Let me put it this way, if I had to chose between going to bed with you and having you like me and think I was a nice guy, I'd take the latter." When she didn't respond, he said, "Do you accept that?"

"Let's put it this way, Reverend—we need each other."

He thought about that for a while. "You know, I don't like that an awful lot."

"Of course you don't. It's mutual. Men don't like anything that's truly mutual."

Hmm, he thought, *this cookie is sharp.* "You see right through me, don't you?"

"Your guilt made it easy," she replied. "All I ask is help with my father. The rest doesn't matter."

Dane glanced over at her. Infatuation, he realized, could be a cruel and terrible thing.

"They aren't fucking going to the mountains for a picnic," Hap said as he stared down the highway at the Camry, a quarter of a mile ahead and about to disappear around a curve. "I think that's pretty damned obvious by now."

"I don't care," Rut replied. "Wherever they're going, we're going."

Hap Coleman sighed. "What they're probably doing is going to San Fran."

"Then we will, too."

"But our suitcases and shaving gear is back at that motel in Reno."

"They won't throw it out."

Hap gnawed on his lip. He was starting to get really upset. "Listen, Rut, I know you've been through hell—all those years you spent in the slammer and all. But I want you to listen to me. This chasing around some girl because you got obsessed with her is bullshit, man. It really is. You got to let go of her. This isn't doing you any good."

"I know what I'm doin', Hap."

"No, you don't. You've got to let me help you. Once you get your feet back on the ground, then fine, do what you want. But for now, let me decide for you. What you need is to get laid. Let me turn around and take you back up to the Mustang Ranch. The girls might not be so classy as this Duggan broad, but they ain't bad. After a couple of belts of bourbon, you won't be able to tell the difference. Come on, Rut, listen to your kid brother, just this once."

"I know you're tryin' to help me, Hap," Rut said, lighting a cigarette. "Even if I'm being a son of a bitch, I'm glad I got you on my side. But scorin' with this hot little piece is somethin' I just gotta do. I can't expect you to understand."

"But following her all over the goddamn country's not going to get you what you want."

"Oh, yes it will, little brother. Somewhere along the way she's going to walk past an alley, fat, dumb and happy, and I'm going to be waiting. She can't avoid me forever. And this guy she's with won't always be around." Rut gave him an affectionate slap on the arm and then inhaled deeply from his cigarette. "Now come on, we're falling too far behind. They could pull off into a rest stop or something and we could go sailing right on past."

Hap shook his head with regret. He wouldn't tell his brother, but losing them would be the best thing that could happen.

* * *

They had been riding along in an unsettled silence for some time and he began to wonder what she was thinking. But then she surprised him.

"Mind if I ask you a personal question?" Mary Margaret said as a couple in a Porsche went zipping past them, the woman's long hair streaming out the sunroof.

"No, ask anything you want."

"Why did you become a minister?"

His relief was palpable. A topic he could deal with easily. "I guess the answer is I like pondering the meaning of life," he replied. "Ultimately, that's what religion is about, you know."

She considered that. "So, what's the meaning of life?"

There was a slow-moving truck ahead and Dane eased into the passing lane. They swiftly went by it. Mary Margaret was watching him, waiting. Talking about religion or philosophy outside of church was always a tricky proposition.

"You don't have to talk about it if you don't want to," she said. "I was just curious what you believe in."

"I believe in the goodness of life, of all creation."

"How about God?"

"Call it God, if you like."

"Do *you* call it God?" she asked.

"I don't think it matters."

"You'd never hear a priest say that."

"No, I expect not," he said.

She pondered his response. "How do you keep your faith?" she asked finally. "I mean, don't you wake up some mornings and say to yourself, how did I ever buy into this crap?"

"No," he said.

"No? Never?"

"Well, you see, Unitarians don't have to accept on faith what somebody else says, because what matters is what's in your heart. In my case, it's a belief in the importance of love and of doing justice to my fellow man. I try to be understanding and accepting. And that kind of faith isn't lost easily, though I admit it is always a struggle to live up to it."

"That's it? No angels and devils? No miracles?"

"No heaven, no hell—except for the heaven and hell we

make for ourselves on this earth. And as for miracles, life is miracle enough. I do believe things happen for a reason, that there's something out there far greater than me, a grand design, but whether it's serendipity or the hand of God, I'm not sure."

Mary Margaret returned to her contemplation.

"I hope you aren't shocked," he said.

"No…"

"It's not the sort of thing you hear in most churches, I realize."

"That's for sure."

Dane thought perhaps he'd offended her in some way and she was being too polite to say so. On the other hand, she'd made it clear she wasn't orthodox about religion. In his experience, a person could be deeply spiritual in a nonconventional way. But maybe she wasn't spiritual at all.

God knew, Kathy hadn't been. She hadn't even liked uttering the word, *God*, except in anger. Science and rationality were all she needed and all she wanted. "There is no conflict between what I believe in and science," he'd often told her. But Kathy could not even accept the fact that a beautiful sunset or a walk among the redwoods could touch a person's soul.

He went around another truck. Mary Margaret was off in her thoughts again.

She was aware of him watching her. He seemed disconcerted. The poor man had to be wondering what in the hell he'd gotten himself into. But if he was confused, it was because she was confused. She felt like a yo-yo. One moment she was intrigued by him, distracted by his pale blue eyes, the next she resented him for being a man like all the others.

"So, how about you?" he said. "How do you see the meaning of life?"

The meaning of life. No one had ever asked her that one before. So why was he? Because he cared what she thought? She was skeptical, though she didn't want to be. "I guess I don't think about it much, to be honest. When you're struggling just to survive, worrying about how to get the rent money, you tend not to be philosophical."

"I don't mean to press."

"No, I don't mind. You said some nice things, beautiful things. Things you just don't hear people say much. At least not at the High Chaparral." She hesitated, then added, "I'd like to think it's you and not just something ministers say."

"What do you mean?"

"All this talk about love and beauty and spirituality is great. But then I wonder what the hell happened to Stephen Ragsdale? Where was *his* love when he did what he did to me and Donna Lee?"

"I have no intention of defending him."

"I know. And I'm certainly not blaming you or your church for what he did. But it isn't easy to be philosophical when your father's in prison for something he didn't do, and every guy you meet's interested in just one thing—getting you in bed."

She'd spoken a little more forcefully than she'd intended. And she figured she must have hurt him because he fell silent. Now she was sorry she'd opened her mouth. Why was she picking a fight, anyway?

Then he said, "Maybe you should tell me how you feel about him."

"What are you, Dane? Some kind of masochist?"

"Something like that. But here's your chance. Vent a little," he said.

She hesitated, then decided, why not? "Okay. For a long time I thought Ragsdale killed Donna Lee. But after he died, I began hoping it was someone else. It's hard to get the truth out of a dead man."

"Well, somebody still cares about what really happened," Dane said. "Otherwise Elena Perez wouldn't have been threatened. I interpret that to mean the truth didn't get buried with Stephen Ragsdale."

"I hope you're right."

Dane surprised her then by reaching over and taking her hand. He lightly caressed her fingers. "We'll do what we can to prove that your father is innocent," he said.

Mary Margaret shivered at his touch, enough that Dane noticed. She didn't move, she just stared at his long slender fingers for several moments. It was affection, not a sexual thing like usual, and it felt good. Somehow right. Still, after a moment, she pulled her hand away.

The traffic began to slow. The signs indicated there was work ahead. Dane let up on the accelerator. Coming up behind a line of vehicles, they stopped.

After a while the traffic began inching ahead. Mary Margaret had remained mute. Dane wondered if maybe there'd been a little too much talk about religion. There were probably things she'd rather discuss. "So, what are your passions?" he said.

"My passions?"

"Let's talk about something that interests you."

"I guess I'm obsessed with my father, but we've already discussed that."

"Pick another subject, then."

She gave it some thought. "Since we've been morbid, how about former spouses?"

"You do like to wallow in misery, don't you?"

"You said I should pick."

"All right," he said. "What about former spouses?"

"Did you divorce your wife or did she divorce you?" she asked.

He might have known. The old "What happened, anyway?" question.

"You don't have to answer that if it's too personal," she said.

"Oh, I don't mind. I *love* talking about my ex-wife," he said, not sounding the least bit sincere. "Let's see, which of us got the divorce ball rolling? Hmm. I'd say the impetus came from Kathy, but I was not an unwilling participant."

"She pushed the button, in other words."

"I guess you could say that."

"Men tend not to unless they've got a honey in the wings," she said. "After all, why be inconvenienced?"

He heard it again, an edge to her voice. "You really have a problem with men, don't you, Mary Margaret?"

"Marriage will do that to you."

His heart stopped. He felt a pang of pure agony. "Married? You mean married, as in married *and* divorced, or just married?" He was almost afraid to hear her answer.

She laughed. "What did you think? That I'm married?"

He tried to act nonchalant, but without much success. "One is occasionally caught unawares by this sort of thing."

"Does my marital status matter?" she asked.

"I much prefer that you're single."

"That's more honesty, I take it."

"Yes."

"Well, you can relax. I'm divorced. Thank God. But I was only married for about fifteen minutes. It was one of the bigger mistakes of my life."

He was relieved, if not elated. But he also wondered about her experience—enough that he had to ask. "What happened?"

"The marriage never got off the ground. It was downhill from our wedding night."

"You mean he was inept?"

"God no. Anthony was a hell of a lover. When he wasn't drunk, that is. Booze and Anthony Casagrande did not get along. To make a long story short, he had too much champagne at the reception and basically raped me on our wedding night."

"*Raped* you?"

"Tied me up with the bedsheets and did what he wanted. Some of it wasn't very pleasant. It's not like I was a virgin or anything, but a girl doesn't expect to be abused on her first night of marriage."

"I guess not."

"Anthony and I did not see eye to eye on what a wife was supposed to be. That was more the problem than his drinking and the rough stuff, to be honest."

Dane ran that through his mind as they passed the spot where the Cal Trans crews were repairing the road. The traffic began moving more swiftly. Each bit of information put Mary Margaret in a new light. His illusions were fading. Oddly, he found that comforting. He didn't want to be attracted to the fantasy showgirl. He wanted to know the real woman.

"You're so beautiful and glamorous, a person tends not to associate the ugly things in life with someone like you."

"Believe me, people in show business get their share and more. We're real people with real lives. We've been raped and maybe shot. We've been swindled and cheated on, slapped around and deserted, impregnated and deceived, same as everybody else.''

"And yet you can be stoic about it," he said.

"The only other choice is to go off in a screaming rage, but where does that get you? No, if your husband's an ass, you divorce him and tell yourself you'll be more careful next time—if you've got the stomach for a next time."

Mary Margaret was bitter. He could hardly blame her. He'd been fairly accepting of what had happened to his own marriage, even though the divorce had hurt him. True, Kathy hadn't been the monster Mary Margaret's ex had been, but she'd deceived him, if not herself, which he'd resented. Yet, unlike Mary Margaret, he wasn't prepared to dump her without at least making an effort.

"I feel badly for you," he said.

"I don't want pity."

"What do you want?"

She blinked. That was not a question she'd heard very often. "I don't know, a little breathing room, I guess. To be able to do something that matters and feel good about myself."

"That's a worthy aspiration."

"Let me ask you something," she said. "Do you try to sound different than most men, or are you really different?"

"I don't know that I'm all that unique. Maybe I'm just not like the other men you've known."

Her silence told him that maybe she agreed.

San Joaquin County, California

Elena Perez went into the back bedroom where her dear little Juanita was sleeping and kissed the child on the temple. Murmuring her love, she returned to the front room where her husband, Miguel, and her nephew, Efrain, were watching a football game. As a small boy in Guadalarja, Efrain had played soccer incessantly, but since he had come to California, all he seemed to care about was American football.

"Already the Raiders?" she said, taking her purse from the

table and checking to make sure everything she needed was inside.

"It is a preseason game," Miguel said absently.

"But it is so important you must watch it, right?"

"I work hard all week," her husband said.

"Well, I hope the Raiders are not so important that you do not forget your daughter. You are lucky she is sleeping so late."

"Yes, yes," Miguel said. "Don't worry, Elena."

It was only the pregame show, but she knew there was no competing with football. Taking her purse, she went to the door. "Efrain, don't let your uncle neglect your little cousin," she said in Spanish.

"*Sí, sí, Elena,*" he replied. "I'll watch him watch her."

She shook her head and left the house. Though it was mid-morning, the sun had already burned off the dew and the temperature was rising. Fortunately, the hospital where she worked was nicely air-conditioned and she never suffered like at home, especially in the kitchen, where the effects of the small window unit in the living room could not be felt.

Standing at the foot of the steps, Elena peered up and down the country road. There was no sign of a vehicle. The bright sun shone on the cornfield across the way. Once again she feared that he was out there somewhere, watching her. The previous morning, when she'd gone to her car, there had been a note under the windshield wiper. "Go home to Mexico," it said. Elena wondered if maybe they should, if it wasn't too dangerous to stay. But Miguel had told her the bad people, whoever they were, simply wanted to test her courage. "How can what you've done be so serious that they would hurt us?" he said when she showed him the note. "If they can make you go easily, they will."

Elena knew her husband was more concerned than he let on. But since he wouldn't let her go to the police, he had no choice but to put up a brave front. "It was too hard to come here," he said. "That I should give America up so easily is crazy. We will not give up our life because of some old woman's dying words."

And so, that had been that. Of course, Miguel wasn't the one who had to face the man with the harelip who was so evil-looking and frightening. If Miguel had seen him, he might understand.

Elena was relieved that there was no note today. Even though Miguel had said he'd checked, she did not trust that the man might not come back. Unlocking the car door, she got in. She was relieved when the engine started easily. This was her last day of work before she had two days off. She could hardly wait until she was home again with her family—and this before she'd even left the house.

Elena backed out of the drive and started down the road, headed for the highway, which was two miles from the house. From there it was another twenty minutes to the nursing home in Lodi. Twenty minutes in which she would be looking at the rearview mirror as much as the road ahead.

She'd only gone a quarter of a mile or so, when a large car came up right behind her, driving very close. Dangerously close. Her heart choked. She tried to pull over to the edge of the road, thinking the car wished to pass, but it followed her right over to the shoulder. It was then she realized the driver's intentions were to harm her, not to pass. *"Dios mío!"* she cried, her heart beginning to pound wildly.

Terrified, she stepped on the accelerator, but the other car stayed right with her, only a few feet from her rear bumper. Elena gripped the wheel tightly, certain he was going to make her crash. She tried to slow down and when she did, the big car bumped against hers, making it lurch forward and swing wildly back and forth from one side of the pavement to the other. She cried out, fighting the panic building inside her. She told herself she had to go faster, to try to escape before he killed her. But she couldn't get away.

She glanced from time to time in the rearview mirror, but never got a very good look at the driver. It was a man, perhaps the same man, the one with the harelip. That was all she could say.

The speedometer went above sixty. In her mind's eye, Elena kept seeing herself die. She began crying, certain her life was over. Her poor child! But then, the next time she looked in the mirror, the big car was gone. Had he crashed? Or simply disappeared?

She let up on the accelerator, her heart racing. Holy Mother, why were they doing this to her?

At the highway there was a small store with a gas pump out front. There was also a pay phone on the side of the building. After checking to make sure the big car hadn't returned, Elena pulled into the parking area in front of the store. A cloud of dust was still swirling around the car as she climbed out and ran to the phone, her purse in hand. Fumbling for coins, she finally extracted a quarter and put it in the coin slot. Her fingers trembling, she dialed.

"*Miguel,*" she screamed into the phone. "He tried to kill me!"

"Elena? What? What are you saying?"

Her chest heaving and tears streaming down her cheeks, she told him what had happened. "I am telling you, Miguel," she said between sobs, "I can't do this anymore. Either we go to the police or we must take vacation time and go to Mexico for a while. I could have been killed. And if I was, what would happen to Juanita?"

"Elena," he husband said, "there is no point in going to the police. It is because of them that this man found you in the first place. The priest told the police and somehow this man found out."

"So what will we do?" she said, her body shaking with fear.

Miguel did not answer immediately, then he said, "Okay, ask your supervisor for some time off. And I will try calling my boss. If we can get a few weeks, then we will go to your mother's."

"And what about Efrain?"

"Once he leaves the country, it will be very difficult to return."

"Then he must find another place," she said resolutely. "We must think of our own lives and our daughter."

"Yes," Miguel replied. "And there will be no more talking to the priest."

Auburn, California

Dane stood at the gas pump, filling the tank of the Camry. He kept looking across the parking lot at the fast-food place where Mary Margaret was getting them coffee. She'd only been gone a few minutes, but he was already eager to see her. In the few short hours they'd been together, he'd fallen for her, tripped right over his libido. His feelings transcended sexual attraction. It had become complete and total infatuation, the type a kid in high school would get.

He knew exactly what was happening, of course. And he was perfectly aware he couldn't trust it. But it felt so good, and it had been such a long time since he'd been this way—helpless, giddy, embarrassed and aching inside. The ache was poignant and very real, even though he knew it was nothing but fancy.

As the hose clicked off, he saw her come out of the door of the restaurant. His heart began to lope. She walked toward him with all the grace of a fashion model, her long legs swishing as she came toward him, one of those little cardboard trays in her hand. Her hair shone brilliantly in the sun; there was a smile on her lovely face. She was a vision—such a compelling one that it filled him with longing.

He put the nozzle of the hose back in place as she arrived.

"Two coffees and two apple tarts," she said with a tone of gleeful decadence.

They looked into each other's eyes for an extra-long time. He saw something new, a hint of joy perhaps. "You seem to be in a chipper mood all of a sudden," he said.

"It isn't all of a sudden. I've been gradually feeling better."

"Why?"

"Maybe because I like you," she said brazenly.

"How nice. It's mutual, by the way."

She extended the tray toward him. "Hungry?"

"Gee, I don't know if I can eat two," he said.

She gave him a look. "You know, you men are like male lions. You think all the food's for you. And if there's any left over..." She slid into the seat.

Dane leaned over, looking in at her. "I take it you're into equal relationships."

"We might be friends, but I won't be dragging home any dead carcasses for your dinner."

"But we're just getting acquainted, Mary Margaret."

"Go pay for the gas and hope there's a tart left for you when you get back."

He reached in and pinched her cheek. "I like your subtlety."

Smiling, he headed for the building. The euphoria he felt was welcome, like the first warm day of spring—pleasant and full of promise. He was so caught up in it that he scarcely noticed the dour man standing outside the door, smoking. It was the guy's glare that caught his attention more than anything. Dane almost did a double take, thinking that to engender such a response they must be acquainted. But then the man looked away, flicking his cigarette onto the pavement.

Dane went inside and paid for the gas. When he came out, the man was gone. Without another thought, he dismissed him from his mind and went to the car. Mary Margaret had taken the lids off the coffees and had the tarts open on her trim thighs. He felt a pang of appetite, as well as deep yearning for her.

"Looks wonderful," he said, privately enjoying his secret meaning.

"Just to show my maturity, I share everything fifty-fifty. Want some now, or do you want to wait until we're on the road?"

"I think I'll wait."

They left the station, squeezing out the driveway between a blue van sitting at the entrance and a car that was coming in. He noticed the man who'd glared at him was in the passenger seat of the van. Dane guided the Camry onto the freeway ramp, merging easily with the traffic. Mary Margaret handed him one of the tarts. He took a bite out of it before handing it back. Then she gave him a cup of coffee.

"It's hot," she warned.

Dane took a cautious sip.

"So, would it be all right if I went to church today and heard you *preach?*" she asked.

Dane was thrown completely off balance by the question. "You want to hear me preach? Today?"

"Sure, why not?"

He shrugged. "I'd be happy to have you at the service, if you like."

"Am I dressed all right? I've got nicer clothes in my case, if this is too casual."

"No, people come dressed very informally. Especially in the summer. Anyway, you look great."

"I'd really like to hear you."

"Why?"

She looked at him thoughtfully. "I don't know, I just would."

He felt his blood begin moving smartly through his veins. Kathy had only heard him preach once—a sermon he'd given at the Berkeley church when he was still in seminary. She'd complimented him begrudgingly, saying the pop psychology elements, while not original, were used effectively. That was her sole comment. It thrilled him, though, that Mary Margaret would want to hear him speak. "Is it curiosity?" he asked.

"Sort of."

"What do you mean, 'sort of'?"

"Don't take this wrong, but I want to see if you're boring when you preach."

Before they'd stopped for gas, she'd asked him why Kathy had divorced him and he told her his theory that one of the reasons was she'd found him boring. "I was a little too normal for her taste," he'd said. "Kathy wanted a craziness in her relationships that I couldn't provide. She needed danger, if only emotional danger. My boat was a little too steady." Mary Margaret had allowed that was pretty weird and he'd told her she probably felt that way because she was pretty normal herself. She'd replied, "I don't know the woman, but I bet her problem is she's spoiled. Did she grow up going to the country club?" Dane admitted that she had. "Well," Mary Margaret had said, "no mystery there." But now she wanted to check out his "boring quotient" herself.

"Great," he said. "It's not enough that this is my maiden sermon, but I'm going to have you out in the audience, examining my every word for boredom."

She'd eaten her tart and was licking her fingers. "Don't sweat it. If you want, I won't say a word after."

"No, if you're going to be there, I'll have to have your honest opinion."

"Why?"

"Because I care what you think."

"You don't even know me," she said.

"Don't you care whether I thought you were graceful or awkward on stage yesterday?"

"That's different."

"No, it's exactly the same," he said. "Everybody cares what people think of them. Especially their friends. And we *are* friends, Mary Margaret."

She handed him his tart and he took a big bite, chewing as he glanced over at her, waiting for a reaction. Her expression was surprisingly serious. But he saw a softness, a vulnerability, that was compelling. He again had that strong desire to touch her and have her touch him. He could imagine her putting her head on his shoulder, ruffling his hair, any number of things. Had he the courage, he'd pull over right then and there and kiss her. Right by the side of the road.

He finished the tart and took the napkin she handed him. After wiping his mouth, he traded that for the coffee cup, from which he took a couple of quick sips. Then, as he stared at the road ahead, he tried to get his feelings into perspective.

"I wonder if we could be thinking the same thing," she asked.

"I don't know."

"Tell me."

"You may not like what I say."

"I'm willing to take a chance," she said.

He screwed up his courage. "I was thinking I'd like to pull over, take you in my arms and kiss you."

His words were received with a deafening silence. But after several moments she said, "I thought so."

"You aren't upset?"

"No."

"So what were *you* thinking?"

"That if you pulled over, you'd make us late for church. And I wouldn't want that on my conscience. So then I thought, maybe if I give you a kiss on the cheek, a friendly kiss, we'd both be content."

He desperately hoped she wasn't making fun of him. "Is that true?"

Loosening her seat belt, she leaned over and took his jaw in her slender hand, despite the fact they each were holding a cup of coffee. She pressed her lips to his cheek, her breast touching his arm. His heart went wild. He even felt the first stirrings of an erection.

Dane could smell the soft scent of her hair and had to struggle to keep his eyes on the road. His gut ached for more. Why wasn't there a rest stop when he needed one? Would the shoulder of the highway do? But Mary Margaret settled back in her seat and refastened her belt.

"Don't make too much of that," she said. "I like you very much, and I meant it in a friendly way. It wasn't a come-on."

"Thanks for making that clear."

"Dane," she said with a laugh, "surely you aren't one of those guys who needs it all to be satisfied."

"Who, me? Of course not."

"Liar. There's not a man alive who won't keep going until he's stopped."

"And there's not a woman alive who doesn't enjoy stopping him." He finished off the coffee and stuck the cup in the side pocket.

"You know, I like you very much," she said. "As a man, you're definitely in the top ten percent. The problem is the circumstances."

"Hmm."

"Hmm, indeed," she said.

"Circumstances do change."

"They can. But this isn't a good time to speculate."

"So, what's the bottom line?" he asked.

"That you'd better wipe the lipstick off your cheek before climbing into the pulpit."

Laurel, California

As they entered town, Mary Margaret began to get nervous. During the drive down, she'd been adjusting to Dane Barrett, the person and the man, the hunk that Janine had drooled over and the minister who wanted to help her father. Once they'd settled on who they were and where each of them was coming from, she had relaxed—at least enough to decide she liked him. Kissing him, even though it was just a friendly kiss, had probably been a mistake. There was no way he wouldn't misread her intentions. Not that she was all that clear on them herself. But what was done, was done.

Now that they were in Laurel, her entire state of mind changed. It was her first visit back since her father's trial, and she'd underestimated the emotion the place held for her. Dane had been a prince since that little kiss. He hadn't tried to press any advantage he thought he had, maybe because he sensed this was emotional for her.

"I'm going to have to change clothes for the service," he said, "so unless you'd rather I drop you off someplace, we'll go to my place first."

"I have no place else to go," she replied. "Your house will be fine."

Mary Margaret looked at the quiet tree-lined streets of Laurel, feeling a curious mixture of nostalgia and rage. This was now enemy territory and she'd come back blithely, having suppressed the depth of her feelings. Her father had been judged a monster, and her loyalty to him meant she was found lacking, too. Whether the people of Laurel still thought of her that way or not, she still very much felt like an outcast.

"I guess you recognize that place," Dane said as they passed the neat old brick building where Stephen Ragsdale had preached and where she and her father had lived in the basement.

When they'd turned onto the street, Mary Margaret had actually started feeling ill. Once again she was the child of the man who'd murdered Donna Lee Marshall. Getting no response, Dane reached over and put his hand on hers.

"You all right?"

"This town holds some unpleasant memories," she said, refusing to look at him. She didn't want him to see that her eyes were all teared up.

"I'm sure it does. Happily, I'm not part of them," he said, giving her hand a squeeze.

It was true, and a nice thing to say. But a tear did squirt out of her eye just the same. She wiped it away, hoping he wouldn't notice.

They went around the corner and a short way down the next street over before he pulled into the driveway of a tidy little bungalow. Though decades old, it seemed homey. Many times Mary Margaret had walked the streets of Laurel, looking at the houses where her classmates lived, wondering if someday she'd live in such a place. The home she'd shared with her mother in the Sunset District of San Francisco was only a flat. At least she'd had her own room, albeit a tiny one that had once been a storage area.

"This yours?" she asked.

"I rent it from one of the trustees of the church at a favorable rate. The house I own is in Berkeley. Kathy and Toby lived in it before they went to Japan for a year. Now it's being rented out."

"Who's Toby?"

"My son. Didn't I tell you about him?"

"No."

"Toby's a great kid, the love of my life. He's four. We have a wonderful relationship. The only problem we have is his mother. She likes to manage everything, including the way Toby and I relate to each other. But I'm sure you have no desire to hear all that."

She was truly surprised. Dane noticed.

"What's the matter?" he said. "Was I sounding like a horse's ass? Sometimes I do when I talk about my ex."

"No, that's not it at all," Mary Margaret said. "I'm trying to picture you as a father. Until now it wasn't part of the image."

He groaned. "Don't tell me you hate kids."

"No, I guess I'm neutral toward them. They haven't been much of a factor in my life one way or the other."

"That's the way it was with me until Toby came along. No, that's not right," he said, correcting himself. "Actually, kids might have been a negative. Screaming little buggers have ruined more than one restaurant meal. But as a baby, my son never bothered me. I guess people feel differently when the brat is their own."

"You amaze me, Dane," she said.

"How so?"

"I don't know, you keep coming out with these revelations about yourself."

"For the better, I hope."

"Let's just say I think it's nice that you love your son and are close to him."

She could tell he wasn't sure about her response.

"Well," he said, "I've got to get inside and change."

They went in, receiving a begrudging welcome from Dane's cat. But when Mary Margaret bent down to pet him, he scampered off.

"Don't take it personally," he told her. "Mead's Toby's cat and my son's the only human being he will let pet him. Kathy and I are qualified to feed him, but that's pretty much it." He waved broadly toward the living room. "Make yourself at home. I'll run upstairs and get ready."

She wandered into his rather Spartan front room. The bookshelves immediately caught her eye. She gave the bookcases a quick once-over, deciding from the titles that his taste was eclectic—the word Colleen used to describe her own library. Dane seemed to have more history, philosophy and books on religion than Colleen which was to be expected—but there were also a number of books on business.

Hearing a sound behind her, she turned and saw Mead watching her from the doorway. "Looking for company, kitty?" she said to him. "I bet you're not as shy as they think."

She sat in an easy chair and watched the cat. Soon it ambled in her direction. Finally it sat back on its haunches at her feet.

"I'm not going to get on the floor with you, kitty," she said softly. "If you want some loving, you'll have to come up here."

Mead cocked his head, reading her. After a minute of vacillation, he jumped onto her lap and made himself comfortable. Mary Margaret lightly rubbed his soft fur, closing her eyes as she remembered her own childhood cat. A poignant sadness filled her, a sort of homesickness for those days, that life, and the people who'd loved her.

"Well, I'll be damned," Dane said.

Mary Margaret's eyes popped open and she saw him standing at the door, looking real sharp in a dark blue, double-breasted suit and red tie. His dark hair was neatly combed. There was delight in his pale blue eyes.

"I never thought I'd see the day Mead got friendly with a stranger."

"Cat people are never strangers for long," she said, stroking the cat's fur. "I had a calico growing up. My father gave her to me after he got back from Java, so that's what I called her. She got hit by a truck right in front of my eyes the same week my father was arrested for burglary. My mother said I'd see Java again in heaven, but I didn't believe it. That's why I never got another cat."

Dane stared at her for a long time, then said, "I think Mead senses all that."

"We've had a little chat," she said.

"Obviously Mead is as susceptible to your charms as I am."

The compliment pleased her. "Speaking of charms, you're looking pretty cool. And not too much like a minister, if you don't mind me saying so."

"It's a carryover from my days as a stockbroker. I still have some of my business duds," he said, ambling over to where she sat.

Her eyes rounded. "You were a stockbroker?"

"For five years. Before I went to seminary."

"Another surprise."

"I'm thirty-four, Mary Margaret. It didn't take me ten years to get through college and graduate school," he said, scratching Mead behind the ears.

The cat hissed at him. Dane laughed. Mary Margaret purred at Mead and stroked his back to calm him.

"You've seduced him, all right," Dane said.

"So, why did you leave the brokerage business?"

"That's a whole sermon in itself. Suffice it to say my two biggest clients were my parents and that didn't seem a very worthy way to spend my life."

"Your family's really rich, then."

"More than comfortable, let's put it that way."

"I thought so."

"Why's that?" he asked.

She looked down at Mead as she stroked him. "The first time I saw you I thought you were pretty classy, sort of aristocratic."

He threw back his head and laughed. "Oh, so that's why you put that gun to my head!"

Mary Margaret blushed. "Yeah, when you're a murderer's daughter, all rich guys become the enemy...or at least they become *them.*"

"Don't say that, Mary Margaret, even in jest. You're not a murderer's daughter."

"I am in this town."

Dane brushed her cheek with his fingers in the same affectionate way she stroked the cat. "Not to me, you aren't."

She regarded him, her eyes shimmering. There was a big lump in her throat. She wanted to tell him thank you, but instead she said, "You're going to be late."

Dane left, telling her he'd see her at the church. Mary Margaret sat there for a long time, petting Mead and thinking about what Dane had said. First her eyes got glossy, then she started to cry. She wasn't sure why, except for the fact that she was back in Laurel and felt clingy toward Dane. She was starting to like him an awful lot and that wasn't wise. Friendship might be possible, but there was no place beyond that for it to go—at least no place she'd be interested in.

Dane probably had notions, but that didn't mean anything because it was what *she* wanted that mattered. Dennis Malloy, the first boy to try to have sex with her, had taught her the premier lesson of dealing with men—a woman should never start anything she wasn't willing to finish. Her playfulness in the back seat of Dennis's car had cost her a good blouse and him three stitches under his eye. But she'd profited in the long run. Since then, many a man had called her a cold bitch, but it was far better than being everyone's patsy.

The important thing was she still had control. And fortunately, Dane was gentleman enough to respect that. This trip was not about him and it wasn't about her. It was about her father. She had every intention of being civil, and they might even have a little friendly fun along the way, but Mary Margaret was under no illusions. And if Dane had illusions, then it was up to her to see that they wouldn't get in the way.

Mary Margaret walked up the steps of the First Unitarian Church of Laurel, wondering why she'd thought coming here was a good idea. She'd been curious and she had wanted to please Dane, but she'd also overestimated her ability to forget. She wasn't going to back out, though. That wasn't her style. So she told herself to buck up and see it through, if only for Dane's sake.

Inside the church she was greeted by the lady at the welcoming table. Mary Margaret gave her name.

"Oh, I thought I recognized you, Miss Duggan," the woman said. "How nice that you've come to visit us." The woman seemed sincere, if a touch embarrassed, but Mary Margaret harbored no ill will toward anyone here. By and large, they'd tried to help her and her father, at least until Donna Lee was murdered. Still, had it not been for Dane and the fact that she hoped to do some good for Jimmy's cause, she would never have returned to Laurel.

As Mary Margaret entered the sanctuary, the piano prelude commenced. She took a seat two-thirds of the way back from the front, an empty place on either side of her. She actually knew surprisingly few of the congregants, though most who'd been around a decade ago probably remembered her, if only as a social experiment that had gone awry.

There had been a low buzz as the word moved from person to person in the hall. These people were known for being more tolerant than other townspeople, so there were no hostile looks. Mostly they seemed surprised and curious to see her.

Mary Margaret tried not to think about that. Instead she listened to the piano music and glanced around at the vaguely familiar hall with its colorful flags of the world's religions. She realized she had never attended a service in this church and the only other time she'd been in the sanctuary was with her father—when he was cleaning. Jimmy had sent her to Saint Aubin's a few times, mainly because he thought it was what her mother would have wanted. He was trying to meet his parental responsibilities, though she hadn't fully understood it at the time.

Being in the place where her father had worked, she suddenly felt his presence. A clear recollection of the day they'd arrived in Laurel came to mind. Her mother had been dead six months, so it was just the two of them. Jimmy was all she had. The alternative was a foster home. "Poor kid," he'd said to her as they sat on the old beat-up old sofa in their basement apartment, their suitcases at their feet. "Hell of a thing for a girl to be stuck with a father like me."

"Daddy," she'd replied, "you can think whatever you want, but don't ever say that to me again. You're my father and that's all that matters."

Jimmy had cried after that because he'd felt so inadequate. Mary Margaret understood, because her mother had taught her to feel compassion for her father. "Your dad's got a good heart, Mary Margaret," she'd once said. "He just doesn't know how to be a good husband and father. He wants to, and he does the best he can, so we've got to love him for that." Though Mary Margaret didn't fully understand her mother's love for Jimmy Duggan, she took it as her own. As Moira was dying, she told Mary Margaret that Jimmy would need her as much as she needed him. Her last words were: "Forgive him."

A wave of sadness went through her and Mary Margaret tried to ease her father from her mind. If she dwelled on his predicament, bitterness and resentment would surely follow.

Just then Dane entered the sanctuary from a side room. A flutter of excitement went through her. He was so handsome in his dark suit, seeming for all the world like one of those brooding male models in a *GQ* ad for fancy Italian suits. He looked like anything but a minister. Yet he was. She shouldn't forget that...and neither should Dane. No matter how hunky he was, or how liberal his beliefs, they were coming from very different places. And yet, he refused to make it easy for her. He was a kind person, but not so kind as to let her off the hook.

Mary Margaret saw that he had spotted her. They made eye contact and, unless it was her imagination, his thoughts weren't very pastoral. His smile almost seemed sacrilegious. That made her blush.

But the more she thought about it, the more she'd come to realize that Dane's religion wasn't nearly so important as who he was. Their backgrounds couldn't be more disparate. He'd told her he'd gone to Europe before he was ten and had attended private school. Clearly, he'd had every advantage, whereas she had been lucky to get a new pair of shoes each school year, considered a ride downtown on the N Judah Muni Line to be a big deal, and grew up thinking food stamps were the same as grocery-store coupons.

The prelude concluded and Dane stepped to the pulpit. He slowly looked around, his presence drawing people's attention. Then he began to speak, his manner smooth and self-assured. A humorous quip got a chuckle from the congregation, which seemed to put everyone, including her, at ease. He ended his introductory comments with a request for patience with him, tolerance for one another and love for the world.

Could that really be the man who'd gone to see her dance last night, the man who professed to be her friend, the one she'd kissed in the car? Was that Dane Barrett, or was Dane Barrett the man in the pulpit? Uncertainty boiled up from within, making her wonder what in the hell was she doing here. But then he smiled at her, momentarily stilling her heart.

After the service Dane was deluged by well-wishers. Glimpsing toward the rear of the hall, he saw Mary Margaret moving toward the exit. They'd agreed to meet out front, but he was anxious about her going out the door just the same.

The service had gone well. There were a few minor glitches, but for a maiden voyage it wasn't bad. He'd found himself speaking often to Mary Margaret, wondering if they were connecting.

The comments he was getting as he shook hands with congregants indicated the overall reaction was positive. A few gushed their compliments in glowing terms. But what did *she* think? Was she put off? Or bored? For all their rapport during the drive down, was the reality of who he was a disappointment? If the reviews weren't good, there wasn't a lot he could do about it. He was who he was.

Helen Conroy, the president of the board of trustees, buttonholed him, praising his sermon and passing along compliments she had heard. Dane knew he should be savoring every moment of this, but his heart had already gone out the door with Mary Margaret.

"Listen," Helen said, clearly oblivious to the fact he was dying to get away from her, "the executive committee of the board is going to lunch, and since you're now an ex officio member, we thought you'd like to join us."

"I would, Helen, but I have a pastoral commitment that I should be tending to right now, as a matter of fact."

Deep furrows knit the brow of Helen's long face. "No one's ill, I hope."

"No, no, it concerns..." he hesitated the briefest of moments before deciding the truth wasn't too good for a minister in the throes of an infatuation "...Jimmy Duggan's daughter. You may have seen her this morning. I'm trying to assist her with developments in her father's case that have come to my attention."

"Oh." She looked truly astonished. "That was all so long ago. I'm surprised you're even aware of it."

"Believe it or not, the priest at Saint Aubin's descended on me with the problem my second day in town. Father Muncey. Used Catholic guilt on me, and I'm embarrassed to say it worked." Smiling, he patted her hand. Hand-patting, he'd discovered, came very naturally, a fact which no doubt would have given his mother fits. "So, if you'll excuse me, Helen," he said, "duty calls."

He exited the church, leaving a stream of unfulfilled congregants in his wake. To his great relief, Mary Margaret was standing at the sidewalk in the shade of a big elm. She'd changed into a blouse and skirt after he'd left, and looked every inch a proper lady—even if her hem was pleasingly short to his eye. It was quite warm. By the time he reached her side, there was a fine sheen of perspiration on his brow. The temperature and the suit he was wearing were only partly responsible.

"Good," he said, showing his relief. "You didn't leave."

She raised her brows with surprise. "Why would I have left?"

"I don't know...boredom...whatever." He glanced around at the half dozen or so little gatherings of people chatting, some discreetly eyeing him and Mary Margaret. "I hope people were friendly."

"The few I spoke with were very nice. Mostly they left me alone. It was partly my doing. I kept as low a profile as I could."

"I considered making a comment about you being there from the pulpit, but decided I might embarrass you."

"You would have. Thank you for restraining yourself."

He looked into her clear green eyes. She was so very pretty. One of those welling urges to kiss her rose in him again. He restrained himself from looking to see if people were noticing. God, he almost didn't care.

"Are you hungry?" he asked. "I'm famished. Preaching does that." He took her arm and started leading her up the sidewalk. "Let's go back to my place and get my car. I'll take you someplace for lunch."

"Okay," she said. "Under the condition you let me pay. You've provided the transportation and that's more than your share."

"Nonsense," he said. "I won't hear of it. This is my town. Sometime when I'm in Reno, you can throw an extra hamburger on the grill."

"Janine would be ecstatic."

"I'd rather *you* be ecstatic."

They'd come to the corner and he took her arm as they crossed the street. "I thought about you during the service. I was worried that being back at the church might be difficult...bring back memories," he said. "But I didn't want to bring it up for fear of planting the wrong seed."

"Frankly, I wish you had, not that there was any need to plant seeds."

Dane kept hold of her arm even after they reached the other side of the street. He was glad for the excuse to touch her. "Was it difficult?"

"It was okay. Don't worry about it."

"I am worried. I brought you here," he said.

"It was my idea to go to the service. Frankly, I'm more concerned about you."

"Me?"

"People saw us leaving the church together," she said.

"Oh, I can guarantee you the tongues are wagging already."

"Doesn't that bother you?"

"I refuse to let my great good fortune in knowing you be a problem, Mary Margaret. It's a small price to pay."

She came to an abrupt stop. "Dane, you and I have to get something straight. You've been kind to offer to help me with my father. I'm grateful we're friends. But friends look out for each other. I don't want you messing up your career because of me. This is your first job as a minister and it's very important you start off on the right foot."

He grinned, amused.

"What's so funny?"

"You're going to hate hearing this, but you remind me of my mother."

"Oh, God."

"It's not as bad as it sounds. Mother has some admirable qualities. Realizing I'm a big boy now is not one of them, however. Which is another way of saying, let me worry about myself."

They started walking again. Mary Margaret didn't speak. Dane wondered if he'd been too abrupt, cutting her off. They'd gone a block, the uneasiness growing. He decided he had to say something. "So, what did you think of my sermon?"

"Oh, I meant to tell you, I really liked it."

"You aren't just saying that?"

"No, I did. It was very good."

"You weren't bored?"

"Not at all. I do have trouble seeing you in a pulpit, though. All due respect, but it was a little creepy, even though you were very good."

Dane knew she was trying to compliment him. Still, he was disappointed. It wasn't Kathy's voice he heard, but it was a form of rejection, just the same. "That's unfortunate," he said, trying not to sound as dark as he felt.

"No offense," she said. "It's me, not you." She glanced over and seemed to pick up on his mood. "What I mean is that I can relate a little better to the guy in the car."

"I understand."

They walked a bit farther.

"*Do* you understand, Dane?"

"Yes."

Mary Margaret groaned audibly. He could tell she felt dreadful and he didn't want that.

"I only said all that because I care about you," she said almost pleadingly. "But you're thinking about your wife hating your work, aren't you?"

He gave her a wan smile. "Not really."

"Come on, you are, too. Admit it."

"All right," he said, relenting. "So it did cross my mind. No big deal. The point of your coming to Laurel wasn't to stroke my ego, it was to find out if we can help your father. Right?"

"Yes."

"Fine then, let's focus on that," he said, realizing it was up to him to get things back on track. "But the first order of business is lunch. What kind of food do you like?" He tried to sound upbeat.

"I like just about everything," she said. "But that's not the issue. It's what I *can* eat that matters. Artie Heartman, our director, doesn't care what we put in our mouths, so long as it doesn't have calories in it."

Dane laughed. "The guy's all heart."

"You have no idea."

As they neared his place, Dane managed to bring his expectations back down to earth and Mary Margaret appeared less anxious. He was glad, but also skeptical. He'd been here before.

Lodi, California

Dane pulled over before they reached the next intersection and checked the map again. "It's the street after this," he said. "Almost there."

Mary Margaret had been tense ever since they'd left the restaurant. Dane had phoned Elena Perez's home and was told by a boy with a strong accent she was at work. Though it probably would have been easier to speak with her at home, they'd decided to go to the nursing home to see if they could get a few minutes with her there.

"I'm nervous," she said honestly.

"We'll do the best we can and hope something comes of it," he said. "But it's probably a good idea to keep your expectations low."

She liked his reassuring manner and appreciated his support, but he simply didn't understand how impossible that was. This was the first glimmer of hope she'd had since the jury had come in with a guilty verdict.

They arrived at the nursing home, a low building set back from the street. It seemed to ramble over a wide area. There weren't many vehicles in the parking lot. Dane parked the Camry in a visitor's slot near the entrance.

"Here at last," he said, giving her a reassuring smile.

They got out of the car and went inside. There was a receptionist behind a glass-enclosed counter. The woman, youngish and heavyset, asked them which patient they were there to see.

"Actually, we're here to see someone on the staff," Dane said. "Elena Perez."

"Is it business?"

"Yes," he replied. "It's concerning one of her former patients."

"And you're..."

"Dane Barrett and Miss Duggan."

"I'm not sure where Elena is at the moment, but let me see if I can find her," the receptionist said. "Please have a seat."

Mary Margaret and Dane retreated to a grouping of sofas near the window. The place was bright, modern and pleasantly decorated. But it still had an institutional feel, not your usual sort of hospital, but close enough. Ever since her mother had died, she'd hated hospitals. The only time she'd been in one since was to have her jaw x-rayed after Anthony had slugged her, the day she'd told him she was getting a divorce.

Dane was sitting very close, their knees almost touching. Her wary expression must have aroused his compassion because he took her hand. "It'll be fine," he said.

She didn't say anything and Dane filled the void by recounting the time he'd broken his arm in Italy. He'd gone with his parents so his mother could school him on European art and the antiquities and he had ended up falling off a block of granite in the Colosseum. "In my eagerness to see where the lions ate the Christians, I took a header," he explained.

"That's one lesson that'll probably stay with you."

"Actually, the thing I remember best about the incident is the nurse at the hospital. She had enormous breasts, which rubbed against me as she worked. We'd celebrated my tenth birthday in Florence the week before, so I was still prepubescent, but the experience left a lasting impression."

"Apparently so."

The double doors leading to the wards opened and a short, plump Hispanic woman in a uniform appeared. She had a tight, worried expression that turned even more grim when her eyes fell on them. After hesitating, she slowly moved in their direction, appearing very unhappy. Dane got to his feet and Mary Margaret did, as well. She decided Elena Perez's demeanor did not augur well.

"Mrs. Perez?" Dane said.

"Yes."

"I'm Dane Barrett."

"The minister Father Muncey told me about."

"Yes, and this is Mary Margaret Duggan."

Elena Perez looked back and forth between them. "I know you have good reasons for coming here, but I can't talk to you. I should never have said anything to Father Muncey because I have nothing but trouble ever since. Please go away and leave me alone."

"What's happened?" Dane asked.

The woman hesitated before answering. "They are trying to frighten me and I'm afraid for my family."

"The man who threatened you?"

"Yes. And this morning he tried to kill me—tried to run my car off the road when I was driving to work."

Mary Margaret and Dane exchanged looks.

"I cannot live with this," Elena said, on the verge of tears. "My husband and I are taking time from our jobs and we are going with our daughter to the house of my mother in Mexico. Please don't speak with me. I am too scared. I want to forget this forever."

She started to turn away and Mary Margaret stopped her. "Elena," she said, moving toward her, "I can see you're very upset and I don't blame you. This is not your problem, yet you are suffering. But my father is in prison for a crime he didn't commit. I don't want you to risk your safety, or the safety of your family, but won't you speak with us for just a few minutes?"

Elena agonized, her eyes brimming. Mary Margaret could see she was a decent woman who wanted to do the right thing.

"The man with the harelip warned me not to speak of it," the woman said. "He said bad things would happen to my family. He would send Efrain back to Mexico."

"I know," Mary Margaret said, gently clasping her arm, "but I promise you, no one will find out you spoke with us. If you'll just tell us everything Ledi Hopkins said, we'll go away and never bother you again."

"I told Father Muncey what I know."

"But he's not familiar with the case. Just give us a few minutes."

Elena bit her lip. "Okay, but then I must return to work."

Mary Margaret and Dane returned to the sofa. Elena Perez sat opposite them, perched on the edge of the cushion.

"It is not much," Elena began. "Ledi Hopkins told me very little. It was not so much her words that made me go to Father Muncey, it was her voice, her emotions."

"But she said my father was innocent," Mary Margaret said. "Is that right?"

"Yes, over and over, many times before her stroke, and also after, though it was hard for her to talk then. She worried that he would be executed for something he did not do."

Dane leaned forward, his hands clasped. "Is that all she said, that Jimmy Duggan was innocent?"

"She mumbled different things. Usually I didn't understand. Mostly it was that I should tell them so that the man who was innocent would not be executed."

Dane turned to Mary Margaret. "Ledi was under the mistaken impression that your father had received a death sentence."

"Perhaps she was crazy and it means nothing," Elena said. "Perhaps this is for nothing."

"I don't think so, Mrs. Perez," Dane said. "The man harassing you is obviously afraid of something. He doesn't want Ledi's change of heart discussed."

"Believe me, I know."

"Elena," Mary Margaret said, "can you remember any of the things Ledi said? Even if it made no sense to you, what were her words?"

The woman thought for a moment. "She talked about her sister a lot. Thelma? Was that her name?"

"Theo," Dane said.

"Yes," Mary Margaret added. "Theo Bledsoe."

"I guess because Theo had died the year before, Ledi was concerned that she was the last one alive who knew the truth," Elena went on. "She was very upset about that and often mentioned her sister."

"No one else?"

Elena hesitated. "There was one time near the end, I think the morning of the day she died, when she took my hands and said, 'Tell the police to talk to Theo.' I reminded her that her sister was dead and she said, 'Well, Benny knows. He was there.'"

"Benny?" Mary Margaret said. "Who's Benny?"

"I don't know. She only said it once."

"Are you sure that was the name?" Dane asked.

"Yes. I remember wondering if she was confused or, if because of her difficulty speaking, I did not hear her well. And I said, '*Who* knows?' And she repeated the name. 'Benny,' she said. 'Benny.' That was the last she said about it. She spoke of something else next and before much longer nothing she said made any sense."

Mary Margaret and Dane regarded one another. Was this important, a possible break in the case, she wondered, or simply the confused rambling of a dying woman? She decided the same thing must be going through Dane's mind.

"Is there anything else you can tell us, Elena?" she asked.

"No."

"What about the man who's been threatening you?" Dane asked. "You have no idea who he is?"

A dark look came over her. "No."

"You said he has a harelip. You mean, surgically repaired?"

"Yes."

"Can you describe him?"

"He was big. Not fat, but like a football player. His eyes I did not like. They were very cold. I thought at first he was perhaps a policeman. He had a very official manner, like someone connected with the law."

"A policeman," Mary Margaret said.

"Yes," Elena replied.

"But you've never seen him before?" Dane asked.

"Never. And I hope this is the last." She looked anxiously toward the double doors. "I cannot talk longer," she said. "I am working. My supervisor will be mad."

"We'll let you go," Dane said.

They all got up. Mary Margaret reached out to the woman, taking her hand. "Thank you so much for speaking with us," she said. "I promise we won't make any trouble for you. You've been very helpful and I'm so very grateful."

"I am sorry for what has happened to your father," Elena said. "But my daughter is young and I must think of her."

"I know. I don't blame you."

"Well, goodbye then, *señores,*" Elena said.

They watched her disappear behind the double doors, then faced each other.

"Benny knows," Mary Margaret said, repeating Ledi Hopkins's words.

"Yes," Dane said. "He was there, apparently. Know who he might be?"

"I have no idea. But I'd sure like to find out."

"*If* he exists."

"It could be another witness," Mary Margaret said. "One who can exonerate my father."

"Let's hope so."

He took her arm and they headed for the door. Mary Margaret felt as if she was in an oven as they stepped out into the full afternoon sun. It could get hot in Reno, but not like the unrelenting heat of the Great Central Valley. She was glad that they'd taken the time to change out of their church clothes, even though she'd been impatient with Dane when he'd suggested it.

"Now what do we do?" she asked as they walked toward his car.

"See if anyone else knows who Benny might be, I guess."

Dane got out his keys to open the passenger door. Mary Margaret stared across the parking lot at the heat waves rising from the asphalt. Unlocking the door, he pulled it open, holding it for her. As she slid into the seat, she caught a glimpse of a vehicle sitting under a tree on the far side of the lot. She looked over at it while Dane went around to the driver's side. Why did that blue van look familiar? she wondered. Then she recalled that van she'd seen that morning at the trailer park, the one that had been illegally parked. It was also blue, as she recalled, but she couldn't say it was the same one.

Dane climbed in beside her and put the key in the ignition. He started the engine. Mary Margaret welcomed the rush of cold air, but she was looking past him at the van. Dane backed out of the space and headed for the street. She saw a puff of smoke come from the exhaust of the van. When they got to the street, the van began moving slowly in their direction.

"You know," Dane said, "I wonder if maybe we should swing by the police station in Laurel and see if they can tell us anything that might lead us to Benny."

"Sure," she said, "if you like." She glanced back and by the time they'd gone half a block, the blue van was exiting the parking lot.

Dane looked into the rearview mirror. "What's the matter?"

"Do you think that van could be following us?" she said.

"Why?"

"I think I may have seen it at the Desert Rest this morning, and it was sitting across the parking lot just now...like whoever's in it was waiting for us to leave."

Dane checked the mirror again. "You think we were followed from Reno?"

"I don't know," she said. "It's just that I noticed that van this morning, too. Or one like it. I suppose it could be a coincidence.''

"Well," Dane said, "let's make a few turns and see what happens."

Mary Margaret tensed. She gripped the door handle. At the next corner Dane made a left. After they'd gone a ways, she peered back up the street. The van made the turn.

"Lord," she groaned, "they *are* following us."

"Let's make another turn or two," he said.

Dane effected his maneuvers. The blue van stayed half a block behind them.

"Suppose it's the guy with the harelip?" Dane said. "Elena's friend?"

"Not if it's the van I saw in Reno."

"You have a point."

She fiddled nervously with her fingers, wondering if it could be Rut Coleman.

"I'll head back to Laurel," Dane said. "If the van follows us, I'll take that up with the police, as well."

Mary Margaret sighed and leaned back in the seat. Why couldn't anything ever be easy?

Laurel, California

By the time they reached the edge of town, Dane and Mary Margaret had determined that there were at least two men in the vehicle. Whoever the guys were, they were trying to be discreet and probably hadn't yet figured out that Mary Margaret and Dane were on to them.

Dane could tell Mary Margaret was upset. He wasn't exactly in a carefree mood himself. One thing was certain, though, he had to do something about it. As they drove toward the police station, he realized it would help if they had a license-plate number. But every time he slowed down, the van did, as well. Their intent clearly was to survey, not harass or intimidate.

"Do you think it's the guy your father warned you about?" he said.

"I can't imagine who else it would be. I'm sure now we didn't pick them up at the nursing home."

"No. I might have seen them on the road, now that I think about it," Dane said. "Maybe when we stopped for gas. A guy at the station gave me the evil eye, and I think I saw him in a van, but it didn't register at the time that he could have been following us."

They'd reached the center of town and stopped at a light. The van pulled over to the curb half a block back. Glancing over, Dane saw that the Camry was next to a police car. The officer was doing paperwork, probably just having issued a citation. On an impulse, Dane backed into the space behind the police car.

"What are you doing?" Mary Margaret asked.

"I'll see if I can get the officer to go give our friends back there the what-for." Jumping out of the car, Dane strode up to the police car. The driver's-side window was down. "Excuse me, Officer," he said, "but I have a problem."

The cop looked up at him, squinting in the sun. "What kind of problem?"

"There's a van with two men in it parked half a block back that followed me and my friend over from Lodi. In fact, we think they may have followed us down from Reno this morning."

"Yeah? You know who it is?"

"No, but it may be somebody who's threatened my friend."

The cop looked into his side mirror. At the same time Dane glanced down the street. The men in the van, evidently sensing that something was amiss, made a U-turn and headed away in quite a rush.

"Stand back, if you will, sir," the cop said, starting the engine of his patrol car. "I'll check this out."

"We'll be at the police station. I wanted to talk to Sergeant Jones anyway."

"Fine. Give Granville any particulars. License number, if you got it."

The officer put on his emergency lights and moved ahead, but the light was against him. By the time he got headed back down the street, the van was out of sight. Dane returned to the car.

"The cop is going to question them," he told Mary Margaret. "Assuming he manages to catch up with them."

"I feel better knowing something is being done, whether he catches them or not."

"Yeah, me, too."

He could feel an energy ebbing and flowing between them. A closeness that was new.

"Poor Dane," she said. "When you drove up to Reno to be the Good Samaritan, I guess you had no idea what you were getting yourself into."

"Wouldn't have missed it for the world," he said, pulling into the street.

"Oh? You mean you like being followed by God knows what kind of crazy characters? I won't even mention being mugged by the woman you were trying to help."

"Gee, I'd nearly forgotten that."

"Yeah, sure."

"Actually," he said, "I was thinking about the pleasant drive and the pleasant conversation."

"Thanks for not mentioning the show last night."

"That's what I was going to bring up next."

Mary Margaret gave him a playful whack on the arm.

"I cannot tell a lie," he said.

"Who do you think you are, George Washington?"

They'd arrived at the police station. Dane took a parking spot right in front.

"I'd be happy just being the Good Samaritan," he said. "Helping out any way I can." He touched her hand.

"You're a good friend, Dane."

"Even if I am a minister?"

"Nobody's perfect," she said.

They got out of the car and headed up the steps. Dane glanced admiringly at her backside. The physical aspects weren't easily forgotten.

Minutes later, they were in Granville Jones's office. The officer, wearing civilian clothes, motioned for them to sit, then hitched up his trousers before taking his chair.

"You folks are damned lucky to catch me in. The wife

drove up to Sacramento to see her sister after church. When the Raiders' game was over, I decided to come in and catch up on paperwork." He ran his hand over his slicked-back hair. "Annual review's coming up so it's no time to fall behind," he said with a rat-like grin.

Mary Margaret shifted uneasily. Dane had sensed the tension in her the moment Granville Jones had come to greet them. Jones, for all his idiosyncracies, seemed to be on the ball. "Hello, Miss Duggan," he'd said even before Dane had a chance to introduce them. "Guess I shouldn't be surprised to see you. All kinds of folks have dropped by the station on your behalf. I figured it was only a matter of time before you showed up, too."

"Mary Margaret has lots of friends," Dane had said to take the burden of an explanation off of her.

But she hadn't flinched. "I hope seeing me is not too unpleasant for you," she'd said to Jones.

"No, ma'am. Not at all."

After that she remained silent, letting Dane take the lead.

Jones leaned back in his chair, clasping his hands behind his head as he looked back and forth between them. "So," he said amiably, but with a hint of condescension, "you've turned up something new in the Donna Lee Marshall case."

"A name that hasn't surfaced before. At least to our knowledge," Dane said.

"Oh? What name?"

"Benny."

"Benny who?"

"That's all. Just Benny," Dane said. "We don't have more."

"Well, what's the connection? How does this Benny figure in?"

"We think he may be a witness of some sort. At least someone with knowledge of the crime. Does the name mean anything to you, Sergeant?"

Jones pondered the question. "Can't say that it does."

"It's possible Benny might have been at the murder scene," Dane said with a glance at Mary Margaret.

She was maintaining a discreet silence, but Dane could tell

emotion was boiling inside. She did not like Granville Jones
and the sergeant had to sense her animosity.

"I think that's highly unlikely, Pastor Barrett," Jones said.
"All due respect."

"Why?" Mary Margaret asked.

"To be blunt, Miss Duggan, if there'd been anyone else
around there, we'd have turned up some evidence of it. I've
never been at a crime scene that got checked out as thoroughly as that one. We talked to everybody living within a
six-block radius of the Marshall place. Nobody named Benny
was mentioned. I can guarantee you that."

Granville Jones rocked in his chair, his expression moderately complacent.

"If an innocent man was convicted for a crime committed
by somebody else, isn't it possible some important evidence
was never turned up?" Mary Margaret shot back.

"You're making some assumptions I'm not inclined to
agree with, Miss Duggan."

"I'd hope you'd at least be open-minded about it."

"If you've got evidence, ma'am," Jones said, color rising
in his neck, "I'll listen. True, you've given me a name. But
that's not proof of anything."

"We don't have any evidence at the moment," Dane interjected. "We were told Benny knows about the events surrounding the murder. That he was there. The reason we came
here was to see if you could help connect us to a person."

"Unfortunately, Pastor, I can't. But it might help if you
told me where you got your information."

Dane and Mary Margaret looked at each other. How much
could they reveal without breaching Elena Perez's trust? he
wondered.

"Ledi Hopkins was the one who made the statement,"
Dane said.

"The old lady who died after claiming Jimmy Duggan was
innocent," Jones said dryly.

"Yes."

"No offense intended, folks," he said, again running his
palm over his slicked-back hair, "but I put as much stock in
this Benny business as I do in her saying Jimmy Duggan was
innocent. I mean, she wasn't even in a position to know."

"Based on your understanding of the case," Dane said.

"Based on what the jury concluded from the evidence."

"We're wasting our time, Dane," Mary Margaret said, getting to her feet. "These people made up their minds about my father long before the facts were in. They're going to believe what they want and nothing we say will ever open their minds."

Granville Jones turned red. "You bring me some hard evidence, Miss Duggan, and I'll listen."

"One of your own witnesses recanted her testimony!" Mary Margaret snapped, her voice rising.

"The ranting of a senile old woman does not qualify as recanted testimony," Jones replied, maintaining his cool, but just barely. "Anyway, all Ledi Hopkins did at the trial was place Duggan at the murder scene. After changing his story a couple of times, your father admitted he was there anyway. So what Ledi Hopkins testified to doesn't matter. And saying your father was innocent or guilty is a conclusion, not a statement of fact. What she *saw* is what matters."

"This is useless," Mary Margaret said to Dane. "If you want to listen to it, fine, but I'm going to wait outside."

Dane got to his feet and she started for the door just as the officer they'd seen in the street appeared.

"Excuse me, Granville," he said, "but Betty said these folks were back here talking to you. I wanted to let them know about that van."

"What happened?" Dane asked.

"Sorry to say, it slipped away. I never got a look at it. Did you get a license number?"

"No," Dane said, shaking his head.

"Well, my guess is they left town. There were two other cars patrolling and we covered most of the streets. No sign of the van anywhere."

"Thank you, Officer. They were evidently spooked, and if they left town then they're out of our hair, which is really what we wanted. We appreciate your effort."

"What's this about?" Granville Jones asked, standing.

"It seems an ex-con from San Quentin, a former cell mate of Mary Margaret's father, has taken it upon himself to harass her," Dane said. "And we think they followed us down from Reno."

"You sure?"

Dane realized then they'd made some assumptions. "We're not positive, but it's a strong possibility."

Jones gave him a knowing smile, but refrained from making a critical remark. "Well, I'm sorry," he said, hitching up his trousers. "If you see them again, let us know."

"We may not have any hard evidence that my father is innocent and that somebody named Benny can provide proof of it," Mary Margaret said from the doorway, "but someone is very concerned that the truth might come out, a man with a harelip, to be exact. All I can say is it would be nice to know that you were just as impressed by that fact as we are." With that, she turned and left the office.

Jones looked puzzled. "What the hell was she talking about?" he said, scratching his head.

"Word has gotten out that Jimmy Duggan's guilt is being questioned," Dane said, "and it's got somebody in a dither."

"Somebody with a harelip?"

"Whether that's the interested party or an agent of the interested party, we don't know," Dane said. "But I've heard enough to conclude that the jury didn't have all the facts." Nodding politely, he said goodbye and left.

When Dane got outside he found Mary Margaret sitting on the fender of his car. Seeing him coming, she unfolded her arms long enough to wipe the tears off her cheeks.

"Those bastards are half the problem," she said bitterly.

"Cops are bureaucrats when you come right down to it."

She looked up at him from under wet lashes. Dane gazed into her eyes, the protective instinct in him so strong he took her by the shoulders and lifted her to her feet. Then he did what he'd been wanting to do all day, what he'd been wanting to do from the moment he'd first laid eyes on her—he wrapped his arms around her and held her close.

Mary Margaret hesitated before putting her arms around him. She pressed her face against his neck. "Oh, Dane," she lamented, though the reason for her lament wasn't at all clear to him. Was it the situation? Or what she was feeling for him? But as long as she was in his arms, it hardly mattered.

Her scent raised a heat in him. She aroused him so easily, he was surprised. Maybe she sensed that, because she separated herself from his embrace.

"Sorry to be a crybaby," she said. "It's so frustrating. One step forward, then one step back."

"Hey," he said, lifting her chin, "how about I buy you an ice cream?"

She gave him a sad smile.

Then he did the second thing he'd wanted to do all day long—he kissed her lightly. It was brief, but it clearly disconcerted her. She looked around the empty street.

"What if somebody in your congregation saw?"

"I guess they'd see the guy they hired, being himself."

"Sure that's what you want?"

"Come on, worrywart," he said, leading her to the car. "Let's get that ice cream."

Highway U.S. 99

"Come on, Rut," Hap said, checking the side mirror. "Don't get pushed out of shape about it. Following her around like that was stupid. They were bound to notice us eventually."

Rut Coleman was hunkered down in his seat, puffing on a cigarette, his dark countenance darker than ever. He wouldn't reply, hardly having said a thing since blowing his top and pounding the dash.

"You'll be glad later if you aren't now," Hap insisted.

"Button it, Hap," Rut said after a moment or two. "I don't want to hear that crap."

"No, I'm not going to button it," Hap snapped, his own anger flaring. "I've been giving you your way and that's what nearly got us in trouble. No telling what might have happened if that fucking cop had caught up with us."

"The bitch is going to pay!" Rut spat, shaking the hand with the cigarette for emphasis. "I swear to God she is."

"Forget the broad, for chrissakes."

"I won't!" Rut shouted. "So you can forget that shit."

Hap Coleman drove, holding his tongue. He checked the

mirror again. There had been no sign of cops since they'd left Laurel. He turned to his brother. "Listen, here's what we're going to do, man. I'm taking you to Nevada, back to the Mustang Ranch. I'm going to buy you a girl, my treat, and you're going to fuck your brains out. So be thinking about that, okay? Not Mary Margaret Duggan."

"Okay, okay. We'll do it your way," Rut said, drawing on his cigarette, inhaling deeply and holding his breath. "But you might as well know," he went on, the smoke spilling from his nose and mouth, "I'm waiting for the bitch to come back to Reno. And I'm not leaving until I've fucked her."

Laurel, California

"I guess I was a bitch back there," Mary Margaret said. They were stopped at a traffic light.

"What do you mean?" Dane said.

"With Granville Jones. I mean, I was rude, wasn't I?"

"Hell, Mary Margaret, you're entitled, considering what you've been through. I was kind of annoyed with the guy myself. But if you believe the police are involved in some kind of conspiracy against your father, I think you're wrong."

"Why?"

"Because...well, most alleged conspiracies are just the paranoia of the victim."

"Oh, great, now I'm paranoid on top of everything else."

The light changed and he started up. "I'm not saying that. What I am saying is that it isn't helpful to think the whole world's against you. We've just got to convince them that Ledi Hopkins's deathbed assertion, the business about Benny and the threats to Elena Perez, mean something."

Mary Margaret was skeptical, but she wasn't going to whine about it. She'd been negative enough. "I hope we're successful," she said mildly.

As they drove past the park, Mary Margaret spotted a Good Humor truck. "There's some ice cream!" she enthused, seeing an opportunity to be more upbeat.

"I was thinking of a nice cool, air-conditioned ice-cream parlor. Sure you want to get back out in this heat?"

"I haven't had an ice cream from a Good Humor man in years. It's worth sweating a little, if *you* don't mind."

Dane pulled over behind the truck.

"But it's my treat," she said. "I insist."

They got out and walked to where the driver was serving a small group of children. Mary Margaret was surprised how excited she was.

"Brings back memories, doesn't it?" Dane said, smiling at her, his pale blue eyes bemused, happy.

"Yes." She thought it nice that they both felt that way.

They watched the kids trying to decide what they wanted. Mary Margaret speculated right along with them.

"I remember stealing some quarters from my mother's purse so I could go with the other kids to Golden Gate Park and buy an ice-cream cone," she said, shaking her head at the recollection. "Then my conscience got to me. I thought I was going to burn in hell."

"You didn't go to confession and get absolution?"

"God, no. I was more afraid of the priest than hell."

Dane laughed.

The children ran off and it was their turn. Mary Margaret looked at the pictures of the items for sale, knowing Dane was watching her.

The vendor, a stringy-haired kid soaked with sweat, appeared bushed as he waited. He wiped his forehead with the back of his hand, though he somehow found the energy to check her out.

"What are you having, Dane?" she asked.

"That's easy. A fudge bar."

"I used to like those, too, but I think I'll go for a Nutty Buddy."

"That it, then?" the kid said. "A fudge bar and a Nutty Buddy?"

"That's it," Dane said.

The boy, who was probably eighteen or nineteen, fished their selections from the bowels of the truck, and Mary Margaret paid him over Dane's objection. The kid gave her a crooked grin as he gave her change, obviously grateful for the reprieve from yammering kids.

As they walked away, Mary Margaret suggested they sit in

the park rather than get back in the car. Dane agreed, so they made their way toward a bench under a large shade tree as the Good Humor truck went off, it's musical jingle eliciting memories of childhood.

Mary Margaret plopped down on the bench and licked the edges of the cone where the ice cream had already begun running. Dane sat toward the other end, but put his arm on the back of the bench, half facing her as he crossed his legs.

"So what do you think? Has the trip been worthwhile?" he asked.

"I think it's too early to tell."

"You're probably right."

Mary Margaret took a huge bite from her cone. Dane watched as she ate. His expression was oddly peaceful.

"You make me nervous when you watch me," she said.

"*I* make you nervous?" he said. "Thousands of guys can watch you dancing with hardly a stitch on, and *I* make you nervous watching you eat ice cream."

"Yes, this is much more personal."

He laughed, then his face filled with admiration. "You're adorable, you really are."

She blushed violently.

"Your ice cream's running," he said, gesturing toward her cone.

Mary Margaret caught it just in time. Dane observed every flick of her tongue, seemingly entranced, which only embarrassed her more.

"Well, wouldn't you know it," he said. "Look who's coming."

Mary Margaret turned behind her to see an older woman coming along the walk in their direction, with a small child on a tricycle in tow. The face was vaguely familiar, but Mary Margaret couldn't attach a name to it. "Who is it?"

"Claudia Rosenfelter, the church secretary. That's probably her granddaughter with her."

Then Mary Margaret remembered. The woman had been a staunch defender of Reverend Ragsdale and therefore a natural enemy of her father. It was about then that Claudia spotted them, her mouth forming a little O of surprise. Shepherding the child along, she approached them.

"Well, Reverend Barrett," she said, "just the person I want to see."

Dane got to his feet. "Good afternoon, Claudia." He turned toward Mary Margaret. "You remember Mary Margaret Duggan, don't you?"

"Of course. Hello, Mary Margaret. So nice to see you back in Laurel."

Her tone was transparently insincere. Still Mary Margaret answered pleasantly. "Thank you."

Claudia returned her attention to Dane. "I wanted to tell you that during the service this morning you had a long-distance call from a Tom Muncey in Los Angeles. I tried to find you after the service but I was told you'd left with Mary Margaret."

"What did Tom want?"

"Just that you call him. He said it was urgent."

"Thank you, Claudia. I'll get in touch with him."

"Oh, yes, I nearly forgot. You had a caller this morning, as well. A gentleman came by the church office asking for you."

"Who was it?"

"He wouldn't give his name, which I told him was quite impolite, but it seemed to have no effect."

"What did he look like?"

"Large man. I'd say fortyish. Gruff. Wanted your home address, but I wouldn't give it to him. He went off in a huff. Rude. Very rude. I certainly hope he wasn't a friend."

"The guy didn't have a harelip scar, by any chance."

"Yes, as a matter of fact, he did."

Dane glanced over at Mary Margaret. She could see they were thinking exactly the same thing. Claudia Rosenfelter clearly noticed there were unspoken messages passing between them.

"Well," she said, "I've done my duty. I'll leave you to your socializing." She glanced around, looking for her grandchild, then noticed that the curly-headed munchkin had wandered down the walk on her tricycle.

"Alicia!" she called after the child. "Come back!"

The little girl, seeing her freedom was being threatened, took off in the other direction at full speed.

"Oh, good heavens," Claudia said. "She's going to make me chase after her in this heat."

"I'll get her, Claudia," Dane said. "You sit and rest."

He took off in pursuit of the child and Claudia sat down on the bench with a weary groan. She gave Mary Margaret a sideward glance before taking a handkerchief from her purse and dabbing her lip.

"It seems you've charmed our new minister, Mary Margaret."

"I don't think charmed is the word. I've taken advantage of his kindness in wanting to help me with my father."

"I may be old," Claudia said, "but I'm no fool. And I'm not blind."

Mary Margaret shifted uneasily. "I can't control what you think, but I know what I'm doing and it's definitely not charming Dane Barrett."

Claudia dismissed the comment with a wave of her hand. "I won't quibble with you, but for Dane's sake, I'd like you to think very carefully about what you're doing. He's recently divorced, alone and quite vulnerable. A pretty girl like yourself would naturally appeal to him."

Mary Margaret bristled. "I'm not sure what you're suggesting, but if it's that I'm using him, you're dead wrong, Mrs. Rosenfelter."

"Heavens, it's perfectly understandable. He's attractive respectable, and from a very substantial family. I can hardly blame you. But if you have any compassion for the man, you'll let him be. Nothing good can come of the relationship, but there's lots of potential for harm."

"I may not be good enough for Dane," Mary Margaret said, her eyes narrowing, "not even good enough to be his friend, but I can tell you this—you sure as hell won't be the one to decide that."

Dane was returning with little Alicia. Claudia got to her feet, eyeing Mary Margaret a final time. "Nothing can be done about the past," she said under her breath, "just be aware that Dane's future—his career—might very well rest in your hands. Search your heart." With that she went to meet Dane and her grandchild.

Mary Margaret sat trembling with anger as she watched the church secretary going off with Alicia.

Dane sat down with a sigh. There was chocolate running down his hand. He licked off the dribbles and gave her a warm smile. She took a last bite of her cone and gazed off across the park, not wanting to engage his eyes.

"Are you all right?" he asked.

Mary Margaret couldn't bring herself to tell the truth. "I'm fine," she said, not too convincingly.

"No you're not. Did Claudia say something to upset you?"

"Just that she was worried about you."

"Worried?"

"Because of the man with the scar on his lip. She sensed he was dangerous, and she's right. I didn't explain why, though."

Dane looked off in the direction the woman had gone. "Claudia means well, but she's a bit of a busybody."

"We both know that man *is* dangerous, Dane. And if he's looking for you, it can only mean trouble."

"Well, I'll deal with it," he said.

"And if something should happen to you because of me, imagine how I'd feel."

"Guilty, I imagine."

"Exactly."

"Why don't I absolve you in advance, that way you won't have to worry about it."

"Now you're being a smart-ass," she said.

He grinned. "I never said I was perfect."

"Come on," Mary Margaret said, getting to her feet. "Take me back to Reno...or to the bus station, which would be fine with me, too."

Dane got up. "No, I'm going to drive you home, but would you mind if we went by my place and fed the cat first?"

"No, of course not."

"And I'll buy you dinner on the way."

They started walking toward the car. "By all rights, I should buy *you* dinner," she said.

"Nonsense," Dane said. "You bought the ice cream."

"Big deal."

"Well, you're *my* guest."

Mary Margaret took his arm, hating herself for it, but doing it just the same. A woman was entitled to be confused, she told herself, though she knew a statement like that would have sent Colleen into a fury. On the other hand, Janine would have thought it was just fine, because she was in favor of taking all the pleasure you could from a man, so long as you kept your guard up. And as for Claudia Rosenfelter, Mary Margaret hoped she was off in the bushes, watching. Mary Margaret had no more desire to see Dane hurt than Claudia did, but she'd be damned if she'd let the old gossip have the satisfaction of cowing Jimmy Duggan's daughter.

Looks like you've made a lifelong friend,'' Dane said when Mead came running up to her as soon as they entered the house.

Mary Margaret swooped the cat up into her arms and rubbed his furry head against her cheek. "How did your son come up with the name Mead, anyway?"

"He didn't," Dane said, closing the door. "That was Kathy's doing. She's an anthropologist."

"So she named the cat after a lake?"

He laughed. "No, he's named after Margaret Mead."

"Who?"

Dane looked puzzled and Mary Margaret immediately realized she'd made a gaffe. "Maybe I should know, but I don't," she said. "Whoever she is, she wasn't in my high-school curriculum."

Dane went into the living room and got a book off the shelf, *Webster's Biographical Dictionary*. He handed it to her. Mr. Williamson, her English teacher in high school, used to do that and it always infuriated her. Dane's expression wasn't smug, but he was at least mildly amused.

"You college boys think you're pretty hot shit," she groused. "I probably know a couple of things you don't."

"Mary Margaret, that's not a budding inferiority complex I hear, is it?" he quipped.

His grin got wider as her eyes narrowed. "Ever see this at the country club, Master Barrett?" she said, giving him the finger.

Dane roared. "Mary Margaret, you're priceless. An original."

"You've never been flipped off by a woman before?"

"Sure I have."

"But only by guttersnipes, I suppose. Bet your wife never gave you the bird."

"Oh, but she did. Her preference was the European style, using the entire arm."

"I guess you've got to expect that, marrying a cultured woman."

Dane chuckled, shaking his head. "Well, make yourself at home, and learn all about Margaret Mead while I make my phone call."

Mary Margaret sat in the easy chair, allowing Mead to curl up on her lap while she paged through the biographical dictionary until she found the entry. She discovered, not surprisingly, that the woman was an anthropologist. Seeing all the books she had written, Mary Margaret realized the name was somewhat familiar after all, but she knew nothing about Margaret Mead herself, which was nearly as bad.

Dane had found her ignorance amusing, but she wondered if deep down he didn't think it was pathetic. The man had been married to a college professor, so how could he find anything to admire in the mind of a showgirl who made her living sweating it out under the hot lights every night? She was being self-deprecating, which normally wasn't her style, but the truth was that she was feeling inadequate. And it was all Dane's fault for drawing attention to her stupidity.

On the other hand, he was probably used to being able to have an intelligent conversation without having to hand a dictionary to the other person every five minutes. Kathy was obviously very intelligent. The two of them probably talked for hours like a couple of professors showing off their IQ's. So what interest could he possibly have in *her* besides her tits and her ass?

Mary Margaret didn't want to think that he was slumming—amusing himself at her expense. If he thought she was an original, it was because he hadn't spent that much time with regular girls. She knew she wasn't dumb, but neither was she a professor of anthropology. High kicks and bumps and grinds—that was her field of expertise.

Appalled by her own train of thought, Mary Margaret eased Mead off her lap and returned the dictionary to the shelf. While she was at the bookcase, she checked out his collection a little more closely. Spotting a thin volume entitled *Siddhartha*, she took it from the shelf, recalling him saying she ought to read it. She returned to the chair, letting Mead onto her lap, and began to read about the handsome Brahmin's son who by the river bank, bathed at the holy ablutions, the shadows in the mango grove passing across his eyes as his mother sang and his father conversed with the learned men about the art of meditation and contemplation.

"What have you found?" It was Dane returning from his call.

"Siddhartha," she replied.

"Ah, one of my favorites."

"I know. You told me I ought to read it."

He joined her, sitting on the arm of the chair. "What do you think?"

"I've only read a few lines," she said, "but I can see already this is you."

"What's me?"

"Siddhartha, the Brahmin's son."

"You think so?"

"Yes, and I didn't even have to look up the word *Brahmin* to figure it out," she said with a whiff of indignation.

"I offended you earlier, didn't I?"

"No, but you might as well know I'm not completely illiterate. I just have big blank spots. I don't know a damned thing about theoretical physics, for example. Or linguistics. Or anthropology. But I've read every novel Thomas Hardy wrote."

"Mary Margaret, I didn't mean to be critical. And I certainly wasn't making fun of you. I find you very bright."

"Please don't patronize me," she said, getting to her feet so abruptly that Mead had to leap to the floor. "It only makes it worse."

She went to the window and peered out at the street. Her heart was pounding hard, and she wasn't even sure why. It didn't take much thought for her to realize she'd overreacted. Turning to face him, she saw he looked a bit crestfallen.

"I guess I'm letting my insecurities show, aren't I?" she said. "Sorry if I snapped."

"I wasn't much help," Dane said contritely.

She felt a need to reach out to him. "I hope you don't laugh, but I've got academic aspirations of my own."

"Oh?"

"I want to teach literature. Can you picture it? Me an English teacher?"

"Yes, I can picture it. Very easily."

"You're just saying that."

"No, I'm not," he said, brightening. "I think you'd be great!"

"How would you know?"

"How many hours have we talked today?"

Mary Margaret slowly walked back to the chair where Dane was still propped on the arm. "A lot, but not about books," she said, handing him *Siddhartha*.

Dane leafed through the slender volume and handed it back to her. "You keep it. It's yours."

"But it's one of your favorites."

"I can pick up a copy anytime. That's the third or fourth one I've owned."

He gazed at her, emotion in his eyes, concern. "I talked to Father Muncey," he said somberly. "He had somewhat disquieting news."

"What happened?"

"It seems Tom also received a warning not to get involved in the Jimmy Duggan case."

"A warning from who?"

"He got a call from his bishop. There are more pressing matters in his parish requiring his attention, according to the bishop. Jimmy Duggan does not come very high on the list."

"Bastards," she said. "It's a miracle the whole world hasn't gone Protestant or Jewish or something."

"Curious, isn't it?"

"What do you think it means?"

"Tom and I discussed it. All we came up with is that people in high places have passion about the case."

"Who?"

"God only knows."

"That's about as high as you can get," she groused, not fully able to enjoy her own cleverness.

"Very good."

"If it wasn't so pathetic, it might be funny."

Mead meowed and rubbed his body up against her legs. "I don't know about you, Dane," she said, "but I'm starting to feel outnumbered. It was the same during the trial. I'm not even sure Lloyd Haskell was a hundred percent on board."

"The attorney who represented your father?"

"Yes."

"Why?"

"There's nothing specific, just a feeling I had. Maybe paranoia," she added with a laugh.

"If it helps, Tom and I have decided to press ahead with our inquiry," he said.

"And do what?"

"I thought I'd have another conversation with the police chief, Carl Slater. Seems to me there's been enough going on that he could look into our friend with the harelip, if nothing else."

She sighed. "I have to tell you, I have mixed feelings. Part of me wants to charge ahead full speed and…"

"The other part's afraid," he said, giving her an understanding smile. "I know what you're going through."

"You know what? I believe you do. In fact, sometimes I think you know what I'm thinking."

"It comes with friendship."

"None that I've ever had."

"You don't look pleased," he said.

"You're a little scary, to be honest, Dane. Nobody—except maybe my mom—has ever been able to do that with me. It's like I have to be careful what I think around you."

"I can be very discreet," he said, giving her a puckish smile.

"Was it that way with your wife?"

"No. Never. Oh, Kathy and I communicated, but we also communicated with our professors."

"You didn't even feel a connection when you were discussing Margaret Mead?" she teased.

Dane grinned and reached out, playfully tapping her jaw with his fist. "You aren't going to let me forget that anytime soon, are you?"

"A woman always has to have something on a man, Dane. There's not much we can do that truly scares you guys, so we have to get our leverage where we can. And I've discovered what scares a man most is a woman who's determined."

He contemplated her. "You're very wise. Beyond your years."

"Is that a compliment or more patronizing."

Dane took her chin in his hand. "A compliment." His face hovered near hers.

"You know, I've got that urge to kiss you again."

"I know," she said. "I can tell."

He leaned forward and lightly kissed her lips. She lowered her head, knowing that it was a mistake to allow this, but damn, she did enjoy the affection. Dane inhaled her scent and ran his thumb over her cheek.

"I believe you wanted to feed Mead," she said, clutching the book he'd given her to her chest.

"Yes," he said softly. "I did." Then, calling the cat, he went off to the kitchen, his heels thumping on the hardwood floors.

Mary Margaret returned to the front window, holding the book, unconsciously running her thumb over the edge of the pages. Her mind, though, was on Dane and the kiss he'd just given her. Something important had just happened, though she wasn't ready to say what.

Mary Margaret gazed out at the lengthening shadows of the afternoon. How long had she been up? For hours and hours and hours. And yet the sun wasn't anywhere near setting. She couldn't believe how long the day seemed—like a week at least. And she felt she'd known Dane Barrett twice that long. By the time they made it to Reno, she was sure it would seem as if they'd had an entire relationship. And in a way they would have.

She slowly riffled through the pages of the book, liking the notion of having something he treasured. Yet she felt guilty taking it, just as she felt guilty liking him. She could only end up being hurt, which was what she'd been trying to avoid from the beginning. Damn.

After a couple of minutes he came back into the front room. Mary Margaret turned from the window. "Ready?" she asked.

"Yes, but I've been thinking I'd like to go by the Marshall place, check out the neighborhood where Donna Lee was killed. Talk to the neighbors, maybe."

"What for?"

"To satisfy my curiosity. See if anyone knew somebody named Benny. If you're right about the police being close-minded, we can hardly rely on them to follow up on a lead. Granville Jones as good as said he's not interested."

"Yes, I know."

"So anyway, I was wondering if you'd like to go with me."

"When?"

"When do you have to be back at work?"

Mary Margaret saw what he was getting at. The wheels were turning. "My next show is Tuesday night."

"Then why don't you stay over? We can do some sleuthing tomorrow before I take you home."

"I was wondering if that was what you had in mind."

"What do you think?" Dane asked.

She knew staying over was a bad idea. But how did she explain there were a number of problems, not the least of which was her financial difficulties? She decided to be direct and honest.

"Dane, I'll be blunt. I caught up on what I owed Anthony, but that's left me flat broke. Between the money I've paid my father's lawyer and the private investigator who worked on the case, I got myself in a hole. I can scarcely afford to buy groceries. I just can't afford a motel."

"You're welcome to stay here."

He said it in an offhand way, as though it was a perfectly reasonable suggestion, but there were implications, whether he appreciated that fact or not. The kiss he'd given her wasn't a casual handshake, and Dane had to know that as well as she.

"That's not a good idea," she said.

"Are you afraid how it would look?" he asked.

"Among other things."

"Then I'll put you up at a motel."

"I can't accept that. You're sweet to offer, but you've done so much already."

"Really, Mary Margaret, I'd be happy to—"

"No," she said, cutting him off. "I won't."

He looked disappointed. "Would you like to go over to the Marshall place now, then, before we head back to Reno?"

"You're going to be getting home late as it is."

"Hey, this is important. We've turned over some rocks and found a few bugs. I'd like to find out if this Benny business means anything or if, like the police claim, it's just the incoherent rambling of a dying old woman."

"Okay then," she said. "Let's go have a look at the scene of the crime."

He looked concerned. "Will it bother you to be there?"

"If you mean because of my father, why should it? He didn't kill Donna Lee."

He'd scarcely opened the front door a crack when Mead made a dash for freedom.

"Hey, you little bastard," Dane called after him, "come back here!" But it was too late. "Damn," he said. "We don't have time to chase him down, and he could be gone for hours."

"Let's come back after we go by Donna Lee's house," Mary Margaret said. "He may be ready to go inside by then."

"Good idea."

Dane locked the door and, as he turned, she put her hand on his arm in a gesture of caution. He looked out at the street and saw what she was staring at. A large man in a white polo shirt was leaning against the fender of the Camry, his arms folded over his chest as he glared in their direction.

"Looks like we have a visitor," Dane said as a spurt of adrenaline washed through his veins. He'd been an athlete in high school and college—basketball and crew—and though he had a competitive streak, he'd never been a fighter.

"What are we going to do?" Mary Margaret said under her breath.

"See what he wants, I suppose."

He descended the steps and walked toward the car. Mary Margaret was at his side. He sensed her nervousness, sharing it.

As they drew near, Dane saw that the man sported a distinctive harelip scar. He'd suspected as much. The man did not move except for his eyes, which focused on Dane. He virtually ignored Mary Margaret.

"The car's not for sale," Dane said amiably, "if that's what you're wondering."

The man, whose brownish-blond hair was close-cut and flat as a tabletop on the crown, did not smile. He wore the dour expression of a drill sergeant, his bulging chest and arms a symbol of stubborn defiance. "I've got a message for you, Reverend."

"Oh? From whom?"

"From me."

"I'm listening."

"Your talking to Elena Perez is complicating her life, if you get my drift. I suggest you butt out."

"I'm afraid I don't get your drift, Mr...."

"It's not good for her to be talking," he rejoined, ignoring Dane's implied request for his name. "It's not good for you to be talking, either. Matter of fact, it's not good for the town. If you don't want trouble, cool it before things get nasty."

"Hmm," Dane said, stroking his chin. "If you didn't look like such a decent upstanding individual, I'd be inclined to think you're threatening me."

The man stood, drawing himself up, his hard expression unwavering. He was large, a couple of inches taller than Dane, who was six-one. The glistening skin on his scar couldn't help drawing the eye. Dane made himself engage the man's flat gray eyes.

"Think what you want, Reverend," the man said. "The point is, nobody's interested in having some do-good clergyman stirring up people's emotions over an old murder case. Like I say, butt out."

"And if I don't?"

"You'll regret it."

"Well, let me tell you something," Dane said, his voice hardening. "Vague threats from someone too cowardly to identify himself don't cut it. Frankly, your attempt to intimidate me is having just the opposite effect. You're obviously afraid of what I might discover, which tells me it's all the more important I find out what it is."

"I guess you want to impress your girlfriend," the man said, glancing at Mary Margaret for the first time. "But I promise you, you'll regret it. Ignore me at your own risk. If you don't give a damn about your own ass, fine, but do the macho gig and others will pay. Trust me on that. And believe me, it won't be pretty." The last he said, glancing at Mary Margaret again.

"Listen, you slimy bastard," she said stepping toward him and jabbing a finger in his direction. "If you think you can keep an innocent man in prison by trying to intimidate people, you've got another think coming. I'm going to find out who really killed Donna Lee Marshall if it's the last thing I do. So tell whoever sent you here that this hard-ass shit won't cut it with us. And after that, go crawl back under your rock."

He glared. "You've got a smart mouth, bitch. And, believe me, it'll cost you. Just wait and see." He started to move past them, pausing long enough to tap Dane firmly on the chest a couple of times with his knuckles. "I assume you've got more brains than Kewpie doll, here. If you can't muzzle her, at least mind your own P's and Q's. Word to the wise, mack."

"I don't mean to disillusion you, my friend," Dane replied as calmly as he was able, "but you've just convinced me that Jimmy Duggan doesn't belong in prison. We're going to prove it, too."

"Then you're a bigger fool than she is." Giving Dane a little shove for emphasis, just enough to throw him off balance, he walked away, heading up the street.

"I hope you rot in hell!" Mary Margaret called after him.

The man made an obscene gesture over his shoulder and continued walking. They watched him go. Dane's muscles were taut, his blood full of unspent adrenaline. He couldn't remember the last time he'd been like this. Next to him, Mary Margaret stood shaking.

"Bastard," she muttered under her breath. Then she looked at Dane, her eyes glistening with anger. "That's the kind of lowlife we're dealing with," she said bitterly. "And it's people like that who put my father in prison."

Dane put his hand on her back and rubbed it. She continued to tremble.

"What arrogance," she said, continuing to rant.

"Whoever he's speaking for is scared to death. That was not someone coming from a position of strength."

"Yes, but how can we take advantage of it?" she asked.

"It might help if we could find out who this guy is."

The man had reached the corner and turned, disappearing from sight.

"Come on," Dane said, going to the car. "Let's see if we can get a license-plate number or something."

He opened the car door and Mary Margaret jumped in. Then he ran around to the driver's side. He had to make a U-turn to head in the direction the guy had gone. When they got to the corner, they saw a car going up the side street at high speed. It turned at the corner and was gone. Dane decided not to chase him.

"Damn," he muttered. He pulled to the curb and regarded Mary Margaret. "What happened doesn't change my thinking. How about you?"

"You know how I feel about my father," she said. Then she ducked her head with embarrassment. "But I'm afraid to say anything else. Shooting off my mouth like I did, I nearly got you beat up."

Dane chuckled. "If he was going to beat anybody up, it was more likely going to be you."

She flushed. Dane reached over and stroked her burning cheek with the back of his fingers. Mary Margaret felt oddly close to him. And grateful.

"I apologize for my dirty mouth," she said. "I know I'm not much of a lady."

"I've heard it before. You're not that different from anybody else."

"Oh, don't lie, Dane. It's unbecoming to a minister."

"I'm not lying," he said.

"I suppose all the girls in Santa Barbara sounded like me."

"Some did. But I wasn't on many dates where I got into confrontations with underworld types."

"See, it matters who you hang around with."

"Hey," he said, taking her chin and turning her face toward him. "Why the sudden self-doubt? You're the girl who lives her life the way she wants to. The girl who's not afraid of anything."

"Maybe I care...what you think of me," she said self-consciously.

Dane couldn't help himself. He took her in his arms and squeezed her body really hard against his. It wasn't at all surprising how good it felt.

"Thanks for not hating me, Dane," she said as she pressed her head against his shoulder. "And thanks for being my friend. It means a lot."

His heart beat nicely. He had that helpless feeling of someone who was smitten, in the grip of a powerful desire. *Friend*, he thought ironically. If she only knew.

And then it occurred to him that maybe she did.

She took his hand. "Look, if you just want to take me back to Reno right away, that's fine. I don't want to be a problem." Then she laughed. "I guess saying that's sort of like closing the barn door after the horse has fled, isn't it?"

"I'm not eager to take you back to Reno, Mary Margaret."

"What do you want to do, then?"

His body wanted to say, "Let's go back to my place and go to bed," but the son his mother raised, the socialized man of culture and the cloth, said, "I'd like to press ahead with our investigation, but the choice is yours. He's your father and it's your decision. I'm here to help."

She touched his face, sparking in him another paroxysm of desire. "Let's go over to Hemlock Street," she said.

The street looked like any other in a small town. She had only visited it once before, not long after she'd first arrived. Donna Lee was one of the first girls to invite her to her house and Mary Margaret had gone. But it had soon become apparent that Donna Lee was desperate to have a friend. She'd dug her stash out of her closet and offered Mary Margaret a joint, the mark of real friendship. Mary Margaret had been reluctant to mess with drugs, but she'd taken a drag or two, mostly out of fear of insulting Donna Lee. She was, after all, the new girl in school and living with a father who was an ex-con. Friends wouldn't be easy to come by. But when she'd gone home that afternoon, she'd decided Donna Lee was trouble and that she stood to lose a lot more than she stood to gain, even if she'd end up with no one. It was the end of their budding friendship. Sadly, Donna Lee took it harder than she had.

Staring at what had once been Donna Lee Marshall's house, Mary Margaret remembered that day, but she was even more aware of the fact that it had been the place where the girl had died, a place her father was seen leaving, his clothes covered with blood. The association bothered her more than she expected, and she began regretting that she'd come, just like church that morning. But when Dane got out of the car, she did as well.

They were parked under a huge tree, so he stayed in the shade, leaning against the fender as he stared across the street at the house. Mary Margaret came around the car, joining him.

"This two-story white house next door must have been Theo Bledsoe's place," Dane said, "judging by the placement of the Marshalls' driveway."

"I suppose," she said.

Mary Margaret continued to stare at the house where Donna Lee Marshall had been brutally murdered. It was a single-story frame house, pea green in color and needing a paint job. It looked shabbier than she remembered it. At the moment there were a couple of tricycles on the patchy lawn.

"I wonder if there's any point in talking to the occupants," Dane said.

"The detective I hired, Robinson Palmer, said that it's been occupied by a series of renters since Donna Lee's mother moved out after the murder. The Bledsoe place was purchased by a couple of young motorcycle types." She pointed to the motorcycle parked on the side of the big white house. "Everybody's gone who knew anything."

"That's the trouble with this case," Dane said. "The principals are dead—Ledi Hopkins, Theo Bledsoe, Stephen Ragsdale and his wife. About the only one still alive who was directly involved is your dad…and the police, the judge and the lawyers, of course.''

"One of whom went on to be attorney general and will likely be our next governor," she said.

"Scott Wainwright."

"Right."

"But we're forgetting Benny," Dane said. "Assuming he isn't dead, too."

"Or he isn't somebody who grew out of Ledi Hopkins's imagination."

Dane nodded. "Sure, that's always possible."

Despite the heat, Mary Margaret shivered. She'd spent so many years alternately agonizing over these people and trying to forget them, that this visit to memory lane was proving to be a lot more painful than she'd have thought.

"Dane, can we go?" she said as a panicky feeling welled up inside her. "There's nothing we can do here, is there?"

"I thought maybe the name Benny would ring a bell with someone," he said, looking up and down the quiet street. "Since we're here, don't you think it's worth checking out?"

"What were you planning to do? Knock on doors?"

"Isn't that what investigators do in the movies?"

"Is that what you want to do?" she asked.

"Sounds like you don't."

"I guess it's silly not to do what we can."

"Come on," he said, taking her hand. "You can pretend you're a Girl Scout selling cookies."

"That's a great one," she said as they went around the car. "Me a Girl Scout."

"I was a Boy Scout. Made Eagle Scout, as a matter of fact."

"Why am I not surprised?"

"That wasn't an altogether approving tone," he observed.

"You're my first Eagle Scout," she said. "Most of the boys I grew up with either went to trade school or the reformatory."

"Now you know somebody who can teach you every knot known to man."

"I knew something useful would come of this trip," she said with a laugh.

The first house they went to, situated directly across from the former Marshall place, was closed up, the shades drawn. Half a dozen yellowing newspapers lay on the porch. Dane knocked on the door anyway.

"The occupant's probably on vacation," he said.

"Or dead."

He gave her a look. "How do you do on the Rorschach test?"

"The what?"

"You know, the psychological test where they show you a series of inkblots and you're supposed to tell what you see."

"Oh, that. I always see vampires and ghouls and dead babies."

"Aha, a regular Mary Poppins type."

"Yeah, right."

They went back down the steps and headed toward the next house. Seated in the corner of the wide porch in a wicker chair surrounded by a jungle of potted and hanging plants was a little old lady in a pink-flowered sundress. She was leaning on a cane, which she clasped in both hands. Despite her rather grumpy expression, she looked like a potato doll.

"I don't need brushes, I don't need encyclopedias, I don't need real estate and I don't need Jesus," she said as they climbed the steps. "So you can save your breath."

"But could you spare a few minute of your time?" Dane asked. "No obligation, no strings attached, nothing to buy."

"I don't do surveys either, young man, unless you're willing to pay like the Nielsen TV folks."

"We're paying a buck an interview for residents who've lived in the neighborhood at least eight years. Do you qualify?"

"Been here in this house for sixty," she said. "Guess that means I do."

"Wonderful. May we ask you some questions?"

The woman gave them both a wary look, then gestured for them to approach. "Let's see your money, son."

Mary Margaret couldn't help laughing. But Dane dutifully produced his wallet, extracting a crisp new dollar bill. Holding it out, he approached the old lady, who snatched the bill from his hand and stuffed it down the front of her dress. Mary Margaret had to bite her lip to keep from tittering.

"So who are you? Is it a TV survey?" the woman said.

"No, ma'am. We're researching the neighborhood. My name is Dane Barrett, by the way, and this is Mary Margaret Duggan."

The old lady gave Mary Margaret an especially appraising look. "Duggan?"

"Yes, ma'am," Dane said. "And you're..."

"Agnes McBain."

"How do you do, Mrs. McBain."

"You children care to sit down?" she said, gesturing toward the wicker love seat under the window.

Mary Margaret found the woman a hoot and had to struggle to keep a straight face. But since Dane seemed to be doing well with her, she kept silent.

"You say you've lived in the neighborhood for a number of years, Mrs. McBain," he said. "Have you ever known anyone in the area by the name of Benny?"

"Benny? Benny who?"

"Just Benny. Presumably it's a given name."

She thought for a moment or two. "Can't say that I have." She was still checking Mary Margaret out. "What's this concerning?"

"We're conducting a private investigation of the Donna Lee Marshall murder."

"Oh, that. Then this young lady must be kin to that Catholic boy they convicted for the crime. Jimmy Duggan, wasn't it?"

"Yes," Mary Margaret said. "He's my father."

"Glory be. I heard tell you were pretty. I see now the stories were true."

"Thank you."

"No point in thanking me. I didn't have anything to do with it. Anybody who looks at you can see what you look like." She frowned. "I understand you work in some honky-tonk up in Nevada."

"I'm a showgirl in Reno."

"On TV, are you?"

"No, I work at the High Chaparral."

"Can't say I know it," Agnes said. "William and I—he was my husband—went to a honky-tonk up in Sacramento a few times after they lifted Prohibition, but when he passed in '38, I never bothered going again. I understand now they don't play anything but that Elvis Presley music. Can't see how you dance to it myself."

"It's a challenge."

"I expect it is."

"Mrs. McBain, Ledi Hopkins claimed that someone by the name of Benny may have witnessed Donna Lee's murder," Dane said, getting right to the point. "Do you have any idea who she might have been referring to?"

"Ledi Hopkins?" Agnes said. "Lord, I wouldn't trust a word she ever said. She was might near as nutty as her sister. Theo used to live right over there in that big white house until she skulked away in the middle of the night a few years back."

Mary Margaret felt the same old stab of disappointment in the pit of her stomach. Just what she needed to hear.

"Where did she go?" Dane asked.

"Moved to Fresno. Died there a few years later, from what I understand."

"You knew Theo well, I take it," Dane said.

"We lived within spiting distance of each other for fifty years, but it was rare a civil word passed between us. In the early days, we shared a common interest in dogs, but after she had that affair with the deacon in the Baptist church, she turned into a recluse. Never was the same. Some folks said her sin got to her. Wouldn't surprise me."

"She had an affair?"

"Lord, yes. It was common knowledge. During the war while her husband was off fighting the Japs. Poor soul got killed while Theo was playing hanky-panky with the Baptist boys. Guilt got to her, obviously."

"I thought Theo was a Unitarian," Dane said.

"Not until the Baptists kicked her out. Theo was partial to churchmen, no question," Agnes said. "Before he shot himself, the Unitarian preacher was hanging around her quite a bit, too."

"Reverend Ragsdale?"

"Theo seemed to attract them like flies, though I never figured out her appeal."

Dane glanced at Mary Margaret.

"Of course, he was a ladies' man," Agnes added, "and probably not too particular."

"What do you mean, ladies' man?" Mary Margaret said.

"I expect I'm the only one in the neighborhood he wasn't courting while his wife was ill. It was scandalous the way he was always calling on the Marshall girl. She was just a child, even if she was a hellion."

"What?" Dane said. "Reverend Ragsdale called on Donna Lee?"

"He was over at the house all the time. Whenever Loretta, the mother, left, he'd show up fifteen minutes later. He'd stay an hour or two, then sneak away."

"My God."

"And the cops wouldn't listen to me about him," Mary Margaret said bitterly.

"Mrs. McBain," Dane said, "did the police interview you at the time of the murder?"

"Lord, yes. They talked to everybody."

"Did you tell them about Reverend Ragsdale's involvement with Donna Lee?"

"Yes, but they didn't seem to put much stock in it. I was away at the doctor's the day the girl was killed, so not being a witness to anything they dismissed me as a gossip. I told them Donna Lee and Theo had a few run-ins, but they didn't seem much interested in that, either."

"What do you mean, run-ins?" Dane asked, his curiosity aroused.

"The Marshall girl was a hellion, like I say. After her father left, she always seemed to be getting into trouble. I'm not sure exactly what it was between Theo and Donna Lee, but they had more than one screaming fight over the fence. Once I heard them going at each other like a couple of alley cats. Personally, I held Theo responsible. A child doesn't know any better. But then, everybody knew Theo was strange.

"Loretta was the one I felt sorry for. First her husband left her, then she had her hands full with that child. But imagine having your baby murdered in your own house. The woman had a lot to bear."

"What happened to her?" Dane asked.

"Loretta moved up to Placerville after the trial. She married a plumbing contractor by the name of Richard Casagrande." Agnes began fanning herself with her hand. "Loretta was always nice to me, one of the few people in the neighborhood who was. I still get Christmas cards from her."

Agnes stopped talking long enough to take a couple of breaths and fanned herself some more. Her face looked a little red.

"Are you all right?" Mary Margaret asked.

"The heat gets to me more than it used to, honey. All this talk has got my heart racing."

"Why don't you stay inside? You have air-conditioning, don't you?"

"Unit broke down again. The repairman won't come till tomorrow."

"You poor thing," Mary Margaret said. "Don't you have a friend you could visit during the heat of the day?"

"I'm eighty-nine, child. All my friends are dead except for one or two in rest homes. The young folks around don't even notice I'm here, except on Halloween when the little ones come for candy. This is the third time the air-conditioning's gone out this summer, so I'm getting used to it. I fix a pitcher of ice water and come out here on the porch at the end of the afternoon when the temperature inside is higher than out here. And that way if I croak, somebody's likely to notice."

Mary Margaret felt sorry for the old woman. "Is there anything we can do?"

"Nothing to do, honey. Unless you'd like to put some ice cubes in my water pitcher. What's in here melted an hour ago."

"I'd be glad to," she said, getting to her feet. "It's all right if I go inside?"

"Door's unlocked. Kitchen's in back."

Mary Margaret took the pitcher and went inside. The furniture was a bit shabby and liberally strewn with knickknacks and memorabilia. The tiny front room was cluttered and could use a good dusting. The kitchen was dated, the refrigerator ancient, but overall the room was clean and tidy. She imagined the woman mostly lived in the kitchen and the bedroom. It was stifling hot inside.

Mary Margaret discovered there was no ice maker. She'd have to get ice from the trays. As she ran water over them from the sink, she thought of what Agnes McBain had told them. The news about Stephen Ragsdale and Donna Lee came as no surprise, though their involvement seemed more extensive than she thought. It made her even more suspicious of the clergyman. Maybe he *was* the one who'd killed Donna Lee! In a jealous rage, perhaps.

But the story about Donna Lee and Theo fighting also gave Mary Margaret pause. Could there have been enough animosity between them that Theo would have been driven to murder? Agnes McBain said Theo was nutty. It wasn't beyond the realm of possibility.

When Mary Margaret returned to the front porch, Dane and Agnes were chatting about the Unitarian church and Theo Bledsoe's involvement with it.

"This young man is the minister at First Unitarian," Agnes said, sharing her incredulity with Mary Margaret. "Never would have guessed."

"Yes, and he's quite a preacher," Mary Margaret said as she filled Agnes's plastic glass with ice water. "I heard him this morning."

"I don't have much use for any church, but Theo was enough to keep me away from the Unitarians," Agnes said. She took a long drink of water. "Thank you, honey, for fetching this for me."

"My pleasure," Mary Margaret said, taking her seat next to Dane.

"I think the thing that bothered me most about Theo," Agnes said, returning to the topic of conversation, "was the way she mistreated those dogs of hers."

"What do you mean?" Dane said.

"For starters, she kept them locked up in that house. In thirty years I don't think she ever so much as took them for a walk. I say dogs because in all that time she had to have several. They had the same thing in common though—they all whined. Summers when the windows were open you could hear them. Somebody called the humane society once, and there was a big to-do, but nothing ever came of it. Don't know exactly what happened in the end.

"Theo must have kept the dogs locked up in an upstairs bedroom most of the time because the motorcycle gang that moved in said the room wreaked of urine and excrement. I'm not surprised she took off in the middle of the night when she did go. In my opinion, she was crazy, that one."

Dane turned to Mary Margaret. "In the trial, did it come out what Theo was doing at the time of the murder?"

She could see that his thoughts were moving in tandem with hers. She found that fact gratifying. "As I recall, she said she was napping and didn't awaken until her sister rang her bell. Ledi was at the front door when she saw my father leaving Donna Lee's place."

"That's right," Agnes chimed in. "It didn't all come out in the trial, but Theo was taking medication for her heart, which made her drowsy. She slept a lot."

The question had been burning in Mary Margaret's brain and she saw no reason to be shy, so she came right out with it. "Mrs. McBain, do you think Theo could have killed Donna Lee?"

The old woman considered the question. "She was crazy as a hoot owl, like I say, but I have no idea if she was capable of murder. She was pretty ill. Her heart was really giving her problems. Hard to believe a frail old lady could overcome a heathy young girl, pursuing her out of the house and stabbing her repeatedly without getting a scratch herself."

Mary Margaret's disappointment was palpable. She sensed Dane shared it. That was the trouble with this case, every time she saw a glimmer of hope, she was invariably disappointed. As always, it made her want to jump up and get the hell out of there. After her father's conviction, she hadn't been able to get out of Laurel fast enough. Now, here she was, eight years later, suffering the same disappointment.

"Mrs. McBain," Dane said, "you've been very helpful. We appreciate your time."

"I have nothing to do but sit here and broil," she replied. "It was nice to talk to somebody for a change." She reached inside her dress and removed the dollar bill Dane had given her. "You take this back, son. I only took your money because I thought you was one of those rich TV fellas."

"No, you keep it, Mrs. McBain. I insist."

She returned it to her dress and gave him a sly smile. "You seem like a mighty fine young man," she said. Then she glanced at Mary Margaret. "Don't you think he's nice, young lady?"

"Oh, Dane's very nice," she replied, doing her best to mask her amusement at the old woman's manner.

"It's none of my business, but you two make a mighty fine-looking young couple. How is it that you're together, anyway?"

Mary Margaret and Dane both hesitated.

"We're friends," he said.

"You both single?"

"Yes."

"I don't expect it'll be just friends for long," the old woman said, looking back and forth between them. "I've got an eye for such things, you see."

"I live in Reno," Mary Margaret said. "And Dane lives here."

"Lord, when did something like that ever make a difference? When we was courtin', William used to drive down here to see me twice a month from Medford, Oregon, and the roads weren't half of what they are now."

"You make a very convincing case, Mrs. McBain," Dane said.

"I reckon it's that pretty young thing next to you that needs to hear it, Reverend, not me."

"I think maybe we've taken up enough of Mrs. McBain's time," Mary Margaret said, her cheeks beginning to burn. She got to her feet. "You've been very helpful," she said to the old woman. "Thank you so much."

Dane rose, as well. Agnes McBain looked disappointed.

"Well, thank you for dropping by," she said.

"It was nice meeting you," he replied, shaking her hand.

Mary Margaret shook Agnes's hand as well. "Goodbye."

"Come back anytime," she called to them as they went

across the porch. "And maybe I will come to church. Might even drop this dollar you gave me in the collection plate."

"I look forward to it," Dane said, looking back at her from the top of the steps.

"Good luck, children."

They went to the sidewalk.

"You certainly have a way with little old ladies," Mary Margaret said, gently chiding him.

"Yes, and I'd trade it all for having a way with beautiful young showgirls," he said, giving her an endearing smile.

She chortled. "I have a feeling you do just fine with just about any woman you choose, Dane Barrett."

"Mrs. McBain seems to think we make a right smart couple. Suppose I should put any stock in that?"

Mary Margaret refused to look at him. "She only said it because you gave her a dollar."

"Money well spent."

"You're gloating," she said.

"Yep. It sure feels good."

"I think it's time you take me home."

They started walking toward the car.

"Mrs. McBain was a wealth of information," he said, his voice taking on a more serious tone. "I see you and I were both thinking along the same lines with regard to Theo Bledsoe."

"Yes, but it's always such a disappointment when a promising lead fizzles."

"I'm not so sure Theo isn't worth pursuing."

"Dane, she's dead!"

"Yes, and whoever killed Donna Lee might be dead, but that doesn't mean we can't uncover the truth." He opened the car door. "The minister at the Unitarian Universalist church in Fresno is very nice. I'll call her and see what she can tell me about Theo Bledsoe." He went around the car and got in. "It's certainly worth a try."

He started the car and they headed for his place. "That business about Stephen Ragsdale and Donna Lee," he said. "I wonder if it was true or if Agnes might have exaggerated. He supposedly was counseling her, but if half of what Agnes said was true, then something smells."

"The whole case has smelled from the beginning, but that didn't stop them from sending my father to prison."

"Maybe I'm naive, but it's hard for me to believe there was a conspiracy."

"With all due respect, Dane, I think you *are* naive. I've always thought my father was set up."

"To protect who? Stephen Ragsdale? The cops would have hung him as readily as your father."

"I can't explain it or my dad would already be out of prison. But if that man who threatened us and Elena Perez proves anything, it's that the case is still open."

"That's one thing we agree on completely," he said.

They went a few blocks.

"You know," Dane said, breaking the silence, "if we work together as well as we look together, we just might break this case."

Mary Margaret laughed. "You're not one to let an opportunity pass, are you?"

"A fella's got to seize every one he can."

She wasn't going to tell him so, but the notion that they made a pretty good team had occurred to her, as well.

They went to the front door with no sign of Mead. As Dane put the latchkey in the lock, they could hear the telephone ringing. He quickly opened the door and ran for the phone.

"Would you mind checking the back door and see if Mead is there?" he called over his shoulder. "The last time he was on the loose, that's where he showed up."

"I'd be glad to," Mary Margaret said.

As she was closing the front door, Dane picked up the receiver.

"Hello? Ah, Mother, how are you?"

Mary Margaret caught Dane's eye and smiled slyly.

"No, Mom, I was going to call you," he said, "but I just haven't had a chance. It's been a really hectic day."

She made her way toward the kitchen, amused, but also curious. A conversation with his mother had to be revealing.

"Yes, it went well," he was saying. "Very well, I think. At least they didn't throw me out of the church."

Mary Margaret had reached the kitchen but she could still hear him.

"Listen," he said, "I can't talk now, I'm here with a friend and we..."

She lingered just inside the door, wanting to hear, even knowing she was eavesdropping.

"No, a lady friend.... No, not anyone at the church. She's from out of town.... Look, Mother, this is not the time to discuss it. Why don't I give you a call tomorrow?"

Mary Margaret chuckled. Dane Barrett was definitely the dutiful son. She could tell by that little snatch of conversation. And she was sure the woman adored him. What mother wouldn't want a son like him?

Mary Margaret unfastened the security chain on the back door, pulled it open and nearly screamed at the grisly sight. On the outside of the screen door, Mead was hanging from a link of cord tied around his neck, his lifeless eyes bulging.

Stepping back, she clasped her hands to her mouth, stifling a scream. After gathering herself, she went to find Dane. He was still on the phone. She stood in the doorway, waiting.

"I know exactly how you feel, Mom," he said. "And I want to discuss it, but at a better time when we can talk.... Yes, I promise to call tomorrow.... Right. Bye, Mother."

Shaking his head, he hung up the phone.

Then, seeing Mary Margaret, he said, "Is it just my mother, or do they all want to talk about your former spouse every chance they get?" The smile faded when he saw her expression. "What's the matter?"

"It's Mead. Somebody's killed him."

"What?" There was horror on his face.

Dane came to the kitchen, Mary Margaret stepping aside so he could pass by. He'd only gone a few steps before he saw.

"Oh, my God."

He opened the screen door and, as she watched, he untied the cord and lowered the cat's body to the porch. There was a note tied to the cat's collar which he removed. Mary Margaret joined him.

"What does it say?"

He unfolded the small piece of paper. "If you're nosy, even nine lives aren't enough," he read.

Mary Margaret shivered. "It's that man, the one with the harelip."

"Yes," Dane said darkly. "I guess he didn't appreciate us not taking him seriously."

He peered down at the cat and Mary Margaret knew he was thinking about his son. She didn't know the child, but tears filled her eyes just the same.

"Oh, Dane, I'm so sorry. I should have kept my damned mouth shut."

"It's not your fault. I told the guy I wasn't going to be intimidated. He decided to send a stronger message in response to what *I* said." Dane glanced down at the cat again. "Well, I'm not letting this pass. What that bastard did was a crime. I'm going to report it to the police."

"Do you think they'll do anything about it?"

"They'd better."

His shock had turned to anger. She could tell by the set of his jaw that he was determined. More determined than ever. It was obvious that the issue had broadened. There'd been another death—only a cat, it was true—but for Dane it was a grievous loss. They were at war. The only unknown was who, exactly, the enemy was. It wasn't the man with the scar on his lip. He was only an agent.

"Believe me, sir," the deputy said, "I take this very seriously. I've got dogs myself. It's a manpower problem. It's a Sunday night, we're short-staffed. We've got a big accident working over on the highway. Tomorrow morning's the soonest a report can be taken."

"I don't care about a report. I want you to arrest the guy with the harelip," Dane said.

"There's not much that can be done about that tonight, sir. I'll suggest they send over an investigator in the morning. In the meantime, I'll have the animal-control people come by for the cat. They'll know what's needed for evidence."

They were in the kitchen. Mary Margaret listened from the

front room where she was curled in the easy chair where she'd petted Mead. The men came into the room.

"I know it's frustrating," the deputy said, "but we do the best we can with the resources available."

Dane said no more as he walked the officer to the front door.

"Good evening, ma'am," the deputy said.

"Goodbye," she replied.

After shutting the door, Dane came over and plopped on the sofa opposite her. He looked beat. "Proposition 103 at work," he said glumly. "The taxpayers get what they're willing to pay for, and no more."

"I'd rather be mad at the bastard who killed Mead," she said.

"Yes, I guess blaming everything on politics is a liberal kneejerk reaction, isn't it?"

"Hatred, I understand," she said. "Politics, I don't. I'd never voted until Colleen, my neighbor, made me go down and register so that whenever there's a feminist issue or candidate on the ballot, I could vote."

"That's not a bad reason. I'm a feminist myself—or at least a fellow traveler."

"Why?" She was genuinely curious.

"Empathy, I suppose."

"Oh."

Dane, she decided, was an unusual man. She'd known smart, educated men, but their brains hadn't made them any less egocentric and exploitive. In some cases it was the reverse—the more intelligent they were, the more superior they acted. She wasn't quite sure she'd figured Dane Barrett out.

"We've got a problem, though," he said. "Mead's murder has complicated our schedule somewhat. I could run you up to Reno now, but it would be a whole lot easier if you let me take you back tomorrow."

"Yes, I know. You've got a lot to contend with."

"We still have to eat dinner, which means I wouldn't be home until close to sunrise."

"I'm willing to stay over," she said.

"I'll be happy to take you to a motel. But if you think you

can trust me, you're welcome to stay in Toby's room—the bed's full-size. And there's a lock on the door.''

"Are you suggesting I'd need to keep the door locked?" she asked, arching a brow.

"Wasn't it Robert Frost who said, 'Good fences make good neighbors'?''

"Yes," Mary Margaret said, "and the rest is, 'Before I built a wall I'd ask to know...what I was walling in or walling out.'''

"Hmm." Dane seemed to like that.

She was very proud and glad Colleen had lent her a volume of Frost's poems.

"What *are* you walling out?" he asked.

"You were the one who brought up the lock on the door."

"Just keep the door locked tonight," he said. "Then there won't be any questions."

"What about the neighbors and your parishioners?"

"I hate the thought of living my life according to the dictates of other people's prejudices and fears."

"Unitarians are a lot different than Catholics," she said.

"Don't kid yourself, Claudia Rosenfelter would have a field day with the news that you're staying over."

Mary Margaret smiled to herself. How well she knew. "So maybe I should go to a motel."

"No, Mary Margaret. I can be as practical as the next guy when pragmatism is called for, but I've got a stubborn streak in me, too. Sometimes, I just can't get past principle and I've got to do what I think is right."

"What's the principle involved?"

He thought for a moment. "That there's nothing wrong with us being together. It's nobody's business but our own."

"In other words, you like living dangerously," she said.

"I suppose you could say that."

"You wouldn't make a very good gambler, Dane."

"Why's that?"

"One of the basic rules is the reward has to justify the risk. In this case, there's no payoff."

He smiled. "You'd be surprised how little it takes to satisfy me.''

She smiled back. "You'd be surprised how little you'll find available."

He rolled his tongue back and forth from cheek to cheek. "How does spaghetti sound for dinner?"

"It sounds good."

"I must warn you," he said, "I'm not much of a cook."

"I'm not, either."

"Boy, I'm continuously amazed how much we have in common."

Mary Margaret laughed. "Just to show you what a feminist I am, I'm going to read *Siddhartha* while you fix dinner."

"Well, just to show you how enlightened I am," he replied, "I'm going to let you."

Dane got up and, giving her a wink, went off to the kitchen. Their easy banter pleased her. It amazed her how comfortable it felt to be with him. And it was surprising because there was no reason why it should be so. They couldn't be more different in background, life experiences and lifestyle. He couldn't have any idea what her world was like, and she had only the most superficial understanding of his. And yet, she felt as if they knew each other very well. Maybe it was physical attraction. That could make a lot of things seem unimportant. Of course, that was a danger, too.

True to her word, she did spend the next half hour reading. The simply beauty of the story fascinated her, but her mind wandered. Every clank of a pot or rattle of a dish brought her mind back to him. After a while she began feeling guilty about her feminist belligerence, and she put down her book and went to the kitchen door. Dane bustled about, looking a bit awkward, before he noticed her. As luck would have it, he caught her checking out his derriere.

"So, the hunger reflex tore you away from pursuits of the spirit," he said.

"It's a very good book. Different than anything I've ever read."

He carried the pot of spaghetti from the stove to the sink. "I'm glad you're enjoying it."

Dane had set the kitchen table, but he'd forgotten the napkins so Mary Margaret took some from the cellophane package on the counter, folding them the way her mother had taught her. She didn't often think of her mother, but she did now, maybe because she was feeling so protective of herself.

Moira Duggan had been a strong, deeply principled woman, who was as unshakable in her conventionality as Mary Margaret was in her independence. Until her dying day she'd been convinced that Jimmy Duggan's true failing was that he'd strayed from the church. Mary Margaret's chief misgiving about her life was what her mother would think of it. There was little doubt she'd be scandalized. Mary Margaret's divorce, though, would have upset Moira much more than the fact she performed without her clothes on. In one of their last conversations, her mother had said, "When you marry, darling, be sure the man you choose is Catholic, a good Catholic." Mary Margaret had gotten the first part right.

She couldn't begin to imagine what Moira Duggan would think of Dane. At one level her mother couldn't help but like him. Dane was everything a woman would want for her daughter except, in this case, the sanction of the Catholic Church. And that he was a clergyman on top of everything else would almost certainly make him an Antichrist in Moira Duggan's eyes. But when Mary Margaret looked at Dane Barrett she saw a man, a good man, not a devil, and if she knew one thing about him, it was that she'd rot in hell before she'd condemn him for his beliefs or for being the person he was. On that point, if no other, she and her mother would have parted company.

She caught Dane contemplating her, his gaze inquiring. "So, does Hesse have you rethinking your life? That book has had that effect on more than one person."

Mary Margaret was amused. How could she tell him that if anyone had her rethinking her life, it was *him?* Well, of course, she couldn't. "It has me thinking," she said.

"We'll have to talk about that."

She felt the same rush she'd experienced when she and Colleen talked about Jane Austen or Thomas Hardy. But with Dane Barrett, a part of her still held back.

Dane brought over two heaping plates of spaghetti topped with meat sauce from a can. It was three times what she'd normally eat and she told him that so he wouldn't think she didn't finish because of his cooking. There was broccoli on side plates. She hated broccoli and wondered if she could gag down a few sprigs so as not to hurt his feelings, but decided that was dishonest.

"Don't take this personally, Dane, but I've never met a piece of broccoli I like, even when it's buried in cheese sauce."

"Hmm," he said. "Our first crisis. I love broccoli. Can this relationship endure?"

"Considering it only has to make it through lunch tomorrow, I'm optimistic."

He chuckled, shaking his head. "Has anyone every told you you're a difficult person, Miss Duggan?"

"I'm not an easy lay, if that's what you're really trying to say."

"No, I've already discovered that. I think what I'm referring to is your...I don't know...Victorian attitudes, maybe."

The comment struck her as ironic considering what she'd been thinking only moments earlier about the contrast between herself and her mother. "I'm careful, Dane, but hardly Victorian. I'm in a survival mode and have been all my adult life...and, I guess, some of my childhood, as well."

"I think what bothers me is that you're fighting yourself as much as you're fighting me," he said.

"Of course I'm fighting myself. I've got hormones, the same as you. And you've got a nice butt, Reverend. I'm human. But I do try to be practical and set aside impulses that aren't in my best interest."

"The old risk-versus-safety conundrum," he said.

Mary Margaret realized he was right. But what really surprised her was how much she seemed like her mother. What did that say about her? she wondered. Or, more important, what did it say about Dane?

Mary Margaret took her first bite of spaghetti. Dane did, as well.

"Hey, this is good," she said, chewing.

"Thank you for your forbearance and generosity, but I'd hate to think your palate isn't more sophisticated than this."

"Janine and I live on potato chips, Dr Peppers, an occasional bowl of soup or a hamburger and lots and lots of carrot and celery sticks. Sorry if that's disillusioning."

"You aren't philosophically opposed to good, healthy cuisine, I assume."

"Forgive me for being blunt," Mary Margaret said, "but whenever a guy asked me to some real fancy French place for dinner, you know the first thing that went through my mind? I'll give you a hint. It wasn't curiosity about what sauce they put on the frogs' legs."

"No, I suppose it was whether it was worth having to go to bed with the guy."

"Exactly." She took another bite. "That's the real reason I never developed a taste for snails."

She glanced up to see Dane giving her a wonderful, warm smile. He savored that for a moment or two, then said, "Oh. I forgot the wine. There's a jug of red in the cupboard. Can I interest you in a glass?"

Her first impulse was to decline, but then she decided she didn't want to seem *too* Victorian. "Maybe a little...if you're having some."

She watched as he got the wine and poured them each a modest glass. When he'd returned to his seat she studied him, her curiosity about him growing.

"So tell me, what was dinner like when you were married?" she said. "Did you discuss conundrums every night over glasses of red wine?"

"Hardly. Kathy and I connected about as well as a Ph.D. candidate and her orals panel."

"That must mean not good."

"You've got that right. How about you and Anthony?"

She took a long sip of wine, then another. "You know, I don't think Anthony and I ever talked about anything but money and his sexual needs. I mean, I'd be putting beans on his plate and he'd say something like, 'So, how about I tie you up tonight?' or 'We got any whipped cream left for the bedroom?'"

Dane stroked his chin. "Sounds like the creative sort."

"Anthony knew what he was doing when it came to sex. Love, though, was a little more confusing."

"He didn't love you?"

"He didn't know the difference between sex and love."

"Did *you* love *him?*"

"How could I?"

"You married him."

"I was running from my unhappiness and didn't manage to escape," she said, taking a forkful of spaghetti.

As she ate, he watched her.

"You know," he said, "you deserved better."

"I always thought so, but thank you for saying it, anyway."

There was mutual appraisal, but things remained innocent. She decided this was going smoothly, maybe too smoothly. There were as many lines as there were men and since she hadn't been around guys like Dane Barrett all that much, she couldn't be sure how much of what he said was calculated for effect. She had little doubt that he'd gladly take her to bed, but she didn't want to think that was the reason he'd said what he'd said.

"Not the best subject to discuss while eating," Dane volunteered.

"Former spouses?"

He nodded.

"Then let's talk about today."

"All right."

"So what do you think?" she asked.

He chewed the bite he'd taken. She waited.

"One discouraging possibility has occurred to me," he said. "Do you suppose the Benny Ledi Hopkins was referring to was her sister's dog?"

"Her *dog?*" she said.

"Yes. Remember Agnes McBain talked about Theo's having a dog. Maybe Ledi, in her senile confusion, thought of the dog as a witness to whatever it was that transpired."

She had a sinking feeling. "That never occurred to me."

"I could be wrong. I hope I'm wrong. But it probably should be considered."

Mary Margaret reflected on that as she toyed with her fork. "Yeah, but Ledi Hopkins was still saying that he'd seen something that proves my father was innocent. Maybe that's what we should focus on. Unless it's already too late. A lot of time has passed."

"Having raised a negative I don't want to leave things on a down note," he said. "I'm firmly convinced that if we keep at it, something's bound to turn up."

"We can't do any worse than the detective I hired, I suppose." She turned the stem of her wineglass.

"Was he able to find anything?"

"Not much. Just that the police files were sloppy. I don't know what that was supposed to mean—maybe that he was anal."

"Who was this guy, anyway?"

"His name's Robinson Palmer. Works out of Sacramento. I guess he did a thorough job. When he didn't turn up anything, I assumed it was because there wasn't anything to turn up."

"In fairness, he didn't have the advantage of Ledi Hopkins's dying words."

"You really think it's an advantage?" Mary Margaret asked. "Or are we kidding ourselves?"

"I can see one of my greatest challenges will be keeping your spirits up."

She laughed. "It's cute the way you're always upbeat."

"Cute," he said. "I'll have to remember that."

"Sorry, but you *are* cute."

They stared at each other. Mary Margaret felt a curious closeness, an intimacy. Maybe it was their common endeavor. Or maybe it was something more, something that went beyond the physical chemistry.

Dane pushed his plate away. "In all the excitement, I forgot about calling Sheila Warren, the minister of the UU church in Fresno. I'd better do it before it gets too late."

"You think it's worth the trouble?"

"I'm hoping I can get some useful insights about Theo Bledsoe. If Sheila was around Theo at the time of her death, something may have been said that would help us."

Mary Margaret really did admire his enthusiasm and determination. It gave her heart. "Whatever you think."

"Listen, I'll go dig Sheila's number out of my directory and give her a call. While I do, how would you like to dish up a couple of bowls of vanilla ice cream? I believe there's chocolate syrup in the refrigerator."

"Artie would die."

"The hell with Artie. You can live dangerously for just one night, can't you?"

Dane caught the double entendre about the same time she did. Grinning, he went off to make his call.

Monday

August 12th

Laurel, California

Dane checked Mary Margaret's door again after he'd had his shower. It was still closed. He wasn't surprised. When he'd gotten up in the middle of the night, he'd noticed her light was on. She'd gotten hooked on *Siddhartha* to the point where she'd hardly said a word about anything else after dinner.

He hadn't minded. Actually, it had been a rather nice evening despite what had happened to Mead. They had read. A couple of times she had asked about Buddhism, but mainly they'd enjoyed a kind of mutual tranquillity.

He and Kathy had spent many evenings reading, too, often in the same room, but without the contentment he'd felt with Mary Margaret. Though Kathy had never said so, he sensed that she always wanted to be somewhere else...with someone else.

Yet in spite of the ease he felt being with Mary Margaret, they'd both been self-conscious when it was time to go to bed. He'd gotten her a towel and then shown her his badly stocked linen closet where he kept the shampoo and the hair dryer and other things she might need. She'd assured him she was just fine. Then, beating him to the punch, she'd given him a quick kiss on the cheek and thanked him for all he'd done before she'd disappeared into Toby's room. He hadn't seen her since.

Considering she was accustomed to sleeping in, he reckoned that it could still be a while before he saw her, so he made himself a cup of coffee, drank some juice and had a soft-boiled egg on toast. He'd make her breakfast when she got up.

Dane relished the thought of spending the day with her. It would be their third—not much time at all in the greater scheme of things—and yet each moment with her was becoming precious. He knew it was infatuation, but he didn't care. It felt wonderful. And though it was early in their relationship, he had hopes the connection they'd formed could lead to more.

Dane sipped his coffee. Mary Margaret Duggan had changed his world. She had renewed him, given him hope for something he couldn't fully define. But still, he had enough of his father in him that he wasn't quite ready to abandon all reason.

Besides, there was Jimmy Duggan's case to be considered. Before falling asleep, he'd wrestled with the bits and pieces of evidence. He sensed that Theo Bledsoe was somehow pivotal, though he wasn't sure why. Unfortunately, his best chance of learning more about the woman was from Sheila Warren, the UU minister in Fresno. But he hadn't been able to reach her. The best he'd been able to do was leave a message on the answering machine at her church.

He'd be gone most of the day, so he figured he should alert Claudia that Sheila might call. Since there were a couple of other matters he wanted to discuss with the church secretary, as well, he decided to run over to the church before they left for Reno. The question was if he had time to go before Mary Margaret woke up.

A neighborhood dog began barking and Dane remembered poor Mead. During those sleepless hours after he'd gone to bed, he had also worried about how he was going to break the news to Toby. Kathy would find a way to give him grief over it—she had a propensity for finding ways to make him suffer. Her game was punish him whenever she could, probably because she blamed him for whatever guilt she felt.

Of course, Mead, not Kathy, was his immediate problem. Which reminded him that he was supposed to be getting a visit from Laurel's finest sometime that morning.

After refilling his coffee cup, Dane telephoned the police

station to make sure the issue of Mead hadn't slipped through the cracks. The dispatcher told him that Granville Jones was on his way over. Dane thanked him and, as he hung up the phone, he heard a car door slam outside.

Coming out of the bathroom, Mary Margaret thought she heard voices. She stood silently in the hall and listened. One voice was Dane's. The other she recognized to be Granville Jones's.

"It could have been the guy you had the confrontation with," Jones was saying. "It's probable. But it's also possible it was some neighborhood kids playing a prank."

"Sergeant, you can't believe that," Dane said.

"I didn't say I believed it. But in police work you've got to be careful about jumping to conclusions."

Yeah, Mary Margaret thought, like jumping to the conclusion that my father killed Donna Lee.

"Well, I want that man arrested," Dane said, his voice growing louder. "There's no doubt that he threatened me."

"Yes, but from what you said, the guy was vague in his threat."

"The message was very clear."

"A jury would look at the exact words. And they would have to be proved."

"Mary Margaret was there. She heard what he said."

"Well, any decision to arrest would be Chief Slater's and any decision to prosecute would be made by the D.A."

"Are you saying you aren't going to do anything, Sergeant?"

"No, Pastor Barrett. What I'm saying is, it's difficult to make charges like that stick. The guy gave you a little shove, but he didn't hurt you. Juries don't like to put people in jail for that sort of thing, let alone for using strong language."

"He killed my cat. Cruelty to animals is a crime."

"Yes, but it must be proved."

"Sergeant Jones," Dane said, "if I didn't know better, I'd say you don't want to do anything about this."

"I'm going to recommend we pick the guy up, if he's seen

around town. And yes, there is justification for questioning. Beyond that, I can't make any promises.''

"I suppose that's something, but I see now it's going to take a dead body—like mine, for example—to really pique your interest.''

"We deal with the facts, Pastor, not possibilities.''

"Yes, I've come to understand that,'' Dane said.

"I know when people get all emotionally involved it's hard to be objective, but as police, that's what we have to be—objective.''

"I don't mean to be critical,'' Dane said, "but in just one day Mary Margaret and I have turned up several pieces of information regarding Donna Lee Marshall's death that seem to have escaped your objective attention.''

"Such as what?''

"Apparently, Stephen Ragsdale spent a lot of time with Donna Lee. According to one of the neighbors, he went over there whenever Donna Lee's mother left the house.''

"We knew he was counseling her.''

"You consider that counseling?''

"Pastor Ragsdale had an alibi at the time the girl was murdered. He didn't have blood on him and he wasn't seen leaving the scene of the crime.''

"Were you aware that Ragsdale had a relationship with one of your witnesses?''

"Who?''

"Theo Bledsoe.''

"She was a member of his church.''

"Yes,'' Dane said, "but she was also a recluse. Her sister was about the only one she ever saw in her later years. Her sister *and* Stephen Ragsdale. He visited her at her house, which no one else ever did.''

"He was her pastor. You, of all people, should understand that.''

"I hate to say this, considering Reverend Ragsdale was one of my predecessors at First Unitarian, but the more I learn about this case, the more I'm convinced he was in this a lot deeper than anyone in the police department realized. With all due respect, Sergeant, I'm getting the impression that the department did a half-assed job on the Donna Lee Marshall murder."

Mary Margaret gave a silent cheer for Dane, shaking her fist as if to say, "Right on!"

In the living room, Granville Jones was fumbling. "What do you mean, half-assed? You may be a pastor, but—no offense intended—who are you to say?"

"The detective Miss Duggan hired said your files were sloppy. And from what I've seen, I'd feel very uncomfortable knowing I'd put a man away for life, if I were in your shoes."

"You're entitled to your opinion."

"You honestly don't think there's reason to doubt?" Dane asked.

"We're only human," Jones said. "I expect errors were made. But that doesn't mean we got the wrong man. Besides, we didn't convict Jimmy Duggan. The jury did. Ted Gotchall did a hell of a job gathering the evidence. He's as good as anybody in the state and doesn't have a dishonest bone in his body."

"If he was so good, why was the file sloppy?"

"That wasn't Ted's doing. The slipup must have been made by a clerk."

"What slipup are we talking about?" Dane asked.

"I assume you're referring to the misnumbered pages in the lab report. That's what that detective pointed out when he was going through the file."

"The pages were misnumbered?"

"He thought maybe a page was missing. I wasn't in on the lab side of the case, so I didn't know. Chief Slater told me to check with the county criminal lab. Their files were the same as ours, so we figured some clerk slipped up. A simple human error. But that's a long way from saying the wrong man went to prison."

"Maybe so, Sergeant, but then again, maybe not. I wasn't on the jury, I grant you, but from the jury box I'm sitting in now, I'm starting to think there's a reasonable doubt."

Mary Margaret again thrust her fist in the air. Her heart was tripping with glee. She hadn't felt this kind of joy in years.

"I'd like to see proof," Granville Jones said. "That counts more than opinions."

Mary Margaret pictured Jones's little rat face and wanted to smack it, but Dane seemed to be doing a pretty good job with verbal jabs.

"Proof is what I'm after," Dane told the man. "It's a shame Mr. Gotchall isn't around. The first time we talked I believe you said he's retired."

"Teddy was living in the Bay Area near his daughter, but from what I understand he had a stroke this past spring and he's been in a nursing home."

Mary Margaret rolled her eyes. God, they were dropping like flies. With their luck, he probably died a week ago.

"Do you know where, Sergeant?" Dane asked.

"No, but I could probably find out."

"Would you be willing to share the information?"

"Sure. If Teddy doesn't care, I sure don't. I'll check with him."

"I appreciate your cooperation, Sergeant Jones," Dane said, sounding very pastoral.

Mary Margaret pictured him putting a hand on the man's shoulder and giving him a beneficent smile. Show business came in more than one form.

"I'm going up to Reno this afternoon," Dane said, "but maybe I can check with you in a day or two."

"I'll do what I can," Jones said. "Now, unless you've got something else, I'd better go. We've still got statements to take regarding that big accident last night."

"No, you've been very helpful."

She could hear the front door open.

"Sorry about your cat, Pastor Barrett," Granville Jones said. "I don't mean to sound like I don't care, but I have a job to do and I do it the best way I can."

"I understand. But if you can find out who that man with the harelip is, it would go a long way in telling us who is so nervous about the Duggan case."

"I take your point."

"Goodbye, Sergeant."

Hearing the door close, Mary Margaret was about to dash to the living room, when she realized all she had on was a

T-shirt. Remembering the terry robe she'd seen on the back of the bathroom door, she quickly grabbed it, cinching the belt as she went down the hall. She was in such a hurry that she didn't see Dane until she practically ran in to his arms.

"I heard you talking to the cop," she said, gathering herself together. "You were great."

"Thanks, I mean to please."

Mary Margaret saw special meaning in his eyes. A warm feeling went through her. "Maybe something will come of this, after all," she ventured.

"I have a hunch it will...not that I have any special insight," he said. "It's just a feeling."

He peered into her eyes. Her sense of him was very strong.

"I'm afraid to hope," she said honestly.

"Your fear's the problem," he replied, "not the hope."

Dane took her by the shoulders, his hands gentle. He seemed so good to her, so kind. The most natural thing in the world would've been to hug him. He must have been thinking the same thing because the next thing she knew, he had folded her lovingly into his arms.

She smelled the brace of his cologne and felt the warmth and strength of his arms. It seemed so natural to be with him like this, and yet she couldn't deny feeling a spark of apprehension.

"This robe looks familiar," he murmured.

She blushed, pressing her face into his shoulder. "I heard you talking and I was so excited that I grabbed the first thing I could put my hands on."

He took her by the shoulders again and held her at arm's length. "This robe has never looked so good."

She colored even more. "You embarrass me more than any man I've ever known," she said, lowering her eyes.

"Why do you suppose that is?"

"Now you're teasing me."

"No, it's a serious question."

"I suppose because you're a clergyman."

"A clergyman with a great butt?" he teased.

She turned absolutely scarlet and tried to pull away, but Dane wouldn't let her go. He laughed.

"You're not as nice as I thought," she said, avoiding his eyes. "In fact, you're downright mean."

"*You* were the one who commented on my butt, remember?"

"Well, you didn't have to bring it up. What kind of a gentleman are you, anyway?"

"One who finds you nearly irresistible."

She did look into his eyes now. "Irresistible?"

Dane smiled as a quietness settled over them both. "Let me put it this way," he said. "I hope you have something on under that robe."

She swallowed hard. "I do."

"But not much, I bet."

She shook her head.

His fingers tightened. "Oh, God," he said. The question "What to do next?" was in his eyes.

Fear and hope clashed inside her. Mary Margaret asked herself what it was that she truly wanted. She knew she didn't have long before he'd take matters into his hands. She also knew what she had to say.

"Don't hate me, Dane," she said, "but I'd like you to take me home now."

His face registered disappointment. His grip loosened, then his hands slowly fell away. He managed a face-saving smile. "If that's what you want."

"It is," she said earnestly. "But don't take it personally."

"That's the only way to take it," he said with a small laugh. "I know you don't mean it unkindly, though."

Her heart was suddenly heavy.

"I'll fix breakfast while you dress," he said, sensible and practical sounds overlaying the hurt.

"I don't need anything. I usually start with lunch."

Mutual embarrassment had set in. They were behaving like a couple of kids at a dance—standing together but not knowing quite what to do.

"Not even coffee?" he said.

"Coffee's okay, I guess."

"I'll fix you a cup, then."

"Great."

"Then, maybe while you're getting ready, I'll run over to

the church for a few minutes," he said. "I need to talk to Claudia."

She almost said, "Lucky you." But she caught herself in time. "No problem, as long as I get back in time to go to work."

There was an unmistakable look of regret in his eyes, but he didn't complain. He simply kissed her on the temple then headed for the kitchen. "You take your coffee black, don't you?"

"Yes."

She followed him. He filled a mug with coffee and handed it to her.

"I won't be long," he said. Then, touching her hair with his fingertips, he left the room.

When Mary Margaret heard the front door close, she wandered into the living room, making her way to the big picture window. Dane was already out of sight, but he wasn't out of her mind. Something important had happened between them, though on the surface it seemed little more than simple affection.

The phone rang then, startling her. At first she ignored it, thinking the answering machine would pick it up. But after a few rings she realized Dane had neglected to put it on. She expected the caller to give up at any moment, but the ringing persisted. Then it occurred to her that it might be the man with the harelip. On an impulse she snatched up the receiver.

"Hello?"

There was silence on the other end of the line. Then she heard a woman's voice. "Is this the Barrett residence?"

"Yes."

"Is Dane there, please?" There was a certain businesslike crispness to the voice, but also suspicion. The quality of the sound seemed a bit hollow and there was an echo.

"No, I'm sorry, he just left. May I take a message?"

"Who's this?" The voice definitely had an edge.

Mary Margaret was taken aback. "Who's calling?"

"Dr. Kathy Allston. I'm Dane's ex-wife."

Mary Margaret gulped, feeling as if she'd been caught red-handed, though she knew that the woman had no grounds for indignation. "Oh, hello."

"And you're...?" Kathy said.

"Mary Margaret Duggan."

"Not the housekeeper?"

"No, just a friend."

"Hmm. Dane doesn't let any grass grow under his feet, does he? How long's he been in town? A week?" She cleared her throat. "So tell me, Mary Margaret," Kathy said, her tone patronizing, "do you expect Dane back anytime soon?"

"Yes, but if it's urgent you can reach him at the church. He won't be around this afternoon. He's leaving town."

"Damn." Kathy sighed with exasperation. "I'm about to go out myself and I do need to talk to him. It's important. Do you have a number you can give me?"

There was a phone book next to the answering machine and Mary Margaret quickly flipped the pages. "Just a second, I'll look it up."

"I am calling from Japan, in case you're not aware," Kathy said, her tone edgy, impatient.

"Yes, it should only take a second. Let's see..." Mary Margaret found the number. "Here it is." She read it off.

"Thank you so much."

"No problem."

"I know it's early morning there. Hope I didn't wake you."

Mary Margaret heard the sarcasm and was taken aback again. Was it hostility? Or was Kathy just a bitch? God knew, she had no bone to pick with the woman, but she didn't much appreciate the innuendo.

"No," she replied with a breezy tone. "I was just having my morning coffee."

"I hope you're the one making it, honey. Dane never could. But then, maybe that's why he's got you. I assume you also cook in addition to taking care of his libido."

Mary Margaret couldn't believe it. But she took a calming breath. "Oh, no, I don't even know how to use a microwave," she said sweetly, "Dane keeps me around because I'm good in bed. The poor bastard hasn't had any decent sex since his bachelor days."

There was a stunned silence, then, "You're a regular little tart, aren't you?"

"It's all relative," Mary Margaret said evenly. "Dane had no way to go but up."

On the other side of the Pacific the phone was slammed into the cradle. Mary Margaret enjoyed momentary elation before she stopped to consider what she'd done. Then the stupidity of it began to sink in. Sure, the woman was a bitch, but Mary Margaret didn't have to rise to the bait. Her indignation for Dane's sake had gotten the best of her—which made no sense because he didn't need her protection, and she certainly hadn't done him any good. She agonized. God, if this ended up causing him trouble, she really would have to shoot herself.

She began pacing, uncertain what to do. Should she call the church and warn him, or simply let nature take its course? Anything she did would probably only make things worse. She'd really blown it. Dumb, dumb, dumb!

Mary Margaret had always had a smart mouth, and also a tendency to lose her temper, which, as her mother had frequently pointed out, served no worthwhile purpose.

She agonized, gnawing on her lip. Well, if nothing else, it gave Dane a good reason to send her packing. But what if this caused him trouble with his kid? *That* was no laughing matter. "Shit," she said out loud. "Shit."

It was another sunny day, the temperature still moderate, though Dane knew all too well it wouldn't be long before the overpowering heat of the afternoon set in. For the moment, the air was pleasant and fragrant with the scent of flowers.

As he neared the church, he brooded over the possibility that Mary Margaret might let everything they had going between them slip away. He knew she was afraid...and fear and disillusionment weren't easy to overcome.

Arriving at the First Unitarian, he found Claudia Rosenfelter working on the flower beds surrounding the patio outside the church office. She'd told him that she considered keeping the beds attractive to be one of her responsibilities, even though there was a full-time custodian/gardener.

"Good morning, Dane," she said, looking up from her perch on the garden stool she used to save her knees.

"Good morning, Claudia."

She pushed back errant strands of coarse gray hair. "You've had a call from the Fresno church already this morning," she told him. "The secretary there wanted you to know Reverend Warren was on vacation and wouldn't be back for a few more days."

"That's unfortunate," he said, disappointed. "I wanted to speak with her about Theo Bledsoe. In fact, the main reason I came by was to let you know I was expecting a call from the reverend."

"Oh?"

Dane could see the wheels turning. He knew Claudia was protective of Stephen Ragsdale's memory, but he decided to run a few questions by her anyway. "In the course of my investigation into the Duggan case," he began, bemused by his own stilted syntax, "I turned up some pretty surprising bits of information."

"Did you really?"

"For example, I understand Reverend Ragsdale and Theo Bledsoe were quite friendly."

Claudia smirked, putting down the box of plants perched on her knees. "Theo was having a lot of problems toward the end of Stephen's life, and he did his best to minister to her, despite his own burdens."

"I understand he called on her regularly."

"I believe he did. Theo hadn't been to church much in years, but had the need for ministerial intervention. Stephen gave of himself and was very generous in that way."

"Didn't it seem a little odd?" Dane asked. "I mean, I understand Theo was a virtual recluse."

"She was strange, no question about it. But I believe Stephen's feeling was she was needy and it was his duty to help."

"Did he ever discuss the nature of Theo's problems with you?"

Claudia was a trifle indignant. "Heavens, no. Stephen was extremely discreet, as was proper. If there was anyone who behaved improperly it was Theo."

"What do you mean?"

"I probably shouldn't say anything, but considering they're

both dead I don't suppose it's the end of the world. And I *am* speaking with a clergyman, after all."

"You can count on my discretion," he assured her.

Claudia appeared relieved. "Well," she began, "shortly after Stephen was killed and everybody was all upset and in a tizzy, I came to the church office and found Theo going through Stephen's files."

"Going through his files? His personal files?"

"That's right. Naturally I was shocked. I asked what she was doing, and she told me that she'd shared personal information with Stephen in the course of their counseling and she had no intention of it ever becoming public. I assured her the files were secure, but she would have none of it. She dug out what she'd been looking for, showed me that her name was on the manila folder and left with it. I never saw her again."

"That's very interesting," Dane said. "I wonder what was so sensitive that she'd come out of seclusion to make sure no one got a look at it."

"Believe me, I've often wondered myself."

Dane decided she was telling the truth, though it would have been conceivable that she felt the need to protect Ragsdale even in death. "I assume Theo got everything, that nothing was overlooked," he said.

"To my knowledge, yes. Whether there was anything in his personal diaries, I have no idea."

"What personal diaries?"

"Stephen kept a diary of his ministry, thinking he might want to write a book someday. Not many people were aware, but he confided that in me."

Dane's interest was piqued. "What happened to the diaries?"

"His daughter, Sally, got them, I imagine, along with his other personal effects."

"I see." Dane stroked his chin, noticing a tabby cat slinking along the edge of the beds at the far side of the patio. It made him think again of poor Mead. But it wasn't the time to worry about that. "Do you have any idea if the police looked at Reverend Ragsdale's diaries?" he asked Claudia.

"I don't know. After Sally returned to settle her father's affairs, the church hasn't had any contact with her, to my knowledge. Things were so emotional when she was in town that I didn't discuss the diaries with her."

"Hmm."

Claudia waited for his next question.

"Do we have an address for Sally?" he asked. "What's she doing now?"

"Sally's married. Her married name is Nesbit. She lives in San Francisco. I have an address for her. I assume it's current, but I'm not sure. Shall I get it for you?"

"Yes. Leave it on my desk, if you would. I've got to get back to the house. I'll be leaving town, by the way," he added. "I don't expect to be back until late tonight or tomorrow morning."

"Business?"

Somehow it didn't surprise him that she would ask. "Yes."

"It's concerning the murder, isn't it?"

Dane could see she didn't lack for chutzpah and wondered if a lecture was forthcoming. If so, he wasn't in a mood to hear it, so he decided to preempt her with some questions of his own. "I've only been looking into the matter for a couple of days, but it's amazing how much we've managed to turn up."

"You and Mary Margaret, you mean?"

"Yes, and Tom Muncey, the priest."

"People in a small town love to gossip," she said, somewhat ironically.

"Yeah, right. Come to think of it, maybe I can ask you a question I've been asking everyone else. Does the name Benny mean anything to you?"

"Benny? As in Jack Benny?"

"Or possibly a given name. Might you have heard it in connection with Theo Bledsoe?"

Claudia stopped to think, wiping her brow with the back of her fingers. "Benny," she said, repeating the name. "You know, that sounds vaguely familiar."

Dane brightened. "It does?"

She pondered some more. He wondered if at last some independent confirmation of Benny's existence might be forthcoming.

"Theo Bledsoe," she said vacantly. Then she nodded.

"You know, that day Theo came to get her files from Stephen's office she was muttering a name. It may have been Benny. The reason I think so is because I have a cousin, Benjamin, we all called Benny. He and I were very close growing up, and there was an incident several years ago where the name Benny was mentioned and I thought of my cousin. I'm sure it was around the time of Stephen's death and that the person was Theo—that day she was here."

"Does your cousin live in the area?"

"Oh, no. Benny retired to Florida from Chicago and died ten years ago."

"But you think Theo was muttering the name the day she was here."

"I believe so."

"Did you get an impression of who Benny might be?"

Claudia shook her head. "Frankly, I'd forgotten about it until you mentioned it just now."

"Hmm." Dane knew it wasn't a tremendous breakthrough, but it was independent confirmation of a name Ledi Hopkins had mentioned on her deathbed. It at least took the utterance out of the realm of delusion. Maybe.

"Is it significant?" Claudia asked.

"I don't know. Another piece in the puzzle, I guess."

The phone rang inside the church office and they both turned toward the sound. Claudia got up.

"Excuse me, Dane." She went inside the building.

While he waited, he looked at the flowers Claudia had planted and he pondered their conversation. She returned after a few seconds.

"It's your ex-wife, calling from Japan," she announced.

Dane went to his office to take the call. Despite himself, he felt a wave of apprehension. Kathy was frugal, and any call she made from Japan would not be good news.

"Hello, Kathy. What's up?"

"Who you sleep with is your business," she said without ceremony, "but I'm telling you this in no uncertain terms, as long as that little bitch Mary Margaret, or whatever her name is, is in your house, I won't be sending Toby there."

"What on earth are you talking about?"

"I called your place several minutes ago, asking for you, and she—she insulted me!" Kathy sputtered.

He could tell when Kathy was angry, really angry, because she sputtered and her voice got thin and high. But this was a surprise. "Insulted you? Mary Margaret doesn't even know you."

"Then she must have gotten her hostility from you!"

Dane felt the all too familiar bite of Kathy's indignation, not liking it. "What did she say?"

"That I was sexually inadequate, among other things. I suppose she was trying to justify herself as a sex toy."

"Sex toy? Mary Margaret?"

"I have no intention of discussing this further," Kathy said. "Not on my nickel anyway. Just be advised I won't have Toby exposed to that. If she can talk to me that way, God only knows what she might say to him. Frankly, Dane, considering your piety, I'm surprised you want her around."

His temper flared. "Look," he said, "I don't know what went on between the two of you, but you're not telling me who's going to be in my place and who's not when Toby's with me. It's none of your damned business, Kathy. And you're out of line to suggest it, just as I would be out of line to tell you to get rid of Osvaldo."

"Osvaldo never insulted you!" she shot back.

"Osvaldo is an embarrassment, but that's only my opinion. Until now I didn't think I still had a vote when it came to your private life."

"You don't."

"Then you don't, either."

There was a wounded silence. He knew she was seething. Kathy hated it when he tripped her up on logic.

"Well, I don't have time for this," she said. "I called for another reason. I'm going to be in Berkeley in a couple of days on business and I was wondering if you could meet me so we can discuss something."

"Discuss what?"

"I'd rather not talk about it over the phone. Since I'm going to be there for a few days anyway, it's a good opportunity for us to meet and come to an understanding. It's very important."

"Wait a minute, you aren't going to tell me you have to see me and then not say why, are you?"

"I'm afraid so. It's not something that should be discussed over the telephone—"

"It's Toby," he said, cutting her off. "What's wrong?"

"No, it's not Toby. He's fine."

"Are you bringing him with you?"

"No, it's silly to put him through two long, grueling flights over the course of a couple of days. He's finally adjusting to being away from you. I don't want to confuse him."

"Confuse him? Jesus Christ, Kathy, he's my son. I think you're the one who's confused. Better he spend a couple of days on a plane than stay with Osvaldo who isn't even capable of taking care of himself!"

"Dane," Kathy said, her voice growing firm, "Osvaldo is gone. He went home to Lima yesterday."

He was stunned. The woman still had the ability to amaze him, though any pleasure he'd once derived from that fact was long gone. Now she just made him crazy, pure and simple. "What do you propose to do with Toby, then?"

"I'm leaving him with our housekeeper. Miyuki is good with him and she's a dear, sweet person. Very reliable. She has a few words of English. They're able to communicate."

"Jesus, Kat," Dane said, exasperated, "you're leaving my son in a foreign country with a servant who barely speaks English? What if Toby has an attack of appendicitis?"

"Dane, don't get all emotional. He won't. He's very content."

He didn't know whether to believe her or not. His instincts told him the woman had lost it. First, she rants and raves about Mary Margaret, then she says Osvaldo has split and that she's coming back without Toby, albeit for only a few days.

"Listen, Kathy," he said, trying to sound as calm and reasonable as possible, "why not just tell me what's going on? How can it make any difference whether or not you're looking in my eyes when you say what you have to say?"

"Remember when I told you I wanted a divorce?" she said, her tone taking on the same calm, reasonable tenor as his.

"Yes."

"Well, imagine if I was in Athens or someplace at the time and I'd done it over the phone. I don't think you'd have appreciated it, would you?"

"In the long run I don't know that it would have mattered," he replied.

"Sometimes the short run counts, too. This is such an occasion. Trust me on this, Dane."

He didn't want to, but he didn't know that he had a lot of choice. "All right, but be advised, I'm coming to the end of my rope. If I don't like what I hear, I may have to take matters in my own hands. If necessary, I'll go to Japan and bring Toby home."

"I'm sure you'll agree that isn't necessary," she said.

Outwardly she sounded self-assured, but Dane could hear a hitch of emotion in her voice.

"I'll call back when I know my exact schedule," she added. "Perhaps we can meet on campus. I'll stay at the faculty club, so if that's all right, we can meet there."

He did not like it at all, but his hands were tied. "Okay, fine."

"Good," she said, sounding relieved.

Dane resolved then and there not to give her the same latitude he had in the past. Originally he had thought that the less he and Kathy fought, the easier it would be on Toby, so he'd done whatever it took to be accommodating. But now he was beginning to realize that nice guys just got screwed.

"There's one more thing," Kathy said, "before I let you go."

He winced, expecting another bombshell. "What?"

"I apologize for what I said about your friend. I've been very emotional and anxious lately and...well, I guess I let her get to me. In fact, I was probably just as responsible for what happened, if not more so than she."

"I'm sure it's just a tempest in a teapot," he said, trying to respond to her conciliatory attitude.

Kathy hesitated. "I don't mean to pry, Dane, but is...it serious?"

The question caught him flat-footed. How did he answer?

What was the honest response? He looked into his heart, then said, "Yes."

"Oh."

He started to qualify, but then held back, thinking to himself, what the hell.

"Well," she said, "congratulations."

"Thanks."

"Will you apologize to Mary Margaret for me?"

"Certainly."

Oddly—especially for Kathy—she seemed in no hurry to end the conversation. "I'm pleased," she said, "because it may make our conversation easier. In fact, I think everything's going to work out extremely well. I'm happy for us both!"

That was sufficiently vague that it told him nothing. But he knew there was no point in questioning her. Kathy always had to be in control.

"This is costing me a day's salary," she said. "I'd better go."

"I'll be looking forward to your call," he replied. "If for some reason I'm not home, I'll put on my machine."

"If you don't forget." It was an inside joke, and a little too familiar for comfort. Kathy quickly backed off. "Talk to you later, then."

"Bye," he said. Dane put the phone back in the cradle.

Getting up from his desk, he noticed that the window was slightly open. Not far away, Claudia Rosenfelter labored in the flower beds. He went back outside. She glanced up at him, shading her eyes from the sun with her hand.

"I trust everything is all right," she said.

"Yes, everything's fine," he replied obliquely. Then, checking his watch, he said, "Well, I'd better run, or I'll be late."

"Do you have an out-of-town meeting then?" Claudia asked, rising from her stool.

"No. I have to take Miss Duggan back to Reno."

Claudia's expression turned grim. She brushed back her hair from her face. "Oh. She stayed over."

Dane figured that having likely overheard his conversation with Kathy, Claudia had a good idea what had been going on. Enough of his dirty laundry was in public view that forging full speed ahead was probably as good a strategy as any. "I was supposed to take her back yesterday afternoon, but there was an incident last night that required me to talk to the police this morning and it set us back," he said. "So she stayed in my guest room."

Claudia's expression turned dark. "Dane, I don't mean to tell you your business, but every minister who's been here while I've been church secretary has relied heavily on my advice. I consider it my duty to tell you what I think."

He groaned inwardly. After Kathy he hardly needed this, but people didn't always get to choose when they got advice. "You apparently don't approve of Mary Margaret staying at my house."

"This is a small town. We have a reputation to maintain and the way our minister is regarded is a large part of how we're seen in the community. I would not advise you to have pretty young women as houseguests."

"Are you saying that if Mary Margaret was old and ugly, it would be okay?"

She grimaced. "I believe you know what I mean."

"I certainly wouldn't do anything to embarrass the church intentionally," Dane said. "But you might as well know that nothing transpired that would compromise either my morals or Mary Margaret's. I regard her as a friend and someone whom this congregation owes a certain degree of compassion."

"That's all well and good," Claudia said, "but she *is* a showgirl and your good intentions might be easily misconstrued."

"Forgive me for bringing scripture into this," he said, becoming annoyed, "but I've always felt it wasn't an accident that Jesus socialized with prostitutes, adulteresses and other outcasts. I think the point he was making is that we're all God's children."

Claudia Rosenfelter turned bright red and began to sputter.

"But I know we're not talking about *your* views," he said. "You're worried about what others will think. Well, to them I say we're an open, welcoming congregation that turns no one from its door. We respect the worth and dignity of each individual and look for goodness in everyone. Should anybody be scandalized by Mary Margaret and me, I suggest you tell them that, Claudia." He turned. "Now I've got to run. Don't forget Sally Nesbit's address, please," he said over his shoulder. "I'll get it tomorrow."

Reno, Nevada

Hap Coleman ordered two medium-size Pepsis and handed the girl a fin. She gave him his change and went to fill the order. A couple of young women were standing in line next to him, giggling. He glanced at them, annoyed by their chatter. He couldn't even get excited about the fact that one of the girls had bazoombas the size of honeydew melons bulging out of her halter top. Christ, after Rut got them thrown out of the Mustang Ranch for roughing up that whore, he'd had his fill of women for a while. Too damned bad Rut didn't feel the same.

Hap was in a foul mood. Rut was giving him fits over this fucking obsession with the showgirl. His ass was rump-sprung from sitting in the goddamn van. It seemed like it had been a week. They hadn't had a decent night's sleep in days. Jesus.

When the girl brought him the soft drinks, he took them and headed for the door, bumping one of the bimbos in the next line who'd taken a step back as she was horsing around.

"Hey, watch it," she complained.

"Fuck you," he replied without bothering to turn around.

The heat outside was like stepping into hell. Hap had had his fill of Nevada. He was going to give Rut one more night, then he was heading back to Oakland, with or without him.

Hap walked along the highway, cursing under his breath. The entrance to the trailer park was across the street and a hundred yards up. He'd made the trek to the fast-food joint when he'd gotten their lunch, so this was his second trip and it was even hotter now than before. Rut had refused to go because he didn't trust Hap to watch the entrance carefully enough. "I've seen every fucking rig that's gone in and come out and I know she ain't come back yet. But she will. And I'll be waitin'.''

When Hap got back to the van, which was parked in the lot of a little strip shopping center, facing the street, Rut was gazing steadily at the entrance to the Desert Rest, a cigarette hanging from his lip, his stony face bearing the same grim determination it'd had since the morning he'd walked out of Quentin. "So," Hap said, climbing into the driver's seat, "no sign of the broad, I guess." He handed Rut one of the Pepsis.

"No, but she'll show. Unless she quit her job."

"I hope so because one way or the other I'm leaving for home in the morning."

"Don't worry," Rut said with assurance Hap didn't fully understand. "Tonight's the night. I feel it."

Hap Coleman pried the lid off the paper cup and took a long drink. He was sweating and so was Rut. The van smelled like a goddamn gym.

"Mind telling me what you plan to do, exactly? You haven't said two frigging words except that you want to fuck her."

"Soon as her roommate leaves, I'm going inside the trailer and wait for her there."

"What if she's with the guy?"

"If she is, I'll take care of him."

Hap guzzled some more Pepsi. "And then what?"

"Ten minutes after she returns, or after the guy leaves, whichever happens first, you bring the van to the trailer and have the back door open."

"Then what?"

Rut took a last drag on his cigarette and flicked the butt out the window. He removed the lid from the Pepsi and threw it out the window, too. "Then you do what I tell you, dumb nut."

"I don't know," Hap said, shaking his head. "You're asking a lot of me for nothing."

"You can fuck her, too, after I'm done with her."

"I don't want to fuck her."

"Then keep your goddamn head down and she'll never even know you were there. Nobody will, 'cause the van can't be traced. You spent the last four days fishin', haven't you?"

"Just the same, I don't like it," Hap said.

"Nothin' will go wrong 'cause I'm the one takin' all the chances."

"Maybe, but you might as well know, if she doesn't show, it's adios for me. I'm splitting first thing in the morning."

"She'll be here. She's gotta prance that little butt of hers around at the High Chaparral. Could be she'll be otherwise engaged when the curtain goes up, though," Rut said with a laugh.

"I hope so," Hap replied. But he didn't really. In fact, just the opposite. He'd had a bad feeling about this all along. He'd humored Rut because of what his brother had been through, but he knew Rut was letting his cock do his thinking for him, and that was never good. It was downright dangerous. And if they weren't careful, it could end in disaster.

Laurel, California

Mary Margaret had gotten more and more anxious as she waited for Dane to return home. The conversation with Kathy weighed on her. She hadn't felt this guilty since...well, since she'd threatened Dane with the gun. If she'd been able to, she'd have written him a note and grabbed the first bus out of town, praying never to see him again. But she had to face the music. She owed him that.

When the front door finally opened and he appeared, she was in the middle of the living room, wringing her hands. They exchanged a long meaningful look before Mary Margaret said, "Did she get a hold of you?"

"Kathy?"

"Yes."

He nodded. "She was so pissed, I never did figure out what happened between you two. Something about her sexual inadequacy was all about all I got out of her."

Mary Margaret buried her face in her hands, wanting to die. "I did something really stupid, Dane. I blew it."

"You told her we were sleeping together?"

She dropped heavily into the easy chair, avoiding his eyes. "Not in so many words, but I guess that was the effect."

"Why did you do that?"

Mary Margaret sighed helplessly. "I don't know her from Adam, and she got all pissy about me being here. She made a few snide remarks implying I was a slut, so I let her have it. I said something like you hadn't had any decent sex since your bachelor days. It was really a dumb thing to do."

Dane began to laugh, really laugh.

"What's so funny?"

"You telling Kathy to stuff it," he said, wiping his eyes. "That's classic. It's something I should have done a long time ago."

"You mean you aren't pissed off?"

"No, I'm sure she deserved it."

Mary Margaret was relieved. "I was sure I was going to mess everything up, cause problems for you with your son."

He went over to the chair where she sat and took her chin, lifting her face to him. "It would take more than telling Kathy how the cow ate the cabbage to do that. Besides, Kathy may have learned a lesson. Toward the end of our conversation, when she was being conciliatory, she actually asked me to apologize to you."

"Really? Or are you just making that up?"

"No, it's the truth."

"Then everything's all right?"

"It's fine." He took a deep breath. "At least I hope it is. Kathy never did tell me why she called. She said her boyfriend has gone back to South America and she wanted to see me in Berkeley in a few days. She insisted we had to talk face-to-face."

"Maybe she sent her boyfriend packing and has had second thoughts about divorcing you," Mary Margaret said. "Maybe she wants a reconciliation. That would explain why she got upset with me. She was jealous to think you were with somebody else."

"No, that's not Kathy's style."

She studied him, trying to read his thoughts. A man's eyes seldom lied when he was talking to one woman about his feelings for another. "What makes you so sure she's not interested?"

Dane sat in the sofa across from her. "I was married to

the woman for several years," he explained. "Kathy's not one to play games, at least not that kind."

Mary Margaret decided she believed him. But the real question was whether he was right. Men could be very naive when it came to women's true motivations.

"How do *you* feel about it?" she asked.

"What do you mean?"

"What if she surprises you...says she's thought it over and realizes that leaving you was the wrong thing to do and now she wants another chance?"

"It won't happen, Mary Margaret, trust me."

"But say you're wrong," she insisted.

Dane rubbed his chin. "I'd say it was too little, too late."

"Why, because you're bitter?"

"No, because it's over. We don't belong together. To her credit, she figured it out before I did. That relationship is definitely history."

"You loved her once."

"And you loved Anthony once," he replied.

"No, I didn't. Not for one minute. I married on an impulse because I was confused and probably feeling self-destructive."

"Well, be that as it may," Dane said, "I'm older, wiser and maybe a different man now. I'm positive Kathy feels the same."

Mary Margaret studied him, deciding he meant it. He could still be wrong, but she didn't detect evidence of deception, even self-deception. "I'm glad for you," she said.

Dane gave her a little smile. "I'm glad, too. For everybody's sake."

She could tell by the look on his face he was thinking of her, not Kathy. Oddly, she found that disconcerting and sensed things might be moving too quickly, and in a direction she wasn't sure she wanted to go.

"Dane," she said, craving relief, "it's late. I have to get home."

"I was afraid that's what you were going to say next."

"My bag's packed and by the door."

He glanced over at it. "So it is," he said, his voice cheerless. "So it is."

Placerville, California

The waitress had refilled Mary Margaret's ice-tea glass a
second time. The rest of the dishes had already been cleared.
Dane silently watched her, his heart sad. She was staring out
the big glass window at the cars passing on the highway,
reflecting, distracted, unaware of his observation. She'd been
like this since they'd left Laurel.

"I'm trying to decide if you're thinking about that conversation we had last night about *Siddhartha,* or if you're still
brooding about Kathy," he finally said, hoping to draw her
out.

Mary Margaret looked at him, so lost in her thoughts it
took a moment or two for her to fully comprehend. "Huh?
Oh," she said then, understanding. "Neither, really. I thought
of something else we can do about the case, but you've sacrificed so much already, I hate to ask more of you."

Dane was embarrassed. Of course she was thinking about
her father. "What is it?"

The waitress happened by. He asked for the check.

"This is the town where Donna Lee's mother lives," she
said. "Remember, Agnes McBain said Loretta had remarried
and moved to Placerville?"

"Yeah, I remember."

"Do you think it would be worthwhile talking to her?"

"Do you?"

"I don't know," Mary Margaret said. "But it would probably be a hassle trying to find her. I have no idea what her
address is."

"Do you remember her married name?"

"It's Casagrande," Mary Margaret said. "I think his first
name was Richard."

"You've got quite a memory."

"I can hardly forget Casagrande. It was my married name,
too."

"Oh, yeah. Do you suppose Loretta's husband is any re-
lation?"

"I doubt it. The name's not uncommon. Anyway, Anthony's family's all in Texas."

"I don't suppose it matters, either way."

"No," Mary Margaret said. "What bothers me is how Loretta is likely to react to a visit. She was very bitter about Donna Lee."

"Who could blame her?"

"Right. Obviously she hated my father. But she also hated Reverend Ragsdale and the Unitarian Church."

"In that case, it doesn't sound like she'd welcome either of us with open arms."

"Probably not. And I have no idea if there's anything she could tell us that would be useful," Mary Margaret said. "But driving up here, I realized that I never made my peace with her."

"Do you feel the need to?"

"I know I'm not responsible for my father, whether he did anything to Donna Lee or not," she said. "But I have some guilt over something that happened before Donna Lee was killed."

Mary Margaret seemed surprisingly anxious. He decided that whatever was bothering her was pretty serious, and that she was asking for help. "Want to talk about it?"

She looked relieved. "If you don't mind."

"No, of course not. Being a good listener is my job. But there's always room in my heart for my friends. Tell me what happened."

The waitress passed by, dropping the check on the corner of the table between them. Dane pulled it to him, but kept his eyes on Mary Margaret.

"It was shortly after that time I'd gone to Donna Lee's house," she began.

"The time you smoked her pot."

"Yes. Anyway, I ran into Mrs. Marshall at the stationery store. She told me she was glad I was Donna Lee's friend, because she didn't have many, except for boys who were trying to use her. She said I seemed like the kind of person she wanted Donna Lee to associate with. She asked me—almost begged me—to come back."

"That's nice."

"Yes, but I never did, Dane. In fact, I snubbed Donna Lee."

He could see she felt guilty about it and he felt sorry for her. "You were just a kid, and kids don't think about those things."

"I didn't, that's for sure. It never even entered my mind again until the trial. Then I started thinking about it. Loretta went to every court session, and so did I. We sat on opposite sides of the visitor's gallery, but I often looked at her and I found myself thinking about that conversation in the stationery store."

Dane was surprised to see Mary Margaret's eyes well. The next thing he knew, tears were running down her cheeks.

"I guess I've felt guiltier than I realized," she said, wiping her eyes. "If I had been nicer to Donna Lee, been her friend, maybe none of this would have happened. Maybe she wouldn't have been killed, maybe my father wouldn't be in prison."

He took her hands. "Mary Margaret, you can't blame yourself."

"Oh, I'm not really. But I feel badly about Loretta. I'd like to tell her I'm sorry about what happened. I never did that, and I've always regretted it."

"Let's try and look her up, then. And who knows, she may be able to add a piece to our puzzle."

Mary Margaret reacted as though a burden had been lifted. She slid out of the booth and drew herself up, squaring her shoulders with renewed energy. She'd changed into shorts and a tank top for the drive back and was a remarkable sight to behold. But Dane could no longer think of her as he had at first, when she was synonymous with her beauty. Now she was a person...a friend...the woman he was coming to care for very deeply.

They walked together to the cashier, Dane touching her waist as she drew the eyes of the men at the counter. She was obviously used to lots of attention, but he wasn't used to being with someone who got it. The result was a curious blend of pride and jealousy.

He gave the woman at the register the check and a twenty. As she gave him his change, he asked if there was a pay phone around. She told him there was one back by the rest rooms. Unfortunately there were a couple of teenage girls using the phone and it didn't look as though they'd be getting off anytime soon.

"I've got a cell phone in the car," he told her. "Let's use it."

Once they were back in the Camry, Dane got the phone from the glove compartment and gave it to Mary Margaret.

"Call information and they'll connect you directly," he said. Then he started the engine so that they could have air-conditioning.

As she spoke to the operator, he studied her mouth. A woman's lips told a lot about her. More even than her eyes. The mouth was the thing. It could be sensuous or contemptuous, sweet or profane, but rarely duplicitous. Mary Margaret's said good things about her.

"Damn," she said, turning off the power. "The number's unlisted. Well, I guess that's fate saying I need to bear my guilt a little longer."

Dane thought for a moment. "Agnes said that Loretta's husband was a contractor, didn't she?"

"Yes, I believe she said a plumbing contractor."

"We ought to be able to track them down that way. Come on," he said, putting the car in gear. "Let's go find some Yellow Pages."

They headed down Main Street until Dane spotted a plumbing company. There was nothing on the sign to connect it with Richard Casagrande, but he figured that someone inside would know the guy. He went inside and sure enough it was a friendly competitor. "Dick's shop is at his home out on the edge of town," the man told him. "On Coon Hollow Road." Dane got the exact address and directions from him.

"It's just as well I drop in on her," Mary Margaret said when he got back in the car. "If I call, she could hang up. This way I've got a chance of getting in a few words."

"You think she'll be hostile after all this time?"

"I guess I won't know until we get there."

Mary Margaret was nervous, but she was also determined. The importance of talking to Loretta had been taking on greater and greater proportions. Maybe it had been buried in her subconscious all these years and was just now finding its way out.

Coon Hollow Road branched off of Highway 49 at the edge of town. They didn't follow it far before they came to the Casagrande place, a large white house close to the road. Behind it, they could see a shop and other outbuildings. Dane pulled into the driveway and stopped.

"Do you want to go up alone," he asked. "Or do you want me to go with you?"

"My instincts tell me this is best handled one-on-one," she replied.

"All right, I'll wait here."

She took a fortifying breath. "In addition to making my peace with her, I'll find out if she has any idea who Benny might be."

"Good idea."

Mary Margaret looked at him and had second thoughts about going in alone. Peering into his eyes, she wanted to tell him how good it felt to be with him, but she'd confused him enough already. She got out of the car and headed toward the house.

There were a dozen steps leading up to the porch. Mary Margaret climbed them slowly, her heart picking up its beat. She knew it was possible Loretta would scream at her. If she did, Mary Margaret told herself it would simply be something that had to be done. It was better she know how the woman felt than be in the dark.

Reaching the porch, she noticed a bicycle leaning against the railing. It had never occurred to her that Loretta might have had more children. Then she realized the oldest a child by her second husband could be was six or seven, and probably younger than that. A stepchild perhaps?

Mary Margaret knocked. The door opened. A boy of about twelve in baggy shorts and with a baseball cap on backward stood looking at her.

"Yeah?"

"Is Loretta home?" she asked.

He turned toward the cool interior and, without answering, called, "Ma, it's somebody for you. A lady."

Moments later Loretta Casagrande appeared. Her dark hair

was shorter. She was heavier, but she had the same long face and round, deep-set eyes as Donna Lee. She was barefoot, wearing plaid shorts and a plain white blouse. Loretta stared at her, an awareness slowly building.

"Loretta," she said, her dry throat producing little more than a whisper. "I'm Mary Margaret Duggan."

The woman clasped both hands to her mouth. "M-my God," she finally stammered.

"I'm sorry to barge in on you," Mary Margaret ventured, "but I was passing through and felt a need to talk to you. It's long overdue."

Loretta thumped her chest with her hand. Mary Margaret didn't know if the door was about to be slammed in her face or if she would be invited in. "Sorry, it's taking me a minute to get over the shock, but come in," the woman said. "Please."

Mary Margaret let out an inaudible sigh and stepped into the cool interior. The large front room was littered enough to prove it was well lived in. Two children sat on the sofa—the boy she'd seen earlier and a little girl of about four or five. They were watching television.

"This is my stepson, Brett," Loretta said. "And my daughter, Cindy."

"Hi, kids," Mary Margaret said.

"Brett, why don't you take Cindy upstairs and watch the TV in your dad's and my room?"

"Oh, Ma," the boy groaned. "Do I have to?"

"I'd appreciate it."

"Can we lay on the bed?"

Loretta didn't look very happy. "Well, this once," she said. "But be sure and take off your shoes."

"All right. Come on, Cindy," the boy said, getting up.

"No, I don't want to," the little girl protested, folding her arms over her chest in a defiant pose. "I want a snack."

"Cindy," Loretta said firmly, "you can have your snack later. Now run on upstairs."

To punctuate the statement, she went over and turned off the TV. The children offered no more resistance, running from the room. Loretta gave Mary Margaret an embarrassed smile and picked up a couple of the kids' books from the sofa, then folded part of a newspaper that was open on the coffee table.

"You'll have to excuse my housekeeping," Loretta said, "but two children in the summer when there's no school are a lot to handle. And I can only devote myself to it part-time because I also keep the books for my husband's business." She pointed to the adjoining dining room that was set up as an office.

Mary Margaret could see a computer running and file cabinets with open drawers, and ledgers stacked on the desk. "I'm sure you don't relish my intrusion," she said, "but I won't take much of your time."

"No, I don't mind at all," Loretta said. "Really." She gestured toward the sofa. "Please sit down."

Mary Margaret sat at one end, Loretta at the other. It was awkward looking at each other sideways, they both did a half turn so that they were practically facing each other.

"So, where are you living now and what are you doing?" Loretta said, as though Mary Margaret were just any old person from her past.

"I'm in Reno," she said simply. She wanted to avoid saying she was a showgirl, because it always led to a long discussion.

"Oh," Loretta said. "Of course you wouldn't stay in Laurel. I couldn't."

Mary Margaret shook her head. She began formulating her next speech. As she did, all the painful memories flooded her mind. "Loretta," she said, her voice husky with emotion, "I never told you how awful I felt about what happened to Donna Lee." She choked back a sob. "It was a terrible, terrible thing and I feel so badly about it still."

Tears shimmered in her eyes and Loretta's got misty, too. "I say that sincerely," Mary Margaret went on, "though I know with every fiber of my being that my father was not the one who killed her." She wiped her nose with the back of her hand. "I'm sure it doesn't matter to you what I believe, but I—I just wanted to…"

Mary Margaret couldn't help herself. She broke into sobs and she pressed her hands to her face. Loretta got up and brought a box of tissue from the top of the TV set. Carrying it back, she put the box on the cushion between them.

"Here," she said, wiping her own eyes with a tissue. "Take one."

Mary Margaret dabbed her eyes, then blew her nose. "Sorry."

"Mary Margaret," Loretta said, "I'm past the bitterness. And though I still love Donna Lee and think of her often, my life in Laurel is over."

Mary Margaret took an uneven breath and cleared her throat. "I don't mean to bring things back and cause you pain," she said, "but there's something I did I'll always regret, and that's not being a friend to Donna Lee."

Loretta seemed perplexed.

"Don't you remember that time I saw you in the stationery store and you asked me to be Donna Lee's friend?"

The furrows on Loretta's narrow forehead deepened. "*I* asked you to be her friend?"

Mary Margaret couldn't believe it. "Don't you remember? It wasn't long after my father and I moved to Laurel."

Loretta shook her head. "I'm sorry, Mary Margaret, but I don't."

Mary Margaret let out a sigh—part relief and part disbelief. "Lord, imagine all the grief I could have spared myself."

"I'm sorry I don't remember, but Donna Lee was such a problem, and I talked to so many people about her," Loretta said.

Mary Margaret was incredulous. "Well, it just goes to show how much suffering is in a person's head, doesn't it? All this time I was sure I'd hurt you and Donna Lee terribly by letting you down."

"I try not to dwell on painful memories," Loretta said thoughtfully. "You shouldn't, either."

It was a Buddha-like comment, though Mary Margaret was sure Loretta would have had no idea of that. Dane, it seemed, had altered her awareness in an important way. "I know you're right, Loretta," she said, "and I appreciate you saying it." Mary Margaret realized she had an opportunity and decided to take advantage of it. "Would it be too painful if I ask you some questions about the case?" she asked. "You see, there's been new evidence pointing to my father's innocence. A friend and I are trying to get Dad's case reopened."

"I'll talk about it," Loretta said, "but there was so little I knew, even at the time. The police were rather disgusted because I couldn't tell them a thing about Donna Lee's secret life. Maybe I was sticking my head in the sand." An awareness came over her. "Look at me, I'm a terrible hostess. Can I get you something cool to drink? Ice tea? Lemonade? I think we have some soft drinks if the kids haven't drunk them all up."

"No thanks. I had something when I got to town."

"Okay, what is it you want to know?"

Mary Margaret pressed her hands together prayerfully as she gathered her thoughts. "Does the name Benny mean anything to you?"

Loretta thought for a moment, then shook her head. "No, I can't say that it does."

Mary Margaret felt herself deflate. "In connection with Theo Bledsoe, maybe?

"Ugh, her. What an awful woman."

"You didn't like her?"

"What was to like?" Loretta said. "In the six or seven years I lived in that house, she only spoke to me once and that was when she called to complain about Donna Lee."

"Oh? What did she say?"

"It was a week or two before…Donna Lee was killed," Loretta said, her voice faltering. "She told me Donna Lee was parading around naked in the backyard and that I better put a stop to it or else."

"Or else what?"

"I don't remember her exact words, but it was a vague threat. Maybe I didn't take it as seriously as I should have."

"How did you respond?" Mary Margaret asked.

"I think I told her not to look if it bothered her. Her tone was so nasty I had no sympathy for her at all. But I did ask Donna Lee about it. She told me that Theo had yelled at her when she was sunbathing. I asked if she'd had her suit on and she said she had, though she might have taken the top off so she wouldn't have stripes. I dismissed the incident as the ranting of a prudish old woman." Loretta sighed. "But then I guess I was too permissive. Donna Lee pretty much did what she wanted."

"Back to Benny," Mary Margaret said. "Do you think he might have been Theo's dog?"

"Lord, with that woman, who knows? Frankly, I paid as little attention to her and that house as I could. Donna Lee was intrigued by her, though, probably just because she wanted to annoy her."

"What do you mean?"

"It was just a silly childish thing."

"What was?" Mary Margaret insisted.

Loretta shifted uncomfortably. "Donna Lee claimed the house, the Bledsoes' house, was haunted and that Theo was some kind of witch."

Mary Margaret's brows rose. "Why would she say that?"

"It was so silly, I'm embarrassed to mention it."

"No, please tell me."

"Well," Loretta began, "I wouldn't let Donna Lee smoke in the house so she used to go outside. She'd tell me that at night she often heard strange sounds coming from the Bledsoe place. They were cries and moans, whining."

"Maybe it was Theo's dog."

"I don't know. I didn't hear the sounds. Donna Lee was such a storyteller that I dismissed most of what she said."

"What else did she say?" Mary Margaret asked.

"One night, she claimed to see a ghost, or I guess the hand of a ghost is more accurate."

"The hand of a ghost?"

"Yes, she said she was walking back and forth along our driveway, smoking. It was a hot night and she just had on this little teddy. I didn't like her going out dressed that way, but Donna Lee was headstrong. Anyway, she said she heard that same moaning sound she'd heard before, and she looked over and saw this hand protruding between the curtains in the second story window of the Bledsoes'. She said the palm was pressed flat against the glass."

Mary Margaret shivered. "How strange."

"I didn't think much of it. Donna Lee was always making up wild stories."

"Was there anything else about Theo Bledsoe you can tell me, Loretta?"

The woman shook her head. "Not that I recall."

Mary Margaret reflected. "Forgive me for bringing up a sore subject, but what about Reverend Ragsdale? What was your sense of his relationship with Donna Lee?"

"I was disappointed. I had high hopes that getting her into the church youth group might straighten her out, but if anything she seemed to get worse."

"What do you mean?"

"More independent. Toward the end, I couldn't do a thing with her. She kept telling me she was a woman and could live her life any way she wanted."

"Do you think Reverend Ragsdale had anything to do with it?"

"Well, he didn't help, let me put it that way," Loretta said. "He called me once toward the end of the school year and asked if I minded if he counseled Donna Lee. I gave my permission, but I never got any feedback. I wasn't even sure if Donna Lee kept her appointments with him."

Mary Margaret could see Loretta was still either oblivious to what had gone on or she'd repressed it. "I'd like to ask you something else, Loretta," she said. "It may be painful, but I've got to know." She drew a fortifying breath. "Did Donna Lee ever mention my father?"

Loretta shook her head without hesitation. "No. Not once."

"Do you know of any reason why he would have killed her?"

Again Loretta shook her head. "Maybe it shows my failing as a mother that I didn't have a better handle on my child's life, but the fact was, I simply couldn't control her." Her eyes began to fill again and she reached for a tissue. "The police insisted I had to know something, but I didn't. The prosecutor grilled me at length about Donna Lee and your father. All I was able to do was identify the knife used to stab her as one of my kitchen knives." Loretta dabbed her eyes. "I felt like such a failure." She blew her nose. "That's why I'm trying so hard with the two I have now. But believe me, it helps to have a father in the picture."

Mary Margaret felt compassion for the woman. So many people had suffered and continued to suffer. She reached over and took Loretta's hand.

"You weren't a failure, Loretta. That time you talked to me in the stationery store I could tell you cared about Donna Lee and wanted what was best for her."

Loretta wiped her eyes again. "That's really sweet of you to say so."

The front door opened just then and a slender man in a gray work shirt and pants appeared. "Loretta," he called before he saw them, "who's the guy in the...car out front..." His voice faded when he saw Mary Margaret.

"That's my friend," Mary Margaret said.

The man, who she assumed to be Richard Casagrande, closed the door and moved his eyes back and forth between them, looking baffled.

"Richard," Loretta said, getting up, "this is Mary Margaret Duggan, a friend I knew in Laurel."

He approached the sofa, wiping his hand on the front of his shirt. Mary Margaret stood, offering her hand.

"Hello, Mr. Casagrande."

"Nice to know you." He didn't leer, but it was apparent he didn't expect to walk into his house and see anyone like her. He smiled at his wife. "What's going on, honey?"

"I was passing through and just stopped by to say hello. I'm sure Dane's roasting out there, so I'd better go," Mary Margaret said.

"Have him come in," Loretta said. "I'll fix us all some ice tea. Wouldn't you like a cold drink, Richard?"

"No, really," Mary Margaret insisted, "I've got to get back to Reno. I'm scheduled to work tonight." She headed for the door, smiling at Loretta's husband as she moved past him. Her hand on the doorknob, she turned to face Loretta, who'd followed her. "Thanks for talking to me," she said. "And I'm so glad you're doing well."

"I appreciate the visit," Loretta said. "I truly do."

Mary Margaret gave her a hug and then she left. Her eyes shimmered as she hurried down the stairs. Poor Dane looked as though he was on the verge of heatstroke when she got to the car. All the windows were down and he was fanning himself with a road map.

"Sorry," she said, climbing in. "You must be dying."

"I've been cooler," he said, starting the engine. He raised all the windows and the cool air was soon flowing over them. "So, how'd it go?"

Mary Margaret thought for a moment, then said, "I think I learned something about suffering."

"Oh?"

"Let's just say some practical experience confirming some of the things you said about Buddha last night."

Reno, Nevada

As they came down out of the mountains, the late-afternoon sun reflected off the glass of the high-rises downtown. Dane did not feel good about returning to Reno. He sensed the coming of a *Casablanca*-type ending to what had once been a promising relationship. But then, maybe he'd been deluding himself. Maybe there'd never been a promise—only titillation. True, he'd gotten to know the person, the real woman, but there was also reality to contend with, the sort of reality Kathy had injected with her call.

"As I see it, we've got three things to follow up on," he'd told Mary Margaret earlier when they'd discussed what to do next. "One is to talk to Stephen Ragsdale's daughter about his diaries. The second is to talk to Ted Gotchall, the retired detective who handled the murder case. The last is for me to learn what I can about Theo Bledsoe from Reverend Warren at the Fresno church. Can you think of anything else?"

"Not unless you want to try to interview the ghost."

She'd told him about her conversation with Loretta, and they'd had a good laugh. "That's one for a medium, not a minister," he'd replied.

After a minute, he added, "That reminds me, I don't think I told you that Claudia said she'd heard Theo mention the name Benny once, though she had no idea who Theo was referring to."

"Oh, really?"

"We know Theo was nuts, so it might not be significant."

"Maybe Benny's a ghost," Mary Margaret said.

"Maybe so, but it'd be hard to sell to a jury."

"And hard to get him to testify," she'd added.

They'd agreed on that, but he still wasn't sure if they would continue as Nick and Nora Charles, or if their joint escapade in the world of crime detection had come to an end. And so, he'd come right out and asked her if she was game for another round.

"You've already volunteered a bunch of your time, Dane," she'd replied, "and I hate to take advantage of your generosity any more than I have, especially considering you've got Kathy to contend with."

"Kathy's not an issue. The point is I'm willing to keep after this thing, if you are."

"The question is when I can do it," Mary Margaret had replied. "Getting time off in my line of work isn't easy. And I can't afford to lose my job."

"How about we run down to the Bay Area next week on your day off?"

"Perhaps," she'd said, but she seemed hesitant.

He wasn't sure if it was out of fear of imposing or out of fear of him. "Why don't I give you a call later in the week and we'll discuss it," he'd suggested, offering her a face-saving way out.

Mary Margaret had seemed happy to get off the hook. "Good idea."

The rest of the way to Reno there'd been a little small talk and a lot of long silences. Dane kept trying out speeches in his mind, never coming up with one he felt comfortable with. The harsh reality was, he wanted to see her again, but finding a way to say so wasn't easy. The words he could make himself utter, but putting them in a way that would get the desired result was the challenge.

As they passed the downtown exits, he knew time was running short. Mary Margaret had already gotten a little antsy. She didn't like having to rush over to the casino. That meant dinner was not in the cards. The way it was playing out, he'd be dropping her off, then turning around and heading right back to California.

In his frustration, Dane had toyed with the idea of staying over and taking in her show again, but he realized it would be worse than torture. No, the real telling moment would come when he called her later in the week.

"You know," she said, filling the silence, "in spite of what we've been through, it's been enjoyable—the getting-to-know-you part, anyway."

Dane's flagging hopes took an upward turn. "Really?"

"Really."

"I've enjoyed it, too," he said.

"That's good."

"I hope the fact that I developed a little crush on you wasn't too upsetting," he ventured, amazed that he'd actually said it.

"A crush?"

"It's a little premature to call it true love," he said with a good-natured laugh. "I've always felt that the important things about a person are deep inside and it takes a while to uncover them."

She said nothing.

"You're really pretty," he said, his mouth again off and running, "but I think the thing I like best about you is that you wanted to read *Siddhartha* and talk to me about it."

"That's not so unusual, is it? I thought it was an interesting book, different…and I don't know a thing about Buddhism."

"That's what I mean."

"Well, I'm no intellectual," she protested.

"I think you're very intelligent."

"You're trying to flatter me, aren't you?" she said.

"Yes, I suppose I am. But it's sincere."

She looked troubled. "Well, don't do it. Please."

"I guess I'm trying a little too hard, aren't I?"

She didn't say yes and she didn't say no, which he took as confirmation. They'd gone a ways down Highway 395 and she directed him off at the South Virginia Street exit. He felt the last grains of sand in the hourglass dropping beneath his feet. He saw hints of grim resolution on her face. It reminded him of a high-school girl dreading an impending good-night kiss.

Once on South Virginia they went the few blocks to the

entrance of the Desert Rest Mobile Home Park. He moved into the left-turn lane, his blinker like a warning light at mission control. Ten...nine...eight...seven. The Camry glided under the arched entryway. He realized his run of the dice was coming to an end.

Dane turned into Date Palm Lane. They rolled to a stop in front of Janine Russo's double-wide. He turned off the engine. Mary Margaret glanced at him nervously.

"I'll get your bag," he said.

"You don't have to. I can get it," she said.

But he'd already opened the door. It was easier to say goodbye standing up. He got her overnight case from the back and walked around the car, where she stood waiting, her hands clasped in front of her. He forbade himself to look at her legs though he wanted to badly. She took the case from his hand. Her pretty smile was self-conscious and apprehensive.

"It's been fun," he said, thrusting his hand toward her.

Mary Margaret took it, relieved. "Thank you, Dane. For everything."

He held her hand a bit longer than was required, before letting go. "I'll call," he said. "And if for some reason we don't manage to get together, I'll keep you posted on whatever turns up in your father's case."

"Great. I'd appreciate it."

He nodded. He smiled. He did everything but grab her and kiss her, which was what he wanted to do. Mary Margaret headed for the trailer. He allowed himself one last, long, languorous appraisal of her backside.

But then she stopped suddenly and turned on her heel. Marching back, she came right up to him, put her hand behind his neck, pulled his face down and kissed him firmly on the mouth. "Coward," she hissed, then turned again and went to the house.

Dane's heart tripped nicely. What could be better than *her* kissing *him?* He wanted to take it as a signal that she didn't consider the relationship at an end. It was a small thing, maybe, but he was happy.

He went around and got in the car. Glancing toward the house, he saw her at the door, fumbling with her keys, those long legs of hers sheer poetry. Sighing, he turned the ignition key and, when the engine fired, he put the transmission in gear. God, he said to himself as she disappeared inside, maybe there was hope after all!

Mary Margaret's heart was racing as she pushed the door open and stepped inside. She'd just shut the door when something large bumped up against her from behind and a hand clamped over her mouth. The *thing* surrounded her, a tentacled arm clamped over her breasts, the hot, moist body radiating stench. There was no scream in her, only terror, panic, suffocation. She couldn't breathe and what little struggle there was in her was futile. It—*he* was so large and strong.

Deep within her she heard a voice telling her she was going to die. And another voice saying, but what can I do? There must be something, the voice reasoned. She couldn't bite, she couldn't scratch. She could barely move her elbows. No violent blows to the solar plexis possible there. Then she remembered her feet. Her legs were totally free so she lifted her knee as high as she could and brought the heel of her sandal down as violently as she could on his foot.

The man screamed with pain, releasing his grip just enough that she managed to squirm free. She practically leaped to the door, but before she could pull it open, a fist the size of a brick caught her on the side of the head, knocking her against the wall and buckling her knees. But before she hit the floor, he was on her, a heavy, wet, smelly ape, smothering her again.

Lifting her to her feet by the torso, he grabbed her hair with his free hand, yanking it back so hard that all she could see was the ceiling. "Listen, you little bitch," he snarled in her ringing ear. "Just for that you're gettin' it in the ass, the mouth and any other goddamn place I can find to put it."

Mary Margaret started to black out, but drifted into consciousness again. Her head throbbed. She knew then she was defeated. Sobs heaved from her throat like vomit, but the man ignored her. He was peering out the window, grumbling, his rancid tobacco breath stinging her nose. She was nothing but a huge rag doll, limp in his arms. Even though she was only half-conscious, she knew it. And so did he.

Dane jammed the nozzle into the mouth of his fuel tank and peered back up the street toward the Desert Rest Mobile Home Park. What, exactly, had she meant when she'd called him a coward? That he'd been afraid to kiss her? Or that he'd been afraid to make her see him again? No, *demand* that she see him again.

He hated self-doubt. It was crippling. But this falling-in-love business was even more crippling; it could confuse the most levelheaded of men. He *had* realized a victory of sorts, though. *She* had kissed *him* when they said goodbye!

As he alternately questioned and congratulated himself, he saw a vehicle come sailing out of the Desert Rest onto Virginia Street, weaving as it headed his way. It seemed in an awfully big rush, but it wasn't until it roared past the service station that Dane realized it was a blue van, the same kind of blue van that had followed them back in Laurel.

The horrible certainty hit him that they were fleeing for a reason and the reason was Mary Margaret. Had she spotted the van and called the police? Or— A god-awful terror went through him like a blade...had she not seen it in time?

Dane had no idea if she was in the van, but he knew he couldn't go back to the park to find out. The van went around the corner, disappearing from sight. Pulling the nozzle from the car, he threw it on the ground. Ignoring the cap to the gas tank, which was sitting on the roof of the Camry, he ran to the driver's side and, as he pulled the door open, hollered to the startled woman at the next pump to tell them he'd be back.

The Camry raced into the street, barely missing a passing UPS truck. Dane jammed the accelerator to the floor, narrowly avoiding a collision with a car going his way. He made a right turn from the center lane, cutting off two other vehicles. There was a cacophony of horns.

The freeway entrance was half a block over, but the van was out of sight by the time he got there. Which way did they go? North or south? The odds were fifty-fifty.

Dane uttered his first desperate plea to God since the birth of his son. The Divinity or Mary Margaret or Father Muncey's spirit shouted *south* and he pulled hard on the steering wheel, swinging to the right. The Camry sped along the southbound ramp.

Her head throbbed, but the most immediate discomfort was in her neck where clawlike fingers dug into her flesh, pinning her facedown into the mattress. The next worse thing was the knee pressing into her kidneys. She could only breathe enough to sob.

She hadn't yet seen the monster's face, but the reek of his body and foul tobacco breath would be burned into her brain forever. The only words he'd uttered since dragging her into the van were, "You so much as turn your head and I'll kill you." Mary Margaret already felt half-dead.

For some reason, she was aware of the thumping of the tires every time the van went over the lane dividers. She assumed they were on the freeway. It occurred to her she should try to remember that, in case she lived to tell the police what they'd done to her.

She didn't know how many of them there were, but there had to be one other at least, the driver. Though the monster pinning her to the bed was evil incarnate, she had a sense that the man driving was at least human enough to be afraid. She could hear him muttering under his breath, "Jesus Christ, Jesus Christ, Jesus Christ," over and over and over again.

The monster, who could be no one but Rut Coleman, lowered his mouth to her ear and spoke in a low, raspy voice. "Listen, sweetheart, I'm going to let go of you, but if you want to keep that pretty face in one piece you won't move a fuckin' inch. Understand?"

Mary Margaret nodded. He let go of her then and she weighed the pros and cons of spinning around to get a look at him. It would enable her to positively identify him in court, but it could also get her killed. She knew now she was beyond the point of resistance. That was for alleys and parks, where there was a chance of attracting help. She'd learned the hard way that she couldn't beat him off. No, she decided, she would turn off her mind for the duration.

But then she got a sudden jolt when something was abruptly yanked over her head. Her eyes flew open, but the sack—it felt like a pillowcase—was being gathered at her neck. She heard the sound of tape being pulled from a roll and the next thing she knew it was being wrapped around her neck, cinching the pillowcase at her throat. Then, grabbing her by the shoulders, Coleman flopped her onto her back. He pressed his knee into her abdomen to keep her from moving as he wrapped something—rope, she thought—around first one wrist, then the other.

As he secured her hands, one to each side of the van, panic rose through the numbness of her brain. She began gasping for air, thinking she'd suffocate. But after a minute she realized she could suck oxygen through the cloth. And though it was dark, she could see enough through the pillowcase to make out the contours of Coleman's body. Her mind clearer now, she began trembling with fear, but she willed herself not to panic, telling herself it was the best way to survive.

In the front, the "Jesus Christs" were getting louder and more insistent. She thought of her Catholic childhood and began muttering Hail Marys.

Coleman was kneeling close to her. She could still smell him despite the pillowcase. But then, when she heard the sound of a metallic click, she tensed. It was a knife. She knew it was a knife. When he grabbed the neck of her tank top and pulled it taut, she let out an involuntary scream. But the blade didn't pierce her skin, it slit open her shirt. Again she had to fight back panic. Especially when he grabbed her bra, lifting the band and sawing on it until the blade cut through and he was able to pull the cups away from her breasts.

"I'll be damned if you don't got sweet tits," he muttered, pinching her nipples and laughing.

Mary Margaret trembled violently. She cried, helpless in her misery as he put his hand between her legs and began rubbing. "Think I can get you wet, sweetheart?" he asked, still laughing.

"No," she said, even as she was aware she shouldn't speak.

"Well, you'd better believe I will. You're going to be dripping before I'm done."

Deep sobs racked her body then and she lost it, pleading for him to leave her alone. It only made him rub her all the harder.

"We ain't going to kill her," the man in front shouted.

"Shut the fuck up!" Coleman screamed at him.

"Nobody gets killed," the man insisted. "I'm not going to the goddamn gas chamber just so you can get laid."

"Shut your mouth and drive the goddamn car, you ignorant piece of shit! And get us off the fucking highway."

The anger, the evil in the man, frightened her even more than what he was doing to her. Would he kill her? Worse, did she want to live?

"South on 395," Dane shouted into the cell phone. "That's all I can say for sure!"

"Try to stay calm, sir," the dispatcher said. "Give me some landmarks. Have you come to Washoe Lake yet? It'll be off to your left."

"No, I haven't seen a lake."

"How about the Virginia City turnoff? Highways 341 or 17?"

"I haven't noticed any signs, but I'm not sure. I was going ninety trying to catch them."

"But you have the van in sight?"

"Yes, it's fifty yards ahead."

Dane was breathing heavily. His heart was pounding so hard it hurt. But at least he'd found them!

"All right," the dispatcher said. "Keep them in sight, but don't get too close. We've got units on the way."

Units on the way, he thought. Yeah, but from where? Vegas? If Mary Margaret was in that van, God only knew what was happening to her. He hadn't told the police he wasn't sure she'd been kidnapped. And if it turned out she wasn't, he'd look like a damn fool. But it was a chance he was willing to take.

For the first couple of minutes after he'd gotten on the freeway, he thought he'd guessed wrong, or that they'd already exited, but when he'd passed a semitrailer and seen the blue van sailing along, he'd almost cried for joy. The trouble was, the sun had set and twilight was coming. Some vehicles already had on their lights. Once darkness fell, the van would be harder to follow. Lord, surely the police would be here before then.

The van was cruising at seventy and Dane was keeping pace. He knew the police considered this helpful, but he wanted to do more. He was mulling over his options when he passed a road sign for the Virginia City turnoff.

"Hello," he said into the phone. "Are you there?"

"Yes, sir," the dispatcher said. "I'm with you."

"We're coming to the Virginia City turnoff. And it looks like the van is exiting," Dane said. "He's got his blinker on."

"Stay with him, sir, but keep your distance."

At the foot of the off-ramp the van made a left turn and crossed under the freeway overpass. Dane followed. "East on 17," he said into the telephone. "Toward Virginia City."

"Roger that."

Dane pulled a little closer. He didn't like this, not knowing what was happening to her. He wondered if it was better to let Coleman know he was there. It might at least divert his attention from Mary Margaret—assuming she was in the van. God, he hoped she wasn't. He wanted very badly to come out of this looking like a horse's ass.

"All right, sir, do you hear me?" the dispatcher said.

"Yes."

"We've got a sheriff's deputy headed west on 17 about twelve miles from your present location. He's going to try to stop the van. When you see that happen, stop immediately and stay clear. The nearest state police unit is about ten minutes south on 395. He'll be behind you. Do you copy?"

"Yes, I do."

Dane didn't like being treated like a child, but he couldn't fault their intentions. Still, he felt there had to be something constructive he could do.

They'd gone about half a mile when the left blinker of the van went on and they made a turn onto a side road.

"Hold on," Dane said into the phone. "They're turning, making a left."

"Where?"

"It's the first road we've come to, I think. Yep, they're headed north."

"Can you see a street sign?"

Dane made the turn, following the van. "No."

"Landmarks?"

"Housing development on the right."

"That must be Miraloma Road," the dispatcher said. "Hold on."

Dane was losing patience. This was taking too long. This meant both the sheriff's patrol and the state police unit were behind him now. "What do you have that's ahead?" he asked.

"Checking."

Dane agonized. He was twenty or thirty yards behind the van now and wanting to ram it. Damn.

"All right, sir," the dispatcher said, coming back on the line. "Our nearest units to the north are on Interstate 80. Eastbound at Clark. And I've got municipal units in Sparks."

"How far away's that?"

"Twenty miles."

"Jesus."

"The road you're on goes through rugged terrain, so be careful and keep your distance. We've got air units on the way."

Dane figured this could drag on forever. He didn't think Mary Margaret had that long. "I'm not waiting," he said. "I'm going to try to stop them."

"Sir, I wouldn't. It could be dangerous for the young lady as well as yourself. Let us handle it."

"You boys keep coming. I might need you," he said. Then he tossed the cell phone onto the seat next to him.

Mary Margaret tensed as he kneaded her breasts. He was squeezing hard and it hurt. She was stiff as a board, the muscles of her legs and stomach and back aching. Every time he touched her between the legs she felt she was going to be sick, but then she imagined herself choking on her own vomit. Intermittent sobs continued to rack her body, but they were also gasps for air.

"Fuck it," Coleman said, unfastening her belt. "Time to get down to business." He brusquely unzipped her shorts and began yanking on the waistband. "Lift your goddamn ass," he growled.

Mary Margaret complied but it wasn't her nature to be passive. Once when Anthony had hit her, she'd kicked him in the balls, which only made him hit her harder the second time, but afterward she was glad she'd done it. Reason told her with Rut Coleman it could be fatal. She wanted to hurt him anyway.

"Now that's more like it," he said, dragging her shorts down off her legs.

Mary Margaret held her breath, straining to see him through the pillowcase. She felt his hand as he pressed his fingers against her pubis. Again she thought she'd be sick.

"You know, watching you dance, I wondered what this would feel like. I bet it smells pretty good, too." She could see him lean over and press his face into her crotch. Bile rose in her throat and she fought it down. "Ah, baby," he said. "Aren't you sweet."

Then he sat up, bracing himself as the van made a sharp turn. The way they kept being thrown from side to side, they had to be in the mountains. He took off his shirt and moved between her legs. She tried hard to see, but it was getting so dark only the faintest outline was visible. His back was to the rear door of the van.

Mary Margaret pictured herself putting her foot in the middle of his chest and shoving him. She pictured the rear doors flying open and his body sailing out of the van, spattering on the pavement. Chances were the door wouldn't open, that he'd simply crash against it, but she couldn't resist trying. When he leaned forward and grabbed the waistband of her panties, she brought her feet up and shoved against his chest as hard as she could. Coleman went flying back, just as she'd envisioned, but the door didn't open. There was simply a crash, a stunned moment of silence, then a scream of anger.

"You goddamn bitch!"

The van negotiated a sharp turn, throwing Coleman against the side of the compartment. About the same time there was a blast of a car horn. Then another blast. It was coming from behind them.

"Jesus Christ," the driver shouted. "Oh, shit."

"What?" Coleman said. "What?"

"There's a goddamn car behind us. I think it's her boyfriend. The Camry."

The honking continued. Mary Margaret grew hopeful even as Coleman seemed to panic.

"What? What?" he kept saying.

"Jesus, it's him!" the other man lamented. "His lights are flashing!"

Coleman stumbled past her to the front of the van, which was swinging back and forth, making turns a little too fast, so the tires squealed. The honking continued.

"What the hell's he doing?" she heard Coleman ask.

There was fear in his voice and Mary Margaret was glad. She started yanking on the ropes, trying to free herself.

"Go faster!" Coleman shouted.

"I can't, Rut. I'm going as fast as I can!"

"Well, go faster anyway, dammit!"

There was a loud thud and Mary Margaret felt the van lurch forward.

"The bastard rammed us!" the driver cried.

Mary Margaret started crying, too. But for joy. She squirmed and rolled her head back and forth, trying to loosen the tape, but it was too well secured. "Dane," she started mumbling. "Oh, Dane."

There was another sharp jolt and the horn blasted again and again.

The men in front were yelling at each other and cursing.

Then she heard a different sound, an air horn, a terrifying blast coming from in front of them, followed by the hideous screech of tires, a violent crash and the whole world began spinning and tumbling and bumping as she was jerked from side to side, up and down by giant invisible hands.

Then all was still. There was a sudden, yawning silence. Nothing. The world had gone from chaos to tranquillity. For several moments she thought she was dead, but then she felt a terrible burning on her wrists where the ropes had torn her skin. And the back of her head hurt where it had banged the metal floor. The mattress was no longer beneath her, but was lying across her legs. Through the pillowcase she smelled dust and sage. Maybe they were all dead but her. Once again she began to cry, wailing like a child.

The guy in the dump truck looked dazed but, judging by the way his arms were wrapped around the steering wheel and his head rested on his forearms, Dane concluded he was all right. But that was not who he was concerned about. Dashing to the edge of the road, he peered down the slope where the van had disappeared.

The sun had long since dropped behind the mountains. The sky was a palette of vermilion and orange and violet and pink, giving off barely enough light to make out the contours of land. Half a mile below were the lights of a few homes scattered along a road that ran along the base of the mountain. Farther west, in the center of the valley, perhaps four or five miles away, he could see the string of headlights on 395 stretching north to Reno. But his attention was on the deep shadows of the mountainside where he searched until he finally spotted the crushed roof of the van, sitting in a shallow draw, perhaps two hundred feet below him. It was just emerging from a dust cloud that drifted slowly off to the south.

Dane plunged down the slope, following the path the tumbling van had taken, past flattened sage, torn shrubs and scarred slabs of sandstone. Finally, he scrambled over the hip of the little draw to the spot where the mangled vehicle rested, its crown dented, the windows shattered. His heart racing, he ran to the driver's side and peered through the smashed window. The crumpled, contorted body of a man lay bent unnaturally across the front seat. In the faint light he could see a dark streak of liquid issuing from the corner of his mouth. The way the head was twisted told him the man's neck had been broken. There was no other body in the cab. The door on the passenger side had been torn off.

Dane tried to see into the back of the van, but it was too

dark. Then he heard a sound. A whimpering sound, the sound of a woman crying.

"Mary Margaret?"

There was silence, then, "Dane...help me."

He tried to pull the door open, but the frame had been too badly twisted. He rushed to the rear and found one of the doors bowed, but ajar. He managed to free it. Dust still hung in the air, but he could see arms lashed to either side of the van. A head lifted from the floor. It was encased in a sack.

"Oh, my God," he murmured and scrambled inside.

He tore frantically at the tape as she wept, finally removing the pillowcase from her head. Her tear-streaked face was red, her eyes beseeching him from the darkness. He started to work on the knots binding her wrists.

"Are you all right?"

Through her crying she managed to tell him she was. When he finally had her free, she grabbed hold of his neck and clung to him like a terrified child. He'd been vaguely aware that she was naked, but it wasn't until he rubbed her back and felt her smooth skin under his palm that it fully hit him.

Sitting down beside her, he stroked her head and held her tight and told her she'd be all right. He didn't know if she'd been raped, but he did know she needed him and he gave her all the solace and comfort and protection he could.

After a few minutes she pulled her head back and looked into his eyes. "Where are they?" she said, as though she'd just remembered the cause of her agony.

"One guy's in the front seat, dead. I haven't seen anyone else."

She shivered violently, though the air was still quite warm. Then she clutched her arms over her breasts, shielding herself.

Dane quickly unbuttoned his shirt and put it on her. She sat shaking then, clutching it closed at the neck, still hunched over.

"My shorts and shoes are around here somewhere," she said vacantly, her brain obviously fuzzy.

Feeling around in the darkness, he found her shorts and one sandal. He was about to give up on the other, but finally located it in front. Moving with the deliberateness of a sleepwalker, she managed, with his assistance, to dress. Then he helped her out the back of the van. He had his arm around her to support her and she clung to his waist, glancing up at the starry sky. It was then they heard the first siren.

Mary Margaret lifted her face to him and said, "Dane, you saved my life."

He pulled into the little market back down on the Virginia City highway and got out of the Buick. Another siren sounded and he turned to see another state police car coming from 395. It turned on Miraloma Road and raced into the night, its emergency lights flashing. Shaking his head, he went to the pay phone and dialed the number on the slip of paper he'd taken from his wallet. He waited.

"Yes?" came the familiar deep voice.

"Well, you won't believe what I've just seen," he said.

"Pray, what have you seen?" the voice intoned.

"Barrett brought the girl back to Nevada, like I figured, drops her off at her place then goes to get gas. I figure I'm going to be following him back to Laurel, but no, all of a sudden the S.O.B. jumps in his car—doesn't pay for the gas or anything—and goes racing off like it's a Hollywood movie or something. Anyway, I follow him and turns out he's chasing a van. I don't know what the hell's going on, but I'm chasing Barrett, who's chasing the van.

"Finally, we get on this mountain road and the van gets hit by a dump truck and goes down the side of the mountain. I'm just coming around this curve when it happens."

"And Barrett?"

"He avoids the collision, but goes running down the mountain after the van."

"Curious."

"Before long I hear sirens and the cops start coming from all directions, so I skedaddle. This is maybe half an hour ago. Beats me what was going on."

"The girl was probably in the van," the voice said dryly.

"You think?"

"What else?"

"Never occurred to me," he said.

"That's why I don't pay you to think."

He was annoyed. "Fine. So what now? What I've been doing doesn't seem to be working."

"Turn the screws up a notch. Let him know it's his last chance."

"Okay, fine," he said. "One more turn of the screw, but I'm telling you right now, this guy doesn't listen. On their way up here, he and the girl stopped to see somebody in Placerville. She went inside. I don't know if it was her old cheerleader friend or something to do with Jimmy Duggan, but the sign said Casagrande Plumbing."

"I'll check into it. You keep your eye on Barrett."

"Right, I will. But you might as well know I'm almost at the end of the line. I'll jab him in the ass one more time, but if you decide you want to get really serious with him, you'll have to find yourself a heavy, somebody with serious mustard. I'm not your boy."

"I'll take your suggestion under advisement."

"Yeah, fine, you do that."

"I'll be waiting for your next report," the voice said.

"You'll get it. And it'll probably be my last."

It was eleven-thirty by the time the police dropped them off at Janine's. They'd taken Mary Margaret to the hospital, but the emergency-room doctor couldn't find much wrong with her. He said she might have gotten a minor concussion when her head had banged against the floor of the van. She had rope burns and minor abrasions on her wrists, one shoulder had been wrenched and her cheek was puffy where she'd been slugged, but that was pretty much it. "You were probably lucky you were tied up," the doctor said. "Otherwise, chances are you'd be dead. As it is, a couple of aspirin should make you right as rain."

"I guess I should ask to be tied up every time I get kidnapped," she'd told Dane, struggling for a light moment, but not quite succeeding.

He was glad she was trying to hold it together. It was a good sign. She'd been pretty clingy ever since he'd found her, refusing to let him out of her sight, even when she was being examined at the hospital. When the doctor had suggested she spend the night for observation, she'd declined, holding Dane's hand tightly so they wouldn't try to take her away. In the police car, both leaving the scene of the accident and on the way home from the hospital, she'd lain her head on his shoulder and told him she was still afraid. "He was going to rape me," she said several times. "And then kill me. I'm sure of it."

Dane had stroked her head and kissed her fingers and assured her she was safe now, that he wouldn't let anything happen to her. But she was hanging on by a thread. At any moment she could fall apart.

As far as Dane knew, they still hadn't found Rut Coleman. That concerned him—if only for Mary Margaret's peace of mind. Until they found the guy's body or had him back behind bars, she'd be uneasy. The body in the van, they'd discovered, was Hap Coleman, Rut's brother. The police speculated Rut had been thrown from the vehicle and was lying in the bushes. They were searching for him when the decision was made to take Mary Margaret to the hospital.

She'd had the presence of mind to have a police officer call the High Chaparral and inform them she'd been in an accident and wouldn't be making the show. A call coming from a cop or a doctor always had more punch. Artie hated it when somebody got sick or hurt. "Why does it always have to be at the last minute?" he'd complain. "People die at the last minute, too, Artie," one of the girls told him. "So lighten up."

A police sergeant named Calloway was waiting for them at the trailer, having brought back Dane's car. He went with them inside. "I wanted to update you folks on developments," he said, standing just inside the door. He was a short man with a fringe of close-cropped gray hair, balding on top, his face reminding Dane of his own father. "Unfortunately the news is not good," he said. "We believe Rut Coleman survived the accident. A pickup was stolen at a ranchette half a mile from the accident scene, and blood was found on the ground. We think it was Coleman's."

"Oh, shit," Mary Margaret said.

"Most likely he's in need of medical attention," Calloway went on, "but we can't be sure about the severity of his injuries. We've alerted hospitals, but we have to assume that he's dangerous.''

"No kidding," Mary Margaret said.

Dane gave her shoulder a squeeze.

"Now I won't be able to sleep," she said, pinching the bridge of her nose.

"With luck, we'll be picking him up soon," the sergeant said. "I'll keep you advised, though I assume you won't want a call until morning."

"Call the minute you arrest him," she replied.

"Yes, ma'am. And I want you to know I'll keep a patrol in the neighborhood. The chances of him coming back here are zilch, but we won't take any risks."

"Thank you, Sergeant," Dane said. "Thank you for everything."

Calloway gave Dane's car keys to him, and told Mary Margaret they would return for a more detailed statement when she was feeling better. Then he left.

The two of them sat there for a while in silence. Mary Margaret stared off blankly, shivering every once in a while. Dane continued to hold her, rubbing her upper arm.

"You see," she said, "I wouldn't make a very good Buddhist. There's no rising above this."

"No, of course not. You had a terrible, terrible experience."

"I'm afraid," she said. "I know it's over, but I'm still terrified. I just can't get it out of my mind."

She was wrestling, not just with Rut Coleman, but with all her demons, he could tell. "I know you're having a rough time," he said, kissing her hair. "You're entitled."

"I want to take a shower," she announced, shivering. "I want to get clean."

"Okay."

She got up tentatively and slowly walked to the hallway that led to the bedrooms, glancing over her shoulder at him a couple of times. When she finally disappeared from sight, he slumped, feeling completely drained. It had been a rough night for him, too. He could only thank God things turned out as well as they had. He didn't even want to consider what might have happened.

* * *

Mary Margaret edged her way down the hallway, her fingers gliding along the wall. There were a few years when she was quite small that she'd been afraid of the dark and could still remember vividly the terror a dark room held for her. That was exactly how she felt now, except that the terror was more real—perhaps even more immediate.

Nearing the bathroom door, she stopped. She couldn't go in. She couldn't make herself move another step. She was frozen. This was ridiculous, she told herself. She was an adult, not a child. But knowing that didn't help.

Leaning against the wall, she closed her eyes and tried as hard as she could to pull herself together. She wanted badly to wash herself where Rut Coleman had touched her with his filthy hands, but she couldn't even make herself reach in and turn on the bathroom light.

"Dane!" she called, doing her best to fight back her growing panic. "Dane!"

He came to the hallway. "What's wrong?"

"I'm afraid," she said, her teeth chattering. "I know it's stupid, but I can't move."

He took her in his arms and she very nearly began to sob. But she felt safe again and her taut muscles began to relax slightly.

"Would you turn on the bathroom light for me?" she asked.

"Sure."

He didn't ask why. He seemed to understand her need.

"I know I'm acting like an idiot," she said. "But ever since that cop said Coleman got away, I picture him around every corner."

"It's natural," he said. "I'd feel the same."

"Thank you for being the way you are. I can't tell you how much it means to me."

"I'm here for you, whatever you need."

"I really want to take a shower. Will you come in with me? Talk to me? Let me hear your voice?"

"If that's what you want."

He stepped into the bathroom and turned on the light. Mary

Margaret stuck her head in and peered around the small space. It seemed safe enough.

"I need to get some clothes from my room. Will you come with me?"

"Sure."

They went to her room. Mary Margaret gave him back his shirt, keeping her back to him as she slipped into a robe. She could see red marks on her breasts where Rut had pinched her nipples. And her stomach and inner thighs had a couple of scratches. She would bruise. She shuddered, hating that the mark of that man was still on her. It was as if Rut had branded her. She felt sullied. Dirty.

She shivered, pulling the robe tight at her throat. As she did, she thought of Rut taping the pillowcase around her neck, remembered her fear of suffocating or choking on her own vomit. Shuddering again, she knew she had to get in the shower. More than anything, she needed to wash the feel of his hands off of her.

She turned and gave Dane her hand, letting him lead her back down the hall to the bathroom. Without being asked, he stepped in and checked the room before letting her enter.

Mary Margaret turned on the shower and, his back to her, she got in the stall, closing the frosted-glass door. "Please say something, Dane," she said over the rush of the water. "I want to hear your voice."

"I'm right here. And I'm not going anywhere. I'll make sure you're safe."

"Keep talking."

"I hope this is the last adventure we have for a while," he told her. "I don't think I can take any more excitement."

"*You* can't?"

"I'm damned grateful you're all right," he said. "If something had happened to you, I'd...well, I don't know what I've have done."

"Talk about something else," she said. "Tell me about Toby."

"I really want you to meet him, Mary Margaret. I'm not objective, of course, but he's a super kid. I think you'd like him even if you aren't big on children. In fact, I'd be very interested in how you'd react to him."

"Why?"

"I don't know why, I just would. Maybe it's because I respect your opinion."

He was trying hard to distract her. His earnestness touched her.

"Mary Margaret?"

"Yes?"

"Would you like to meet Toby?"

"Yes," she said. "I guess so."

"I could tell you stories about him all day," he said.

"Tell me some."

Dane went into a long monologue. She tried to concentrate on what he was saying, but as she began soaping herself down, she recalled the feel of Rut Coleman's hands on her body. She scrubbed herself hard, trying to wash the memory away. The harder she washed, the more desperate she was to exorcize every last trace of him.

"He can be really comical at times," Dane was saying. "When he wakes up before I do, which is most mornings, he thinks he's doing me a great favor by coming in to tell me it's time to fix breakfast."

Mary Margaret was standing under the showerhead now, letting the water pound her. For the first time in what seemed like forever she felt halfway clean...almost decent. And the sound of Dane's voice, the steady rhythm of it as he spoke of everyday life, was such a comfort. He understood her need, not just to be protected, but to be reminded that life could be good and decent. Normal. Even if it wasn't.

"I bet you're a soft touch," she said, trying to keep up the conversation. "Sounds to me like the kid has you wrapped around his finger."

"I suppose he does. But I am capable of being firm if necessary."

She pictured Dane trying to be stern, and smiled. "I'll bet Kathy's the disciplinarian." It was the first time she'd mentioned his wife since they'd talked about Kathy's call. The effect was surprising. She felt somewhat grounded just thinking about the woman, probably because their relationship had been adversarial.

"She is," Dane said. "Kathy says I've got no guts when it comes to getting tough with my kid."

"Don't take this wrong, Dane, but she may be right."

"I guess my mother was a pretty bad role model," Dane said. "She spoils Toby even more than I do. And by her own account, she spoiled me."

"I can believe that, too."

"Hey," he protested. "You must be feeling better. You're starting to sound like your old feisty self. Or is it my imagination?"

She actually smiled in response, until the reality of her circumstances came to mind. Dane could distract her only so long. The water was starting to get cold and she couldn't hide in the shower forever. It was time to pull herself together and face what was waiting for her out there. She was a survivor, she told herself. Anthony had beat her, but she'd refused to be a victim then and she'd refuse to be a victim now.

If only Coleman had been killed or captured. That was what terrified her—the thought that he might come back. The question was, how did she get over the fear of being grabbed every time she walked into a room or climbed in bed? If Dane weren't out there, she'd probably be afraid of getting out of the shower. Rut Coleman could be standing there, just as he had been when she walked in the front door.

"Mary Margaret?"

"Yes?"

"That was a question."

"I'm sorry, I didn't hear."

"I just asked if you were all right."

"Yes, I'm fine," she said. "I'll be getting out now. I think I've just about drained all the hot water out of the tank."

"I've got a towel waiting."

She turned off the water and reached her hand out the door. He put the towel in it. She began drying herself off in the crowded confines of the shower stall.

"Would you like me to step out of the bathroom?" he asked.

She was over the worst of her panic attack and was probably going to be all right, but having him nearby had been such a comfort that she didn't want to give it up. "Would you mind just turning around?"

"Sure, why not?"

"I'm asking a lot of you, aren't I?"

"No, not at all. I'd like to think I'm of help."

"You'll never know," she said, peeking out.

He was dutifully facing the door, his back to her. Mary Margaret stepped out and quickly finished drying herself. Then she had him hand her the robe. She put it on.

"Okay, you can turn around."

He did, checking her out from her wet hair to her bare feet. "Always good to see you, Miss Duggan."

He was being so nice and she really appreciated it. "I made a decision while I was in the shower," she said.

"Oh?"

"I'm not going to let what happened tonight ruin my happiness. I'm going to pull myself together and move ahead."

"That's the spirit."

"But I do want to ask another favor. And this one you might refuse. I wouldn't blame you if you did."

"Shoot."

She took a breath to respond, but lost her nerve. Dane waited, his expression compassionate, his eyes understanding. "No," she said. "It would be unfair."

"What would be, Mary Margaret?"

She lowered her head and he lifted her chin.

"Tell me what you want."

She took a fortifying breath and blurted it out. "I want you to sleep with me. Not to have sex," she hastily added. "Just to be with me."

Though he tried to hide it, Dane looked surprised, if not shocked. "It's not an unreasonable request," he said. "Given the circumstances."

"But you'd rather not."

"If it's what you want…"

Mary Margaret hugged him. "You're a saint."

"That may be a premature judgment," he said, chuckling. He stroked her head.

Dane could say what he wanted, but she knew that he cared

about her, cared about her as a person. She wasn't used to that. And it made her wonder if this was what it was like to be loved, truly loved.

Tuesday

August 13th

Reno, Nevada

"You two should write a book," Janine said, pouring them coffee. "I work late, come home dead tired and I see this banged-up Camry sitting out front and say to myself, 'Oh, shit.' I almost woke you up to find out what happened, never dreaming…"

"If you could have seen me last night," Mary Margaret said, "you'd realize I'm a completely different person."

"Ditto," Dane said.

"A good night's sleep does wonders," Janine said with a wry little smile.

"Well, we didn't have sex," Mary Margaret said, annoyed by the innuendo. She hated the way Janine was coy sometimes. "I might as well make that clear right up front."

"Did I ask?" Janine said, sitting at the table with them. She all but gave Dane a wink.

Dane lifted his right hand. "She's telling the truth."

"I guess you'd know," Janine quipped.

"Glad you two are having fun with this," Mary Margaret said, "because I was the one who almost got raped last night."

Janine reached out and took her hand. "Hey, kid, I'm sorry. Maybe I'm trying too hard to keep it light. I know how horrible it was, because I've been there. Remember?"

Mary Margaret sighed. "I'm sorry for being testy. I guess I'm still confused. And I really hate it that they haven't ar-

rested Coleman. I'm just fine until I think he's out there someplace, waiting for me.''

"They'll get him," Janine said.

The telephone rang and Janine went off to answer it. Mary
Margaret looked at Dane.

"I guess it's hell being a gentleman, isn't it?" she said.

"There are worse fates."

"I admire you an awful lot, Reverend Barrett."

"I admire *you* an awful lot."

She gazed steadily into his eyes, recalling how wonderful
it was to fall asleep in his arms. "Mutual's nice," she said.

"Mutual's *very* nice."

Dane reached out and touched her puffy cheek. The injury
was better and her head was only faintly throbbing. Her wrists
bothered her the most, but they weren't terrible or anything.
She liked his touch, though.

Janine returned. "That was the police," she announced.
"They asked me to tell you Rut Coleman's still at large. They
believe he robbed a convenience store in Carson City last
night and he has a gun, apparently from the pickup he stole.
They suggest you be very careful."

"Oh, Jesus," she said, putting her head in her hands. Suddenly the pain in her head got worse. "If it's not one thing,
it's another."

"I think there's a solution," Dane said. "You've got to
leave here."

"And go where?"

"Someplace with me."

She studied him, searching for his meaning.

"I've been as supportive as I can," he explained, his tone
resolute, maybe even a touch angry, "but I think it's time I
assert myself a little. You do not need to be here. In fact, you
shouldn't be here. And not just because of Coleman. I want
you to call the casino and tell them you need a few days off.
Then you're going to come with me."

"Where?"

"I don't know. L.A. Santa Barbara...no, not Santa Barbara." He thought for a moment. "How about the northern
coast? Do you like the ocean?"

"I grew up within a dozen blocks of the Pacific."

"I know this romantic getaway up near Mendocino. Took Kathy there once. It was too quiet and she hated it. But I loved it. I always said I'd go back with somebody who appreciated it, but I never have."

Janine rinsed out her cup. "A romantic getaway sounds pretty good to me," she said. "Not that anybody asked my opinion."

Mary Margaret's cheeks colored. She wasn't sure what to think. Surely he didn't mean romantic in the usual sense.

"They allow *innocent* romantic getaways," he said, intuiting her concern perfectly. "Besides, you'll be with a gentleman."

Something stirred inside her, something as powerful and pure as any feeling she'd ever had for a man. She realized, with sudden clarity, that she was falling in love with this guy. *That's* what she'd been feeling. It was love. Not just romantic love, or the love of a friend, but the all-encompassing kind of love that touched the soul. The kind of love that lasted forever. It was the plain old simple love that Mama used to talk about and Mary Margaret had lost faith in. Until now...assuming she wasn't deluding herself.

He picked up the receiver but waited for a jet to ramble down the runway before dialing the long-distance number.

"Yes?" came the voice, resonant and vaguely annoyed.

"You're getting your last report earlier than I expected."

There was a pause. "I'm listening."

"This guy, Barrett, is something else. An hour ago he takes the girl to the airport where he charters a small plane and off they go."

"Really?"

"Really."

"Where to? Las Vegas?"

"No. Mendocino County," he said. "I poked around. The flight plan was for the Mendocino County Airport. Never knew they had one. From here it's the better part of a day's drive, so by the time I get there they could be anywhere. If you want to step on him, it may be time to call out the shock troops."

"You may be right. But as it is, it'll take me a while to get some people up there."

"Well, it's in your hands, boss. I'll be sending in my final statement."

"Okay, but remember the procedure."

"I will," he said. "Discretion is my middle name."

"It'd better be your first and last name, as well."

"You've got it."

"There's something else."

He felt his stomach tense. "Yeah?"

"I'll see that there's an extra five thousand in your pay envelope. I'd like you to spend a couple of months in Mexico or someplace."

Now that was a surprise. "Any particular reason?"

"Yes, my people tell me there's pressure in Laurel to have you arrested. The water might be better in the San Joaquin County jail, but in Mexico there'd be distractions, if you take my point."

He swallowed hard. "I take it."

"Adios, my friend. I hope never to see you again."

"Yeah, right," he said uncertainly. "Adios."

Little River, Mendocino County, California

She stood at the corner of the deck and peered out at the sea. A quarter of a mile from landfall, the ocean and fog blended into a seamless film of gray, whereas the pine-festooned hilltops behind her were still dappled with sunlight. During the fifteen minutes she'd stood there in a near-hypnotic state, the brilliance of the day had been succumbing progressively to the mists. She had inhaled the salt air and listened to the whoosh and rumble of the surf, coming very close to forgetting who she was. For the first time in her life she imagined herself emptying, her soul uniting with the universe, just as Dane had said it did when he meditated.

Eventually the nip in the air reminded her that she had a body, that there had been a yesterday and, yes, that she was mortal and feeble and had reason to be afraid. But by coming here with him she was both renewed and, in some way, a different person. That van and all the horrible things that had happened were best forgotten. She would fill her senses with so much beauty that there wouldn't be room for the ugliness.

Flying through the clouds that afternoon, she had experienced the first definitive hints of liberation from the horrors of the previous night. Dane had made her feel secure, but it wasn't until they were airborne that she'd had a complete feeling of freedom. She had held his hand the entire way, forgetting everything except that something special was happening—she was in love.

Dane couldn't have picked a better place to bring her than the Heritage House. The main lodge was at the top of a lawn that swept to the edge of the sea cliffs ringing a cove. Cabins were clustered in little groups among the trees or perched on points with perspectives of the sea. Theirs was in the Vista Group and featured the most spectacular panorama of all. From their deck, she could see up and down the coast, as far out to sea as the fog would allow, the cove and mountains. It was an eagle's-nest view. Especially intriguing was a gazebo, which sat on a jut of land above the cove, a few hundred feet below her. At the moment, a couple was standing in it, arms around each other as they watched the waves crashing on the rocks.

When she'd stepped outside to commune with creation, as Dane called it, he had been lighting a fire. Turning to check his progress, she saw that the fire was blazing. He was sitting in an armchair, staring at her through the sliding glass door.

Mary Margaret had on jeans and a heavy green cotton sweater, the latter having been brought at his insistence. Summers in San Francisco could be cool enough to keep polar bears happy, but after years in the desert, she'd nearly forgotten how cold August could be on the coast. "Dinners at this place require dressing up," he'd told her, which had been more of a problem for him than for her. To her surprise, on the way to the airport in Reno he'd stopped at the shopping center and bought a cheap sport coat, a couple of shirts, two pairs of pants and a tie. "When it comes to dress codes, it's the thought that counts," he'd explained.

She went to the sliding door and opened it. "So what are

you doing sitting there, looking like Abraham Lincoln in his memorial?''

He chuckled. ''Mary Margaret, that's a first for me. Never have I been compared with Abraham Lincoln.''

''It's the way you're sitting. What have you been doing?''

''Admiring your backside.''

Her smile turned puckish. ''Wasn't it George Washington who couldn't tell a lie?''

''Would you rather I tell a lie?''

She stepped inside and closed the door. Then, going right to him, she plunked herself down onto his lap, put an arm around his neck and gave him a kiss. ''No, I'm glad you were looking at my backside.''

''What is this?'' he said, giving her nose a pinch. ''Are you testing my gentlemanly resolve?''

''Maybe. Or maybe I'm testing mine.'' Giving him one of her ''devil grins,'' as her mother called them, she jumped right back to her feet and went over to the fire, where she bent over to warm her hands. ''Forgive my rear end,'' she said, ''but my hands are cold.''

''Forgive it? I lust after it!''

''Dane!'' she said, spinning and giving him an admonishing look.

''I know,'' he said. ''That's a terrible thing to say, but sometimes the truth gushes out and I can't do anything about it.''

''Maybe it's my fault.''

''You *are* such a tease, Mary Margaret.''

''I guess I'm testing myself because I don't like being damaged goods.''

''Hey, you're not damaged goods. You've had a terrible experience. There's a difference.''

''What if I never want to have sex again?''

''It'll be a tremendous loss to mankind.''

''I'm serious.''

''So am I.''

She went to the bed, sat down and crossed her legs. She looked at him and he looked at her. ''If I ever have sex again, it'll only be with one special person.''

''Why's that?''

"Because I've had enough experience to know what I want. And when he comes along—Mr. Wonderful, I mean—that'll be it."

"You sound very sure of yourself," he said.

She grinned. "I'm getting the hang of it, I guess."

"So, tell me," he said. "What's Mr. Wonderful going to be like?"

"Like you."

He blinked. "Pardon me?"

"I don't mean *actually* you," she said, immediately back-tracking. "I mean somebody with your better qualities."

"Which are?"

"Well, let me see. A gentleman. That's very important."

"Yes, I agree."

"Hey," she protested, "this is *my* fantasy. You don't get an opinion."

"Sorry." He grinned. "Go on. A gentleman, you said. What else?"

"Well," she said, laying her index finger across her cheek, "he's got to be smart."

"Why?"

"Because I am and it's nice to be challenged every once in a while."

"I can buy that."

"Can you?"

"Mary Margaret, I've come to appreciate your mind as much or more than the rest of you, and that's saying a lot."

"About whom?"

He looked her over provocatively. Then, lilting a brow, he said, "Maybe about both of us."

"Smart and smart aleck are not the same, Mr. Barrett."

"You're right, of course. Forgive me. I got us off track. What else about Mr. Wonderful? So far we've got an erudite gentleman."

"He can be assertive, but he's got to know when to back down."

"Like when he gives self-important speeches serving nothing but his ego?"

"For example."

"Okay, I'm with you. Continue."

"Kind. He's got to be kind, like you. That's very important. And sensitive. Somebody who can cry with me when I cry."

"I see."

She had surprised herself talking this way, but words just seemed to flow from her heart. No sentiment seemed too dangerous. Well, almost no sentiment. "So, what do you think?"

"I think that's a hard fantasy for a guy to live up to," he said. "What about religion? What's Mr. Wonderful's position on that?"

Mary Margaret surmised the question was more serious than the lighthearted manner in which he'd stated it. "That's a toughy," she replied. "Mother said I should marry a Catholic since we'd have a lot in common. But my father was Catholic and Anthony was Catholic. So much for marrying guys with the same religion."

"Then where are you on the religion issue now?"

Again his tone was light. She watched his expression carefully. "Coming from a clergyman, that's not a casual question, is it?"

"It isn't a trick question," he replied.

"I guess the truth is, religion isn't important to me, so it shouldn't be important to Mr. Wonderful, either."

Dane considered that a moment.

"That isn't the answer you wanted, is it?" she said.

"I can't program anyone to feel what I feel and like what I like. I know that. But I do care deeply about the fundamental issues of life. And I like the idea of having someone to share them with."

"Kathy didn't, did she?"

"No. And maybe that explains its importance."

"I know what you mean," Mary Margaret said. "After Anthony, I'm grateful when I find a guy who's willing to talk about *anything* besides sex and money."

Dane gave her an inquiring look. "So, would you be put off by a guy wanting to discuss the meaning of life?"

"As long as it wasn't in the middle of 'E.R.,'" she quipped.

He smiled. "I'm putting you on the spot by asking this, I

know, but is my philosophical side off-putting? A lot of people feel uncomfortable around clergymen.''

"It's definitely different than what I'm used to."

She kicked off her shoes and swung her legs onto the bed, lying on her side, facing him, her head propped on her hand. Dane's eyes swept up and down the length of her body, and it struck her as odd that there should be this sexual awareness between them while they were talking about religion.

"You didn't really answer the question," he said.

"I don't want to disappoint you," she replied.

"The truth works best in the long run. It took a marriage for me to figure that one out."

"Then I have to be very careful what I say, don't I?"

Dane watched her as he waited for her to formulate her answer. She was taking his question seriously, which he appreciated. It was obvious that Mary Margaret was well aware how important the issue was to him. That was heartening.

But caring wasn't enough. He wanted someone to share his passion and he was fairly certain she cared about him more than the things that moved him. His way of life simply didn't mesh with hers. Mary Margaret had a lively, inquisitive mind. She was tolerant. But God—even his liberal, impersonal, undemanding God—was not part of her life.

"Chalk and cheese," she said. "When you come right down to it, we're chalk and cheese."

"So, my work *is* off-putting," he said.

"Not off-putting," she replied. "Out of my league."

"You underestimate yourself."

"Look, Dane, we're being truthful, right? You want to know who's in my league? Anthony Casagrande. Sure, he's a shit, and it was a mistake to marry him, but at least we ate in the same restaurants. And Kathy might be a bitch, but she speaks your language. The point is, you're a nice guy and I'm intellectually curious, but that's still a long way from saying that we belong together."

"I think we're off to a good start, though. Things can develop," he said, feeling encouraged. He sensed the lady was protesting too much, which was always a good sign.

"Bullshit," she replied. "You're rationalizing."

"Am I?"

"Yes."

"So, I bore you."

"No," she said. "You don't bore me at all."

"And you don't bore me."

A frown creased her brow. "Is there a point to this?"

"I care about you and what you think, and you care about me and what I think."

"Which means we should go to bed together?" she said with a dollop of sarcasm.

"No, but that caring can lead to greater things."

"Oh, Dane." Mary Margaret sighed, letting her head drop onto the bed. She stared at the fire as he stared at her. She was wary and afraid. He understood that, but he also figured they could get past it. What he wasn't sure of was how deep her intellectual curiosity ran and, more important, how enduring it would be. Kathy had indulged him at first, too. And then, when she lost her interest in the things he cared about and turned hostile toward them, he'd rationalized. Mary Margaret was accusing him of rationalizing now. His biggest fear was that she was right.

"What is it about men?" she said, sounding almost sad. "They can't even think about God without working sex into it somehow?"

He laughed. "You think that's what I'm doing?"

"Maybe not consciously."

"Believe it or not, Mary Margaret, at the moment I'm a lot more concerned about what you think of my soul than what you think of my body."

She propped her head back up on her hand and contemplated him, giving him a long, intense look. "You know, I half believe you."

"It's true."

"Are you saying this connection I feel is to your soul?"

"I'd like to think so."

"I don't want to hurt you, Dane," she said, "but I've got to tell you straight out that if you're looking for someone to sit with you under a Bo tree, I'm not your girl. I like my creature comforts. I like bubble baths, a nice foot massage. Even sadness isn't all bad. A good cry every once in a while can feel real good. I guess what I'm saying is a person can be *too* enlightened. Forgive me if that offends you, but that's how I feel.''

He got up and went over to the bed. She rolled onto her back as he sat beside her.

"Mary Margaret Duggan," he said, looking into her eyes, "you're adorable."

She gazed up into his eyes, wondering what that meant. He seemed happy, which could only mean she'd said what he'd wanted to hear, but she didn't know what that was. Men could be such fools and that concerned her. Sure, women often made poor choices, but it wasn't because they were delusional. Mostly it was because they were desperate.

"I'm afraid to ask what you're thinking," he said.

"Don't."

"You leave me no choice, then."

With that he leaned over and kissed her—more passionately than before. She was immediately aroused, which surprised her. She couldn't stop kissing him and he couldn't hold her too tightly.

Finally their mouths parted and she ran her fingers up the back of his neck and into his hair. He'd excited her, but she was also anxious. It was awfully brazen of her to allow this, considering.

"Dane," she whispered, "is this wise?"

"How does it feel?"

She cocked her head. "I think that should be obvious."

"All's well that ends well."

"I'm not so sure."

He touched her cheek. "You want me to state my intentions."

"No," she said. "I *know* what your intentions are…"

"Maybe you do and maybe you don't. I'm on the path to enlightenment, but I don't aspire to sitting under a Bo tree. And I'm certainly no saint. In fact, the thoughts going through my mind at the moment are anything but saintly."

"Thank you for not sharing, then."

He gave her an admonishing look, then checked his watch. "Guess what, Miss Duggan? You have just enough time for a bubble bath before dinner."

"That sounds good, actually."

"Out of deference, I won't ask to join you."

Funny, but the very same thought had just gone through her mind. It was terrible how temptation could be so insidious—wanting one thing and knowing you had to do another. She really hated the word. There were too many hurdles on the way to happiness as it was. Why did fighting yourself have to be one of them?

"Christ," the Russian said to his partner. "Why is it the priest he could not fuck her in a city hotel like a civilized person?"

"Romance, Yuri," the driver said.

"For this romance we must drive halfway to Canada? I think we should kill him for the trouble he makes."

"If he doesn't cooperate, fine."

They made two tight turns in succession, the wheels of the big sedan squealing on the pavement. Arnold glanced over at the huge sulking Russian.

"I am hungry. I am bored and I must piss," Yuri said. "We find this priest. We kill him now and we go back to San Francisco. It saves the trouble later."

"The boss man said if we scare him good, we don't need to whack him."

"My way is easier, Arnold. You know this."

"Twenty Gs says we do it the hard way."

"You Americans do *everything* the hard way. How you win the Cold War, I do not know," Yuri said, looking out at the night.

Arnold braked for another curve, but he didn't reply. Yuri was ruthless, he did what he did for the sheer pleasure of it. He fancied himself Rambo's evil twin. For him, hits were a blood sport, like bullfighting. Yuri didn't go so far as to cut off ears, but he'd take a cuff link or a pinkie ring, anything to remind himself he'd met a challenge and won.

"So, where is this fucking Hermitage House?" the Russian said.

"*Heritage* House," Arnold corrected. "The guy's a preacher, not a monk."

"Monk? In our Hermitage in Leningrad there are paintings. So what is heritage?"

"A place to screw, Yuri."

"Like a cathouse?"

"Upscale," Arnold said with a grin. "Just help me watch for the sign, okay? The guy at the airport said it's right along here somewhere."

"Better we find a McDonald's."

"We'll get you a hamburger after we find the hotel."

They drove for a while in silence. Yuri was clearly getting restless. Arnold knew how important the guy's stomach was to him.

"Tell me our plan, Arnold," the Russian said, obviously trying to get his mind on business.

"First we check things out, get a lay of the land. Once we find them, we look for an opportunity. Dramatic's good in situations like this."

"Dramatic like I beat the shit out of him?"

"Maybe something more subtle." Arnold slowed as lights came into view through the trees. Then they saw the sign clearly. Heritage House. "Eureka!" he said.

"About time," Yuri said, slapping his gut.

They pulled into the drive that sloped down from the highway to the main building, stopping about halfway down. The front of the ivy-covered building was all they could see clearly.

"Looks like a real cozy place," Arnold said, thinking it was kind of nice.

"Yeah, so what do we do now?" the Russian asked.

"First we find a bellhop to bribe, then we get a bite to eat. I saw a hamburger joint a few miles back."

"And after that?"

"We'll see if we can find a way to make Reverend Barrett uncomfortable."

"Better we kill him," Yuri said.

"You'll have to indulge me, comrade. First we try it the hard way. If that doesn't work, we'll do it your way."

Dane was only half-aware of having eaten. The food had come, he'd put it in his mouth, chewed and swallowed. The dishes had been cleared, the wine had been drunk. But through it all, he'd savored the sight of her every moment. Yet, he sensed something was wrong. He hated to think he was as delusional about her as she'd alleged. Maybe he wanted too badly for it to be different.

She stared out the large window at the darkness. The candlelight made her satiny skin glow with a quiet radiance. With her fiery red hair done up, her long neck was something Parmigianino might have fashioned.

She was wearing a simple little clingy black dress with a scoop neck. The gold chain around her neck lay lightly over her collarbone, inviting a kiss. The only other jewelry she wore were gold hoop earrings. Everything on her body, including her shoes, couldn't have cost two hundred dollars altogether, yet she had the radiance of a princess. Mary Margaret Duggan was royal and didn't even know it.

But she wasn't a happy camper at the moment. Her mood seemed to have gotten darker as the meal progressed. She'd taken his arm when they'd walked from their room to the lodge, seemingly confident and upbeat, but her glow slowly faded and she'd finally lapsed into a brooding silence. He assumed that once again she was wrestling with the devils that had been tormenting her.

She abruptly turned from the window and peered into his eyes. "When you get quiet like that, I wonder about you," she said, leaning forward on her elbows. It was the first she'd spoken in several minutes.

"*You* were wondering about *me?*" he said. "No, it's the other way around. *I'm* wondering about *you.*"

"Well, I guess we were wondering about each other."

"Hmm," he said. "Funny how that works, isn't it?"

"So, what were you thinking?"

He had a lot to choose from, so he picked the most innocuous. "A moment ago I was thinking about the time I went with my mother to Florence to learn something about art. I was fourteen and saw a neck I fell in love with. At the Uffizi. Parmigianino's *Madonna with the Long Neck*. Tonight, twenty years later, I'm having a similar experience."

Mary Margaret smiled faintly and turned again to the window. Dane peered out into the night, as well. It was so dark they could see nothing but the twinkling lights of the houses across the cove.

"I hope you find that flattering," he said.

"The fact that you said it makes it flattering."

"Do you know Parmigianino?"

"I know the cheese."

His mouth twisted with amusement.

"I'm not kidding," she said. "If you hadn't said 'art' before you said Uffizi, I would have thought you were talking about a pizza parlor."

Her candor was refreshing, but the real message was probably more ominous than it appeared.

"I know you think it's cute," she went on. "But the truth is I didn't go to Vassar. It's important you remember that."

"I didn't go to Vassar, either, so that makes us even."

"Don't make fun of me, Dane," she protested. "You know what I mean."

"You can't let go of that chalk-and-cheese business, can you?"

Mary Margaret drew a deep breath. "We're sitting here in this fancy room," she said, glancing at the chandeliers and the domed painted ceiling of the dining room, "and it's full of guys with gold Rolexes and stock portfolios and ladies with diamonds and charity connections, and I look at you and I say to myself, 'Even in that cheap sport coat and cotton pants, he belongs.'"

"Apparently that's not good." He struggled to keep his tone even.

"Look, Dane, I'm not dissing myself. I've got some good qualities, I know. But let's not kid ourselves here."

"Mary Margaret, you're the most elegant woman in the room. The most elegant woman I've ever known."

"Stop, you're making it worse."

"I'm dead serious."

"You're blind."

"And you're picking a fight," he said, unable to keep the edge out of his voice.

"Maybe I am."

His anxiety began to build. "Why? Just when everything

starts going smoothly, you decide you have to throw a monkey wrench into the works. Why can't you let things flow naturally?"

"Yeah, like right into bed. Isn't that what you mean?"

He was really starting to get pissed. It was all so unnecessary. "Listen, I'm getting tired of hearing about sex. If you want to know the truth, I think you're more obsessed with it than I am."

She gave him a hard look as the soft hum of the conversation of the other diners carried across the room. "I bet Rut Coleman felt the same way."

It was a scathing remark and at first it infuriated him, but then he realized maybe he was the one who'd been insensitive. "That wasn't what I meant."

She lowered her face to her folded hands in a look of prayerful anguish. Then she sighed. "I didn't mean it, either."

"Did I say something to get things off track?" he asked.

"No, Dane, it's not you."

"Look, if you're feeling pressure because things have gotten a little romantic, don't worry about it. I'm fully capable of backing off. Sex wasn't part of the deal."

"It's not that, either."

"Then what?"

She had a terrible look of frustration on her face. Surprisingly, it seemed she was about to break into tears. Dane reached over and took her hand.

"What's wrong?"

She hesitated a moment before plunging ahead. "This is going to sound dumb, but you don't really know me, Dane. You think you do, but you don't."

"Yeah, I know, I'm deluding myself. You said as much before."

"That's not what I mean. What I'm saying is, I'm not what I appear. If you really knew me, you wouldn't feel the way you do."

"What are you talking about, some terrible dark secret?"

"Sort of."

"Then why don't you enlighten me?" he said calmly.

"No, I can't. Just take my word for it."

He leaned back in his chair, annoyed again. "Forgive me, but you can't get away with implying you're depraved or whatever and expect me to accept it."

"Then don't accept it," she shot back. "Just don't press me."

Dane rubbed his chin, fighting the pressure building inside him. He wasn't used to feeling this way. Even Kathy at her worst didn't cause such frustration. Mary Margaret was playing with him as though he were a yo-yo, although that may not have been her intent.

"Okay," he said. "I'll take your word for it. So, unless you have an objection, we'll go back to being friends and try and be as pleasant to each other as possible. Is that acceptable?"

She looked miserable but didn't bother arguing. "Fine," she said. "I'll try to be nice."

"Pick a topic of conversation," he said.

She only hesitated a moment. "Tell me about your mother."

He smiled, finding the request odd and funny both. "You like to go right into the deep end, don't you?"

"If you'd rather not, that's okay."

"Mother's a dear lady, devoted, loyal and very much a snob. Want to know what she'd think of you?"

Mary Margaret brightened, her interest obviously piqued. "Yes."

"She'd be warily impressed until she found out your background. Then she'd think she'd been right to be wary."

"See, that's what I mean."

"You're *my* friend, not my mother's. She's into people's backgrounds, I'm not."

"She may be right," Mary Margaret said.

"My mother's problem is she's too protective. As far as she's concerned, nobody's good enough for me. Kathy wasn't."

"Why not?"

"Her family was all right. They didn't have our kind of money or pedigree, but they had a nice home in Brentwood. Her father was an insurance executive. Her brother was a Rhodes scholar. And of course Kathy had all her degrees. But as far as Mom was concerned, she somehow missed the mark.''

''Your mother *is* a snob.''

''Precisely.''

''Did you think Kathy had class?''

''Kathy was—is very much her own person. The night we came here, for example, she wore a granny dress, a floppy hat and hiking boots. She was making a statement. Not just to the Rolexes and diamonds, but to me.''

''Was she always like that?''

''She always wore hiking shoes and generally eschewed makeup. Basically, she's a hippie academic. Militantly so.''

''You must have liked that, you married her.''

''I made a mistake, like you did with Anthony, but it had nothing to do with her background, it had to do with the person she was inside.''

''Her soul?''

''Yes, Mary Margaret, her soul.''

She averted her gaze again, pondering the lights across the cove. He stroked her long, slender fingers. She turned and watched him for a moment, her eyes shimmering.

''If I didn't like you so much, I'd hate you,'' she said.

''How do I convince you it's all right?'' he asked in a soft voice.

''You can't.''

''Maybe not, but I can still take you for a walk in the moonlight before we go back to the room. Unless the thought of that scares you.''

''You don't scare me, Dane.''

He signaled for the waiter, a wry smile crossing his lips. ''Maybe that's the problem.''

Despite the cool breeze, they strolled across the grounds. He tried to put his disappointment from his mind. Mary Margaret seemed equally willing to set aside their differences. She took his arm but didn't really close the gap between them.

''You warm enough?'' he asked.

''I'm okay,'' she said, and clasped the cardigan she was wearing at the throat. It had been her mother's, she'd told him when they'd dressed for dinner. "Not exactly evening wear, but better than the Forty-Niner jacket Anthony gave me."

Dane put his arm around her anyway and she seemed to appreciate that.

They were following the path that ran along the cliff above the cove. A split-rail fence marked the point beyond which they were not to go. In the past few minutes the moon had risen over the ridge. It shone on the gazebo she'd seen from their deck.

"Let's go out there," she said.

They found the path leading out onto the point. Once they were beyond the protection of the eucalyptus and pine, the wind cut more deeply, making them lean against its force. The power of the sea was more obvious the closer they got to the gazebo. They could hear the fury of the waves crashing against the rocks.

Dane went up on the first step of the gazebo, but Mary Margaret hesitated.

"I want to go out there," she said, waving her hand toward the very end of the point, another ten yards or so beyond the structure. Dane had never cared much for heights and, clearly sensing his reluctance, she said, "You don't have to go."

Clutching the sweater still more tightly over her chest, her hair streaming across her face, Mary Margaret proceeded toward the tip of the land some fifty feet above the dark, roiling sea. "Be careful," he called after her. "That's a strong wind and the rocks could be slippery."

She seemed determined to go, so there was no point in trying to stop her. But he didn't feel good about it.

She took careful steps, but her courage was apparent. He wasn't sure why, or what she was doing, but it seemed she was making a statement.

With each step she took, he wanted to tell her that was far enough. But she kept going. It was as though she absolutely had to stand on the rock at the very end of the point. Finally, she went about as far as she could go. His eyes were fixed on her. She was hugging herself, the hem of her dress fluttering in the cutting wind. It reminded him of the pennants on his father's sailboat when they'd go out into the Santa Barbara Channel on a brisk day.

She stared out in the direction of a light buoy that blinked at her from the dark sea. Then she looked down at the water. For a brief moment he wondered if she might jump. There was no particular reason she would, except that she was gazing down and he didn't want her to be out there. He wanted her to come back. And he would have called to her, but he knew she couldn't hear over the roar of the wind and the sea.

He was so focused on her that he didn't hear them coming. The first he knew of them was when they grabbed his arms, nearly lifting him from the ground. He cried out, looking back and forth between them. They wore ski masks. One was huge, the other Dane's height, but more heavyset.

"What are you doing?" he gasped, his voice on the edge of panic.

"We've got a message for you, Reverend," the shorter man said.

"What message?"

"Leave Jimmy Duggan in peace."

"Because if you don't," the large man added, "we're going to fucking kill you." He had an accent—East European it sounded like. And there was something in the man's voice that said he relished the prospect.

Dane glanced out at Mary Margaret, who hadn't moved. She continued to stare at the water, oblivious.

"If we kill you," the first man said, "you know what that means. We gotta kill the girl, too. In fact, my buddy here would like nothing better than to walk out there and give her a little shove, just to hear her scream when she fell. With the two of you floating in the bay, nobody's left to worry about Jimmy Duggan. Got the picture, preacher boy?"

Dane nodded, the image in his mind all too graphic. He was afraid now that Mary Margaret would turn around and panic when she saw them.

"Take my advice," the smaller man said in a surprisingly gentle voice. "Take poopsie back to your room and fuck her brains out. Forget Duggan. Don't give my friend here the pleasure of carving you up. Make sense?"

"Yes," Dane said, his chest so tight he could hardly breathe.

"You are a lucky bastard," the big man said in his thick accent. "There is only one chance. Now go fuck the woman." With that, he gave Dane a shove in Mary Margaret's direction.

Dane stumbled forward, catching himself before he fell. Looking back, he saw the men were already headed back to the path, peeling off their ski masks as they went. The moonlight was too faint for him to see much of them. Even their hair color was nondescript in the muted light.

He glanced in Mary Margaret's direction just as she turned around. He saw her smile faintly, still oblivious. She walked toward him. He didn't exhale until she was nearly back. When she reached him, he extended his hand and they returned to the gazebo. They went to the windward side, which was enclosed in glass, sheltering them from the wind. Dane immediately took her into his arms and held her tightly, rattled by the image of her being shoved off the cliff. As he rubbed her back, she shivered. He looked over his shoulder toward the path. There was no sign of the men, though they could easily be watching from the darkness.

Mary Margaret's teeth were chattering.

"Had enough nature?" he asked, masking his tenseness as best he could.

She nodded.

"I wonder if that fire's still going in our room."

"Wouldn't that be heaven."

They retraced their steps to the main path. Dane peered warily into the shadows. Reason told him they were safe for the moment, because if harm was their intent, the two men would have killed him out on the point. Still, his muscles were coiled and body poised for a fight. He took Mary Margaret's arm and led her in the direction of their room.

If she sensed that something was amiss, she didn't let it show. He hadn't decided yet whether or not to tell her what had happened. He didn't want to alarm her. Besides, between him and Rut Coleman, she'd had her hands full with men. He searched for something to say.

"What were you thinking when you were standing out on

the point?'' he asked, falling back on what had been in his mind before the men had shown up.

"Funny you should ask. I was trying to decide what I should say to you when we got back to the room."

"Oh? You feel the need to say something?"

"Yeah, I do."

He sensed something ominous, but he didn't question her. Her thoughts were hardly inconsequential, but he couldn't help regarding everything that happened from now on in a new light.

They walked a bit more briskly, though for different reasons. What she wanted to tell him, he had no idea. Nor had he decided what to say to her. Dane checked out each dark corner as they passed, his mind preoccupied with the men. Mary Margaret would have to wait until they were safely behind locked doors.

When they got to their room, he pushed open the sliding door to let her in and glanced back up the road toward the lodge. He saw nothing untoward.

Mary Margaret went to the fireplace. The fire had burnt down to hot coals. He joined her, tossing a couple of pieces of wood onto the grate as she rubbed her hands together. After a minute or two the logs caught. She sat in one of the armchairs. He took the other. She took off her sweater and smoothed her hair. Dane watched her, thinking that nothing would be gained by telling her about the hoodlums. She crossed her legs, then stared into the fire.

Even with her hair windblown, she was the picture of perfection. But he knew there was trouble brewing. He could see it on her face. Finally, she looked at him, and with a sigh of exasperation, she said, "You know I'm a showgirl, but I don't think you know the kind of life I live, the people I'm around, the kinds of pressures and temptations I face on a daily basis."

"You're saying I'm naive," he said.

"Not naive, no. Maybe unaware."

It was clear she was building up to something, probably what she'd been avoiding saying from the start. He could only hope it wouldn't hurt too much.

She got to her feet and began to pace slowly in front of the fire, her expression stormy, conflicted.

"I want to tell you about the girl you saw kicking up her heels and wiggling her ass last Saturday. I want to tell you about the real me," she said.

He had a sinking feeling—as much because of her tone as her words. He waited.

"I did something last week, the night before I met you, as a matter of fact, that I want you to know about." She paced back and forth a few more times, then sat down again, looking weary but resolute. "I've been pressed for money lately," she began. "Bankrupt, to all intents and purposes. I owed Anthony and he's been muscling me because he's been under the gun himself. Literally, probably. The point is, I've been pretty desperate. You get the picture, I think."

"Yes," Dane said, dread building inside him. "I do."

"So anyway, the day I was supposed to pay Anthony the back payments I owe him, I got this offer from a customer, a guy who'd seen the show a hundred times because my boobs mesmerized him and he couldn't get enough of them. In short, he had this thing for me."

He forced a breath. "And?"

"And, Ramon—that's his name—said if I'd come to his room and strip and dance for him and let him feel me up, he'd give me a couple of thousand dollars. That's it. I didn't have to ball him or suck him off or do anything sick, just that, play doctor with him in his room."

She stopped talking then and looked squarely into his eyes, the welling tears and twitch at the corner of her mouth belying her harsh tone and blunt language. The misery on her face was palpable. Dane felt miserable himself.

"And so you did it, I take it."

Mary Margaret slowly nodded. "Yes, I did."

A breathless moment passed. The fire crackled. The wind whistled outside. A tear ran down her cheek. She didn't bother to wipe it away. She was in pain. And so was he.

"Your classy dinner date on another day," she said, her voice cracking. "Now *that's* reality, Reverend Barrett. *That's* me."

He sat very still, his eyes on her. He searched for words

to communicate his feelings. He didn't want to be patronizing or maudlin.

"Well," she said, "aren't you going to say anything?"

"I'm wondering if there's another shoe that's going to drop, or if that's it."

She was taken aback. "Isn't it enough?"

"With all due respect, on the evil and immorality scale that's barely a five."

His response brought her up short. Was he being glib? she wondered. "What are you saying, that you aren't impressed?"

He chuckled. "I hope impressing me wasn't your intent."

"Don't play games with me, Dane," she said, confused by his reaction.

"I don't admire what you did," he said, "but I understand it. Frankly, I'm sorry you had to go through it."

"You're more of a fool than I thought, Dane Barrett. Either that or you want to get laid so badly you don't care."

That wounded him and she immediately realized it.

"Oh, damn," she said. "I didn't mean it. What a bitchy insensitive thing to say."

"I have to agree with you there."

"Don't you see that who I am is a problem, though?"

"Not to me," he said.

"Well, maybe it is to me."

He drew a long breath, slowly exhaling. "You're determined to alienate me, whatever the cost. And you've been that way since the day we met."

"Isn't it obvious why?" she cried, tears spurting from her eyes. She was getting angry because he was being obtuse.

"Maybe it's not," he said, taking his handkerchief from his pocket and tossing it to her. She tossed it right back.

"Take this, dammit!" he said. "You need it. Blow your snotty little nose and stop feeling so damn sorry for yourself. This poor-little-me routine is starting to wear thin."

"Fuck you," she said.

"Fuck you, too," he shot back.

Mary Margaret blew her nose. "It's a relief to know you're a bastard like every other guy I've known. I was getting tired of Saint Dane."

"And I'm glad to see the real you because that halo on your head was starting to look pretty insipid."

"You put it there, not me," she said, blowing her nose again. "That's why I knew you were totally delusional."

"Forgive me if I'm not experienced with inferiority complexes. The etiquette course I took at the country club when I was a kid didn't have a class on dealing with bruised egos."

"You know," she said, dabbing her eyes, "you're a halfway convincing son of a bitch."

"Only halfway?"

"Listen, when it comes to major-league testosterone junkies, I've seen the real thing. You're bush-league by comparison, Barrett. Strictly small potatoes."

"But if I cross your palm with enough bread, I can get anything I want, is that it? Ramon, or whatever his name was, could buy you and so can I—*if* I'm willing to pay."

She blinked.

"Come on, Mary Margaret, your point seems to be that you're for sale, so be consistent. Either you are a slut or you aren't. Which is it?"

"You think you're clever, don't you?"

"Hey, you're the one making the big announcement, not me," he said. "I'm the one who's disillusioned, remember?"

"Screw you."

He laughed. "I thought so."

Mary Margaret studied him. "You laugh, but you don't think I have the guts. You think you outsmarted me."

"I know you *talk* a good game, sweetheart."

"Listen, I was just trying to spare your feelings, but you know what you're doing, you're trying to rub my nose in it."

"Let's be clear," he said. "You're the one giving me this story about being a hooker, more or less. And I'm telling you—sorry, I don't buy it. I'm not impressed. I think you're all talk."

"You're calling my bluff. You don't think I could take money from you."

He grinned. "I'd be happy to pour you some of Janine's champagne if you'd like a little Dutch courage."

Mary Margaret shook her head, her eyes narrowing. Dane didn't try too hard to repress his smile. He had her on the defensive, which was just where he wanted her. She was pissed.

"I don't need champagne."

"Have some anyway," he said.

"I didn't need any for Ramon, why would I need it for you?"

"Maybe stone sober is the only way you're sure of yourself."

"You're going to find out I'm not easy to intimidate, Reverend Barrett," she said, going to her case across the room. "And you're definitely not as tough as you think."

"The game has only begun, my dear."

She gave him a coy smile, then bent over her case, her butt pointed in his direction as if to say, "Take that." Dane was enchanted and bemused. He hadn't expected it to come down to a test of wills, but if this was what it took to prove his feelings, he'd do it. Bizarre as it seemed, her courage, her willingness to be naughty in the face of her insecurities, intrigued him.

Mary Margaret found the bottle and she opened it, letting the bubbles flow over and drop to the floor before she tilted back the champagne and took a big slug. Then she walked over to him and handed it to him. Dane grabbed her wrist and licked her fingers where the champagne had run over them. Then he took a long drink from the bottle and handed it back. Mary Margaret threw back a few big gulps and put the champagne down on the floor.

"So, what's your pleasure, mister? Striptease? A little lap dancing?"

She said it with bald-faced confidence to frighten him, but Dane refused to give in. He was determined that she was going to blink first.

"It's one or the other?" he said. "I have to choose?"

"Oh, I've got myself a big boy, do I?"

"Don't belittle it until you've seen it," he said coolly.

"Ooo," she said, going over and turning off the lamp by the bed. Then she positioned herself between him and the fire. Giving him a pert little smile, she reached back to unzip her dress. The hem of her skirt rose to the top of her thighs. Then, slipping the dress off her arms, she let it slide down her body,

wiggling her hips to get it past them. Stepping out of the
dress, she tossed it aside. All she had on now was her shoes,
panties, bra and panty hose.

Dane swallowed hard as she held her arms out to the side
in a balletic pose, then did a couple of turns.

"See anything you want, Reverend?" she said.

"You've got my interest, I have to admit."

"Your honesty is admirable," she said.

As he watched, she kicked off her sandals and peeled down
her panty hose. Then, she got back in her sandals, making
her long legs look even longer. Swinging her knees back and
forth, she bent over, so that he could see the deep cleavage
between her full breasts, shaking her butt at the fire as she
did.

"Sure you have the guts for this, sugar?" she asked.
"That's a question for a novice from a pro."

"Some pro you are," he deadpanned. "You haven't even
seen my money."

"I can spot a guy with good credit a mile away," she said
with a wink.

With the fire crackling behind her, she began gyrating her
hips, humming, pushing up her hair as she turned to display
her body, then shimmying as he watched. His heart was beating faster and faster. And he was getting hard.

But she continued to perform, pretending she was oblivious, doing her thing as if it was something she did every day.
Damn, but she was tough.

Then, her back to him, she removed her bra, letting it dan-
gle from one hand as she twirled her hips and stuck her derriere in his direction. Dane was really beginning to feel warm.
He loosened his tie and unbuttoned his collar.

Tossing her bra aside, she turned to face him. As she did,
she covered her breasts with her hands, giving him a coquet-
tish smile. He stared at her as coolly as he could, the light
from the fire outlining her incredible legs. Her face was in
shadow, but he could see she'd let her mouth sag open and
she was running her tongue over her lips. She had the act
down to perfection, he had to admit.

She let her nipples slip between her fingers, teasing herself until they were erect. "Kathy do this for you much, Reverend?" she cooed.

"Not often," he said.

"Too proper, was she?"

"She wasn't too inhibited. Maybe it was the audience."

Mary Margaret let her hands drop away and shimmied toward him. Her breasts swung back and forth before his face. He looked into her eyes, grinning.

"You realize we haven't set a price," he said.

"I'm going to make it hard on you," she said. "I'm going to make you pay me what you think it's worth."

"You *are* a clever one, aren't you?"

"Told you, Reverend, you're dealing with a pro."

His whole body ached when she stripped off her panties and danced for him some more. He was afraid to look down to see if his erection was obvious, but Mary Margaret had to know.

She moved toward him and dropped onto her knees, resting her hands on his thighs. "You know the rules of lap dancing, don't you? The customer can't touch the girl. Only the girl can touch the customer."

"A true test of character," he said.

"Or patience."

Grinning, she stroked his cheeks, drawing her fingers lightly down over his jaw, pooching out her lips only inches from his. Close like that, he could see the light sheen of perspiration on her lip, and he could smell the fragrant, womanly heat of her body. He wanted badly to kiss her, to take her face and crush it against his, but that would be giving in.

Then, unexpectedly she dropped onto his lap, her back to him, and began grinding her hips into his crotch. He could hardly breathe. He smelled her hair, her perfume. He wanted with his very being to grab her and carry her to the bed, but he wouldn't allow himself to touch her.

The next thing he knew, she'd spun around and was sitting astride him. She leaned her face close to his, the sweet scent of champagne on her breath washing over him. She ran her tongue over her lips, then arched her breasts and rubbed them lightly against his chest. Dane returned her gaze, maintaining eye contact.

"Hmm," she said. "Maybe you learned more at that prep school of yours than I've been giving you credit for."

He arched a brow. "It's still your mind that impresses me most. No criticism of your professional abilities intended, mind you."

The corners of her mouth twitched. "You are such a bull-shitter, Reverend."

She removed his tie and began unbuttoning his shirt. When she had it half-open, she ran her hands inside it and rubbed his chest, all the while grinding against him.

Then, looking in his eyes, she asked, "So, what am I worth?"

"I'm neither as generous nor as desperate as your friend Ramon. How about an even thousand?"

"Mmm. How generous. But you're not a very shrewd customer. You could get what I just gave you for a hundred bucks in Nevada."

Dane shrugged. "I like your style, but I've got to tell you, in all honesty you strike me more as a wannabe than a seasoned pro. You can put all the paint on your face you want, do the bumps and grinds to perfection, but sweet little Mary Margaret still shines through."

Her eyes narrowed. "You're being hard-assed, aren't you?"

"Am I?"

"Come on, Dane, show me how tough you are. Ask me what it'll cost you to get laid."

He shook his head. "I don't pay for that. And I know damned well you don't sell it."

Mary Margaret flushed, then she got off his lap, picked up her panties and slipped them on. "Asshole," she said, glaring at him. She strode across the room to her case and, digging out a big, oversize T-shirt, she pulled it on over her head. "I'm going to bed," she announced. "Good night, Reverend. You can play with yourself for all I care." She pulled back the covers, then slid under the sheets.

"Good night, Mary Margaret," he said. Then, picking up the bottle of champagne, he took a long gulp, put it back down and gazed happily into the fire. He could feel her glaring at the back of his head and he was pleased. It had taken a herculean effort, but he'd won.

Mary Margaret lay on her side, facing the wall. Dane was undressing. She could hear him undoing his belt buckle and his zipper. She hated him for laughing at her. It was worse than scorn. Couldn't he understand how hard it had been to show him that other side of her? It hadn't been easy telling him about Ramon. And then he had made a joke out of it! Smug son of a bitch.

Dane got into bed. She held herself very still. She heard him give a small sigh like a person does after a hard day when bed feels so welcoming. There was no doubt in her mind that he was going to sleep!

Mary Margaret told herself she didn't care. She'd accomplished what she'd set out to do. She'd gotten everything out in the open, she'd disabused him of his illusions. And he could pretend he wasn't shocked, if that made him feel better. She didn't give a damn.

After a couple of minutes went by, with neither of them moving, the even pace of his breathing told her he was falling asleep. She rolled onto her back and stared up at the flickering light of the fire playing on the ceiling. There was no sign of life coming from Dane. Finally she rolled her head toward him. He lay serenely on his pillow, his eyes closed, a man without a care in the world. It made her seethe.

"Are you asleep?" she asked in a conversational tone.

His eyes blinked open and he rolled his head toward her. "Uh... Well, not now. Why?"

"You obviously aren't as upset by what happened as I am."

"What do you mean?"

"You were being a prick and you know it."

"Oh, that."

"Yes, that."

He didn't respond. When she looked at him again, he'd closed his eyes.

"Dane! Don't go to sleep, we're having a conversation. I'm pissed at you."

He rolled onto his side. Then he propped his head up on his hand. "I'm sorry if you're upset."

"That's all?"

"I'm *very* sorry you're upset."

"Oh," she said, gritting her teeth, "you can be really infuriating."

"Look, I may not have done a very good job of it, maybe I was clumsy, but all I was trying to do was communicate something to you."

"What?"

"That you're not the depraved, immoral being you like to think you are, and I'm not scandalized by your story about Ramon. You're still the person I thought you were, though I have to admit I learned a few things about you tonight."

"Like what?"

"Like you certainly know how to arouse a man."

"That's no revelation."

"To experience it makes it something special, believe me." His voice had taken on a soft intimate tone.

"Well, I learned something about you, too," she said. "And it's not very flattering. You're not the great humanitarian you make yourself out to be. You were cruel, in fact."

"Because I played along with your game?"

"It wasn't a game."

"You were making a point and so was I. You were trying to prove that I didn't know you, and I was trying to prove that maybe I know you better than you think and that I like what I know and see. And frankly, I was miffed you didn't trust me."

"I don't trust anybody."

"That's one of your problems. Your other problem is that you sell yourself short. You're a hell of a lot more worthy than you realize. Plus, it would behoove you to get rid of the inferiority complex or whatever it is. You don't deserve it."

They were harsh words, but they were loving words. She was both surprised and touched. "Is that true, Dane? I don't want you shitting me."

"Is what true? I said a lot of things."

"The part about liking what you know about me and what you see."

"I've been trying to tell you that for days," he said, a touch irritably.

"You've only known me for a few days. And you can't *really* know somebody for a long time. I mean, we only just met."

"I agree. That's why I haven't told you I love you. I'm reserving judgment."

She was stunned. "Love me?"

"Well, it's more than infatuation. And it's more than lust. We've established that, I think. You're my friend, Mary Margaret. I like you very much. Every moment I'm with you I discover something new and exciting. If it feels like love, it just might be love. But then we'll see, I guess, won't we?"

The annoyance she'd been feeling was suddenly displaced by a warm, happy feeling. In the passing of a moment she felt very close to him and she wasn't afraid as she'd been before. Liking him—loving him—had been a very scary proposition. Now it didn't seem quite so threatening.

"What would you think," she said, "if I told you I feel pretty much the same way about you?"

"Do you?"

"Yes, but every time I start to act on my feelings, I freeze up."

"Funny," he said, "but the girl who stripped and did that lap dance did not seem like anyone who was frozen."

"That had nothing to do with love or even sex. Not from my point of view. If anything, just the opposite. I was punishing you, rubbing it in your face."

"Hmm," Dane said, "isn't that interesting."

"For a woman, sex can be a weapon, more so even than for a man."

He touched her face with his fingertips. Turning her head, she kissed his hand.

"I've thought you were really attractive from the beginning," she said. "A big part of me wanted to be with you, that's why I gave all the mixed signals. But now I know exactly what I want. I want to make love with you."

He seemed moved by her words. "And I want to make love with you," he said.

She drew her hand down over his hairy chest and scooted

closer. Dane took her in his arms and kissed her. He kissed her deeply.

The sexual energy she'd been repressing out of fear came gushing out. It seemed the same with him. She'd been physically aroused before, really turned on, but never had the yearning come so deeply from within. Not like this.

"Oh, God," she groaned as he kissed first her mouth, then her neck and shoulders. She pulled away from him long enough to strip off her T-shirt and panties. Then she threw herself into his arms, losing herself in the feel of his body, allowing herself to become overwhelmed.

Dane drew his fingers up between her thighs. She tensed. Her breathing quickened. She desperately wanted more. Taking his wrist, she pressed his hand hard against her, making the sensation spike. For a brief second, she thought she might come, so she held her breath, waiting until the feeling subsided.

It was incredible what was happening, being with this special man who loved her, who wanted her as she'd dreamed of being wanted. She was surrendering out of desire, not need, not fear. So she wasn't holding back.

Dane, too, was ready. He began kissing her stomach. His breath scorched her, making her belly quiver. On the edge now, she couldn't take more. She climbed astride him and guided him into her opening. And when she looked down at him, she felt the same hunger she saw in his eyes.

Somehow she ended up beneath him, surrendering to his power. Within moments she came, he immediately afterward. Her body pulsed for a time, her limbs entwined in his. He lay heavy upon her, spent, without force. But, after a long moment, he managed to lift his head and kiss her moist skin.

"My God, but you're fabulous," he whispered.

Mary Margaret lay still, her eyes closed, her body still throbbing.

"So are you," she murmured, barely managing to speak.

Lying beside her, Dane laced his fingers in hers. They lay motionless except for the rise and fall of their chests. "I think we've found another area of compatibility," he said.

She laughed in agreement. He wanted to tell her he did love her, truly loved her, but he didn't. Instead he pulled her hand to his mouth and kissed her fingers one by one. Mary Margaret was very still. He knew what she was thinking. He knew precisely. She was wondering if this had been a beginning, or the beginning of the end.

Wednesday

August 14th

*Little River, Mendocino County,
California*

Dane awoke, unsure which dream to believe—the one that had begun with Mary Margaret doing the lap dance, or the one ending with him falling from an airplane, pushed by a barbarian with bad teeth and an equally bad accent. Over the course of the past ten hours or so he'd had the premier sexual experience of his life and he'd been threatened with a grisly death. Whoever said life had its ups and downs sure as hell knew what he was talking about.

Mary Margaret was still asleep, her bare leg pressed against his. Dane put his hand on her silky thigh. Just touching her was enough to arouse him. But when he rolled his head toward her, picking up the perfumed scent of her hair, and saw her flawless face, he felt a yearning wrench in his gut. The woman was magic, and her effect on him every bit as immutable as it was unrelenting.

At her initiative they'd made love a second time, an hour or so after the first. It had been much quieter and more loving. Afterward he again wanted to tell her how much he loved her, but still he'd held back, so as not to cheapen it. Eventually, when he did say the words, whether in a week or a month, he wanted her completely free of doubt.

Groaning, Mary Margaret rolled toward him, throwing her arm across his chest and snuggling closer. He'd awakened once or twice during the night and found her glued to him this way—partly, perhaps, because she was cold. But even when he covered her, she stayed nestled close to him, evidently relishing the intimacy. Dane had known other women who were naturally affectionate, but Kathy had not been one of them. Only now did he realize how pleasant it was to sleep with someone who wanted to be physically close.

That was the good side of his night. Unfortunately, he had to worry about the men who'd threatened him. Dane sensed that the situation had become more dangerous. True, it was another attempt to intimidate him, but these men had acted as though they'd just as soon kill him as not. He figured there were two conclusions to be drawn—one was that he was on the right track, the second was it could cost him his life.

He again looked at Mary Margaret. She was incredibly lovely. Drawing a strand of hair back off her face, he considered the fact that she, too, was in danger. So long as they pursued this case together, she was as likely to have her throat slit as he. That possibility he could not conscience. He wondered if they hadn't come to the end of their adventure. After all, he had a life worth preserving, as did she. And he had Toby to think about. Being a hero was one thing, but a man also had to consider his responsibilities.

It was becoming apparent he'd have to tell Mary Margaret what had happened and hope she wouldn't attribute his waiting to the fact he'd wanted to make love with her. He could almost hear her making a remark about men and their obsession with sex.

Mary Margaret groaned, then blinked her eyes open.

"Good morning," he said.

"Dane?" she replied, as though she didn't expect to actually wake up with him there.

"I hope you weren't expecting someone else," he teased.

"No, of course not. But I'm glad it's you."

"That's a relief," he said. "So, are you okay?"

"Hmm. I'm more than okay," she said her eyes twinkling. "And I know now that you're not a novice. Wow!"

"I appreciate the flattery. But you're not so bad yourself."

She studied him. "Does this mean we're lovers?"

"What do *you* think?"

"I think I asked you first."

"Well, I vote yes," he said.

She considered that, then she rolled over, turning her back to him. Dane scooted closer, pressing his face against her, drawing her into his lungs. She smelled so rich, vibrant, immediate. He ran his hand over her shoulder.

"How do you vote?"

"I'm thinking."

"Sorry it's such a tough decision."

She turned to face him. "You have to admit there are implications."

"Do you care to discuss them?"

"Nope. I have to go to the bathroom," she said. Then throwing back the covers, she jumped from the bed, affording him a view of her magnificent backside. She paused long enough to retrieve her T-shirt from the floor, then pranced off. "Brr, it's cold," she said, pulling the shirt over her head as she disappeared into the bathroom.

Dane fluffed some pillows and lay back, putting his hands behind his head. He knew they had issues to consider, but he felt fabulous. He wasn't too worried about Mary Margaret. She needed reassurance, which he could handle easily enough.

When she reappeared, he lifted the covers and she sprinted across the room, virtually diving into the bed. She immediately cuddled up against him, shivering. "That toilet seat could have had ice on it and not been any colder."

"Maybe I should build another fire."

"No, don't leave," she said, snuggling her face into his neck, kissing his skin.

He held her close, wanting to protect her. But it brought to mind that troubling moment out on the point last night. He pictured her, leaning into the wind and staring down at the waves. He recalled fearing she might jump, though he'd had no reason to think she would. Perhaps it was nothing more than the fear of losing something dear that was within his grasp.

"What were we talking about?" she asked.

He had to think. "Implications, I believe."

"Oh." She turned her back to him, but moved close.

"Do you care to discuss it?"

"No," she said, "I changed my mind. Maybe later. This is too nice."

She shimmied her backside against him, evoking in his mind fond memories of their lovemaking. He wrapped his arm around her, taking her breast in his hand. She caressed the back of it with her fingers.

"You liked that I was sexually aggressive last night, didn't you?" she asked.

"Is the pope Catholic?"

"Let's leave him out of this."

"Good idea."

"I'm not always that way," she said uncertainly.

"I'm not always the same either."

"No matter how good it is, people do get bored with each other eventually, you know."

"Is that a warning or a threat?"

"Realism," she said.

"Hmm."

"Don't you agree?"

"If it's only sex, you're right, Mary Margaret. But I'd like to think we have more potential than that."

She looked at him over her shoulder. The question was on her lips, but she left it unmasked. He could tell she wanted to know what last night had meant to him, and he considered making a little speech, but he didn't want to force it prematurely. This was the time for savoring what they had, not drawing conclusions about its meaning.

But he had another problem. Those men. He'd avoided mentioning them last night for the sake of expediency. But he had no excuse now. The only question was whether he should break the mood and get it over with or wait until the subject came up naturally. Over the quiet of his thoughts he could hear the distant surf pounding the rocks. He stroked her hair, wishing he didn't have to say anything, but he knew it wouldn't get any easier.

"What if I said I think it's time for us to give up trying to chase down Donna Lee's killer?" he said to her. "What if I said this adventure of ours is doing more harm than good?"

Mary Margaret turned to face him, giving him a quizzical look. "Is that what you think?"

"I wonder if we aren't out of our league," he said. "Maybe it's time to turn this over to professionals."

"Like who? The police scoff at everything we turn up. Nobody believes in us. I've tried hiring a detective."

"Maybe if we sit down with them and go over what's happened point by point…"

She gave him a long, penetrating look. "I think I understand. Jimmy Duggan's plight isn't so compelling now that you've fucked his daughter."

"Mary Margaret, no!" He took her face in his hands and made her look into his eyes. "That has absolutely nothing to do with it. I swear! Tonight, tomorrow night and the next hundred nights are just as important to me as last night was. To me, you aren't a conquest. You're…someone I care for very deeply. I'm as concerned for you as I am for myself."

"Concerned about what? That you're going to end up hanging on the screen door like your cat?"

He flinched.

Mary Margaret sighed. "I'm sorry. That was an insensitive thing to say. I know how much your little boy loved Mead."

"The point is, I don't know that I can guarantee your safety."

"Why now all of a sudden?"

Dane knew the moment of truth had arrived. He either lied or came clean. He still didn't know what was kindest, what was best. His mother always said, "When in doubt, tell the truth," but of course, she had almost always been intent on finding something out when she'd said it. On the other hand, he didn't want to patronize. Mary Margaret had a right to decide for herself what was in her interest and what wasn't.

"Something happened on our walk last night you were unaware of," he began.

"What?"

Dane recounted everything—holding nothing back. Mary Margaret listened in a stunned silence. After he'd finished the tale, she lay back on her pillow with a heavy sigh.

"I'm sorry," he said. "It's obviously the very last thing I wanted to happen."

"I'm sorry for you," she replied. "It's not your problem,

it's not your fight, but here you are, stuck squarely in the middle of it.''

"Oh, but it is my fight, if only because of my feelings for you. Which is why I don't want to be a coward.''

She retreated into her thoughts, staring up at the ceiling. Dane listened again to the surf and had a sick, empty feeling. The warmth and intimacy they'd been savoring only minutes ago was turning into a quagmire of uncertainty and misgivings.

"I do have one question, though,'' she said after a time. "I don't mean to be critical, but how could you sleep with me ten minutes after somebody threatened your life?''

He groaned, knowing it was coming. "I guess my sex drive is stronger than my sense of responsibility.''

"Well, at least you're honest about it.''

Dane made her look at him again. "What happened here last night was because I feel so strongly about you, and what has happened this morning is also because I feel so strongly about you. The timing was unfortunate, I grant you. But I care about you very, very much.''

"So what are you suggesting we do? Go home?''

"There's no reason we can't stay here another day or two, is there? The whole point in coming was to get away.''

"I don't know,'' she lamented. "I sort of feel creepy about things.''

His heart sank. He was afraid of this, expecting and dreading it both. But he could hardly blame her. Women weren't as good at compartmentalizing their lives. If they were upset about one thing, it tended to infect everything else. Consequently, if a guy screwed up in one domain, he could forget about all the others.

"I'll take you back to Reno, if that's what you want,'' he said, "but I'd feel better knowing Coleman was behind bars.''

"Maybe he is,'' she said.

For the first time, Dane did not find that prospect welcome. A Rut Coleman on the loose better served his immediate purpose—not that he'd go so far as to actually wish for it. "I need to make some calls anyway,'' he said. "When we go to the lodge for our breakfast, I'll telephone and get an update.''

"Strange they don't have phones in the rooms.''

"People come here to get way from everything."

"Too bad it didn't work in our case," she said.

Dane felt badly. They endured their first uncomfortable silence as lovers.

"I hope it hasn't ruined the trip for you." he said after a while.

"No. I can separate things."

She wasn't very convincing. He lay his hand on her stomach. He felt tentative and he didn't like that.

"I think it's time to get up," she said.

"Shall we flip to see who gets the first shower. Or shall we both try to squeeze in at the same time?"

Mary Margaret touched his face, her expression wistful. "No, I think I'll invoke a woman's prerogative and go first. You'll have to wait your turn."

Dane watched as she got out of bed and headed off to the bath. He was once again amazed at how quickly joy could turn to dust.

The waitress cleared away Mary Margaret's half-eaten *huevos rancheros,* poured her some more coffee and left her to watch a forlorn gull soaring in the mist. The dining room was nearly empty, so she was left to contemplate her recent joys and long-standing sorrows in solitude. Dane was making his calls and had been gone for what seemed like a very long time. There had been no reason for him to leave the building so she couldn't imagine any harm having come to him. Yet after the visit from those men, she could hardly take anything for granted.

Dane, she could tell, was not eager to continue the investigation, and she couldn't blame him. What, really, did he have to gain? But she was in a different situation—on the verge of having nothing to lose. Since her mother's death, she'd felt as if her life had been one long series of disappointments. So what was one more setback, one more false start?

The problem was simple. She'd broken with her pattern of going it alone, and complications were inevitable. But regardless of what happened from here on out, her father would remain a problem. The injustice he'd suffered was a cancer on her soul. And Dane understood that, which made it harder for them both. It would be easier for them if Jimmy was placed on the back burner and forgotten, because then they could concentrate on each other. God knew, her father wouldn't squawk. To him, prison was a form of death and being dead was, in his mind, convenient.

Over the past few days she'd wondered more than once if she and Dane could have a relationship exclusive of this crusade. For several hours last evening they'd lived just for themselves and each other. It had been a wonderful, idyllic experience, a dream come to life. In her heart, Mary Margaret knew it wouldn't last, though she hadn't figured it would end quite this quickly or in this way.

Still, she'd done something she hadn't done since...well, since she was a young girl. She'd had visions of cottages with white picket fences, shaggy dogs and kids. She had imagined a life with Dane. It was a rare and frightening thing she'd done and now she was suffering the consequences. It was dangerous, she'd discovered, to want something. Dreams inevitably led to nightmares. Which again made her worry about Dane and why he was taking so long.

Another couple left the dining room and Mary Margaret wondered if she should look for him. The busboys had begun changing tablecloths, removing the toasters from the tables and preparing for the next meal. She decided rather than wait for them to bring her Dane's corpse, she'd go find him. She'd just gotten to her feet when he appeared, walking briskly toward the table. Ominously, he had a sober, if not grim, expression on his face.

"We're going to have to leave," he said, motioning for her to sit. He took his seat across from her.

"What happened?"

"I'll give you the bad news first," he said solemnly. "Your dad was assaulted last evening at the prison and was pretty badly beaten up."

"Oh, my God!" she said, her hands covering her mouth.

"He's all right though, at least it's nothing life-threatening. They have him in the prison infirmary, which I understand is a good sign. If it had been more serious, they'd have taken him to a community hospital.''

She was shaken. "How did you find out?"

"There was a message from Janine at the front desk. I called San Quentin, representing myself as your clergyman. I hope you don't mind the presumption.''

"No, of course not.''

"I asked if we could visit him and was told it might be arranged. We'll have to get down to Marin. I assume you'd rather do that than return to Reno.''

"Yes, of course. But you can't go.''

"Why not?''

"Those men told you to butt out.''

"Visiting a man in prison is not the same as playing Sam Spade.''

"Are you sure?''

"There's no reason for you to go alone.''

She was relieved, but reluctant to let it show for fear of creating a sense of obligation. Her father was very important to her, but so was Dane, and the last thing she wanted was for him to be hurt.

"I've rescheduled our charter," he explained. "And I've got somebody working on getting us a rental car.''

She took his hand, tears of gratitude glistening in her eyes.

"There's more news," he said. "Yesterday Rut Coleman was cornered in the town of Jackson, not far from Sacramento, trying to rob a gas station. There was a shootout and he was seriously wounded. The last Janine heard, he was still alive but in custody.''

The news came as a relief. "I'm not going to shed any tears over him," she said. "That may not be very Christian of me, but it's the way I feel.''

"Even the Christian parts of my soul can't blame you," he said. "All life is sacred, but I suffer over the loss of some lives more than others. Janine, by the way, sends her love. She's happy for us.''

Mary Margaret's brows rose. "What did you tell her?"

"That we've managed to put Rut Coleman from our minds, relax and have a good time. I saw no point in telling her about our little setback.''

"Little setback, huh? It won't seem so little when the bullets start flying."

"Hey, young lady, I thought we were going to try being optimistic from now on."

"*Try*'s the operative word."

He nodded, indicating he wouldn't argue the point.

"Any other news?" she said. "Or have we pretty much scraped the bottom of the barrel?"

"Lots more," he said, brushing some crumbs from the tablecloth. "Claudia said the Laurel police haven't turned up anything on the guy who killed Mead, but she did get an address for Stephen Ragsdale's daughter, Sally. She's in San Francisco and leaving with her husband on a month-long trip to Europe in a couple of days. I thought maybe we could drop by to see her after we visit your father."

"Dane, we can't...or at least you can't. That's just what those men didn't want you doing."

He looked disgruntled. "Maybe we can have one discreet conversation."

"And how do you suppose I'll feel if they kill you because of it?"

"Sad, I hope."

"Thanks a lot. I finally go to bed with a man I actually like and he tells me he's thinking of playing a quick little game of Russian roulette."

"Oh," he said, brightening, "so it's *you* that you're worried about, not me."

"Damned right. Nice guys don't grow on trees."

"I love it when you talk selfish," he teased, patting her hand.

"So, are we headed for the airport?"

"Yes. Turns out I have to be in the Bay Area tomorrow anyway. There was a message on my answering machine from Kathy. She wants me to meet her tomorrow morning in Berkeley."

"God, I forgot about her."

"I did, too."

"Must be something about former spouses," she quipped.

"I have to admit I'm a little curious what she's going to spring on me. Kathy has a sense for the dramatic and likes surprising me—I think because it gives her a feeling of control."

"I'm sure it will be very interesting," Mary Margaret said, fiddling with her coffee cup.

"Claudia also told me Granville Jones got the address for Ted Gotchall, the detective who handled your father's case," Dane said. "He's in a nursing home down on the Peninsula, in San Bruno. Maybe we can find some time to swing by to see him."

She groaned. "God, Dane, you're like a kid who's been told not to do something and that's all he wants to do."

"My only concern is for you."

"What about your son?"

"And for Toby."

"Look," she said, "I want you to go back to Laurel and get to work on next Sunday's sermon. I won't be able to relax until you do. And I mean that."

He stroked her cheek. "God, I love you."

The words came out so quickly that she was sure he hadn't tested them in his mind before he uttered them. She didn't say anything, expecting him to backtrack.

"Was that too candid?" he said after a while.

"I'm taking it in the spirit in which it was intended."

His only response was a smile. She felt such an outpouring from her heart just then that fear surged through her. Fear of loss, fear of hope, fear of failure. Still, she managed to smile back, saved, perhaps, by the fact that tears welled up in her eyes, making it hard to see him.

"I won't be preaching on Sunday, by the way," he said. "There are a few more weeks of summer services. My real work begins after Labor Day. All of which is to say I have a lot of time to devote to you."

"Promise me you won't let anything happen to you," she said in response to a well of desperation. "Promise me, Dane."

"Only if you promise the same thing."

She stared into his eyes, knowing for the first time in her life what it must be like for a woman seeing her man go off to war. Maybe she was being melodramatic, but her concern was not without justification. Mary Margaret had a terrible

premonition that Dane Barrett's optimism could very well
lead to his demise.

San Quentin State Prison, California

Jimmy Duggan lay in bed, listening to the raspy wheeze
of his own breathing as he stared at the barred window across
the room. Instead of seeing five bars, he saw ten. The vision
of his left eye was still blurred and his head was throbbing
to beat the band, but he didn't care. Rut Coleman was in
worse shape and that made it all worthwhile.

Hicks and the others said it was his fault that Coleman was
in the hospital, and so he had to pay. Jimmy didn't tell them,
but it was fine with him. Worth it. Of course, if Coleman was
to die, his own life wouldn't be worth a plug nickel, but he'd
decided long ago it wasn't worth a plug nickel anyway. It
almost didn't matter whether he'd killed that girl or not. Truth
meant less than power. The Rut Colemans and Larry Hickses
called the shots because they could. It was as simple as that.

Despite his pain, though, Jimmy felt about as good as he
had in months. It would only be for a few days, but he was
relatively safe in the infirmary. He could relax. The aches and
pains seemed almost unimportant. Everybody needed a little
peace now and then.

Taking a deeper breath, Jimmy winced. The doctor said he
had a couple of cracked ribs and that he'd have trouble
breathing for a while. Yawning and coughing was a problem,
but as long as he kept his breaths shallow, he was okay.
Maybe Rut Coleman wasn't so lucky.

The door opened and Jimmy saw two figures moving toward the bed. Both were Father O'Grady. The paunchy priest
always wore his collar, but not always his coat. O'Grady was
not a strong individual, which made Jimmy wonder why he'd
been chosen to work in a prison. But he was dedicated and
maybe that's what mattered.

"And how are you feeling this afternoon, Jimmy Duggan?" the priest said.

"Okay."

"That's good because you've got a couple of visitors I'll be bringing in to see you."

"Visitors?" Jimmy was wary.

"It's Mary Margaret, your daughter. And a Unitarian clergyman by the name of Barrett."

"Mary Margaret's here?" Jimmy said, not believing it.

"She is, and I've arranged for her to see you, which took some effort on my part, I might say."

This was like an unexpected Christmas present. Jimmy had seen few of those growing up—with all the brothers and sisters having to share what little his parents had, a few pieces of candy and a rubber ball or a sack of glass marbles was an incredible treat. This was even better because there had been no expectation. But as his heart soared, the reality of his own inadequacies set in. Mary Margaret had been his secret joy, but she'd also been his cross to bear—the most obvious reminder of his failings as a human being. He loved her, but he hated what he'd done to her.

"Are you sure it's a good idea, Father?" he asked, his misgivings growing.

"Don't you want to see her, Jimmy? She's worried and she's come a long way."

The truth was he lived for Mary Margaret's visits. She came to the prison three times a year. They'd face each other through that glass, strangers with the same blood—she wanting a father and he failing to be one. "Can't you just try, Jimmy?" Moira had said one of the times he'd lived with them when he wasn't at sea or in prison. "She's your daughter, your own flesh and blood."

Mary Margaret was about six at the time, an angel who deserved better. He'd taken her to the zoo one day and let her go on the merry-go-round ten or twelve times because it was easier to wave at her as she went round and round than to hold her hand and know she was wondering why it couldn't always be that way.

"Jimmy," Father O'Grady said, "you aren't going to make me send her away, are you?"

Jimmy Duggan rolled his aching head back and forth. "No, Father," he said, his voice barely a whisper. "Tell her I want to see her."

* * *

Mary Margaret was nervous. The prison guard standing at the door didn't help. What did he think? That she was going to smuggle her father out in her purse? But she knew she was in no position to complain. She was lucky to be seeing him at all.

Dane, who sat beside her, had been just wonderful—sensing her need, being there for her. Anthony had given her nothing in the way of support except bus fare one December so she could see her father. "But it's coming out of your Christmas present," he'd said. To Anthony, a relative in prison was something to forget—like a bankruptcy or a case of the clap.

Driving to the prison, she and Dane had discussed how much they should tell Jimmy about the case. "He never wanted to talk about it" she said. "He'd ask about the show, but wouldn't discuss his appeals or his own life. He'd get impatient with me if I brought up the subject. It was as if he were dead."

"But maybe he can be of help," Dane had said. "It's worth asking a few questions, surely."

"Then you talk to him about it. I can't."

Mary Margaret got up and paced, her eyes catching Dane's every once in a while. She remembered him sitting Lincoln-esque in the chair in their room, watching her. Lord, was that yesterday? It seemed a million years and a million miles from where they were now. From heaven to the penitentiary.

The door opened and a doleful priest with a flabby stomach hanging over his belt entered. He approached her, his expression beneficent, his hands extended.

"Hello, Mary Margaret."

"Hello, Father."

"I'm so glad you've come," he said, taking both her hands in his.

She introduced Dane and the men shook hands.

"Does my father know about me being kidnapped by Rut Coleman?" she asked.

"I don't think so. I only learned of it myself this morning, after we got Reverend Barrett's call. I've said nothing to Jimmy."

"There's no point telling him," she said. "He's got enough to worry about. Anyway, I came out of it all right."

"Praise God."

She glanced at Dane, whose demeanor was very ministerial. It was something she had to adjust to, considering the hours they'd spent together in bed.

"Does Mr. Duggan know about Coleman being in the shoot-out?" he asked the priest.

"I believe he found out when he was beaten."

"Do you know who did it?"

O'Grady smiled indulgently. "I didn't ask. Jimmy didn't say. That's the way things are done here, Reverend Barrett."

Mary Margaret and Dane went with Father O'Grady and the guard down a corridor until they came to a gate with bars. The guard stationed there admitted them, then resecured the gate. She shivered at the clang of the heavy steel. It brought home the fact that her father was trapped in this place, caged like an animal.

O'Grady led them to the infirmary. Mary Margaret glanced into the rooms with open doors. In one she saw a man in bed, his leg in a cast, in the next there was a man coughing so hard his face was red. They stopped at the last door. O'Grady opened it.

Mary Margaret looked in, not knowing what to expect. The man in the bed was heavily bandaged. The top of his head was covered except for sprouts of gray hair here and there. So was his torso from the middle of his chest down.

"I'll leave you to talk," Father O'Grady said, slipping away.

She nodded and stepped into the room, approaching the bed. One of the patient's eyes vaguely resembled her father's. The other was a puffy slit and could have belonged to anyone. The mouth she recognized.

"Hi, Dad," she said, trying to sound cheerful, though her inclination was to cry.

"Mary Margaret," he mumbled, the corner of his mouth bending just enough to signal a smile.

She leaned over the bed and gave the least battered cheek a light kiss. "Looks like you've been hanging out in the wrong bar." It was her father's phrase. She'd heard him say it many times when somebody had a problem, especially an injury.

"And the gin wasn't much to brag about, either," he whispered.

Mary Margaret squeezed his hand.

"You all right?" her father asked.

"Couldn't be better, Dad." She glanced back at Dane, who was standing a little behind her. "Oh, I'd like you to meet my friend, Dane Barrett."

"Hello, Mr. Duggan," Dane said, stepping up next to her.

"Jimmy," he replied.

"Dad doesn't trust people who call him Mr. Duggan," she explained.

Jimmy nodded his concurrence.

"So, Dad," she said, "you going to live, or what?"

"I told you Rut Coleman was bad news," her father said.

"Yeah, well, he got what he deserved."

"Now I'm not so sure I want him dead," Jimmy said. "But you're all right and that's all I care about."

"Well, I care about you," she said, sitting next to him on the edge of the bed. "And I've got plans to have your case reopened."

"Don't waste your time," he replied.

"No, there's a chance we can do something," she explained. "Dane has turned up some things. Remember that old lady, the sister of the woman next door to the Marshalls? Her name was Ledi—"

"Mary Margaret," he said, cutting her off, "I don't want to talk about that. Tell me about your show. When will they make you the star? They ought to put you on television, that's what they should do."

"Dad, there's a better chance of you digging out of this place than that happening. I know you don't like talking about the case, but Dane wants to ask you some questions. Just for a couple of minutes. Please."

Jimmy turned his good eye toward Dane and waited.

"Jimmy," he said, "does the name Benny mean anything to you? A possible witness to Donna Lee's murder. Somebody in the neighborhood, maybe."

"I didn't know the neighborhood. That was the only time

I was at the house, the day it happened. I know a guy named
Benny here, but that's not what you're asking.''

"So the name Benny means nothing to you?"

Jimmy shook his head.

"You told the police Reverend Ragsdale asked you to drop
off something at Donna Lee's that day, is that right?"

"Yeah."

"Did he say why?"

"All I remember is he asked me to go by. I don't remember
his words, but I don't think he gave me any big speech or
anything."

Dane and Mary Margaret exchanged looks. She could see
this wasn't fruitful. She patted her father's hand as Dane continued.

"Do you know anything about Donna Lee's relationship
with Ragsdale?"

"She was around the church quite a bit. Once she asked
me where he was. Another time she came down to our apartment in the basement. I thought she was looking for Mary
Margaret, but she said she thought Ragsdale might be there.
A few days later is when I found her in my bed. Where that
came from I don't know. At the time I thought she was nuts.
I ran her out, then a couple of days later...well, you know."

"But you never saw her and Ragsdale together?"

"Sure. Talking. But that's all. I told the cops all this. It's
nothing new."

"Well, I don't want to get your hopes up," Dane said,
"because we're not sure anything's going to come of it, but
the little we've turned up has gotten somebody very nervous.
I've had threats to back off from my investigation, so I know
there's a lot to the story that hasn't been told."

Jimmy was silent for a long time and Mary Margaret
wasn't sure what was going through his mind until he said,
"I'd rather not know."

"I don't blame you," Dane said. "But it's important that
you understand that people care. Mary Margaret refuses to
give up hope and she has lots of support."

"You're a Unitarian minister?" Jimmy said.

"Yes."

"Those people were pretty nice to us. Even Ragsdale. I've

told Mary Margaret this," Jimmy said, "but sometimes being the wrong person can be as bad as doing the wrong thing. Half the black and Hispanic guys here in Quentin will tell you that."

"It's a sad commentary on our society," Dane said, "but doing the right thing is still important. That's why Mary Margaret and I are here. We may not prevail, but it won't be for lack of effort."

With his good eye, Jimmy looked back and forth between them. "You two are good friends, aren't you?"

"Mary Margaret is the finest person I've ever known," Dane said, putting his hand on her shoulder.

She pressed her cheek against his hand.

A little smile cracked at the corner of her father's mouth. "That's the best thing I heard since...well, forever."

Mary Margaret's eyes glistened. "Oh, Daddy," she said.

"So, why don't you leave now?" Jimmy said. "Get out in the sunshine and fresh air. Go stand on Ocean Beach and think of me. I'll think of you there, Mary Margaret, the wind blowing your pretty red hair. That will make me feel good. You want to do something for me. Do that." He gestured with his hand. "Now go on. This place is for the wrong ones, not the right ones."

Mary Margaret kissed him, then she got up. Her eyes were so full of tears she could hardly see. Dane went with her to the door, which the guard opened.

She turned and faced her father. "You and I are going to walk on Ocean Beach together someday before too long, Dad," she said. "I promise you that. Whether you want to hear it or not."

San Bruno, California

Dane wished he'd been watching his rearview mirror more carefully because he had no idea how long the dark brown sedan had been following them. When they'd left Bayshore Freeway just north of the airport and gotten onto Highway 380, the sedan was right behind them. The same when they exited at El Camino Real.

He figured it was probably either the guys who'd threatened him at the Heritage House or somebody connected to them. Seeing how easily they'd found him, he knew he could never feel safe again until this was over. At the same time, seeing Jimmy Duggan had convinced him he couldn't simply close his eyes and walk away. How could he face his son knowing he'd seen injustice up close and done nothing about it? Something in life had to be sacred. But right now he had to decide when to tell Mary Margaret they were being tailed.

"Tanforan," she said, reading the map. "I remember when I was a little girl and my father used to talk about the good old days when he'd watch the ponies running at Tanforan." She laughed. "I thought he was talking about the ponies like the ones in the petting zoo."

"A racetrack, I take it."

"It burned down in the sixties. Now it's a shopping center. It's back the other way, just on the opposite side of the freeway."

She had him make a right onto San Bruno Avenue. Dane checked the mirror. The sedan followed. His level of discomfort went up a couple of notches.

The nursing home where Ted Gotchall was living out his last days was up the hill a quarter of a mile or so, adjacent to a business park. Fortunately, there was an available parking spot right at the front door. Dane pulled into the parking space and turned off the engine.

Granville Jones had told Claudia Rosenfelter that Gotchall was dying of cancer and he wasn't sure what kind of shape his mind was in. When Dane had relayed that to Mary Margaret, she'd said, "I'll bet you dinner he's incoherent."

He'd pinched her cheek. "After meeting your father, I realize where you got your pessimism gene."

"It's a blue-collar thing," she'd said. "You country-club types wouldn't understand. That's why I've been giving you such a hard time."

Dane could only hope she'd be wrong about Gotchall. If the big guy with the accent was determined to do him in, he didn't want to suffer for naught. They'd had one setback already. His call to Sally Ragsdale Nesbit hadn't gone well. First, she'd tried to put him off, suggesting he contact her after she returned from Europe. Then, when he'd pressed her, saying it was terribly urgent, she told him to call back in a few hours. She wanted to discuss the matter with her husband.

Having some time, they'd driven to Nob Hill. Dane got them a room at the Fairmont, but they hadn't bothered going upstairs. He'd suggested they head straight to San Bruno. After their visit to San Quentin, Mary Margaret had been in a funk, but he could tell she was doing her best not to get too down—he suspected as much for his sake as for her own. But now they had the brown sedan to worry about. He decided not to tell her just yet.

They climbed out of their rental car. Dane stretched and looked in the general direction of the big jet taking off from SFO, but he was really studying the brown sedan parked half a block down the street. All he could tell was that there were two occupants, both men. It could have been the boys from Mendocino, but maybe not. At least they were keeping their distance. Dane wasn't sure what he'd have done if they'd come charging up the street brandishing weapons.

They went inside and presented themselves to the receptionist. She directed them to the nursing supervisor, a tiny black woman of about fifty with an authoritative voice and a no-nonsense manner.

"Mr. Gotchall is seriously ill and we wouldn't be allowing non-family members in except that he said he was willing to talk to you, and his daughter concurred," she said. "Come this way, I'll show you to his room."

"What's Ted's mental condition?" Dane asked as they went down the hall.

"Mr. Gotchall is sharper than you and me and the young lady put together," the nurse said. "Nothing wrong with his mind."

Dane gave Mary Margaret a nudge with his elbow and winked.

"Well, I get to pick the place," she whispered.

They stopped at an open door. A large gangly man in his late sixties who looked as though he might have had a lot more meat on his bones at one time, sat up in bed, reading a newspaper. He had an oxygen tube in his nose and a shunt in his arm.

"Ah," he said, seeing them. "You must be Barrett." He let the newspaper settle across his legs. He scrutinized Mary Margaret as they entered. "Jimmy Duggan's daughter, I bet. You were in high school—and about what? Seventeen, eighteen?—the last time I saw you. That makes you twenty-five, six now?"

"I'm twenty-six, Mr. Gotchall," she said.

"We talked, remember? It was in my office. You spilled coffee all over the place. No, it was water. Wasn't that it?"

"I dropped the glass."

"What the hell, you were upset." He offered his hand to Dane. "Hello, Reverend." He motioned toward the chairs facing the bed. "Sit down, make yourselves at home." Gotchall proceeded to fold the newspaper. "Checking to see how my stocks are doing. Nice to know I'm leaving my daughter something of value. She'll have to put three kids through college. Between this lousy ticker of mine and the cancer, I won't be around to see a one of them graduate from high school, but maybe they'll think of me when they put the old diploma on the wall." He laughed. "When hell freezes over. No sentimentality nowadays. Everything's 'What can you do for me?'" He studied them, his affable manner fading. "They tell me you want to talk about the case."

"We have a few questions," Dane said.

"Fine, I'll answer them, but I want to say one thing to you first, Miss Duggan. I gathered the evidence, I didn't convict your father. The jury did that."

"Granville Jones has made that point on several occasions," Dane said.

"Yes, but when Jonesy says it, he's trying to justify himself. I was different than most cops. I always saw it as a puzzle, not a contest with the suspect. I'll tell you right out, if I had to bet my grandkids college money on that case, I'd say your dad did it, Miss Duggan, and the only reason is because the odds dictate it. But I'll be the first to admit it wasn't a very satisfying puzzle."

Dane glanced over and saw Mary Margaret's cheeks turning bright red. "What do you mean, it wasn't a very satisfying puzzle?" he said.

"There were a few key pieces missing as far as I was concerned. Some things that I didn't like much."

"Then why didn't you tell the jury that!" Mary Margaret snapped.

"First, because I wasn't called to testify. Second, because it's the lawyer's job to make the arguments, not the investigator's."

"Wait a minute," Dane said. "You didn't testify at the trial?"

"No. There was no particular reason to call me, though it could have happened. You see, I was in Stockton testifying at a hearing the day of the murder. The crime scene was secured and the physical evidence had been gathered by other officers. I took over the investigation the next day, when I returned, but much of the physical work had been done. And it was a piss-poor job they'd done, too, pardon my French."

"How so?"

"Sloppy. There was only one man on the scene with training. The lab people from the county were disgusted."

"Wonderful," Mary Margaret said. "Why was this never mentioned?"

"Two reasons, Miss Duggan. First, a lot of what I'm referring to is professional kibitzing, insider stuff. And second, again, it was up to your dad's lawyer to raise questions, not us."

"It's always somebody else's fault," Mary Margaret lamented. "What about my poor father? Nobody's willing to take responsibility for what's happened to him!"

Dane was beginning to realize that Mary Margaret's emotional soft spot for her father was boundless. Reaching over, he patted her arm.

"I'm sure I'd feel the same in your shoes," Ted Gotchall said. "But the truth is, I could only do my job. You stick your nose in the other guy's business, you don't have your job for long."

"We're not here to blame anyone," Dane said, "just untangle a few things if we can. You said the initial police work was sloppy. Can you give us specific examples?"

"They moved the victim's body before the technicians got there and somebody covered it. That's a no-no. But the thing

I never really understood, and what surprised the hell out of me, was why the defense never made anything of that extraneous print on the knife."

"What extraneous print?" Mary Margaret said, sitting up straighter. "What are you talking about?"

"The lab found a fingerprint on the knife blade that didn't belong to Jimmy. We assumed at first it was the victim's, but that didn't pan out. Then we thought one of the officers on the scene might have touched it, but we found no match there. We checked Mrs. Marshall, no match there, either. It was one of those things, a piece that just didn't fit."

"For God's sake, why didn't you report this, Mr. Gotchall?" Mary Margaret said. She'd gotten excited again, but was making an effort to keep her cool.

"I did. It was in my report. In the lab report, too. Everything went to the D.A."

Dane and Mary Margaret looked at each other. "The misnumbered pages," she said.

"Yeah," Dane said. "Only they weren't misnumbered. One was missing. I'll bet the information concerning this fingerprint is what was lost."

"What are you talking about?" Gotchall said.

Dane explained how the private investigator Mary Margaret hired found the anomalies in the police report.

"That report was complete when I sent it over to the D.A.'s office," Gotchall said. "If somebody monkeyed with it, it was after it left my hands."

"But who?" Dane said.

"Either the courier or somebody at the other end. I have no idea."

"Wait a minute," Dane said, confused. "Didn't you send a copy of your report to Jimmy's defense counsel, Mr. Haskell?"

"No, sir. That's the prosecutor's responsibility. Everything's done lawyer to lawyer. You'd have to ask Mr. Wainwright."

"But why didn't it come up in the trial?"

"If questions aren't asked, they don't get answered, Reverend. This missing page you're talking about may explain why Mr. Haskell didn't ask about the print."

"Dear God," Mary Margaret said, getting to her feet. "I can't believe this." She went to the window, trembling. "There's your reasonable doubt right there. No wonder the prosecutor didn't want us to see the lab report."

"I'm no lawyer," Ted Gotchall said, "but it's not easy to say what makes reasonable doubt. No question it should have been raised by your father's attorney, though. Had he known."

"Scott Wainwright, or somebody in his office, apparently didn't want it to come out in court," Dane said.

"Yeah. Well, maybe Wainwright wanted a conviction so badly he was willing to suppress evidence, omit a page of the report before he sent it to Haskell," Mary Margaret said. She started pacing. "He made my father a scapegoat."

"Maybe, Miss Duggan," Gotchall said, "but you're skipping along pretty fast there. You have no proof it was Wainwright himself."

"Proof?" she cried. "My father's in prison for something he didn't do. The case smells to high heaven and now suddenly I've got to prove he's innocent?"

"If you've found irregularities, take it to a judge," Gotchall said. "But if I were you, I'd have my ducks lined up pretty good first."

Dane reached back and took her hand. "He's right, Mary Margaret. We have to proceed carefully. If we go off half-cocked, it could backfire on us."

"You aren't suggesting this doesn't count."

"Of course it does. If we can prove evidence was suppressed, your father might get a new trial. But it would be nice to know what, exactly, was suppressed and why. We've turned up a lot more than just a missing page in the lab report."

"Yes," she said, taking her seat again. "What about Benny?"

"Who's Benny?" Gotchall asked.

"We were hoping you might be able to help us with that." Dane explained Ledi Hopkins's deathbed utterances.

"Benny," the former detective said, shaking his head. "The name never came up in the investigation. Not that I recall."

"Dane thinks Benny was Theo Bledsoe's dog," Mary Margaret said, "but I think he's the key to this. Maybe that unidentified fingerprint on the knife was his. For all we know, Benny's the killer!"

"Wait a minute," Dane said. "You checked the print against Donna Lee and her mother and the officers on the scene, is that right, Mr. Gotchall?"

"Yes."

"Did you check it against Stephen Ragsdale's prints?"

Gotchall shook his head. "No reason to. He wasn't a suspect. He had an alibi and there was no reason to believe he was at the scene of the crime."

"We've found out that Ragsdale spent a lot of time at the Marshall place when Donna Lee's mother was gone," Mary Margaret said. "I think Donna Lee and Ragsdale were having an affair."

"I know you thought Ragsdale was the killer," Gotchall said, "but there just wasn't any evidence to support it."

"Did you know about the affair? A neighbor, Agnes McBain, saw Ragsdale slipping into the Marshall house every time Loretta left. Doesn't that make Ragsdale a suspect, at least?"

Gotchall sighed. "Had I known that, I might have gotten prints from him, if only to eliminate him as a suspect. Hindsight's usually twenty-twenty."

"Meanwhile, my father's in prison."

The nursing supervisor appeared at the door, her hands on her hips. "This sounds like a pretty animated conversation going on here. I'm wondering if this is doing my patient any good. The last thing he needs is to get excited."

"What difference does it make?" Ted Gotchall said. "I'll be dead in a month or two."

"I don't see any point in speeding it along," she said.

Dane got up. "We should probably be going anyway. We've gotten our questions answered."

"If you get your father a hearing date, young lady," Gotchall said, "I'll testify as to what was in that report. But if you want my testimony, I wouldn't wait around too long."

"Thank you for your honesty," Mary Margaret said.

"Criminal investigation is an art as much as a science. Gut

instinct's key. For what it's worth, I'm a lot less sure about
your father's guilt than when you walked through the door. I
think you're on to something, but I'd sure like to see more."
He turned to Dane. "And I'd be very careful if I was you.
From what Jones said, it's clear somebody is not very happy
with what's happening. These things have a way of escalat-
ing, you know. Threats tend to become self-fulfilling proph-
esies."

Dane again thought about the car down the street, and a
shiver went through him. "I take your point, Mr. Gotchall."

San Francisco, California

Dane had been watching the rearview mirror constantly.
The sedan was always somewhere back there. Worse, since
leaving San Bruno there had been only one man in the car.
Dane decided that once they got to the Fairmont, he would
give Gotchall a call. If the former detective had a visitor after
they left and the case was discussed, Dane would almost certainly have to pull up the drawbridge.

Since leaving the nursing home he'd been giving serious
consideration to going to the police. The trouble was, he
couldn't give a description of the men who had accosted him.
And unless they could be identified, there wasn't much the
police could do. They certainly weren't going to provide him
with a police escort.

They were heading north on Larkin Street at the moment,
and had just passed the Civic Center Plaza. He glanced over
at Mary Margaret, who'd been brooding silently.

"Hey, kiddo," he said, trying to sound cheerful. "No reason to be so glum. We've made tremendous progress, maybe
even turned up enough to get the case reopened. As a mini-
mum, we can talk to a lawyer about it—somebody besides
Lloyd Haskell."

She reached over and touched his arm affectionately. "I
know. I guess as the prospects improve I'm getting more
tense. Don't take my brooding personally."

"I won't, but I want to remind you we aren't all that far
removed from that little respite we had in paradise."

She gave him one of her prettiest smiles. "You might not believe it, but I've been thinking about that, too."

"Then there's still hope for the home team?"

She leaned over, kissing him on the cheek. "More than hope, Dane."

"I'm going to call Sally Nesbit as soon as we get to the hotel," he said. "If she'll talk to us, then I think we should go take care of that. But either way, I'm going to buy you an extra-special dinner tonight. Then we'll have a nice relaxing evening."

"That sounds wonderful, but *I* owe you dinner, remember?"

"Can't hold you to that. Granville Jones told Claudia, who told me Gotchall was sharp as a tack."

"Dane, you're a liar. You're just trying to spare me."

"I'll pay for dinner," he said. "And you can find a way to repay me. If only in kind," he added with a wink.

She gave him a look. "I shudder to think how much this trip is costing you. Chartering that plane, a rental car, the hotels, meals..."

"I've had a few bucks socked away, Mary Margaret. Personally, I can't think of a better way to spend them."

"What about Toby's education?"

"His grandmother has made a provision for that. And Kathy's parents set up a little trust fund, too. My father managed to keep his money from my hands when he died, but I'll end up with a fairly decent chunk of it through my mother. The long-term result is that I'll stay off the streets. As regards my modest contribution, I'm honored you're willing to accept my help."

"Without you, I'd still be up in Reno, grinding out a miserable existence, trying to pay my bills, with no hope for my father in sight."

"I intend to do something about that money you owe, as well," Dane said.

"No, you won't. Helping my father is one thing, but I won't take any money from you. Absolutely not!"

"Not even for a striptease or a lap dance?"

She swatted him and he laughed. Dane checked the rearview mirror.

They'd come to California Street and made a right turn ahead of a cable car making its way up the hill, its bell clanging. They'd only gone a ways before the brown sedan made the turn, right behind a little VW Beetle. He hoped the guy was just keeping an eye on them, but once it had been confirmed they were sleuthing again, the shit would hit the fan. Dane had little doubt of that.

"Dane," Mary Margaret said, "why do you keep looking in the rearview mirror? Are we being followed?"

"Jesus, you don't miss a thing, do you?"

"Is it them?"

"I don't know. They followed us to the nursing home. There were two. One stayed in San Bruno. I suspect to find out what we were doing there."

"Which means they know."

"Probably."

"Oh, Dane," she said with desperation. "You can't keep doing this. You're going to be hurt."

"I'll have a word with the security people at the hotel as soon as we get there."

"I want you to go home."

"It's probably too late for that anyway, sweetheart. If those men are pissed at me, I won't be any safer there."

"Then get on a plane for Europe or something."

They came to a stop at a traffic light. The brown sedan was a few cars back.

"I'll be just as safe at the Fairmont," Dane said. "Besides, we've got to worry about you, too. These people don't want anybody stirring things up."

"Dane, I've been at this for years. Anyway, he's *my* father."

"That doesn't mean you're bulletproof."

The light changed and they continued up California Street.

"I won't be able to sleep until this is over," Mary Margaret said.

"Not even with me?"

She poked him. "I wish you'd take this threat more seriously."

"I've considered the options. Let's leave it at that."

They were passing Grace Cathedral. The Fairmont was another block up on the left. Dane pulled the car into the circular drive. A doorman opened Mary Margaret's door. Dane climbed out and immediately checked on the brown sedan. It was still on California Street and had pulled over at a spot where the driver could see the front of the hotel. The man, whose face was obscured by a hat, had no discernible qualities—at least, none that could be singled out at that distance.

Dane took the chit from the parking valet and walked around the car. Taking Mary Margaret's arm, they went inside.

"Did you get a look at him?" she asked.

"No, he was being fairly discreet. Could be they'll stop at intimidation."

"I wouldn't want to bet my life on it," she said dryly.

"You've got a point." Then, giving her shoulders a squeeze, he said, "Come on, my love, let's check out the room and I'll call Sally Nesbit."

When Dane got the room key, he was handed a message slip.

"What is it?" Mary Margaret asked.

"A message from Claudia. I told her I'd be at the Fairmont when I called her this morning from Mendocino."

"What does it say?"

"Sheila Warren, the Unitarian minister in Fresno, is back from her trip and would be happy to talk to me about Theo Bledsoe. Claudia says Sheila will be in Berkeley for a meeting at the district office tomorrow and thought I might like to know in case I want to try to catch her before she heads back to Fresno."

"Aren't you meeting Kathy in Berkeley tomorrow?"

"Yes," he replied. "It could work out so that I'm able to see them both in one trip."

"You're pretty lucky your job isn't demanding of your time," Mary Margaret said.

"Yeah, at the rate I'm going I could end up as a full-time detective. A bizarre end to a budding ministry."

They started walking toward the elevator.

"I'd feel terrible if this got you in trouble with your congregation," she said.

"Would you?"

"Of course."

"If I had to guess, I'd say you'd rather I be in just about any other kind of work besides the ministry." It was an off-hand comment, but he was very interested in her response.

"I don't imagine show business would be your first choice for me, either." she said.

"I think you ought to go to college, if you want a candid opinion. You've got a wonderful mind and you deserve an education."

"You're nothing if not diplomatic, Dane."

"That's not a commentary on your work," he said as they came up to the bank of elevators. "I think it's neat you're a showgirl."

"Neat?"

"How many ministers can say their girlfriends dance top-less?"

"The ones who can are probably unemployed," she joked.

"That's the upside to liberal religion," he rejoined.

An elevator car arrived and they stepped inside. They were alone. Dane pushed the button for their floor. The car began its ascent.

"So, if you had your druthers," he said easily, "what line of work would you like to see me in?"

"Wouldn't it be kind of presumptuous of me to suggest anything?" she said. "I mean, who am I to say?"

"I asked your opinion. That's all the reason you need."

"I think people should do what they want to do, what they love."

"You're avoiding answering," he said.

The elevator arrived at their floor and they stepped out.

"Well, I'm not shy," Dane said as they made their way along the hallway. "I think you should get your degree and teach. Either high school or college."

"Oh, you do."

"Yes. I've considered teaching myself."

"What subject?"

He shrugged. "Theology, philosophy, religion."

"Those are things you care about," she said, a lilt in her voice. "I can see you as a professor of philosophy or religion."

It was casual conversation on the surface, but Dane knew his work was a problem for Mary Margaret, at least in the long run. He was in no position to be talking marriage, of course. Their relationship, though heating up nicely, was still in its formative stage. But he wanted badly to know there was a possibility of a future. Maybe Mary Margaret could handle living with a professor better than a minister. The question was if that would be all right with him. Kathy would have preferred the same thing and their marriage had foundered on the issue.

They came to their room and Dane opened the door. Inside they found their bags.

Mary Margaret went over and bounced happily on the bed. "Our second hotel room," she said gleefully.

"I like the trend," he said. Walking over to her, he pulled her to her feet and took her in his arms. "Which reminds me, Mary Margaret, I owe you a thousand for that little performance last night."

"Dane..."

"That was our deal, wasn't it?"

"I'd say we're even."

"On the contrary, I was wondering if you might like to double your money."

Mary Margaret pinched his stomach, twisting her fingers, making him yelp. "You're getting a little overconfident, Reverend," she said.

"We only have so much time on this earth, sweetheart," he replied. "We've got to make every minute count."

"Dane, that's not a very diplomatic thing to say, not in light of the car that was following us today and the threats those men made."

He tweaked her nose. "All I meant to say is I treasure every minute I'm with you."

Her eyes shimmered as she smiled up at him. But she didn't say anything. Her only response was an enthusiastic hug—one that had a hint of desperation in it.

Mary Margaret checked her face in the bathroom mirror, hearing only bits and pieces of Dane's conversation with

Sally Nesbit because the TV was on. She went in and turned down the volume so it wouldn't disturb him. She sat on the bed just as he was finishing his conversation.

"We really appreciate your cooperation, Mrs. Nesbit," he said. "See you at six."

"She'll see us?" Mary Margaret said when he hung up.

"It was like pulling teeth," he said. "But she finally agreed—as long as we come after her husband gets home from work."

"Do you think it'll do any good?"

"I don't know. I didn't want to say too much over the phone out of fear she'd clam up. Better to handle something like this in person."

"Yes, but what if we're followed again?"

"Maybe I should go alone this time."

"Oh, no, you're not pulling that on me, Dane Barrett. He's *my* father and this is *my* fight."

"There's no point in both of us taking a chance."

"Then if anybody goes, it should be me."

"But I was the one who talked to Sally," Dane said. "She's expecting to see me."

"Then we both go because I'm definitely not letting you go alone."

He grinned at her. "You're going to protect me, is that it?"

"I owe you one, Dane, so don't argue with me."

He sat on the bed next to her. She put her head on his shoulder, staring blankly at the TV screen.

"Do you ever think this will end?" she said. "I mean, it seems like we just go from one problem to the next. Do you suppose it's bad karma?"

"No, I think good karma. This is a triumph of spirit. Once it's behind us it'll be like nirvana."

She gave him a look. "Honestly, Dane, you're so full of shit. I don't think you've ever seen a cloud without a silver lining."

"The secret of happiness, my dear."

Mary Margaret hugged him and again laid her head on his shoulder. The news was on and, after a second or two, she became aware that the face on the screen was Scott Wainwright's. Getting up quickly, she turned up the volume.

"To the contrary," Wainwright was saying, his voice deep and raspy, "I'm looking forward to the debate Friday night. The fact that we're running ahead in the polls is irrelevant. The people of California are entitled to see the candidates for governor side by side, so they can decide who they want in Sacramento. I refuse to hide behind favorable polls. With me, the citizens of this state have always come first. I'll be in San Francisco Friday, and I'll be ready."

"Bastard!" Mary Margaret screamed at the television set, her pulse beginning to race.

The reporter came on with further details of the gubernatorial debate. Dane got up and turned off the set.

"I think the mood would be a little more pleasant without Scott Wainwright," he said.

"The *world* without Scott Wainwright would be a little more pleasant," she replied. "I just know he's responsible somehow, someway, for what's happened."

"If he sent Haskell a police report with certain critical elements missing, then you've got to wonder, I grant you."

"Why don't we ask Mr. Haskell instead of just speculating?" she said.

"I thought he was dead."

"God, no. I've been sending him money for years. He's pretty old now and kind of dotty, but he still has his law office and goes in a few days a week."

Dane pointed to the phone. "You want to try and reach him?"

Mary Margaret went over to the telephone. She had to get Haskell's number from information, but she was lucky. He was in his office.

"Oh, Miss Duggan, so good to hear your voice."

Mary Margaret wasted no time. She explained what Ted Gotchall had told them about the lab report.

"There must be some mistake," Lloyd Haskell croaked. "Are you sure Gotchall didn't have his cases confused?"

"No, he was very certain."

"My Lord, I can't believe it. Scott Wainwright wouldn't intentionally withhold evidence, I'm certain."

"Well, was the business about the extraneous fingerprint in the report he sent you?"

"Most certainly not. That would have changed the complexion of the case. There must be a mistake. I can't believe I'd have overlooked it."

"Is there any way you can check?" she asked.

"It'll take a while to find the file. Edna will have to dig for it, I'm sure. Shall I call you back, or do you want to hold on?"

"See if you can put your hands on it quickly," she said. "I'd really like to know."

Lloyd Haskell put down the phone without pushing the Hold button. She could hear his desk chair creak and then his voice as he hollered for his secretary. Glancing at Dane, Mary Margaret put her hand over the mouthpiece.

"He's checking the file."

"And probably praying his malpractice-insurance premiums are up-to-date."

"It isn't his fault, is it?"

"If there is a page missing from the police report, you can argue he should have caught it."

"You know," she said, "I've been wondering. Why would the copies of the report in the Laurel Police Department and at the county lab be doctored, too?"

Dane shrugged. "Somebody probably went to great lengths to make sure this thing wouldn't come unraveled. There's no telling when it was done. If Wainwright was responsible for tampering with the report, he might have waited months to avoid raising suspicion. He could have bribed a clerk or maybe gone in to check the original file under some pretext. Anything's possible."

Lloyd Haskell came back on the line. "Edna's found the file," he said, "and I'm looking through it. Give me a minute."

She waited.

"Hmm. Yes, here we are…. Well, I've got the lab section of the police report right in front of me, Miss Duggan. I'm checking…. Hmm. There's no mention of an extraneous print on the murder weapon. And as near as I can tell, the page numbering is intact…. No, wait a minute. Never noticed this before. The numbers on the last couple pages of the lab report appear to have been altered, like a little patch was put over them when they were photocopied. This *is* bizarre.''

"Mr. Haskell, would you please put that file in a safe place?'' Mary Margaret said. "We're gathering evidence to get a new hearing for my father. Your file might be useful.''

"Of course. Of course. But I still can't believe Scott Wainwright would be a party to an irregularity of this nature.''

"Time will tell,'' Mary Margaret said. "I'll be in touch.''

She hung up the phone and told Dane what had transpired.

"The plot thickens,'' he said.

"Why would Wainwright have changed the page numbers on the report he sent to Haskell, but not the ones in the police department and at the county lab?''

"Probably because he made Haskell's copy and had to deal with the others as he found them. It would have been harder to doctor the originals, but ripping out a couple of pages could be done fairly easily.''

"Jesus,'' she said. "If he did tamper with the files, that would be a crime, wouldn't it?''

"Yes, I suppose so. Suppressing evidence, obstruction of justice—I'm sure there'd be something they could charge him with.''

"That explains what's been going on then!'' she said, growing excited. "Don't you see? The bastard's running for governor from the attorney general's office, right? He's the chief law-enforcement officer in the state. Imagine if an old case came to light during the campaign and it was shown that he tampered with the evidence. It would ruin him!''

"Yes, but can we prove it?''

"Let's think this through. What's the first thing that happened? Ledi Hopkins mumbled something about my father being innocent, right? You and Father Muncey started asking questions. Wainwright gets word that the Jimmy Duggan case is getting talked about. He thinks, 'Shit, that's the one where I suppressed evidence to get a conviction, way back when. Can't have that.' So he sends Harelip down to Laurel to shut the nurse and the priest up. Didn't you say Father Muncey was told by the Church to cool it?''

"Yes.''

"Well, they take care of Elena Perez and the priest, but then you start poking around. You get threatened and you don't back down. More stuff keeps turning up. Wainwright starts getting really nervous. If he knew what we were up to now, he'd probably have a cow."

She noticed Dane's expression turn somber.

"Maybe he does know, Mary Margaret."

"You mean the men who followed us down to see Ted Gotchall?"

"Yes. I was going to phone Gotchall to see if they tried to talk to him. If they did, and he told them about the missing page from his report, we could be up shit creek."

Mary Margaret swallowed hard. As things became clearer, the threat to them became more understandable and the danger more real. She watched as Dane went to the phone. After checking his pocket address book, he dialed a number. "Hello, this is Reverend Barrett. I'd like to speak with one of your patients, please. Ted Gotchall." He glanced at Mary Margaret, his brow furrowed. *"What?"* he said into the phone. He sounded distressed. "When? Oh, no. Listen, is the nursing supervisor there, please? May I speak with her?" Dane put his hand over the mouthpiece. "This is going from bad to worse," he said.

"What happened?"

Dane held up his finger, signaling for her to wait. He spoke into the phone, explaining he'd seen Ted Gotchall earlier that afternoon. Then he listened, going quite white. "Will you keep me advised of his condition?" he said at one point. "I'm staying at the Fairmont Hotel in San Francisco." Finally he hung up.

"What happened?" she said.

"The nursing supervisor said that shortly after we left, a man sneaked into Ted's room and they got into a violent argument. By the time the staff intervened, Ted was having a heart attack. They had to rush him to the hospital. She said his health was far too fragile for that kind of confrontation. The man, needless to say, escaped."

"Oh, my God."

"They got a description of him. He was large and spoke

with an East European accent—the same as one of the men who accosted me up at the Heritage House.''

"Dane..."

"The guy must have demanded that Gotchall tell him what we'd discussed. The question is whether Ted told him."

"Dane, what are we going to do?"

"We could go to the cops, but what do we have besides suspicion and circumstantial evidence? You don't just go waltzing into the police station and say you think the attorney general, who happens to be a candidate for governor, is involved in a criminal conspiracy. We need something that ties Wainwright directly to this."

"A smoking gun."

"Right."

Mary Margaret put her arms around him. "Oh, Dane, I'm scared."

"I am, too. But I feel we're getting close. There's a reason the heat's going up. The police are looking for the big guy. With luck, he'll be arrested."

"Do you still want to go see Sally Nesbit?" she asked.

"It could be more important than ever."

Dane shaved while Mary Margaret was in the shower. They didn't have much time before they had to leave. He was rinsing off his face as she climbed out of the tub. He handed her a towel and, as she dried her neck and shoulders, he put his arms around her, only the towel between them.

"Dane, you'll get wet."

"Seems to me I let you get me wet this morning and things turned out pretty well."

She gave him a playful punch on the chin. "If you're expecting a replay, you'll have to wait until we get back. As it is, I barely have time to get ready."

"You see, you're already getting practical," he said. "The bloom is definitely off the rose."

"Oh, be quiet and quit sounding like a man with a one-track mind."

He kissed her lips. "Do you think danger heightens sexual tension?"

"You'd better hope not," she said. "I don't intend to live this way very long."

"What's the secret, then?"

"Anticipation," she said without hesitating. "All you need to do is think about tonight when we get back."

"Hmm. I'm beginning to wonder if we need to see Sally after all."

"Why am I not surprised?"

Dane gave her bare rump a pat and she went into the other room, wrapping the towel around her. He examined his face in the mirror, wishing he'd bought some cologne along with the razor. This living out of a suitcase was wearing thin.

"You know, I was thinking about Scott Wainwright while I was taking my shower," Mary Margaret said from the other room.

"Just what a guy wants to hear—his woman thinking about another man."

She returned to the doorway. "No, seriously. I was wondering why Muncey would've been warned to back off by his bishop. Isn't that who you said told him to cool it?"

"Yes, that's right."

"Why the Church hierarchy?" she said. "What's their stake in this?"

"You know, I hadn't given that much thought. You're questioning whether there might be a connection with Wainwright."

She shrugged. "It's a thought."

Dane patted her cheek. "Miss Duggan, you're a very clever young lady. Brains *and* beauty."

"Is there a way we can check it out?"

"I think Tom's supposed to be back from L.A. I can give him a call while you finish getting ready. Maybe he has some thoughts on the issue."

"Good idea."

Dane went into the other room, got his address book and dialed Tom Muncey's number in Laurel. The priest's housekeeper answered. Then Muncey came on the line.

"Glory be, my son," he said. "I was beginning to wonder if I'd ever hear your voice again."

"I was intending to give you a full account of my adventures, Tom, and I will when I get back to Laurel. I'm in San Francisco at the moment. But I have a pressing question."

"I have a few questions myself, but you first. Beauty before age and ecclesiastical rectitude."

Dane had to laugh. Muncey always had a quip ready. "We'll discuss that sometime, Tom. Meanwhile, a question about the Jimmy Duggan case. Didn't you say it was your bishop who told you to butt out?"

"Yes, and he's fired another salvo in the interim. Essentially he told me to cease and desist or else. Why do you ask?"

"This may sound crazy, but can you think of any connection between Scott Wainwright and your bishop? Or, for that matter, the Church in general."

"Scott Wainwright? As in the Republican candidate for governor?"

"One and the same," Dane said.

"Well, yes, of course. Wainwright's supporting the Church's position on abortion, as am I, I might add. But it's no secret the Church prefers certain candidates. Nothing new there."

"No, but it's interesting to know that Scott Wainwright might be in a position to pick up the phone and ask a bishop to call off a zealous priest trying to do justice. In fact, I find it very interesting."

"I'm sorry, but I'm having trouble seeing the connection," Muncey said. "What's Scott Wainwright have to do with the Jimmy Duggan case?"

"Wainwright was the prosecutor, Tom. It was before he moved up to Sacramento as attorney general."

"You're kidding."

"Not only that," Dane said, "but we've turned up anomalies in the case. Some possibly exculpatory information in the police lab report—an extraneous fingerprint on the murder weapon, to be exact—seems to have been misplaced somewhere between Wainwright's office and the defense attorney's. We can't prove it yet, but it's starting to look like Scott Wainwright was behind it and now has a lot to hide."

"Holy Mother," Muncey said.

"Exactamundo."

"What do you plan to do about it?"

"That's another reason I called. Looks like we're going to be tied up in the Bay Area for a while, so I was wondering if you'd go by and see Chief Slater. Find out if there's any possibility that a copy of the fingerprint on the knife might have been kept at another location...like in the county or state archives or somewhere."

"Sure, I'd be glad to. But Dane, you said 'we' just now. Would it be impertinent to ask who the 'we' you're referring to might be?"

Dane felt himself color. "Remember when I said you were a *Schatchen?*"

"Yes, it was Yiddish for matchmaker, as I recall."

"Well, Tom, you succeeded beyond all expectation. In fact, you were spectacularly successful."

"Jesus and Mary," the priest murmured.

Dane glanced back at the open bedroom door where he saw Mary Margaret in her bra and panties, doing her hair. "I couldn't put it better, Father."

"You'll be naming your first son Thomas, of course. I mean, it would be heretical if you didn't."

"That's skipping a few steps ahead, I'm afraid. It's only been a week."

"But I understand you Unitarian boys don't stand on ceremony."

"You've got that right, but let's not rush things any more than necessary. Let nature take its course."

Muncey laughed heartily. "Sounds to me like it already has!"

Seacliff, San Francisco

Mary Margaret watched Sally Nesbit pour their tea. She could see a lot of Stephen Ragsdale in the woman, especially around the eyes. Sally was only in her early thirties but had the staid manner of an older woman. Perhaps it was the influence of her husband, a balding insurance executive who was ten or fifteen years her senior. Though Episcopalian, Arthur Nesbit had been chatting with Dane about Unitarian-church politics, having become familiar with the denomination through his wife and his late father-in-law.

"I've always admired men of the cloth," Arthur was saying. "I believe it was why I was so fond of Stephen. Both of Sally's parents were lovely people."

"I'm sorry I never had a chance to meet them," Dane said, sounding sincere. Mary Margaret couldn't help being impressed by his smooth manner. Of course, Dane had no reason to hate Stephen Ragsdale—not the way she did, anyway. So maybe it was a little easier for him to be generous.

She had done her best to be polite, but she sensed Sally Nesbit felt her discomfort. And of course, the murder case itself was an unpleasant reminder of Stephen Ragsdale's problems. His life had gone into a negative spiral after Donna Lee's death.

Sally handed them each a teacup and placed a plate of finger sandwiches on the coffee table in front of them before taking a seat in the wingback armchair next to her husband's. Mary Margaret subtly glanced around the room as Arthur Nesbit finished the point he was making.

She had never been in a house in Seacliff or Pacific Heights or Russian Hill or any of the snobby neighborhoods of San Francisco. Her turf had been south of the park in the Sunset, where she liked to say she'd been born, though the truth was her mother, a Catholic charity patient, had given birth at Mary's Help in Daly City.

Mary Margaret recalled driving around Seacliff with Danny Murphy in his Gremlin when she was a sophomore in high school. "When we get married," he'd told her, "we'll live in one of these places and have ten kids." If Danny's braces and acne hadn't made such a union unlikely, the notion of ten kids had.

She recalled how impressed she'd been by the big houses, though even then she'd wondered what the women who lived in them had endured to get them. Probably nothing like what she'd been through with Anthony, but observing Sally Nesbit and her husband now, she decided everything had its price.

Mary Margaret watched Dane, who was balancing his teacup and saucer on his knee with absolute precision and total insouciance. A wave of insecurity washed over her. What was she doing with these people, she the daughter of charity? Sally Nesbit, she could tell, wouldn't recognize a food stamp if it bit her on the ankle.

Sally sat very still, as though listening to the gentle gurgle of a brook. Her precise, dark hair appeared to be more the work of a portrait painter than a hairdresser. Though only slightly pudgy, she was obviously in the embrace of a foundation garment.

"So, what do you do, Miss Duggan?" Sally said when her husband began telling Dane about his cousin Wilfred's experiences in the seminary.

"I'm in the chorus of *Dream Girls,* the show at the High Chaparral in Reno," Mary Margaret replied without hesitation. "I'm a showgirl."

"Oh, really?" Sally searched for the next gambit. "How interesting."

"It's a living."

"They say dancers keep their figures," Sally said. "The exercise obviously agrees with you."

"Most of the girls sweat off a pound or two every night. It's harder work than you'd think."

Sally picked up her cup, pausing with it six inches from her lips. "I've never been to the High Chaparral. Is *Dream Girls* a musical review?"

"Sort of. A musical-variety show when you come right down to it. Vaudeville, nineties style."

"Fascinating." Sally sipped her tea. "Arthur and I went to the Follies in Paris when we were first married. Is your show anything like that?"

"We do topless numbers, if that's what you mean."

"Oh." Sally replaced her teacup on the saucer.

The men had been listening in silence. Arthur looked as uncomfortable as Dane was serene.

"Mary Margaret is the class of the show," Dane said.

"You've seen it, Reverend Barrett?" Sally asked.

"Yep, and it was great. If you ever get up to Reno, I highly recommend it." Dane gave Mary Margaret a wink and she felt a mixture of triumph and gratitude. She was so pleased by his support that she was willing to forgive him for balancing his cup and saucer on his knee.

"We must keep it in mind, Arthur," Sally said.

"Yes, by all means," her husband replied.

"Well then," Sally said, her tone signaling that the social chitchat had run its course, "we do have business to discuss. I understand, Reverend Barrett, that you have some questions about my father's knowledge of the death of that poor girl."

"Yes," Dane said. "As I told you on the phone, we've turned up evidence that could prove Jimmy Duggan isn't guilty. In fact, I'm convinced he's innocent. The problem is, many of the principals in the case are dead and it's difficult to get firsthand information."

"And more of them are dying all the time," Mary Margaret added.

"We understand that your father kept diaries," Dane went on, "and were wondering if anything in them might shed light on the case."

"I know my father spoke extensively with the police," Sally said, "and I'm sure he told them everything he knew."

"I'm certain of that, as well, Mrs. Nesbit," Dane said. "But we understand that after the murder, Reverend Ragsdale had a counseling relationship with Theo Bledsoe, a neighbor of the Marshalls. Theo figures prominently in the recent developments. She was very reclusive and no one knows what was going on in her home. Your father was apparently one of the few outsiders, and perhaps the only one, to enter the house in decades. We were hoping his diaries might contain some useful information relating to the case."

"I can't imagine what," Sally said.

"I can't either," Dane said, "but we didn't want to leave any stone unturned. Have you read the diaries, Mrs. Nesbit?"

Sally glanced at her husband, who'd remained silent but attentive. "I've skimmed them," she replied. "Especially the ones in the early years when I was still at home. But no, I haven't read his diaries in the latter years."

"Hmm," Dane said, laying his finger across his cheek.

Mary Margaret was seeing the professional side of Dane Barrett. This was a very different man from the one who'd fondled her in the shower, sending her into the throes of ecstasy. This one she didn't relate to as well, but she was beginning to see it wasn't so much a mask as a profile view of the man. If she looked closely, the little tug at the corner of his mouth could be seen, indicating the Dane she knew was still inside.

"Would it be asking too much for you to look through those entries to see if there might be something useful to our cause?" he asked carefully.

"Reverend Barrett," Sally said wearily, "I know your intentions are good, and I would love to accommodate you, but you're asking a great deal."

"I know your trip is imminent," he said, "but—"

"Listen, it's not a question of time or convenience," Sally interjected. "I'll be blunt. The last years of my father's life were very painful. He suffered a great deal. The loss of my mother was difficult for him and...yes, Donna Marshall's death was deeply felt in our family, as well. I wasn't home at the time, I was studying in Italy, but I heard about it from my mother, as well as my father. They both wanted so badly to make a difference in the girl's life and they felt they failed her."

"Did they think Jimmy Duggan killed Donna Lee?" Dane asked.

Sally glanced at Mary Margaret. "You've put me on the spot, Reverend Barrett," she said. "But I suppose you wouldn't ask unless you wanted the truth. The way to put it, I think, is that my parents assumed along with everyone else that Mr. Duggan was the killer."

Mary Margaret kept silent. It was hard, but she didn't want to say anything that would give Sally Nesbit reason to end this meeting.

"What about later?" Dane asked. "Did the problems your father have relate to the Donna Lee Marshall case in any way?"

Sally Nesbit looked decidedly uncomfortable. "As I already said, Donna Lee's death was a burden, but I'm not sure anything is to be gained by further discussion."

Mary Margaret could see that Sally had thrown up a wall. She was that way about her own father at times. It was a natural reaction, but Mary Margaret knew she couldn't let it prevent them from learning what they could.

"Look, Sally," she said, "I know you're being protective

of your father. I don't blame you. I'm protective of my father, too. But there's a painful fact we have to face. Your father's dead and nothing can be done for him. My father is in a living hell, put there by people who may have known he was innocent. All I'm asking is that you help me save his life. If there's anything you can tell us, please share it. Please. I'm begging you.''

"Stephen Ragsdale was a wonderful man," Arthur said, coming to his wife's aid. "He may be dead, but there's no reason to drag his private sorrows into the public eye."

"What about my father's *public* sorrows?" Mary Margaret shot back. "We're all being so goddamn pious here. What about *real* suffering?"

"Now just a minute," Arthur said indignantly.

"No, dear," Sally said, lifting her hand. "It's all right. Mary Margaret has a point. I'm being selfish."

"That wasn't what I was saying," Mary Margaret said.

"Well, it's true, just the same." She sighed wearily. "I'll tell you right up front I don't have any shocking revelations for you. Actually, nothing specific. But I can give you some impressions that may give you cause for hope."

Mary Margaret and Dane leaned forward at the same time.

Sally cleared her throat. "Before his death, my father was distraught about something. It wasn't my mother, it had to do with his work, yet there was a personal dimension. In short, he was plagued by some sort of moral dilemma. I asked him several times what was wrong, but he refused to tell me. The last time I spoke with him—the day before he died—he was so distraught he was practically incoherent. He was mumbling, he even wept." Sally stopped momentarily then and, glancing at her husband, proceeded with a shaky voice. "My father spoke of...Donna Lee."

There was a sudden silence. For several moments the weight of Sally Nesbit's words settled over the group.

"Sally," Dane said, his voice strangely calm, pastoral, "do you think your father might have been somehow involved in Donna Lee's death? Is that what you're saying?"

"Not if you mean criminally. I'm certain of that. He knew something. I don't know what, but my impression was he was in possession of some terrible, damning secret. I think that was his dilemma."

"He knew my father was innocent, didn't he?" Mary Margaret said.

Sally lowered her eyes, smoothing her silk skirt. "Possibly so."

Mary Margaret felt her heart stop. It was as though someone had just loosened the huge steel belt that had been strapped around her chest when the jury had pronounced her father guilty. Someone else had known Jimmy Duggan was innocent!

"But let's be clear," Arthur Nesbit said, filling the breach. "Sally doesn't know that for a fact. It's only an impression. There was nothing concrete to take to anyone. No evidence to offer."

Mary Margaret all but told Arthur to shut up. Everyone, absolutely *everyone,* wanted to shirk responsibility. Fortunately she had Dane to help her.

"You're both very brave to say what you have," he murmured in a priestly voice. "And from what I know of Stephen Ragsdale, any doubts had to be a nightmare for him."

"Thank you for saying that, Reverend Barrett," Sally said. "I want you to know that my father struggled mightily with whatever it was he'd learned. In fact, my distinct impression was that he was trying to do something about it. Or intended to. At the time of his death I was too stunned to think things through clearly. But in retrospect, I wonder if perhaps his death wasn't somehow related to what was going on."

"You're suggesting that someone had a hand in your father's death," Dane said. "Someone who was, shall we say, concerned about what your father was going to do?"

"I had that impression, though I can't give you any specifics. It was in his voice, his tone. The incoherencies he kept uttering."

"What was he saying?" Dane asked.

"It's been so long... A lot of it was gibberish. He mentioned several names. Donna Lee was one. Theo... what's her name?"

"Bledsoe."

"Yes, Theo Bledsoe was another. And there was another name, too."

"Ledi Hopkins," Dane said.

"No, that wasn't it."

An icy hand grabbed Mary Margaret's spine. *"Benny,"* she said. "It was Benny, wasn't it?"

"Yes," Sally replied. "Benny was the name. Father kept saying it over and over."

Mary Margaret closed her eyes. The hand of the Holy Spirit seemed to descend from heaven and touch her. Before she knew it, she'd crossed herself. Twice.

Nob Hill, San Francisco

They managed to return to the Fairmont without incident. As nearly as Dane could tell, they hadn't been followed either going to the Nesbits' or coming back. He'd arranged with the parking valet to pick up the car in the garage and leave directly from there, under the theory that if they were being watched, it would be from the front of the hotel. The strategy, it seemed, was successful.

Even so, Dane had kept a watchful eye on the rearview mirror. The stakes in their investigation were going up rapidly and Scott Wainwright, if he was indeed behind this, had to be growing desperate. Mary Margaret, for her part, had been so elated by Sally's admissions that she'd practically forgotten about the lurking danger. During the drive back from Seacliff, she'd talked nonstop, laughing some and crying a little, too.

Dane had let her go on and on, getting it all out, knowing that's what she needed. But he was all too aware that proof and promise were two different things. It did appear, however, that Benny existed somewhere other than in Ledi Hopkins's mind. That was the good news. But they still had no idea who the man was. That was the bad news. Sally Nesbit couldn't give them any concrete answers, but she'd agreed that the diaries could well contain the information they wanted.

Had it been up to him and Mary Margaret, they'd have said, "Let's go read those puppies now." But Sally was adamant about protecting her father's privacy. There were many things in the diaries that had nothing to do with the case. She'd agreed, though, to begin reading them in the morning. And to call if and when she discovered something of interest.

It was not the most satisfying solution, but it was one they could live with. The first thing Mary Margaret had said when they'd gotten in the car was, "Do you think we can trust her?"

"I don't know that we have a choice," he'd said. "At least not without involving the police. Even then, we'd have to have a pretty convincing reason for a court to force the diaries out of her."

Mary Margaret hadn't liked that. Between the things Sally had told them and what they'd learned about the missing fingerprint from Ted Gotchall, Dane sensed that for the first time Mary Margaret had real hope her father would be proved innocent of the murder. That alone seemed to justify the risk they were taking.

When they picked up their room key, there was a sobering bit of news waiting for them. The nursing home had called to say Ted Gotchall had passed away. Mary Margaret read the message note as they rode up to their floor in the elevator.

"Damn," she said, sagging against the side of the car. "Gotchall's dead because of us. If we hadn't gone to see him, he'd have lived out his days in peace."

"We've also lost a potential witness for your father, if there is a hearing. He might have been the only one who could testify as to what was in the original police report."

Mary Margaret looked positively morose. "Another setback," she said. "See, the minute I start hoping..."

"At least we know part of what the bad guys are worried about. And we know we're on the right track."

As soon as they got to their room, Mary Margaret headed for the bathroom. Dane undressed and stretched out on the bed. It was hard to tell if she would be in any mood for romance, but he was determined not to pressure her. It had been a tumultuous day, to say the least.

The bathroom door opened just then and Mary Margaret appeared in her little T-shirt and those wonderful bare legs. He couldn't look at her without getting butterflies in his stomach. She came over and lay down beside him, taking his hand. His heart began beating nicely.

"Are your guts churning like mine?" she asked.

"Yes, although I'm not sure it's for the same reason."

She rolled her head his way. "Is that a typical male comment, like I think it is?"

"Guilty as charged," he said contritely.

"God, men could be in the middle of having their arm amputated and still want to have sex."

"It's called taking your pleasure where you find it," he said.

"No, Dane, it's called testosterone dependency. Just about every man who hasn't been gelded has it, including the pope."

"My apologies."

"No need to apologize. Testosterone's just another thing women have to deal with—like cramps, wage disparity and menopause. The secret's the same for dealing with all of them. You just outlast it."

Dane grinned and rolled onto his side, facing her. He ran his finger over her lips and chin and down her throat. "Tell me, how did you collect all this wisdom?"

"It wasn't while balancing teacups on my knees, I'll tell you that."

"I thought you felt uncomfortable. I was a little uncomfortable myself."

"Could have fooled me," she said.

"I'm really not a snob," he said. "Just a fellow traveler."

"Thank you for what you said about the show, by the way. You didn't have to do it and I want you to know I appreciate the gesture."

"It wasn't a gesture. What I said was true."

She was quiet for a long time and Dane contented himself with watching her. It was a very easy way to pass the time. He wasn't sure he'd ever grow tired of it.

"Dane," she said, turning to face him, "we're kidding ourselves, aren't we?"

"About what?"

"Our relationship. What reason do we have to think it's more than a hormonal thing?"

He groaned. "There are lots of reasons and I know I don't need to spell them out."

"Tonight at the Nesbits' I felt like a fish out of water. Those aren't my people."

"They aren't mine, either."

"But you looked completely at ease, like you were in your element."

"It's just practice, Mary Margaret."

"I could never do that."

"Nobody's asking you to."

"If I took you to a cast party, you'd feel the same," she said.

"Maybe. Maybe not."

"Dane, you're deluding yourself."

"Oh, I don't know. If you had your degree and you were, say, teaching English at a junior college, would you feel inadequate around the rest of the faculty?"

"No, but that's not me. This is me," she said, tapping her chest with her finger.

"But it could be."

"You know what you want to do, Dane? You want to change me."

"I do not. I'm trying to find a middle ground."

"What's middle about it?" she asked.

"Mary Margaret, for the first time since I entered seminary, I've been thinking about doing something besides being a minister. And lest you've missed it, that's because of you."

"I wouldn't want you to give up something you love," she said, sounding sincere.

"And I wouldn't consider it—unless it was for something I enjoyed as much."

"This talk is crazy. We hardly know each other."

He pulled her hand to his lips and kissed it. "So we table the discussion and concentrate instead on getting to know each other better."

She thought for a moment. "All right, but if you don't mind, I don't want to have sex tonight. Nothing personal, but after what happened today...,"

It was not what he wanted to hear, but it wasn't unexpected. "I understand."

"You know, I never thought I'd hear a man utter those words. I didn't think it was in their vocabulary."

"You and I are a lot more alike and suited for each other than you realize," he said.

Mary Margaret smiled and traced the outline of his lips with her finger. "You're pretty easy to look at, Reverend."

"It's mutual, I assure you."

She put her head on his chest and held him. "I like you a whole bunch."

Her words gave him a lift, but he said nothing. He could feel her soft breath on his face as he waited. Mary Margaret lightly caressed his chest. He didn't move, he didn't so much as flinch.

"I've got to tell you, though," she said, "you are a silky-smooth bastard, if ever I've seen one."

"Yeah, why's that?"

"Every time I make up my mind about you, two minutes later you've got me thinking just the opposite."

"It could be that you don't really mean what you say at first."

She slid her fingers under the band of his shorts. "Maybe."

Dane stroked her hair. Her hand moved lower, making him wonder what was next.

She stopped abruptly. "Can you even remotely picture having babies with me?" she asked. "I mean, is the thought just too weird to imagine? I'm not suggesting anything by asking, I'm just curious."

"It's not weird at all. And yes, I can picture it."

She glanced up at him. "You're just saying that."

"No, I can picture having babies with you even if it meant artificial insemination."

"That's sweet, Dane," she said, kissing his chest. "It really is." There was a sly smile on her lips. "Can I change my mind about tonight?" she asked.

The female mind never ceased to amaze him. "Who am I to deny you?" He was instantly hard, which made anything he said superfluous.

"With you, sex is entirely different," she said, stroking him. "I feel it everywhere, not just between my legs."

"The mind, they say, is the biggest erogenous zone of all."

"Maybe you *should* become a professor," she cooed.

Yes, he thought. *And have babies with you!* His heart swelled. He couldn't stay passive any longer. Capturing her mouth, he bit her lip, wanting her badly, wanting to consume her, swallow her.

Feeling a sudden rush, he got to his knees, reached up under her T-shirt and pulled down her panties, slipping them off her legs and tossing them aside. Then he pushed up her shirt and pressed his face into the soft flesh of her belly. She dug her fingers into his hair.

As he slid his face down over her mound, inhaling her rich feminine scent, she moaned. He blew softly on her, then kissed her moist center. The taste and smell of her was intoxicating. Soon he felt her building toward climax. Suddenly her body stiffened and she arched.

"Make love to me, Dane. I want you in me."

He got up and removed his shorts. He stood beside the bed for a moment, admiring her. With her eyes closed, she was the picture of bliss.

He was about to climb back onto the bed when he heard a faint sound at the door. The doorknob seemed to rattle ever so slightly, as though someone had tested it and, finding it locked, moved on. A maid? No, he thought, she would have knocked.

Mary Margaret opened her eyes. "What's the matter, don't you want me?"

Dane climbed onto the bed, smiling. "You kidding?"

She opened her arms and he hugged her, still in the brace of his testosterone rush. Damn if the woman wasn't right. Somebody could be cutting off his arm and he'd still want her.

Thursday

August 15th

Berkeley, California

They parked on Northside so that he could give her a mini tour of the campus on their way to the faculty club where they were to meet with Kathy and Sheila Warren. For a second time, they'd slipped out of the hotel garage, as best Dane could tell, undetected. There was no sign they'd been followed to Berkeley. It made for a much more pleasant outing.

Dane held Mary Margaret's hand as they went through the eucalyptus grove on the banks of Strawberry Creek. The ground was wet with dew, the menthol-like smell of the trees bracing, though it was nothing like their pungent scent on a rainy winter day.

He recalled a particular rainy night years ago when he'd passed this very spot with Kathy, headed for his apartment. Having forgotten their umbrellas, they'd gotten soaked, which gave them the excuse they needed to strip off their wet clothes and make love under the spell of a flickering candle and incense while a Chopin nocturne played on the stereo, their angry argument over the imposition theory of the patriarchy in human culture forgotten. Maybe it was Kathy's willingness to curse his gender yet allow him to make love with her in the male-dominant position that convinced him to propose marriage that night. It had been a calculatingly impulsive act. He'd often wondered since what would have happened if she'd insisted on being on top.

It seemed strange that he should be going to see Kathy again, at least in the company of a woman who bore no re-

semblance to her physically, morally, emotionally or spiritu-
ally. Of the many differences between the two women, the
one that stood out most in his mind was that Mary Margaret
was comfortable to be with and Kathy was not. The essence
of his relationship with his former wife had been tension—
personal, professional, physical. At one time he'd considered
that a plus—tension as a creative force. Kathy could be vex-
ing, but she was not boring. Time proved to him it wasn't
enough.

"You're thinking about her, aren't you?" Mary Margaret
said as they crossed the Esplanade, the bells in the Campanile
singing high above them.

"Kathy?"

"Yes. Familiar places make a person nostalgic."

"I wouldn't say what I feel is nostalgia," he said.

"This is where you lived with her, where your son was
born, where it all began."

"And ended," he said.

"A little part of you must still regret that it didn't work
out."

"I learned a long time ago not to think of it as failure, even
though that's the tendency. It must have been like that for
you and Anthony."

"I was too busy trying to survive to worry about failure.
Besides, I blamed him. That made it easier."

He put an arm around her shoulder. "Your wisdom sometimes amazes me, Mary Margaret."

"They say the same about Yogi Berra, don't they?"

He laughed, loving her more every minute. The better he
got to know her, the more he saw to care for and respect.
Mary Margaret slipped her arm around his waist.

They crossed the little bridge in the copse of trees at the
foot of Senior Lawn and headed in the direction of Faculty
Glade. The club was dead ahead. Dane pointed it out. Mary
Margaret stopped.

"Listen, Dane, why don't you go on inside?" she said,
checking her watch. "We have half an hour before we're due
to meet Sheila Warren. I'd like to be there for that, but I think
it's best if you talk to your ex alone."

"Don't you want to meet her?"

"I met her on the phone."

"I don't want to twist your arm," Dane said, "but to be honest I was looking forward to showing you off a bit."

"Showing me off?"

"I'm very proud of you and I like having people know you're in my life."

"I'm not quite sure how to take that," she said, looking a little disconcerted.

"In the best possible way."

"We aren't talking about my cup size, I hope."

"Of course not," he said, seeing she misunderstood. " I'm talking about the whole person, your mind, your personality, *you.*"

"Maybe I should have brought my S.A.T. scores with me," she said dryly.

"What were they, anyway?"

"Dane!"

"No, really, I'm curious."

"They were good."

"How good?"

"Does it matter?" she asked, her brow furrowing.

"No, but I'd like to know."

"All right. My score was 1430. Seven-ten in math and seven-twenty in English."

His brows rose. "No kidding?" He expected good, but not that good.

"Yeah, no kidding," she said. "What were yours?"

"I don't know, 1380 or 90, somewhere around there."

Mary Margaret shrugged. "Well, you have a couple of degrees and I don't have any."

Dane took her face in his hands and gazed intently into her eyes. "So come in with me."

"No, there's something else I want to do."

"What?"

"Don't get too excited, but I thought while I was on campus I'd run down to the administration building and get an application and check the admission policies."

He couldn't help the big smile that broke across his face.

"I shouldn't have told you," she lamented. "Now you'll get the wrong idea."

"Hey, I was thinking of dropping by Starr King and seeing what the prospects of a teaching position might be. Wouldn't it be ironic if we both ended up in Berkeley, teaching?"

"Go talk to your wife," she said, coloring. "And point me in the direction of the admin building."

"*Former* wife," he said. "And Sproul Hall is straight down that way on the other side of that tall building."

Mary Margaret turned on her heel and headed off, swinging her ass just a little like a foxy coed who knew she was being watched. "I'll be back in half an hour," she called over her shoulder.

Dane observed her until she made it to the far side of Senior Lawn. As he watched, he saw a young man on a bicycle pass her and look back over his shoulder, swerving off the walk in the process and nearly taking a header. Dane smiled, a thought coming to mind—he could see himself married to Mary Margaret. He clearly pictured the woman with the long legs, now disappearing from sight, as his wife. It wasn't the first time it had occurred to him, but it was the first time he'd imagined it with the feeling of deep certitude that it could be.

Sighing the sigh of a man in love, Dane proceeded to the entrance of the faculty club. He climbed the steps, opened the heavy door and saw Kathy pacing in front of the reception desk, her booted feet thumping on the hardwood floor. She was a dose of cold, hard reality. Seeing him, she stopped and gave him one of her impatient, long-suffering looks, then marched over to him.

"Thank goodness, I was afraid you weren't going to show," she said without ceremony.

"I'm not late, am I?" he said, glancing at his watch. "Well, eight minutes, that's not bad, is it?"

"No, I'm just a little anxious," she said, her small face a bit more pinched than usual.

Thirty seconds ago Dane would have only been able to conjure up a generic image of Kathy at best. But seeing her in the flesh, the smallest details became vivid again, the tiny wrinkles at the corners of her eyes and mouth, the cant of her head when she spoke, her energy, her slender body under her dust-colored chinos and batik-print blouse. She was more nervous than he'd seen her since...well, their divorce hearing.

"What do you have to be anxious about?" he asked.

Kathy pushed back a hank of her dark auburn hair, which was shorter than before. "Let's go sit in the lounge and talk," she said, avoiding a direct answer.

She marched off as though leading a safari through the bush—Kathy was never one to follow. There was one older gentleman in the lounge, reading. They went to the far corner of the room where Kathy dropped into one of the leather chairs and crossed her legs. She immediately began pumping her foot. When Dane sat on the sofa opposite her, she uncrossed her legs, leaned forward, looking him dead in the eye.

"I'm not going to beat around the bush, Dane," she said. "There's been a change in my life. It will affect Toby and I need to discuss it with you as directly, honestly and as openly as possible."

His stomach dropped. He knew the tone. He'd heard it the night she'd told him she wanted a divorce. "What sort of change?"

"I've met someone," she announced. "His name is Ed Lynch, Dr. Edwin Lynch. He's the codirector of the institute in Kyoto. He's a brilliant scholar and a wonderful human being. It was one of those things. It happened instantly. We both knew. As soon as I got Osvaldo on a plane, Toby and I moved in with Ed. He has a magnificent home. You'd be impressed, and you'd like him."

If Dane wasn't taken aback enough by her news, the mention of Toby definitely brought him up short. "I'm sure I would," he said warily. "But…"

"I know you're wondering what the implications are for Toby, but I think it's clear. He'll be with Ed and me."

"So you've come to inform me how things will be and you've left my son with Ed," he shot back. *"Fait accompli."*

"He's with Ed *and* Miyuki. I told you about her, how good she is."

"Okay, fine," he said, growing impatient. "Toby's in good hands. But what's the point, Kathy? You didn't fly all the way back to the States to tell me you traded up from a parasitic graduate student to a Ph.D. with his own place."

She gave him a dark look, but censored the rebuke clearly forming in her brain. "No, that isn't why I came."

"Then why?"

Kathy leaned back in her chair to regroup her thoughts. "First, because of Toby, I felt I had an obligation to keep you informed."

Dane had to admit that was feasible. She was always up-front with him about the things in her life that directly affected Toby and were therefore of concern to him.

"And second," she went on, "I'm anticipating the need for changes in our custody arrangement and I'd like to know now if we have concurrence."

He was beginning to see where this was headed and he didn't like what he saw. "What sort of changes are you talking about?"

"Well," she said, struggling to sound calm and reasonable, "I anticipate Ed's and my relationship will be long-term. We may well marry."

"You don't need my blessing," he replied. "My congratulations ought to take care of it."

"I know, Dane. That's not what I'm getting at. What I'm trying to tell you is...well, I expect to be staying in Japan, period. Ed has been there for twenty-three years. He's as Japanese as he is American. I love him, I love Japan, I love the life I see for us there."

It was now crystal-clear to him. "So naturally, you expect Toby to love Ed, love Japan and love your life right along with you."

"You don't have to be sarcastic," she intoned. "What I'm trying to say is that I see this as more than a one-year proposition. Of course, I'll send Toby home summers to be with you. Consider all the benefits. He'll get a bicultural education. There's a terrific American-Japanese academy in Kyoto that goes right up through prep school. They send their graduates to the best American universities. Ed agrees that Toby would be well served if he attended college in the States, then when he has his degree he can choose where he wants to live and what he wishes to do."

"Ed's got college worked out for a kid not yet in kindergarten? For *my* son?"

Kathy set her jaw and rolled her eyes. "I knew you'd refuse to look at this objectively. Dane, why must you always think in possessive terms like a middle-class Neanderthal? You're smart enough to see this is not about winning and losing, or your manhood. It's about Toby's life!''

He smiled benevolently, trying not to lose his temper. "Kathy, with all due respect, you're crazy if you think I'm going to allow my son to be raised in a foreign country just so you can play anthropological spin the bottle and indulge your libido in the passion play of the hour. You're free to do any goddamn thing with your life you wish and I'm sure as hell not going to second-guess you. But we're not talking about you, we're talking about Toby. You can't expect to take him from his home, his father, his grandparents, his culture and his country just because Ed Lynch makes your ovaries throb! I honestly don't know what you can be thinking.''

"I'm his mother, goddamn it!" she shrieked, drawing the attention of the elderly gentleman from his paper.

"If Toby wants to come and live with you in Japan when he's eighteen, that's his privilege," Dane replied. "And if you'd like to see him summers, I'll be happy to send him over so long as that's what he wishes. In case I'm not making myself understood, the answer to your request to make my son an expatriate is no.''

"You can't dictate to me!" she said. "I have as much right as you!"

"I can't dictate to you, but the courts can and you damn well know it. You won't be given custody if you plan to live abroad. Should you and Ed choose instead to live in the States, somewhere in California, then it's a different matter, of course.''

Her eyes hardened. "This is about power, pure and simple," she fumed. "You're hiding behind the stupid, parochial, chauvinistic attitudes in this country just to deny me my son.''

"No, it's to prevent you from denying me *my* son. You're the one who's trying to upset the status quo don't forget. Just so there isn't any misunderstanding, let me make it perfectly clear, I won't be bullied on this. For Toby's sake, I will do everything in my power to make sure you're a part of his life—short of allowing him to be expatriated. With that condition, the choice is yours.''

Kathy folded her arms in a defiant pose and glared. He

knew that she knew she couldn't win this one by brute force. Her only chance was to outmaneuver him.

"Okay, Dane," she said, "you've got the whip hand. But while you savor your victory, you might consider what you've bought for yourself. If you insist on keeping Toby nine or ten months of every year, you're going to have to raise him. The burden will fall entirely on you. The psychic pleasure might feel good now, but wait until you're staying home with a sick child or passing on a social opportunity to go to soccer practice or a PTA meeting—and I don't mean the ones that are convenient, I mean *all* of them."

"Single parenthood is not easy."

"What about your little friend, what's-her-name?"

"Mary Margaret."

"Yes, Mary Margaret. I have no idea if you intend to marry her, but so long as she's under the same roof, Toby is her problem as well as yours."

"Ed would understand that, I'm sure."

"Ed is a mature person who knows and understands children. He's raised three of his own, very effectively, I might add."

"I'm sure Ed is a delightful fellow who can enrich Toby's life for two months or so each year."

Kathy shook her head. "You can be a real son of a bitch," she said.

"I love my son too much to allow his life to be ruled by his mother's whims and fiats. If our situations were reversed, you'd understand my position perfectly, Kathy, I have little doubt of that."

"All right," she said, getting to her feet. "Round one to the man with the judge in his corner. I will ask one thing of you, though. Give this some careful thought. And talk it over with your little friend, Mary Margaret."

"I will indeed. I'm expecting her momentarily, as a matter of fact."

"What I'm suggesting to you both," Kathy said, "is that in time you may come to realize that letting me carry the burden may not be such a foolish thing to do. I consider the matter still open, hoping you'll think better of it. And now if you'll excuse me, I've got a meeting on campus."

With that she turned and headed for the exit. Dane watched her go. He realized, sadly, that poor little Toby was stuck in the middle once again, but this time there was no room for compromise. It was all or nothing. And lives would be changed either way.

Mary Margaret was elated. All she'd really learned was that admission was not out of the question, but it still gave her a lift. She'd have to retake the college entrance exam and have her high-school transcript sent, but in principle she was as eligible as any eighteen-year-old. It was still a very big step from where she was now to attending the University of California at Berkeley, of course, but it was possible. All she had to do was get in and figure out how to pay for it.

She wasn't about to kid herself, though. Mostly it was a dream, but one that made her feel good. Nearing the faculty club, she saw a woman coming out the door. There was something about the way she was dressed and the way she walked that made Mary Margaret wonder if she might be Dane's ex.

The woman, who Mary Margaret guessed to be in her early thirties, was attractive in a cute, offbeat way. There was a certain verve about her, though she wore a clouded expression on her face at the moment. Wiping her eyes, the woman glanced up as they passed, briefly making eye contact. Mary Margaret had gone only a few more steps when she heard the woman's voice behind her.

"Excuse me!"

Mary Margaret stopped and turned around.

"You aren't Mary Margaret by any chance, are you?"

She nodded. "Yes. You must be Kathy."

"Christ," Kathy said, looking her over from head to toe as though she didn't believe what she was seeing. She began walking slowly back to where Mary Margaret stood. "Pretty, I'd have believed, but..."

"But what?"

"Are you some kind of model or something?"

"I'm an entertainer," Mary Margaret replied obliquely, though her natural instinct was to blurt out the details. But this was Dane's turf, and as she'd blown it once, she didn't want to do it again.

"I see." Kathy bit her lip as though formulating a strategy. "I hope Dane passed on my apology for being so bitchy over the phone."

"Yes, and I owe you one," Mary Margaret said cautiously. "You and I don't have any differences. I was wrong to get into something in which I had no business."

"That's all water under the bridge. It's in both our interests to forget it."

"I'm willing," Mary Margaret said, feeling good about what she was hearing.

Kathy appraised her. "I wonder if you and I can talk for a minute about something else, though."

"What?"

"The future," Kathy said.

Mary Margaret glanced at her watch. "Dane and I are meeting someone in a couple of minutes, so I don't have long."

"I just wanted to ask a favor. Dane and I are having discussions about whether our son should live here in the States with him for the next several years, or in Japan with me."

She hadn't quite expected this. "Oh?"

"You may not consider this your business," Kathy said, "but to the extent you and Dane are together, Toby will be your problem, too. And if you and Dane marry and want kids of your own, you might ask yourself if you want a stepchild underfoot. Marriage is hard enough without that. What I'm saying is, carefully consider what you want. Then tell Dane what you really think. That's all I'm asking."

Mary Margaret wasn't sure what to say. She certainly didn't want to talk about her relationship with Dane, nor would it serve her well to tell Kathy to mind her own business. Ending the conversation gracefully was the best thing she could do. "I regard what Dane does about his son to be his business."

Kathy didn't like that. "Don't take this wrong, but are you trying to be diplomatic or are you the type who thinks a man is boss and should get whatever he wants?"

"Does it matter to you?"

"No, it's actually none of my business and you'd be completely within your rights to tell me to go to hell. I guess that having been down the same road, I feel a certain...I don't know, sisterly affinity, I suppose."

"I have a former husband myself," Mary Margaret said. "Much as I think I know the man, I realize I'm not very objective about him."

Kathy cocked her hip. "Oh, I wouldn't presume to tell you about Dane, I'm sure you're crazy about him. I guess I just have trouble understanding the passive, submissive impulse that so many women get trapped in."

"For me it's very simple, Kathy. If I didn't care for Dane and trust him, we would not be together. I don't want to consider him the enemy. There are too many real ones out there in the world."

"So anything the lord and master wants, he gets?"

"No, the minute I feel my needs and interests aren't being met, I speak up. And I'm never afraid to say what I think, whether I'm asked or not. But because of the way I feel about Dane, I am prepared to give him the benefit of the doubt."

"I can't be that deferential to any man," Kathy said. "Or, forgive me, that naive."

"It's not deferential so long as it's mutual. Dane knows how I feel, so we're both starting from the same place. Call that naive, if you want, but it seems to be working."

"I hope you're right, for my son's sake, if not for yours."

"I have no idea what the future holds," Mary Margaret said, "but just so you don't misunderstand, I want you to know that I would never try to be your son's mother. And I don't think any other woman should, either. That's your place and yours alone."

Kathy bit her lip. Her eyes welled. "If I have my way, you'll never have the chance to be tempted. But thanks for saying it, anyway."

Mary Margaret nodded.

"Good luck," Kathy said.

"Good luck to you."

Kathy left and Mary Margaret continued toward the entrance to the shingle-sided building. She wondered what in the hell had transpired between Dane and his ex that had prompted Kathy's comments and the tears.

She found Dane in the reception area talking to a woman in a long skirt and simple white blouse. His companion was about forty, plain, but with a friendly demeanor. He greeted Mary Margaret and introduced her to Sheila Warren, who was quite cordial.

"Dane was just telling me about you, Mary Margaret," she said. "Good to meet you."

Mary Margaret couldn't decide who Sheila reminded her of, then it dawned on her—the counselor she'd seen at the social services office after Anthony had roughed her up the last time. "You have to make a decision," Alice had said. "Either he's in charge of your life, or you are." Mary Margaret had filed for divorce the next day.

Sheila had the same round face, styleless hairdo and understated, competent manner as Alice. Lipstick and a tiny smudge of mascara were the only concessions to artifice. The major difference, Mary Margaret judged, was that Sheila Warren seemed more at peace with the world. Still, Alice and Sheila could have been sisters.

"Let's see if we can find ourselves some coffee," Dane said.

As they walked back through the building, which was done in dark wood and had the feel of a rustic old hunting lodge, Mary Margaret's mind was more on Kathy than the woman who Dane hoped would be able to help them with Theo Bledsoe and Benny. She wanted to ask him what had happened between him and his former wife, but realized she probably wouldn't have a chance until after their meeting with Sheila. She did glance at him to see if there might be something in his eyes to indicate how traumatic his conversation with Kathy had been. She saw no indication whatsoever.

"I remember participating in the seminar," Sheila was saying to Dane, "but I'm ashamed to say I don't remember you."

"I was one of a couple dozen divinity students," he said. "No reason why you should."

"But now you're in Laurel, filling Jane Shallcross's shoes."

"No small task," he said, as they paused at the entrance to the pleasant dining room overlooking a leafy garden.

There were a couple of people finishing late breakfasts, but the room was mostly empty, the help appearing to be in the cleanup stage. Dane stopped a young Asian man and asked if they could get three cups of coffee. Then they found a table by the window. Sheila sat on one side, Mary Margaret and Dane on the other.

"So, you want to talk about Theo Bledsoe," Sheila said.

"We were hoping you could uncover some of the mystery surrounding her," he replied.

"Theo, rest her soul, takes the prize for being eccentric, I'll tell you that."

"So we understand."

The young man brought them cups and saucers along with a pot of coffee and a small pitcher of cream. "There may be some pastries in back if you want something to eat."

"Not for me," Sheila said.

Dane and Mary Margaret waved him off, as well.

"I've had my morning walk," Sheila told them. "The last thing I want is to undo all the good I've done."

"I enjoy my morning exercise, as well," Dane said, giving Mary Margaret's thigh a squeeze.

She blushed, knowing he was referring to their nude wrestling match that morning when he'd tackled her on the bed, chastising her for "inciting lewd and lascivious acts of sexual misconduct in a man of virtue." She'd fought him so hard and long that she'd been drenched in sweat, all of her strength drained. "Okay," she'd said in the end, panting, as she lay limp on the bed. "So screw me. I hope you're into necrophilia." He'd managed to revive her, though. She'd bucked so hard when she came that Dane had quipped, "If you're this good dead, I'd hate to tangle with you alive."

Mary Margaret returned to the present conversation, hearing Sheila ask what sort of case they were working on, and what it had to do with Theo Bledsoe. Dane gave her a brief rundown of what had been happening.

"Dane is the first person I've run into who believes in my father's innocence," Mary Margaret added when he'd finished. "I owe him a great deal."

"You're very fortunate," Sheila replied. "I don't know what kind of a detective he is, but I've heard good things about his ability as a minister. Laurel's lucky to have you, Dane."

"Thank you. But I've got to tell you, unless we get to the bottom of this case soon, the good folks in Laurel are going to be running me out of town on a rail. I've become obsessed with getting Jimmy Duggan out of prison—almost as obsessed as Mary Margaret."

"I hope I can be of help, then," Sheila said. "What's Theo's connection?"

Dane explained how Theo was a neighbor of the murder victim and how her sister had placed Jimmy Duggan at the crime scene. "Theoretically, she's on the periphery of the thing," he said, "but because of what Ledi said about Benny, we're convinced Theo is the key to unlocking the mystery."

Reverend Warren's mouth sagged open. "You know about Benny?"

Mary Margaret and Dane exchanged quick glances.

"Do *you?*"

"Yes," she said. "But I was led to believe I was one of the few people in the world who does."

Mary Margaret's heart began to race.

"Sheila," Dane said, "all we know about him is that he could be central to the case. The name is really all we have. Who is he?"

Sheila Warren pressed her hands together prayerfully, bringing them to her mouth. "My," she said, looking back and forth between them, "this does present a moral dilemma."

"What do you mean?"

"I swore to Theo that Benny's existence would remain confidential. A sizable endowment is dependent upon me keeping that confidence."

"Sheila," Mary Margaret said, struggling to maintain her composure, "Ledi Hopkins admitted on her deathbed that my father was innocent. This Benny, whoever he is, may be able to prove Dad's innocence."

Sheila shook her head. "I assure you, Mary Margaret, he can't. That much I know."

Mary Margaret's heart sank. "But how do you know?"

"Trust me."

Suddenly this nice woman with the kind manner had become an adversary. Mary Margaret found herself wanting to leap across the table and grab her by the throat.

"I fully respect your desire to honor your obligations," Dane said, "but surely any promises you made to a woman now dead are secondary to the life of an innocent man. We're talking about a gross injustice."

"Of course there are limits," Sheila Warren said. "If I thought I could help, I wouldn't hesitate. But I didn't even know there'd been a murder, or that Theo was possibly involved. And I assure you, Benny could not be a factor. Honestly."

"Don't you think we should have the opportunity to decide that for ourselves?" Dane asked. "If you'd like to share the information in confidence as one minister to another, I'm sure Mary Margaret would be willing to let us speak privately."

Sheila agonized. "A breach of trust on my part could cost the Fresno church tens, perhaps hundreds of thousands of dollars, but if you'll give me your word that you will not repeat what I tell you, then I'll tell you the story."

"With the caveat that the information can be used to exonerate Jimmy Duggan, if that turns out to be the case," Dane added.

"Yes, of course," Sheila said. "But I assure you, that's not likely. What I really care about is doing the right thing, keeping the confidence that was entrusted to me."

Mary Margaret realized right then that amorality had virtue, after all. What could possibly matter except whether somebody would be hurt?

"I think if I tell you the story from the beginning," Sheila said, "you'll understand. I did not know Theo well when she called for an appointment. She only came to church intermittently. I knew she lived outside of town, that she'd pledged a substantial sum to the church, but that was it.

"Anyway, Theo arrived, looking dreadful. She told me her health was rapidly failing, she was essentially alone in the world, and that she was facing surgery and the prospect of a long hospital stay. I assumed she was making a plea for pastoral care, so I assured her I would make myself available, but she immediately straightened me out. It wasn't herself she was concerned about. Rather, she'd had a responsibility she could no longer meet and she wanted my help.''

Mary Margaret was agonizing over Sheila's long buildup but she held her tongue. Dane shifted uncomfortably.

Sheila continued. ''Theo told me that many years ago, while her husband was away at war, she had an affair with a deacon in the Baptist church and got pregnant.''

''*By* him?'' Dane asked.

''Yes. Shortly afterward, she received word that her husband had been killed in combat. Distraught, Theo broke off with the man, then went away to have her child, a son.''

''Benny,'' Mary Margaret said.

''Yes,'' Sheila replied. ''Her son, Benjamin, turned out to be severely retarded. Theo was sure God had punished her for her sin. Not wanting to dishonor the name of her late husband, she decided to keep the baby in seclusion. Nobody but her sister was aware of the child's existence.''

''Sheila,'' Dane said, ''are you saying that Theo hid this child from the world for fifty years?''

''Yes. Needless to say, I was shocked and appalled. If true, it meant Benny had never seen another human being except for his mother and aunt. I realized he'd never had medical care, that he was probably so incapacitated as to be dysfunctional. Later, I discovered that was an understatement at best.''

''So what did you do?''

''I told Theo that Benny would have to receive care immediately and that the authorities would have to be notified. I warned her that questions would be asked and that she could be in for serious trouble. She understood and said her only concern was for her son. She had a great deal of money and she offered me half a million dollars if I would care for him. You can imagine what was going through my mind. I hadn't seen Benny, but it wasn't hard to guess what he'd be like. He was older than I, Dane, a man of fifty probably, with the mind of a three-year-old.

''To make a long story short, I contacted a cousin of mine who is a therapist specializing in developmental psychology.

He told me about a sanitarium in Belmont that treated cases of this nature. He put me in touch with one of the staff psychiatrists, Dr. Patricia Gronke, who expressed a willingness to take Benny into her care. But she told me there was no way to avoid bringing the county mental health people, and possibly the state Department of Developmental Services, into the case. Theo was not pleased, but given the fact that funds were available for private treatment, the necessary arrangements were made. Inside forty-eight hours Benny was at the Belhaven Sanitarium and Theo was in a hospital in Fresno, ready for surgery.''

"Did you ever see Benny?" Mary Margaret asked.

"No, but I was told he was in deplorable condition. Theo had no idea what she'd done to her poor son. He was virtually an animal when he arrived at the clinic. That's why I told you he wouldn't be a factor. Benny is not a functioning human being and therefore couldn't understand your questions, let alone answer them.''

Mary Margaret's heart sank—not just because of the disappointment that Benny wouldn't be useful to the case, but also because his was a tragic, sickening story in itself. She gave Dane a mournful look.

"Sheila," he said, "would it be possible for us to talk to this Dr. Gronke?"

"I could contact her for you and ask. You see, I was made Benny's guardian. Theo never recovered from her surgery. She lived for several months afterward but was hospitalized the entire time. There's a trust fund to pay for Benny's needs and a fund for the Church. When Benny dies, the Church will receive the corpus of the trust.

"Theo herself probably would have been prosecuted, but because of her illness it never came to that. The state was happy to have the case off its hands and, after Theo's passing, the world went on as though nothing had happened. A couple of people at the mental health department in Fresno, the attorney and I are the only ones other than the staff at Belhaven who even know of Benny's existence. That's why I was so surprised when you mentioned his name.''

"There was at least one other person in Laurel who knew about Benny," Dane said. "The UU minister, Stephen Ragsdale. What confounds me is why he didn't do something about it.''

"The real question is if it had something to do with Donna Lee Marshall's murder," Mary Margaret interjected.

Dane nodded. ''You're right about that.''

They drank their coffee, though Mary Margaret could hardly contain her anxiety. She only half listened as Dane and Sheila chatted about the ministerial issues in the case. After a while Sheila asked Dane the time, then said she had to leave soon for her meeting. Dane asked if she had any problem with them driving down to Belmont that afternoon to talk to Dr. Gronke. She was willing and promised to call the clinic, giving her authorization.

Quickly finishing her coffee, Sheila made her excuses and shook each of their hands, saying goodbye. ''I hope you get what you need to prove your father's innocence, Mary Margaret,'' she said. ''Both of you should let me know if there's anything I can do to be of further help. All I ask is that you be discreet.''

"Count on it," Dane said. "Thank you, Sheila."

The woman went off, leaving them facing her empty coffee cup. Mary Margaret fiddled with her own. ''The mysterious fingerprint on the knife,'' she said. ''It's Benny's.''

"I didn't want to say anything in front of Sheila," Dane replied, "but I was thinking the same thing."

"Benny could be the killer, Dane."

"Well, at least we know who the ghost was that Donna Lee saw in the window."

"And who was responsible for the whining and filthy upstairs bedroom," she said.

"But was Benny capable of murder?"

"Maybe Dr. Gronke can tell us."

"That's one of the reasons I thought we should run down to Belmont today," he said, checking the time. "It's what? Twenty miles from San Francisco, thirty from here?"

"Something like that," Mary Margaret said. "I've only been through the town on the train."

"Then it'll be an adventure for both of us."

"Speaking of adventures, what did you tell Kathy about me?"

"What did *I* tell Kathy about *you?*"

"Yes," she said. "I ran into her out front and she asked me to lobby you to let her have Toby, like I had some sort of magical control over you."

"You're kidding."

"No. She basically told me I'd be a fool to play the step-mother role."

Dane shook his head. "The little bitch. She has no shame."

"What did you say to her?"

"Not much. I think Kathy made some assumptions. She's got a new beau she's serious about and kind of projected the same situation onto me, I think."

"She told me the two of you are fighting over custody."

"It's not much of a fight," Dane said. "She wants Toby to stay with her in Japan indefinitely and I said no way." He explained what had happened and what Kathy had demanded.

"She doesn't lack for balls," Mary Margaret said. "I'll give her that."

Dane chuckled. "No, and she'd be pleased to hear you say that, I'm sure."

She studied him, wondering what, exactly, he'd told Kathy. "Dane, why didn't you straighten her out about her misimpression?"

"What misimpression?"

"That we're engaged...or serious anyway."

"Did you straighten her out?" he asked.

"No. Not knowing what you told her, I didn't want to mess things up, so I kept my mouth shut."

He drank the last bit of coffee in his cup. "I didn't think it was important to disabuse Kathy of her misunderstanding. Besides, I'm beginning to think it would be a good idea if we lived together."

"Oh?"

"Don't you?"

"Where? In a motel halfway between Reno and Laurel?"

"You aren't disagreeing in principle," he noted. "That's a good sign."

"Dane, I think we're losing touch with reality here. Consider our situations for a minute."

"So, which one of us is the dreamer?" he said. "Me, or the coed who went to get an admissions application?"

"I never should have told you," she said, coloring. "It's just pie in the sky."

He took her chin in his hand and gave it an affectionate squeeze, making her blush even more.

"I cut pictures of big fancy houses out of magazines, too," she added. "That doesn't mean I'm going out and hiring a real-estate agent."

"I have a suggestion," he said. "As soon as we gather what information we can about Benny and we turn our file over to an attorney, let's go back to Mendocino and do a feasibility study on our relationship."

"Feasibility study? Is that what they call it in academia?"

"Mary Margaret, I'm trying to tell you in the most diplomatic way possible that being with you makes me very happy. I love you. I love your soul. I love everything about you."

Within seconds her eyes flooded and she blinked, hardly able to see him.

"Tears?" he said.

"Nobody's ever said anything like that to me before."

"Believe me, you're going to be hearing it a lot. I hope mostly from me."

Laughing, she took his hands and kissed his fingers. "Oh, Dane," she said, her voice catching as a wave of dread went through her.

"What's the matter?"

"It's too good to be true. I'm afraid."

Shaking his head, he said, "I'm going to break you of that pessimism, young lady, you wait and see."

God, she thought, it would be nice if he could. But no sooner had the thought entered her mind than she was seized with doubt. She had a real bad feeling and she wasn't sure why. Dane wouldn't let her down, she was certain of that. It could only be the dark forces at work—the dark forces that refused to leave her alone.

San Francisco

He watched his own image on the TV screen, liking what he saw. Articulating a public image was an art form, a balancing act that took suppleness and skill. What people didn't realize was that you couldn't be on the popular side of every issue and still get money to run your campaign. The art of politics had become the art of choosing between blocks of votes and blocks of money. You talked loudly if you had the issue and softly if you had the money. Simple as that.

The tape they'd been watching came to an end and Scott Wainwright glanced at the three other men in the room, waiting for their reaction.

"That was super," Ernie Adamson, his media consultant, said. "You've got the balance between firm and caring down to a T. I especially liked the way you finessed the abortion question."

Wainwright nodded and looked at Alec Tolliver, his campaign director. Alec, too, seemed pleased.

"I agree," he said. "Whenever Dunkin starts talking about rights, you counter with morality. You finessed it well on that question about forcing poor women into backroom abortions. I agree with Ernie. The poor don't vote. Just be careful about pontificating, though. What you want the audience to hear is that Dunkin's personal morals are in the toilet, without sounding like you're gloating."

"And without actually saying it," Ernie added.

"Yeah, the object is to take the focus off whether what you stand for is good for women or bad for women. That's the way Dunkin wants the issue framed."

Fritz Strauss, the campaign's polling consultant, concurred. "You do half that well tomorrow night, Scott, and any residual damage from the San Diego speech will be history."

Wainwright was pleased. He was feeling confident, the briefing books were his friends and the tide was moving in his favor. Now, if he could just hold things together until the election. Cal Dunkin might be the other name on the ballot, but Cal Dunkin was not the problem. His problem was that goddamn minister and the stripper. Too bad he couldn't connect *them* to Dunkin. Maybe if it got that far, he'd have to try. But his first priority was to keep the story from coming to light, even if it meant setting a little backfire. And that could be dangerous.

The telephone on his private line rang, but Wainwright decided not to answer it. After the third ring it stopped.

"I think you've done everything you can, Scott," Alec said. "Unless you want to run through the briefing books again with Ernie, I say get yourself some rest."

"You're ready," Fritz told him. "At this point it's just as important to be relaxed."

Wainwright was considering that when the door to the office opened and his secretary, Thelma, stuck her head in.

"Excuse me, Mr. Wainwright," she said, "but you've got an urgent call."

The way she nervously tucked her hair behind her ears, her expression grim, he knew who it was.

"All right, gentlemen, let's call it a day," he said. "Now, if you'll excuse me, I have to take this."

The three got to their feet.

"You might stick around the hotel, Ernie, if you don't mind," Wainwright said. "If I get the urge to do a little cramming, I might give you a buzz later."

"Sure."

Once they were out of the room and the door was closed, Scott Wainwright picked up the phone on the table next to him. "Yes?"

"Somehow, someway, the bastard's found his way to Belmont," the voice said.

"Shit," Wainwright said, feeling a stab in his gut. If they'd gotten that far, the story would be on the front page of every paper in the state within days.

"Must have been something they did last night or this morning when they slipped out on us. Fortunately, we picked them up when they made it back to the hotel a while ago. We're on their tail now. They gotta be headed for the nut farm. It's the only thing that makes sense."

Scott Wainwright felt the perspiration forming on his brow. The chance of them getting the whole story wasn't good. And he couldn't be absolutely sure they were on to him. But they'd spoken with Gotchall and chances were that fingerprint had come up in the conversation. This was definitely getting too close to home for comfort.

Wainwright agonized. Whichever way he went with this, there was danger. For all he knew, it could already be too late. But there was no question that time was working against him. Glancing at the briefing book and picturing Cal Dunkin's face was all it took. The right course of action became clear.

"I think maybe the time has come to bid our friends goodbye," he said, his deep voice trembling slightly.

There was a pause. "The both of them?"

"Yes."

Belmont, California

"Our mistake was going back to the hotel," Dane said, staring at the flashing lights on the railroad crossing gate. "I'm positive they didn't follow us to Berkeley, but they were ready for us when we left the hotel this afternoon. I guess I got complacent."

Mary Margaret glanced anxiously out the rear window at the LandRover, three cars back. Noticing her anxiety, he patted her hand, wanting to give what reassurance he could.

"Dane, let's call the police."

"What can they do?"

"How about arrest them?"

"For what? I don't know for sure that they're the same guys who threatened me at the Heritage House."

"So what do we do, wait until they kill us?"

"We try to be very careful."

"Oh, great."

The southbound commuter train passed and the crossing gates went up. The traffic moved across the railroad tracks. They continued following Ralston Avenue, which ran through the small business district and then on up a canyon between hills studded with trees and houses. Mary Margaret checked the house numbers.

"It's coming up soon," she said. She looked back warily. "And our friends are still there."

Dane wondered if they'd try anything in broad daylight,

and in public. Could the LandRover pull up next to them and open fire with an automatic weapon, or did things like that only happen in the movies? He nervously fingered the steering wheel, knowing it was one thing to risk his own life, but wondering if it was irresponsible to subject Mary Margaret to the danger, as well.

"This might be it on the left," Mary Margaret said.

Sure enough, it was the Belhaven Sanitarium. Dane made a left and entered through the gate as the LandRover continued along Ralston Avenue, much to his relief. The facility consisted of a group of low buildings that rambled among the tall trees on the canyon bottom. He pulled the rental car into a parking slot marked for visitors and turned off the engine. When he didn't get out right away, Mary Margaret looked at him quizzically.

"What's wrong?" she asked.

"I'm wondering if I shouldn't put you on a plane to Reno," he said.

"Why?"

"I don't like the way things are going. These guys following us. The fact that I couldn't get an answer at Sally Nesbit's place when I called this afternoon."

"Do you think something's happened to her?"

"I just hope no one has threatened her."

"But you said you didn't think we were followed last night," she said.

"I don't think we were, but I'm not sure of anything anymore, and if there is a danger, I see no point in subjecting you to it."

"And just hours ago you couldn't bear the thought of us parting. You had us living together, remember?"

"I'd like our relationship to last a long time," he said. "I'd feel better about that happening if I knew you were safe at home. Admittedly, the nights would be lonelier, but I'm trying to take a long-term view."

"Dane, this is my battle more than yours. Besides, what makes you think I'd be safer at home? The last time I was there, as you might recall, I had a rather unpleasant encounter."

"But Rut Coleman's out of commission now. This is a different group."

"You think they can't find their way to Reno? Look, if you're trying to spare me, it's probably too late. They know we're a team. And we've made progress. Why mess with success?"

He touched her face. "Because I don't want anything happening to you."

"I feel safer with you than I would anywhere else. And I'm not just saying that because I like the living conditions."

He drew a long breath, exhaling with a sigh. "You're pretty independent-minded, aren't you, Miss Duggan?"

"I'm not very obedient, Reverend, if that's what you mean," she said, remembering her conversation with Kathy.

"Fine, you win," he said, resigned. "No sense sitting around when we're on the verge of breaking things wide-open. Let's go see what this Benny character has to say for himself."

Patricia Gronke was thirty-eight or nine, attractive in a bookish, sober way. She was very thin and wore her dark blond hair up in a twist. Glasses and a dearth of makeup dispelled any notion that she might be a lightweight. She wore a lab coat, so it was difficult to tell how she dressed. Her shoes were expensive, but she wore no jewelry other than pearl-stud earrings.

Mary Margaret and Dane had been in Dr. Gronke's office for about twenty minutes. Most of the conversation had been between Dane and the doctor.

"I, of course, had no idea any of this had taken place," the doctor said after Dane had given her Theo's background and the details of the murder case. "But I must tell you, a number of things have become clearer. I think I have a much better handle on Benny's foibles, preoccupations and obsessions."

"What do you mean?" Dane said.

"Benjamin came to us with no social skills whatsoever. He couldn't even speak. He was terrified of everything. Once we were able to bond and I supplanted his mother as a maternal figure, we began to make progress. Benny is able to speak in rudimentary sentences now and he's adjusted some to a world with horizons beyond whatever room he occupies. But there are a couple of things in his behavior patterns that I confess have had me befuddled. One is Benny's inability to relate to younger women. Male orderlies have no trouble dealing with him, but whenever he's in the presence of a young woman he's often gotten quite upset, even hostile. The two instances in which he's become violent have involved younger female nurses."

"Are you suggesting that it may have something to do with Donna Lee?" Mary Margaret asked.

"I can only speculate," Patricia Gronke replied, "but the possibility that he was involved in a violent confrontation involving a young female is consistent with some of the behavior I've seen over the months."

Mary Margaret felt a wave of elation.

"Are you saying it's possible Benny murdered Donna Lee Marshall?" Dane asked.

"Possible, yes, but that's a long way from saying he did it. Witnessing a traumatic event could just as easily explain some of the abnormal behavior I've observed." Dr. Gronke took off her glasses and set them on top of her desk, furrowing her brows. "But there's something else besides Benny's sensitivity about young women that gives me pause. Something this murder you've described could explain."

Mary Margaret tensed and she sensed the same reaction in Dane.

"We've known for some time that knives are a special problem for Benny. His first meal here, he took his knife from the food tray and hurled it across the room. No other utensil seems to bother him."

"He must be the killer!" Mary Margaret blurted out, unable to hold her tongue. "It was Benny."

The doctor shook her head. "We can't conclude that. Not on the basis of what I've said. Imagine, for example, that Benny witnessed the girl being viciously stabbed by the murderer, say, from his window. Given his retardation and limited social experience, merely observing such a thing could have been traumatizing. No, it's much too premature."

Mary Margaret sank back in her chair, sick at heart, feeling as though the rug had been pulled out from under her once again. But Dane was still on the edge of his seat.

"Dr. Gronke, isn't there a way to find out what might have happened? You said Benny can talk now. Can't you ask him?"

"The question would be difficult to communicate," she said, "and any answer he might give extremely unreliable. You see, Benny has trouble with temporal issues. Everything is in the everlasting present. He deals in real-time behavior and immediate emotions. Imagine trying to discuss a remote event with a two- or three-year-old and you'll have a pretty good picture of what communicating with Benny is like."

"There must be some way you can get out of him what happened that day," Dane insisted.

Dr. Gronke thought for a moment or two, then said, "There is one possibility."

Mary Margaret's hopes lifted, but almost immediately she began to fear they'd come crashing down again. "What possibility?" she asked uneasily.

"I've recently begun a new type of therapy with Benny, a sort of modified play therapy. Benny is better at manipulating representational objects than verbal symbols. We've used dolls, for example, to represent him and his mother. Through them he's been able to express his feelings more eloquently than with the words at his disposal. What I might do is set up a play table that is representative of his home and the neighbor's house where the murder took place. We can have a Benny doll, a Theo doll, a Donna Lee doll and so forth. With luck, Benny might demonstrate the events he participated in or witnessed."

"When can you do this?" Mary Margaret asked.

"I would think the next day or two is a possibility."

Mary Margaret groaned. "That's the soonest?"

"We're under time pressure," Dane explained. "The sooner we have something we could take to a judge, the better. And if there's any way we can observe, that would be helpful."

Patricia Gronke seemed uncomfortable with the suggestion.

"I'm sure Sheila Warren would have no objection," he said.

"Let me speak with the head of psychiatry and see what we can do."

The doctor put her glasses back on, got up from her desk and left the office. Mary Margaret stared out the window at the towering eucalyptus and the gray-blue sky beyond. She sighed. "Two steps forward, one step back," she said woefully. "It never fails."

"This isn't going at light speed, granted," Dane said, "but we are making real progress. Think where we were only four or five days ago."

To Mary Margaret it was incredible it had only been that long. So much had happened. And not just regarding the case. Dane had told her he loved her and she was starting to feel hopeful about the future for the first time in years. If it wasn't for those men following them and the ominous feeling of dread that welled up from time to time, she'd be positively euphoric.

After a few minutes, Dr. Gronke returned. "I've been given permission to proceed with a therapy session," she announced. "Since Reverend Warren authorized us to cooperate with you, we'll permit you to monitor the session. There's an observation booth adjoining the therapy room where you can watch from behind a two-way mirror."

"Wonderful!" Dane said, giving Mary Margaret a happy smile.

"I don't want you to have overinflated expectations though," the doctor said. "It can take weeks or even months before this sort of thing produces results."

There it was again—a boot in the solar plexis. "What else?" Mary Margaret muttered under her breath. Dane reached over and patted her hand.

"Don't discount the luck of the Irish," he said. "Right, my dear?"

"Not Jimmy Duggan's brand of Irish luck, I hope," she replied.

"Why don't you come with me to prepare the therapy room?" the doctor said. "The more accurate and realistic things are, the better."

* * *

Sitting in the darkened booth next to Dane, Mary Margaret's stomach was in knots. No one needed to tell her that if this went well, if Benny Bledsoe proved to be Donna Lee Marshall's killer, her father would be getting out of prison.

She and Dane had spent half an hour with Dr. Gronke, reviewing the details of the crime, preparing the huge play table. On it were two dollhouses symbolizing the Bledsoe and Marshall homes. There was a Barbie doll in a bikini to represent Donna Lee, a Ken doll ready to play Benny, a somewhat larger doll who would be Theo. A couple of other dolls were prepared to play whatever role Benny dictated. They'd also placed a rubber knife on the table in case graphic inspiration was needed.

The door at the far side of the room opened and Patricia Gronke appeared. Holding her hand was an elflike man who scarcely came to her shoulders. His hair was thin and gray, his mouth sunken, his flabby body stooped. There was no wisdom on his face. Rather, he was the picture of childish wonder and blank stupidity.

A young man in a white uniform entered the room behind them and closed the door, taking a position next to it. Upon seeing the dolls, Benny grew excited and the doctor had to hold his hand tightly to keep him from running to the table.

"Wait, Benny," she said. Her voice was picked up clearly by the microphones. "We'll talk first. Stay calm, please."

Tucking his head contritely, Benny pouted, his lower lip protruding. He looked wounded. "Mama," he lamented, his jaw dropping awkwardly, exposing his toothless mouth.

"You'll get to see Mama in a minute," she said.

Mary Margaret was amazed by the incongruity of the scene. Benny Bledsoe was hanging on to Patricia Gronke's hand like a frightened, cowed little boy when in fact he was practically old enough to be her father. This was the ghost that Donna Lee thought she'd seen, the whimpering animal others thought they'd heard. But was Benny the vicious killer whose cold-blooded act had sent her father to San Quentin?

Benny looked up at the doctor with trusting eyes as they made their way to the table. Despite everything that had happened, Mary Margaret could not feel hatred or bitterness or anger toward the poor creature. If anything, what she felt was compassion. The wretched little man was a victim, too.

Patricia Gronke helped Benny get seated. Already he was smiling, having forgotten the gentle admonition he'd received just moments ago.

"Do you know where we are, Benny?" she asked.

"Hospital," he replied.

"Yes, we're in the hospital, but what do you think these are?" She touched the dollhouses.

"House."

"Yes, they are two houses and they are on a street together."

"Vroom!" Benny said.

"That's right. The cars go by. Whose house is this one?" She put her hand on the roof of one.

Benny shrugged.

"It's Mama's house," Dr. Gronke said.

"Mama's house," he repeated.

"That's right. And who else's house is it?"

"Benny's house." He touched his chest with his hand.

"Very good. Benny's house. And Mama's house. Shall we put Benny and Mama in the house?" she said, picking up the two dolls.

He nodded.

"I'm putting Mama in the kitchen and Benny upstairs in the bedroom," she said. "Now look, Benny. This is a girl. Her name is Donna Lee and she lives in the house next to Mama and Benny. Do you see? She is in her garden."

Benny watched, his expression darkening.

"One day a long time ago, something happened to Donna Lee," the doctor said, picking up the Donna Lee doll. She was in her garden…here…when somebody hurt her with a knife." Dr. Gronke picked up the rubber play knife.

Benny recoiled, his face a curious blend of horror and anger.

"Somebody hit Donna Lee with the knife, Benny. Here she is in her garden. Benny is here at his window. Does Benny see Donna Lee?"

Benny glared, but he didn't answer.

"Benny?"

He refused to look at her.

Mary Margaret was on the edge of her chair, her heart pounding. She stared at Benny, who was staring at the dolls. His toothless mouth was pressed tightly closed.

"Say something, dammit," she whispered. "Say something."

Benny remained frozen. Her heart sank.

"Did Mama hurt Donna Lee, Benny?" Dr. Gronke asked.

He slowly shook his head again.

The doctor picked up the other male dolls. "Did somebody else hurt Donna Lee?"

Mary Margaret waited, her breath wedged in her throat. Benny again did not move. He seemed not to hear.

"Benny?"

No response.

Patricia looked toward the booth.

"Oh, God, no," Mary Margaret murmured. "He's not going to answer."

"Dr. Gronke said it might take a while," Dane said, putting his hand on her shoulder.

She felt bitter. Once more, things seemed headed for disaster.

On the other side of the glass, Benny was virtually catatonic. Patricia Gronke put a maternal arm around Benny's shoulder. He looked up at her then and began weeping like a small child. "Mama, Mama," he cried, finally burying his face in his hands.

Mary Margaret began to cry. She cried for her father, she cried for Benny. She cried for herself.

After a while, when he'd recovered, Dr. Gronke took Benny to another table in the corner of the room where there were coloring books and crayons. Within moments Benny was scribbling and Mary Margaret knew it was over.

Dr. Gronke went to the door, telling the orderly she'd be back in a few moments. She came to the booth, closing the door.

"I know you're disappointed," she said, "but to tell you the truth, we accomplished a lot more than I expected. There may be a fruitful line of investigation here. There's no doubt in my mind Benny has memories of the event. We just can't tell at this point what he recalls.''

"It was worth a try," Mary Margaret said. "I appreciate your effort."

"I promise to pursue this and, if anything develops, I'll be sure to let you know."

"Dr. Gronke…" It was the orderly's voice coming over the speaker.

The three of them looked out to see Benny rising from his chair. His expression grim, his toothless mouth working, he made his way back to the play table.

"What's this?" Dr. Gronke asked.

Benny stood at the table, staring at the dolls. Picking up the Donna Lee doll, he tore at the little bikini top until he'd ripped it off. Then he put it in the backyard of the Marshall dollhouse. Next he took the Mama doll from the house and made it stand near the Donna Lee doll. He made a yammering noise and shook the dolls, face-to-face. Then, dropping the Mama doll, he took the Benny doll from the house and smashed it up against the Donna Lee doll, all the while making a horrible screeching noise. The Donna Lee doll ran into the Marshall house with the Benny doll in pursuit. And there was more crying and lamenting.

Then, flinging the Donna Lee doll to the floor, Benny grabbed the rubber knife and began stabbing the doll furiously. After a while he dropped the knife and began wiping his hands on the front of his shirt. His face was red and again filled with anger and horror.

"Good Lord," Patricia Gronke murmured.

"We just witnessed a decade-old murder," Dane muttered.

Mary Margaret stared through the glass at the motionless body of the Donna Lee doll. Benny had returned to the other table and was quietly coloring in his book. All that remained was for Jimmy Duggan to arrive, take the dying girl in his arms and condemn himself to a lifetime of living death.

It was sunny when they walked out the entrance of the main building, though the stiff breeze had pushed the fog over the hills and down the canyon. They could see misty wisps overhead. Dane glanced toward the street, wondering if the LandRover was waiting for them, knowing it probably was.

When he opened the door for Mary Margaret, she looked at him as though she knew what he was thinking. Dane went around to the driver's side and climbed in. He didn't start the engine. Instead, he took his cell phone from the glove compartment.

"Who are you calling?" she asked.

"A taxi."

"Why?"

"Because I think it would be fun to take the train back to the city, don't you?"

"What about the car?"

"I'll have the rental company pick it up. It'll cost a few bucks, but it's cheap insurance."

"You're worried, aren't you?" she said.

"Just being cautious."

The dispatcher told them it would be fifteen minutes. They could have walked to the station in that period of time, but that would be defeating the point. Dane could tell Mary Margaret shared his concern, but she was also preoccupied with what had transpired in the sanitarium.

"Oh, Dane," she said, gripping his hand firmly, "for the first time I'm starting to believe my father might actually get out of prison, but I'm also afraid they'll find a way to keep him locked up."

"Dr. Gronke's right about Benny being incapable of giving credible evidence, but her testimony about him would go a long way toward raising serious doubts about your father's guilt. If we can just get some physical evidence to corroborate it."

"What do you mean?"

"If Tom Muncey is able to locate a copy of that fingerprint found on the knife, and it turns out to be Benny's, that would give credence to Benny's account of events. Or if Sally Nesbit finds something in her father's diaries that corroborates the story, that would do it, too."

"You mean, like Theo told Ragsdale that Benny killed Donna Lee?"

"For example."

"If that's true, I still don't understand why he didn't immediately go to the police."

"That's the twenty-million-dollar question," Dane said. "We know for sure he was aware of Benny's existence, but that doesn't mean he knew Benny killed Donna Lee. It's clear somebody, probably Scott Wainwright, knows the truth and is doing everything in his power to prevent us from finding out exactly what it is."

"I know it's Wainwright," Mary Margaret said.

"But at the moment we can't prove it."

"I'm afraid he destroyed all the copies of the fingerprint and that he's somehow gotten to Sally Nesbit," she said.

Dane glanced at his watch. "Maybe I should give her another call."

"I'm getting a bad feeling about her," Mary Margaret said. "I don't know why."

He pulled her hand to his mouth and kissed her fingers. "I know why. It's the half-empty-glass philosophy of life."

"In my shoes you'd be a pessimist, too."

"Maybe you've turned a corner," he said.

"You're not going to like this, Dane, but I've also been feeling pessimistic about us."

He couldn't help letting his consternation show. "Mary Margaret…"

"I'm sorry, but I have this horrible ominous feeling. I do. I get this way every once in a while, and something bad always happens."

He held out his hand, face up. "Want to read my palm?"

"Oh, shut up! I'm serious!"

Dane laughed. "I'm going to call Sally." He got out his address book and dialed her number on his cell phone. It rang several times. He was about to hang up when she picked up the phone.

"Hello?"

"Sally? It's Dane Barrett."

"Reverend Barrett, I can't talk now. Call back in half an hour."

Before he could say a word, she'd hung up. He found that strange. And there was something in her voice that was troubling. She sounded afraid. He told Mary Margaret what had happened.

"See," she said. "There's something going on, something ominous."

"She might have had smoke pouring out of her oven or something," he said.

"Yeah, and Scott Wainwright is probably pure as the driven snow." She sighed. "He's going to beat us. I know he is."

"Okay, you can think what you like," he said. "But if you don't mind, I'd rather not give up quite yet—either on the case or on us."

"I know I'm being terrible. But I've been burned too many times." Turning to him, her eyes glistening, she added, "I'm scared, Dane. Scared to death."

He took her into his arms and held her, stroking her head. "You're entitled and I haven't been very supportive and understanding."

Mary Margaret sniffled, wiping her nose. "Don't say that. You've been wonderful." She drew a ragged breath. "I think the problem is I'm beginning to care too much."

"About me?"

She nodded.

"You can't care too much."

She sniffled again. "Yes I can."

A taxi entered the gate and drove up to the main building, stopping in the loading zone right next to them.

"Time for us to make our getaway," he said.

Dane put his cell phone in his pocket and they got out of the rental car. He helped Mary Margaret into the back of the cab.

"Car trouble?" the driver said.

"Worse," Dane replied. "Can you take us to the train station the long way?"

The driver, an older man with slicked-back gray hair, gave him an inquisitive look. "It's half a mile up the road. Straight shot."

"Can't you take us through the hills?"

"We can go up South Road, I guess."

"Let's do it."

They headed for the gate.

"I'll duck down," Dane said. "If they see one person leaving in a taxi, it's less likely to raise their suspicions."

At the street the driver glanced back at Dane, who was hunched down. "You folks spies or something?"

"My former husband is very jealous," Mary Margaret said.

"Oh, one of them deals."

They went down Ralston Avenue for a way, then made a left up the hill. Mary Margaret had been looking back most of the time.

"Any sign of them?" Dane asked, finally sitting up.

"When we came out of the sanitarium, I think I saw the LandRover up the street, but I don't believe it followed us."

"We might as well find out."

He told the driver to pull over. If they were being followed up the narrow, twisting road, the LandRover would be on them before it knew what happened. A minute went by and nothing passed them but a florist truck and some kids in a convertible.

"We seem to be all right," Dane said. "You can take us to the station now."

"Forgive me for saying so, lady," the driver said, "but your ex must be something else."

"You don't know the half of it," she said, giving Dane a little smile.

That pleased him, but when she interlaced her fingers in his and slid over really close, he knew she was still upset. He realized then how badly he wanted this over with. Until it was resolved, they couldn't begin to think in terms of a normal life.

At the top of the hill the driver made a right and they went down Middle Road, which twisted its way back to El Camino Real. From there it was only a few blocks back to Ralston Avenue and the train station. Dane gave the driver a twenty-dollar bill. Mary Margaret checked the schedule.

"Looks to me like we have about a fifteen-minute wait," she said.

They'd been sitting on a bench, waiting for a northbound train for ten minutes, when Dane decided to try calling Sally Nesbit again. She answered on the first ring.

"Reverend Barrett," she said, "I've got a problem. Arthur doesn't want me speaking with you until we've talked to a lawyer."

"A lawyer?" Dane said. "What's the matter?"

"I shouldn't even be discussing this with you. When you called earlier, Arthur was here. He's out walking the dog now. He always does after he changes." She interrupted herself to say something to the maid, then returned to the conversation. "I can't tell you how upset I am by this," she told him. "I've been agonizing all day."

"Sally, is it the diaries? Did you find something?"

She hesitated. "I can't discuss it right now. All I can say is I was shocked. That's why Arthur wants us to talk to an attorney. You can't imagine what's involved. It's terrible. Shocking."

Dane was getting frustrated. "Can you give me a hint?"

"Arthur's going to be coming in any moment and I don't want to be on the phone when he does. Why don't I meet you someplace?" she said. "It'll have to be tomorrow. I've got a luncheon. I can meet you right afterward. Say at two."

"Where?"

"How about in Golden Gate Park? Do you know where the boathouse is on Stow Lake?"

"I can find it. But Sally, Mary Margaret's going to want to know. Is this going to help her father?"

"I'm no lawyer, but I would think so," Sally said. "Tell her I'm going to make copies of the critical pages of the diary. The two of you can do with them as you wish, but if Arthur's adamant, I can't be involved. He's very sensitive about liability issues. He'd be upset if he knew I was doing this."

"Sally—"

"No, I won't say more. I've got to go. I think I hear my husband coming. Please don't call again, Reverend Barrett. Please." With that, she hung up.

Dane turned to Mary Margaret. She searched his eyes.

"She won't cooperate, will she?"

"Yes and no," he replied. "She insisted on being vague. But she is going to give us copies of some of the pages from her father's diaries and she thinks they'll be helpful to your dad's case. We're going to meet tomorrow afternoon in Golden Gate Park.''

"Tomorrow?" she lamented.

"That'll give us an opportunity to line up an attorney and make an appointment. The time has come, Mary Margaret. Whether Sally Nesbit comes through for us or not, we can't sit on this anymore. We know who killed Donna Lee. We just have to hope we can convince a judge.''

San Francisco

They were in the middle of their room-service meal, having just seen the news on TV that Rut Coleman had died in a Sacramento hospital, when Dane got a call from Tom Muncey.

"There's a skunk afoot in Laurel," the priest said by way of introduction.

"Tom, there are skunks all over the place.''

"You want to hear about mine first?''

"Sure.''

"Well," Muncey said, "yesterday I went in and asked Carl Slater if there was any chance of locating a copy of the original lab report, like you asked. He got annoyed and wanted to know what it was about the clergy that they felt they had to stick their nose into things that don't concern them. He told me that he and his staff had been bending over backward to be accommodating, but that we were starting to push a little too hard.''

"Did you tell him about the mysterious fingerprint reported in the missing pages of the lab report and that it was never sent to the defense attorney because someone conveniently exorcized it from the files?'' Dane asked.

"I even went one better. I asked him what in Hades Scott Wainwright had to hide.''

"What did Slater say to that?''

"He was shocked. Said he didn't know what I was talking about. Wanted to know what fingerprint and where I'd heard about it. So I told him. He hemmed and hawed and turned bright red. Kept saying he knew the files were sloppy, but it was the first he ever heard about an unidentified fingerprint on the murder weapon. It all happened before his watch, he said."

"Sounds like he's running for cover."

"He did promise to check into it and see if there were duplicate records somewhere. Told me to give him a call today."

"And?"

"When I dropped by the station, Slater had just left for lunch. I had meetings lined up all afternoon and didn't want this to drag on, so I asked where Slater usually eats. They told me he always meets his wife for lunch on Thursdays at the Laurel House, just up the street, so I figured I'd drop by. To make a long story short, I got there right after Slater. He told me the county crime lab might still have duplicate records in storage, but there was nothing at all in their files. He'd keep on it, but he wasn't optimistic."

"Do you think he was lying?"

"No, but he was upset and I think a little befuddled by the whole thing. But that's not the interesting part. Just as I was leaving, Slater's wife pulls up out front and what do I see plastered all over her Cadillac but Wainwright For Governor bumper stickers. At first I didn't think a thing about it because she has two choices—either Wainwright or Dunkin, right? And I figure the wife of a police chief is more likely to support a Republican attorney general."

"Makes sense to me."

"Well, being a meddling priest, I'm not satisfied with that. So I call up the county Republican headquarters and what do you suppose I discover?"

"What?"

"Mrs. Slater is the county chairwoman of the Wainwright for Governor campaign."

"Sounds like things are getting incestuous," Dane said, glancing over at Mary Margaret, who was quietly playing with her food as she listened.

"I don't think it necessarily means she and Chief Slater are mixed up in any past wrongdoings, but they had good reason to keep the Wainwright people informed about what was happening in Laurel."

"Mary Margaret and I have discovered there's a lot Wainwright would probably want the world to forget," Dane said. "We think today we found out who killed Donna Lee Marshall."

"You did?"

Dane told him what had happened at the sanitarium.

"Holy Mother," Muncey said.

"We're going to see an attorney tomorrow and let the legal system handle this from here on out." He said it as much for Mary Margaret's benefit as Tom Muncey's. She had been in a funk and he took every opportunity he could to inject a note of optimism.

"When this comes out, Scott Wainwright is going to be a very unhappy camper," the priest said.

"He's been unhappy for a while, Tom. And I plan to add to his misery if I can. Especially if it turns out he's known about all this for a long time. Frankly, that's what I expect."

"You know what this means," Muncey said.

"That Scott Wainwright's political career is over. And if we can prove obstruction of justice and suppression of evidence, he could even spend some time behind bars."

"If you know that, so does he, Dane."

"We're being careful."

Mary Margaret glanced up at him when he said that. She did not look pleased.

"There's such a nice lilt to your voice when you say 'we,'" Muncey said. "I hope I'm invited to the wedding."

"You're still premature," Dane said, "but we're thinking along the same vein anyway."

"Ah, she must be an angel."

"She is an angel."

Again Mary Margaret looked over at him and he smiled. She tried, but didn't do well. Dane knew he had to get off the phone.

"I won't keep you then, Tom," he said. "I appreciate your efforts and I know Mary Margaret does, too."

"Kiss her for me, lad."

"I will."

Dane hung up and went back over to the table where Mary

Margaret had been picking at her food. Bending over, he gave her a big kiss.

"That's from Father Muncey," he said.

"I didn't know he and I were on such intimate terms."

"If it wasn't for Tom, we'd have never met."

"Maybe I owe *him* a kiss then," she said.

"You mean you aren't ruing the day I walked into your life?"

"I know I'm being awful," she said, hanging her head, "but I have this terrible foreboding feeling. And for some reason, hearing that Rut Coleman is dead didn't help."

"We'll deal with whatever comes down the pike. Together."

She regarded him, biting her lip, her eyes getting misty. "I think my problem is loving you is not without its complications, Reverend Barrett."

Dane knelt next to her chair and held her, stroking her head. "Complications only mean we've gotten beneath the surface. It's important we love and respect and care for each other as people first."

She shook her head in disbelief. "How did I ever find you?"

"It was destiny, I think."

"You believe that?"

"I don't know how it works or who pulls the strings, but I think there's a certain logic to the universe. Things happen for a reason. I really believe some things are meant to be."

"I wonder if I'll ever be that upbeat," she said.

"Just stick with me, kid."

She kissed his lips tenderly, then tried to look happy, but she didn't quite succeed. "You've got your work cut out for you," she said.

"Honey, you haven't seen anything yet. Trust me on that."

"I want to," she said, hugging him. "I really, really do."

Friday

August 16th

San Francisco

He had not slept well, tormented by dreams of Cal Dunkin lecturing at him from a pulpit, of all things. "Murderer!" Dunkin had screamed at him. "Murderer!"

Scott Wainwright had awakened in a sweat, riddled with anxiety. He had condemned two people to death simply because they were a danger to him. Of course, holding the power of life and death was not new. He made decisions every day that altered the course of lives. And yes, he'd played God. But people demanded that of their attorney general. They demanded the swift sword. They wanted justice.

The death order he'd meted out was ugly, but necessary. He had a campaign to run, a debate to win, an opponent who wanted to crucify him. He had to be strong. He had to be tough.

Wainwright got out of bed and went to the phone. He asked his aide to have breakfast sent up, then he showered and dressed. When he went into the sitting room of the suite he found portly Alec Tolliver waiting, grim-faced. Tolliver was standing. He looked as if he'd been pacing.

"Alec, what are you doing here?"

"We've got a problem."

The campaign director's tone made him uneasy. "What kind of problem?"

"That business in Laurel is about to blow up in our face."

"What are you talking about?"

"I had a call this morning from Carl Slater, the police

chief. He wants to know if evidence had been suppressed in that old case—something about an unaccounted-for fingerprint missing from the police lab report."

"Oh, Jesus."

"Scott," Alec said, "Slater's a friend. If our friends are asking these kinds of questions, what about our enemies?"

"God, I thought I had this under control."

"My sense, talking to Slater, is it's just the tip of the iceberg. Just how vulnerable are we on this thing, Scott?"

"It's not good," Wainwright said, rubbing his jaw. "Let me put it that way."

The color drained from Tolliver's face. "I think it's time for a little candor," he said. "How bad is 'not good'?"

Wainwright thought for a moment. He had a horrible feeling, as though the walls were closing in on him. He looked into Tolliver's bland, puffy eyes, uncertain what he should say.

"Scott? Speak to me."

Wainwright drew a long breath. "How does obstruction of justice sound?"

"Christ. Can it be tied to you personally?"

Wainwright knew he had to be careful. Alec was his best political friend in the world, but Alec had a career, too. A wife and a family. Sinking ships attracted very little loyalty. "I don't think so," he replied.

"You're saying mistakes were made by others, but it was during your watch and so you have some responsibility."

"That would be one way to put it."

Tolliver scratched his head. Then he went and sat on the sofa. Wainwright sat in the armchair. They regarded each other. Wainwright wondered if the minister and the woman were alive or dead. A cold feeling of horror went through him and he thought for a moment he might be sick.

Tolliver didn't notice. He was busy making political calculations. "It may be time to cut our losses," he said after a moment, "make some disclosures before the shit hits the fan. If handled right, a negative can sometimes be turned into a positive."

Wainwright swallowed hard. "It may be too late."

"What do you mean? Nixon was as good as in jail and still clinging to the presidency."

"Let's just say the burglars have been sent to the Watergate. We can only hope now they don't get caught."

Tolliver's eyes narrowed with uncertainty. Wainwright could tell he was wondering if he wanted to know, perhaps deciding he didn't.

"If the burglars can be called back," Tolliver said, "I'd say do it before it's too late. An overzealous act that occurred eight years ago is one thing, a criminal act today is another entirely."

Wainwright pondered that as a sense of doom welled within him. He had acted rashly, he realized now. He'd been desperate, yes, but it had seemed logical and necessary. But maybe it wasn't too late. Maybe he could end this nightmare with one simple phone call. Losing the election was one thing, but losing his freedom, or even his life, was another. A cold sweat broke out on his brow. He could hear Cal Dunkin's accusing voice. "Murderer! Murderer!"

Wainwright got to his feet and silently went into the bedroom. Picking up the phone, he dialed. The phone rang and rang. His heart pounded so hard that the pain went down his arms. "Answer the fucking phone!" he said through his teeth. "Please!"

Finally it clicked and the familiar voice came on the line. "We're not here," it said. "Leave a message." Then there was a beep.

His lips trembling, his entire body shaking, Scott Wainwright said, "Don't do it! I changed my mind. Don't do it!" Then he hung up the phone. Staring at it, he somehow knew it was too late.

Golden Gate Park, San Francisco

Mary Margaret looked out at the trees, the greenery muted by fog as they drove along John F. Kennedy Drive. It reminded her of her childhood and adolescence. She remembered walking alone in the park the morning after Dennis Malloy had nearly torn her clothes off. She'd practically ripped out his eye, but the experience had disillusioned her, and she hadn't been able to put it from her mind for a long time. Maybe there was something to Dane's theory about her half-empty glass.

But she'd learned something else for having known him. Deep down she wanted more from life than what she'd gotten so far. With Dane she'd had a taste of happiness and she didn't want it to end. But she was afraid it would. Somehow, someway, she was going to lose him.

They had spent the morning in their room, eaten a room-service breakfast and working on lining up a lawyer. She'd called the A.C.L.U. attorney she had previously consulted about her father's appeal and had gotten the names of two San Francisco lawyers who'd be good with a politically sensitive criminal case. The first appointment they could get was Monday morning. Mary Margaret was disappointed, but at least they were doing something.

Dane had sensed how uptight she was. They'd fallen asleep in each other's arms, but hadn't made love. And though he'd kissed her when she'd climbed out of the shower that morning, the affection had ended there. There was a compassionate, understanding side to Dane Barrett that rivaled his other virtues. She loved his gentleness.

They'd passed behind the De Young Museum and there was a sign indicating that Stow Lake was off to the left. Dane checked his rearview mirror before making the turn.

Mary Margaret glanced back. There was no sign of a Land-Rover or any other suspicious vehicle. They'd slipped out the back entrance to the Fairmont and Dane had given the parking valet ten dollars to bring the new rental car to the corner of Powell and Clay Streets, a couple of blocks down the hill. The ploy seemed to have been successful.

It was a few minutes before two o'clock as they moved slowly along the drive, passing a couple of women in spandex riding racing bikes. Mary Margaret peered up at the fog. An eerie feeling came over her. She didn't know what to expect from Sally Nesbit—*if* she even showed up. It had to be that Stephen Ragsdale was somehow involved in the cover-up. What else could it be?

They came to the lake.

"I think that's the boathouse," Mary Margaret said, pointing.

Dane pulled into the parking area. There were few other cars. Though it was the height of the tourist season, it was a weekday and once you got beyond the Japanese Tea Garden, the museum, aquarium and planetarium, it was possible to find a quiet corner in the park. Perhaps that was why Sally had chosen Stow Lake.

They got out of the car. Mary Margaret shivered in the damp, cool air. She'd worn a navy linen jacket over a pink silk blouse and white slacks.

There was no sign of a suspicious vehicle as they crossed the road and made their way toward the boathouse. But there were a few people strolling on the walk that circled the lake. Mary Margaret spotted Sally seated on a bench, facing the water. She was in a trench coat and looked stiff and uncomfortable.

Sally saw them coming and got up. She did not smile.

"Hello," she said, acknowledging them perfunctorily. "It's rather chilly. Do you mind if we walk?"

"No," Dane said. "Whatever you like, Sally."

They started off in a clockwise direction around the lake. Three adolescent boys on in-line skates whizzed by. Moments later a jogger passed them from behind. Sally walked between them. She stared glumly at the sidewalk, her mouth in a tight line. Dane and Mary Margaret kept silent, letting Sally set the tone.

"I learned some disturbing things about my father," she said after a minute. "I suppose deep down I expected as much, which is why I've never read his diaries...at least those from the last years of his life." She took a deep breath. "I'll get right to the point. My father had a sexual relationship with Donna Lee Marshall and it ended up costing him his life."

"How so?" Dane asked.

"A few years after Donna Lee was murdered, Theo Bledsoe had what sounded by my father's account like a nervous breakdown. She called Dad and asked for his help. He went to her home and discovered to his shock and dismay that Theo had been hiding a mentally retarded son in her house for nearly fifty years."

"Yes, we know about Benny," Dane said.

"Well, you know then how shocked my father must have been. But that wasn't all. Theo resisted his attempts to convince her to seek help for her son. When he told her he might be forced to take matters into his own hands, Theo threatened to expose his liaison with Donna Lee. Apparently she'd been aware of it and even had some photos of him kissing and fondling the girl taken through the window." Sally shivered. "I can't tell you how hard it was for me to learn this," she said in a thin voice. "This was a man I adored and respected my entire life." Taking a handkerchief from her pocket, she dabbed the corners of her eyes.

"Stephen succumbed to temptation and paid a terrible price," Dane said, "but that doesn't negate the good he did, or what he meant to you."

"A nice sentiment, Reverend Barrett, but I can never forgive him for destroying my trust. He failed me and my mother, not to mention what he did to that poor girl." She cleared her throat. "But it gets worse."

Mary Margaret's heart went out to Sally Nesbit. She herself had been hurt and disappointed by a father, but at least with Jimmy Duggan there had been no illusion, no deception. He'd never pretended.

"I can only thank God my mother never found out," Sally said. "She wouldn't have been able to bear that on top of all her other suffering." She blew her nose. "I'm sorry to be so emotional. Forgive me."

"You've had a shock," Dane said in his most pastoral tone. "Your feelings are understandable."

"Thank you, but I don't want to drag this out. This next bit affects your father, Miss Duggan," she said, glancing at Mary Margaret. "I know it'll be helpful to his case, so I've made copies of those pages of the diary."

"What do they say?"

"That my father learned from Theo that Mr. Duggan wasn't the one who stabbed Donna Lee Marshall—it was her son. Your father was innocent."

"That's the hard evidence we need," Dane enthused.

"Thank God," Mary Margaret replied.

"You see, Sally," Dane explained, "we figured Benny killed Donna Lee, but we couldn't prove it."

Sally seemed relieved. "Well, my father's diaries confirm it."

"That will be a help, thank you."

"Is there any indication why Theo finally let the past come out?" Dane asked.

"She'd been hiding the truth out of fear and guilt, apparently," Sally replied. "Dad wrote that he thought it was the chief cause of her breakdown."

"But he didn't tell anyone because he was being blackmailed."

"No, he struggled with the awful truth until his own mental health started to deteriorate. After a while he began feeling as guilty as Theo. So finally he—" Sally stopped. "Oh, God," she said. "Arthur is going to kill me." Taking a fortifying breath, she went on. "Finally Dad contacted Scott Wainwright and told him they'd convicted the wrong man, that the person who'd killed Donna Lee was the neighbor's mentally retarded son."

"Your father told Scott Wainwright?" Dane said, amazed. Mary Margaret was incredulous.

"That's right. The guilt had worn on him so that he couldn't take it anymore. In his diary he wrote that he wanted to protect me and the memory of my mother, but that our honor and his own pride and self-respect was nothing compared to the lost life of an innocent man. That's another reason I made copies, Miss Duggan. I wanted you to see that in the end my father tried to do the right thing."

"But he never lived to see that justice was done," Dane said.

"No," Sally replied. "He died within days of his meeting with Scott Wainwright. And there's nothing in the diaries to indicate what really happened when he went to the mountains. The tragedy is that he stepped forward with the truth, but ended up dying in vain. Perhaps he was counting on someone reading his diaries someday." Sally stopped walking and faced Mary Margaret. "In that sense, I'm at least partially responsible for your father's suffering."

"But you're brave enough to come forward now," Mary Margaret said, her eyes brimming right along with Sally's. "No one else has done that much."

Spontaneously the women embraced.

"This should be enough to get your dad out of prison, Mary Margaret," Dane said excitedly. "The diary pages together with Dr. Gronke's testimony has to convince a judge to act. I'd be surprised if we can't get some sort of order to have him released within days."

Mary Margaret couldn't believe it. She started crying. Dane put his arm around her. Her tears were tears of joy.

Sally Nesbit dug the photocopies of her father's diaries out of her purse and put them in Mary Margaret's hands. "Here," she said. "And please accept my apologies for the way my family failed you. I hope with all my heart it works out well. But now I've got to get home. I've got Arthur to contend with. He's afraid of repercussions. But I didn't want this on my conscience."

"Thank you," Mary Margaret said. "Thank you so much."

They embraced again and Sally Nesbit headed back the way they'd come. Mary Margaret stood there, the photocopies clutched at her breast, her eyes closed. She'd been waiting for this day for so long.

"Dane," she said, "I can't believe it's finally happened."

He hugged her and she felt so safe, so relieved. A boy passing on a bicycle whistled. They laughed. Then they started for the car, their arms around each other.

"You know what those diaries mean?" Dane said. "We're not only getting your dad out of prison, now we've got proof that Wainwright knew Jimmy was innocent and did nothing. He might have been able to push the missing fingerprint off on somebody else, but not this."

"No wonder he was desperate," she said. "He may be the one going to jail."

"Couldn't happen to a nicer guy."

They returned to the car. It was all Mary Margaret could do to keep from skipping.

"I think I'm going to call the Heritage House when we get

to the hotel," Dane said as he opened the passenger door. "Might as well get our reservations."

"You really want to take me back there?" she said, slipping into the seat.

Dane leaned over to peer in at her, resting his forearm on the roof of the car. "Mary Margaret, I fell in love with you the minute you stuck that gun in my face. But it wasn't until Mendocino that I was able to convince you how I felt. What happened up there was very, very special."

"You mean the striptease?"

He grinned at her. "You know exactly what I mean."

"Barrett!"

The voice came out of nowhere. It was accented and it was harsh and demanding. Mary Margaret saw the surprise in Dane's eyes, maybe a flash of awareness of what was coming. He straightened and turned. The shots came almost instantly, knocking him back against the car and her.

Instinctively she grabbed him, stunned as he lay limp across her lap, motionless.

Looking up, she saw the gunman, a large man with a black ski mask over his face, stepping quickly to the front of the car. He peered through the windshield and, in a surprisingly deliberate way, lifted his weapon, pointing it directly at her head. She flinched, ducking as the glass exploded, raining shards on her and Dane. The bullet had torn through her hair without actually touching her flesh, demolishing the headrest.

Stunned, she was unable to move. Then, through the side window, she saw the gunman running away. Despite her frenzy of confusion, she managed to grasp the fact that the immediate danger was over.

Dane started to slip toward the ground. She grabbed the lapels of his jacket, only then realizing the fabric was soaked in blood, making it too slippery to hold. Fighting the rising panic, she somehow managed to ease him to the ground and clamber out of the car, kneeling beside his body. Until he gave a strange little cough, she was sure he was dead. For a few seconds the horror of that did not fully sink in. But when it finally hit, she began to sob.

"No. Oh, God, no! Please."

Dane lay there, his eyes open, staring blankly at the colorless sky. The only sound he made was a wheezing in his throat. She didn't know what to do. She had to get help. But there wasn't anyone around. Then, in a moment of clarity, she remembered his cell phone. Reaching into the glove compartment, she snatched out the phone and dialed 911. The wait seemed interminable. All she could do was squeeze Dane's hand and stare at his expressionless face, knowing he wasn't fully there, hoping that he wasn't already gone.

At last someone came on the line and she begged the woman to send an ambulance. Then the questions began, the stranger's voice calm, firm, uncompromising. Mary Margaret answered as best she could, but pleaded for the ambulance to hurry. "He's dying," she kept saying. "He's dying."

When the operator assured her that help was on the way, she put the phone aside and leaned close to Dane. She kissed his pallid skin, feeling his breath against her cheek, but getting no response.

"Hang on, Dane," she pleaded. "Don't leave me. We're going to Mendocino, remember?"

His dear face looked so different. There was no sign of his lively, keen intellect. There was no consciousness, no compassion, no pain, no sorrow. Was his mind empty, too? she wondered. Or only his body?

"Dane," she cried, pressing her face to his. "I love you. Don't leave me. Please, hang on. Please."

She heard the siren. It was still some distance away but getting closer. She checked his breathing again and saw that his entire torso was soaked in blood, as were her pant legs. His chest rose and fell ever so slightly, but he was fading fast, she could tell. She kissed his forehead.

"Help's coming, darling," she told him. "They're almost here." Then she did the only thing she could. She prayed to God to spare Dane's life.

St. Mary's Hospital, San Francisco

She had been at the hospital for three hours, the last one in the chapel on the sixth floor, searching for the appropriate deity or spirit, invocation or state of mind that would most likely serve Dane. She had tried the God of her childhood, the Virgin Mary and Jesus, but any supplication for Dane ought, she reasoned, be directed other places, as well. So she meditated on creation, the God-concept that moved Dane. She invoked the name of Buddha, Lord Siddhartha, though it was more a conversation.

Mary Margaret's mother had died at St. Mary's, which she chose not to take as a bad omen. The prayers she'd said for her mother had been a plea for God's compassion and her mother's peace. With Dane the struggle was for survival. And so she spent much of the time trying to commune with him, through the steel and concrete walls, through the matter and space separating them. She wanted her spirit to give him strength, and she wanted him to know he was in her heart.

Practically his last words to her were that he loved her. Whatever happened, she'd always have that. But this would not be the end, she told herself. It had to be the beginning. It had to be. She could not have slept her last night with him at her side.

Mary Margaret was continuing her imaginary conversation with Dane when she heard the doors to the chapel open. A sharp pain went through her. *Oh, Dane,* she begged. *Don't be dead. Please don't be dead.*

Looking back, she saw Sister Cecelia, a diminutive, bespectacled woman, making her way toward her. The nun crossed herself and slipped into the pew next to her. Mary Margaret was about to burst as she waited for the nun's words.

"Reverend Barrett is hanging on," Sister Cecelia said softly.

A million hosannas rose in Mary Margaret's heart. "Oh, thank God!"

"They've decided he's stable enough to try to repair the damage to his lungs and liver. If they wait, he may never be strong enough. The doctor said there's a risk either way," the nun said, taking Mary Margaret's hands. "But he wants you to know Reverend Barrett's facing a few more hours of surgery. We're doing everything we can, but as you know, it's really in the hands of God."

"I've been praying," Mary Margaret said, "but now I think I want to be near him."

"Surgery's on A level. There's a waiting room there. I'll take you down," Sister Cecelia said. She glanced at Mary Margaret's bloodstained jacket, blouse and pants. "Would you like me to find something else for you to wear?"

Mary Margaret shook her head. "No, I'm okay." To some it might have been gross, but Dane's blood made her feel close to him, a part of him. "Did you get a hold of his mother?" she asked.

"Yes," the nun replied. "She's on her way to San Francisco."

Mary Margaret went with Sister Cecelia to a waiting room on A level where three other people sat quietly. A television droned in the corner. The early news was on. The reporter was finishing a story about a threatened teachers' strike in the East Bay. Then the anchor came back on-screen.

"Here in San Francisco, a man was shot and critically wounded this afternoon in Golden Gate Park," he said. "A lone gunman in a ski mask approached the Reverend Dane Barrett, a Unitarian minister from the town of Laurel in the Central Valley, and opened fire at close range. Barrett was rushed by ambulance to a nearby hospital where spokesmen say he is in grave condition.

"No motive for the shooting has been established and there are no suspects. At this hour the gunman remains at large."

"No motive?" Mary Margaret said. "I told the cops exactly who was behind it!"

"Perhaps the police don't want the public to know," Sister Cecelia said.

"Or don't believe me." Mary Margaret hadn't had time to be angry, but her temper flared now. "The bastard," she muttered under her breath.

Sister Cecelia pretended not to hear.

"This evening at the Sheraton-Palace Hotel in San Francisco," the news anchor went on, "the two principal gubernatorial candidates, Attorney General Scott Wainwright, the GOP nominee, and State Senator Calvin Dunkin, the Democratic Party nominee, will face off in the first of three debates. Our reporters spoke to both candidates this afternoon. First we go to Molly Petersen who visited a rested and confident Attorney General Wainwright at his hotel in San Francisco. Molly?''

As the images flickered on the screen, Mary Margaret felt her anger build. When Scott Wainwright appeared, she was seething.

''As I see it,'' Wainwright was saying, ''this election is about two things—the safety of our families and children, which requires moral leadership from the top, and the integrity of government. I think the people of the state should give Senator Dunkin and myself a good hard look and ask which of us is most likely to make our streets safe and bring moral leadership to Sacramento.''

''Hypocritical bastard!'' Mary Margaret screamed, eliciting surprised looks from the other people in the waiting room.

She got to her feet, fists clenched. Sister Cecelia tried to pull her back down, but she'd gotten her choler up.

''That man's not fit to be governor,'' she said, waving at the TV set. ''What gall! First he lets my father rot in prison and now he's pontificating about virtue.''

''Mary Margaret, calm yourself,'' Sister Cecelia said, rising.

Mary Margaret looked at the nun. ''I'm not going to let him get away with it. I can't. Dane wouldn't. I know he wouldn't!'' With that, she marched from the room with determined strides, Sister Cecelia on her heels.

''Where are you going?''

''Downtown. I know exactly what Dane would want for me to do. His hands are full with his own fight. I'll finish the other one.'' She stopped just inside the entrance. ''If Dane is out of surgery before I get back, tell him I'm taking care of Scott Wainwright. And above all else, Sister Cecelia, tell him I love him.''

The nun stood speechless as Mary Margaret went out the door and into the foggy evening.

The Sheraton-Palace Hotel, San Francisco

Mary Margaret didn't think about the blood on her clothes until she was climbing out of the taxi on New Montgomery

Street in front of the hotel. Her initial impulse was to go to the ladies' room and try to wash her pants and blouse. Then she decided Scott Wainwright deserved to see, in graphic terms, exactly what he'd done.

Walking down the long hallways, she felt as if she was in a palace. Between the tall gilt mirrors and the crystal chandeliers, it was like she imagined the Palace of Versailles. As the little Catholic girl from the Sunset District, it wasn't the way she'd wanted to arrive, but this was the hand fate had dealt and she was determined to play it out.

The entrance to the grand ballroom was choked with media people lugging in equipment. She managed to slip in with them, lurking in the back of the hall, amid the cables and support staff. It was half an hour before the debate was to begin. The audience, a small coterie of supporters for both candidates, were mostly in place. The senator and attorney general had not yet made their appearance.

Despite the air of excitement, Mary Margaret was still numb, even as her veins were awash with adrenaline. Miles separated her from Dane, but she could almost feel him struggling. He wouldn't leave her. She knew it with all her heart.

Fifteen minutes before the scheduled beginning of the debate, the two candidates came on to the stage. They shook hands and greeted the moderator, a local news anchor. Mary Margaret's eyes scarcely left Scott Wainwright in his dark blue suit and red power tie. She hated his smug, haughty demeanor, his phony smile. He was everything Dane Barrett was not.

Right then, as she formulated her plan, she realized it didn't matter whether things were half-empty, as it seemed to her, or half-full, as Dane thought. She was going to turn it on its head, make the rich and powerful rethink justice and bring Scott Wainwright to his knees.

When the candidates took their places at their podiums, she took the pages from Stephen Ragsdale's diary from her purse and walked to the foot of the stage, next to the moderator's table. Several media people regarded her quizzically.

"Senator Dunkin," she said in a strong firm voice, "if you

get a chance during the debate, I'd like for you to ask Mr. Wainwright a couple of questions for me.''

Dunkin and Wainwright both peered at her through the glare of the TV lights, surprise on their faces.

"Please ask Mr. Wainwright why, when he was the prosecuting attorney in San Joaquin County, he suppressed evidence that would have exonerated Jimmy Duggan, who was then convicted of a murder he didn't commit. And please ask why a few years later when he was told by Reverend Stephen Ragsdale the identity of the real killer, he began a cover-up that he's continued to this day.''

"Will somebody do something about this woman?'' Scott Wainwright called out. "This is inexcusable.''

"Here's the proof, Senator Dunkin,'' she persisted, stepping to the lip of the stage and handing the papers to the candidate. "Ask Mr. Wainwright why he's left an innocent man to rot in prison while doing everything in his power to keep him there, including threats, intimidation, lying and even attempted murder.''

"This is an outrage!'' Wainwright shouted. "Where is security?''

There were shouts from the back of the room as security guards came running forward. Mary Margaret ignored the commotion and kept talking.

"This blood on me, Senator, is from the body of Reverend Dane Barrett. Scott Wainwright tried to have him murdered so that his attempts to obstruct justice would never come to light. Ask him if he thinks the people of California should have a murderer in the governor's office!''

"The woman's insane!'' Wainwright cried.

Two security guards arrived, taking her by the arms. They started dragging her away.

"All the evidence will be in the hands of the police by tomorrow,'' she shouted. "By Monday, Wainwright will have withdrawn as a candidate and will be under criminal investigation. Ask him, Senator, if he's man enough to apologize to the people for what he's done. Ask him if he's got the guts to do what he can to help Jimmy Duggan. Ask him if he really wants to go on with this charade!''

They had reached the doorway and the guards hustled her

>ut into the hallway. Reporters rushed up to her. The ques-
ions started coming fast and furious. "Who are you?"

"Are you saying Wainwright was behind today's shooting
n Golden Gate Park?"

"Who's Jimmy Duggan?"

Mary Margaret calmly answered the questions, telling the
reporters exactly what had happened. A couple of police of-
icers arrived, pushing their way through the throng of media
>eople.

"Are you Mary Margaret Duggan?" one asked.

"Yes," she said calmly, expecting them to handcuff her.

"There's been an urgent call for you to get back to
St. Mary's," the officer said. "Some kind of emergency."

"Oh, my God," she said, bringing her hands to her mouth.
"It's Dane, isn't it? Is he dead?"

"I don't know," the cop replied. "The call came out to
us. We're just passing the word along."

"I've got to go," she said, starting to push her way through
he throng.

"We can take you there," the cop said, taking her arm.
"If it's urgent, we can get you there faster."

The three of them dashed through the opulent halls of the
Sheraton-Palace. A few reporters tagged along. Mary Margaret felt as though she was being carried by a tide she could
no longer resist. She had lashed out at Scott Wainwright, but
now she was spent. Even Dane and the spiritual bond she'd
formed with him seemed to have slipped from her grasp. He
was gone. He'd left her. She was sure of it.

The Haight-Ashbury, San Francisco

They'd taken Fell Street across town, the lights of the patrol car flashing and the siren blaring. Mary Margaret was in
back, leaning forward in her seat, watching as dusk fell over
the city. Time moved much too slowly. It was the uncertainty
she couldn't bear. Maybe Dane had been depending on her.
The thought made her heart ache.

As they approached Masonic Avenue, a call came over the
police radio. Mary Margaret didn't understand what was said.

"Uh-oh," one cop said to her. "We've got a robbery in progress and that's higher priority. We either let you out here miss, or you go with us."

"I'll get out."

The Panhandle, a long, block-wide strip of parkway between Fell and Park Streets, extending all the way to Golden Gate Park, was on their left. The driver pulled to the curb and let her out. Then the police car swung across traffic and disappeared up a side street. St. Mary's was about six blocks ahead. She looked for a taxi, but none was in sight, so she started running.

After three blocks she was breathing hard and beginning to perspire. Once, she lost one of her flats and had to go back and get it. There were plenty of curious bystanders in the park, but she ignored them. Getting to the hospital was all that mattered.

By the time Golden Gate Park loomed ahead, the air burned her lungs and her legs began to fail. Still, she pressed ahead, not knowing what she'd find when she got there, fearing the worst, afraid to hope.

Reaching the end of the Panhandle at Stanyan Street, she dashed across Fell, barely avoiding being hit by a motorcycle. Her knees were wobbly as she ran up the sidewalk on Stanyan. Arriving at the hospital, she stumbled to the entrance. Sister Cecelia, who was waiting inside the door, seemed dismayed at the sight of her. Mary Margaret, her hair tangled by the wind, her face and neck soaked with perspiration, her clothes bloody, gasped for air as she staggered toward the nun.

"Is he dead?" she cried between breaths. "Tell me!"

"No," the nun said. "No, he's in intensive care. He survived the surgery. But he's still a very sick man."

Mary Margaret fell crying into the poor woman's arms.

"What's happened to you?" the sister said, digging into a pocket for a tissue. She dabbed at Mary Margaret's brow.

"I'm okay," she said, her breath coming a little more easily. "Never mind. Can I see Dane?"

"His mother's here," Sister Cecelia said, taking her by the arm. "She arrived maybe a half hour ago. She's with him now."

They walked through the hospital. Mary Margaret was desperately happy that Dane hadn't died, yet at the same time he felt disoriented and uncertain. How could this have turned out well? Things never went right for her. Maybe this wouldn't yet. He was still in danger, after all.

Arriving at the nursing station in intensive care, they came face-to-face with a tall patrician woman of sixty with silver-treaked, light brown hair. She wore a peach cashmere sweater and cream silk broadcloth pants, a heavy gold bracelet and earrings. Blue eyes like Dane's took Mary Margaret in with an appraising but benevolent look.

"You must be Mary Margaret," she said.

"Yes."

"I'm Constance Barrett."

They were much the same height and looked straight across at each other, eye to eye. There was a slight smile on the woman's lips. It fell short of warmth, but indicated amusement, even pleasure.

"You're every bit as pretty as he said."

"Dane talked to you about me?"

"Not now. The other day on the phone. I believe you were in the shower or something." The corners of her mouth curled slightly.

"Oh." Mary Margaret colored, looking down at herself, embarrassed by the innuendo, not to mention her appearance. She wiped her forehead with her sleeve. "This has been a rough day."

"They tell me you saved my son's life."

"I'm not so sure about that. If it wasn't for me, he'd never have been in this mess to begin with."

"Dane did what he wanted to do. I know him well enough to say that with confidence."

"He's a wonderful person," Mary Margaret said.

"He said the same about you. It's apparently rather mutual."

Mary Margaret blushed again.

"I'm looking forward to getting to know you better," the woman said. Constance Barrett's smile was warmer than Mary Margaret would have expected.

"I feel the same. As soon as Dane's better, I know some-

thing you and I could do. Something that's very important,"
Mary Margaret said.

"What's that, dear?"

"We have to buy a new kitten for your grandson. Toby
may be coming home soon."

"Oh?"

"It's a long story."

"Maybe you can tell me later, then," Constance Barrett
said. "I assume your top priority at the moment is seeing
Dane."

"Oh, yes. Is he conscious? Have you spoken to him yet?"

"It was a very one-sided conversation. I don't know that
he heard a word I said, but he seems to come in and out. The
nurse said that's normal. The next few hours will be critical."
She turned to the nurse behind the counter. "My son's young
lady would like to see him, and I believe it's safe to say he'd
like to see her."

"I'll take her to him," the nurse said.

"Please do."

Mary Margaret touched Mrs. Barrett's hand, then followed
the nurse down the hall. They came to the door to Dane's
room. The woman stepped aside and Mary Margaret peered
into the dimly lit space.

He lay in bed, his head and torso slightly elevated. The
dials of the machines cast a faintly greenish hue over the
room. Dane's dark hair shone against the starkness of the
pillow. His shoulders were bare, his chest heavily bandaged.
Tubes were in his nose, his arms. The beeping sound coming
from one of the machines parroted his heartbeat.

She moved into the room, feeling reverence. According to
the doctor, this was a life that should already have ended.
Reason, science, both said he shouldn't have lived. Yet here
he was, his heart still sustaining him. Beep, beep, beep, even
as he slept.

His eyes were closed, his expression peaceful, calm. His
breathing was shallow and seemed a bit halting. She looked
at the lips that had kissed her, the face that was so dear.
Pushing back her sweat-soaked hair, she leaned over him. He
was so beautiful and now so fragile.

"Dane," she whispered. "I'm here."

There was no response.

"Thank you for not leaving me. Thank you for fighting."

Still nothing.

Tears welled in her eyes. "I love you, Dane," she said softly, brushing her cheek against his. "I really do. With all my heart."

His lashes fluttered and his eyes opened. He looked at her. His expression did not change but she sensed awareness in his eyes. Tears ran down her cheeks.

His lip sagged open after a moment and in a faint, hoarse voice he said, "Mary Margaret. If you're here, this must be heaven."

She bit her lip and said, "Yes, my darling, it is heaven. I realize now you were right. This has been heaven all along."

Despite the tubes and wires and drugs and pain, he managed to smile. "I'm a little tired," he said, "so if we're going to Mendocino, you'll have to drive."

Her tears dropped onto his face and she kissed them away. "I think they're going to keep you overnight, Dane."

His lip trembled, but he managed to speak. "If they do...will you stay with me?"

"I suppose the next thing you'll want is for me to take off all my clothes and dance."

His smile was so broad he winced with pain. "Okay."

"Yeah, well, dream on, buster. I'm thinking of becoming respectable."

"I'll give you...a thousand dollars," he wheezed.

"Ha! I can get that any day of the week!"

He swallowed painfully. "Two thousand."

Mary Margaret gave him a long, hard look. "Now I know what you think I am."

"All right, three thousand," he said. "But that's...my last offer."

She shrugged, giving a world-weary sigh. "A girl's got to eat, I guess."

Somehow he managed a self-satisfied smile.

"Are you gloating?" she asked.

Dane opened his mouth, took a couple of shallow breaths, then said, "Poor Mary Margaret. I'd have given you four."

She nodded, looking just as smug as he. "Poor Dane. I'd have done it for free."

"Really?"

"Really."

"Well," he croaked, "since you've got half my money, you can...pay for the Heritage House."

"I suppose that's fair."

Dane smiled and closed his eyes. Mary Margaret held his hand while he rested. After a minute or two he opened his eyes again.

"Hey," he wheezed, "did you win...or did I win?"

She lightly kissed his lips. "You did, of course."

Dane let his eyelids drop closed. "I thought so."

MURDER, BLACKMAIL AND LIES...

Suspicion

A young law clerk is killed. A high-priced call girl is strangled. Two men are accused of their murders. And defense attorney Kate Logan intends to prove their innocence—even though the evidence and witnesses say otherwise. With the help of homicide detective Mitch Calhoun, Kate discovers evidence suggesting that the two cases may be connected. But when her life and the life of her daughter are threatened, Kate and Mitch realize they have stumbled into a maze of corruption and murder...where no one is above suspicion.

CHRISTIANE HEGGAN

"A master at creating taut, romantic suspense." –*Literary Times*

Available in December from

DIANA PALMER

Was she about to marry the wrong man?

Journalist Wynn Ascot liked small-town news reporting, but she understood the drive that took McCabe Foxe all over the world, courting danger in the search for good stories. Sidelined by a sniper's bullet, McCabe comes home, where he's too close for Wynn's comfort. McCabe is as dangerous as he is exciting for Wynn—a woman who's about to marry another man. And now she has to dig deep to find the truth...in her own heart.

ROOMFUL OF ROSES

Available in December 1997
at your favorite retail outlet.

MIRA BOOKS **The Brightest Stars in Women's Fiction.™**

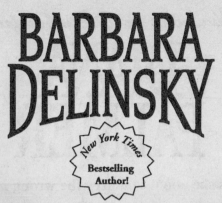

Good Girls

When they were good...

Suzanne, Taylor and Annie:

three Southern women whose lives are
tainted by one man—the charismatic,
ruthlessly ambitious Jack Sullivan—until
he's finally stopped by a bullet.

Welcome to the Old South—
where even good girls turn bad.

Karen Young

Available in January 1998—
where books are sold.

**The Brightest Stars
in Women's Fiction.™**

Look us up on-line at: http://www.romance.net

MKY306